Dav 5/22

**Lena Diaz** was born in Kentucky and has also lived in California, Louisiana and Florida, where she now resides with her husband and two children. Before becoming a romantic suspense author, she was a computer programmer. A Romance Writers of America Golden Heart® Award finalist, she has also won the prestigious Daphne du Maurier Award for Excellence in Mystery/Suspense. To get the latest news about Lena, please visit her website, lenadiaz.com

**Cindi Myers** is the author of more than fifty novels. When she's not crafting new romance plots, she enjoys skiing, gardening, cooking, crafting and daydreaming. A lover of small-town life, she lives with her husband and two spoiled dogs in the Colorado mountains.

Discover more at millsandboon.co.uk

# COWBOY UNDER FIRE

## LENA DIAZ

# MOUNTAIN OF EVIDENCE

## CINDI MYERS

MILLS & BOON

First Published in Great Britain 2020
by Mills & Boon, an imprint of HarperCollins*Publishers*
1 London Bridge Street, London, SE1 9GF

*Cowboy Under Fire* © 2020 Lena Diaz
*Mountain of Evidence* © 2020 Cynthia Myers

ISBN: 978-0-263-28058-6

1220

MIX
Paper from
responsible sources
FSC
www.fsc.org
FSC™ C007454

This book is produced from independently certified FSC™ paper to ensure responsible forest management.

For more information visit: www.harpercollins.co.uk/green

Printed and bound in Spain
by CPI, Barcelona

# COWBOY UNDER FIRE

## LENA DIAZ

To my dad in heaven. You were a true hero and inspiration. It is an honor and privilege to be your daughter. To my amazing mom. This world is blessed by your self less philanthropy and sacrifices for others. In spite of the tremendous hardships you face, you're an unstoppable force of faith, love and hope.
You, too, are my hero.

# Chapter One

Hayley's cold-numbed fingers cramped around the pistol tucked inside her coat pocket as she struggled toward the castle-like house up ahead. Thick mud sucked at her boots like knobby fingers trying to rip them from her feet. Freezing rain slashed her face and hands, seeking out every exposed piece of flesh as if to punish her for what she was doing.

If she'd been looking for a celestial sign about her self-appointed quest, this morning's winter storm was glowing neon orange with bright yellow flashers, warning her to turn back. But retreating to the relative safety of her battered ancient Blazer wasn't an option. It was parked on the shoulder a quarter mile down the road so that anyone driving by wouldn't associate it with this property. She didn't have the strength to make it all the way back to her SUV. She'd end up an icicle in the mud. The lure of the relative shelter of the covered stone porch thirty yards ahead was the only thing that kept her going.

And wasn't that insane—to think of a killer's home as a place of refuge?

Lightning cracked across the sky, whitewashing the hulking two-story structure and its twin turrets. The snow-capped Smoky Mountains of Tennessee framed it like a picture. It really was beautiful, if one preferred a castle over the traditional log cabins that dotted the mountains above Gatlinburg. If she hadn't known who lived here, she would have admired the juxtaposition of ancient and modern, the acres of rolling hills surrounded by miles of uneven, stacked-stone fences that were designed more for rustic beauty than to keep a determined intruder from climbing over them as she had.

She might even fantasize that it was the castle of her childhood dreams, that she was a fairy princess and that a handsome chivalrous knight waited inside to rescue her—at least until he realized she was perfectly capable of rescuing herself. Hayley Nash was no damsel in distress. And Dalton Lynch would never be a chivalrous knight on a white steed. He was the villain of her story, and she was the badass heroine who was going to put him away for a very long time.

If she survived this vicious storm.

She kept slogging forward, but each step was a struggle. The only good thing was that this bone-chilling deluge had forced Lynch to lock his normally free-roaming pack of dogs in the barn—or was it an armory in castle terminology?—before he'd driven farther up the mountain to go to work.

In the months since she'd begun her surveillance of him, he'd predictably gone from home to work with only the occasional trip into town. But the dogs, which seemed more like wolves on steroids than simple canines, were always running around his property, until today. This weather was a gift, a rare chance to breach his personal domain and search for evidence without being mauled. Coming here was still a huge risk. But it was one that she was willing to take.

Because of her best friend since high school, Bethany Miller.

Proving that Lynch had murdered her was far more difficult than she'd imagined when she'd taken leave from her corporate job as a computer programmer. Even temporarily moving from nearby Pigeon Forge to Gatlinburg so she could focus on her friend's case didn't seem to have helped all that much. The police had grown weary of her pleas and refused to discuss Lynch anymore. Maybe because he'd been a police officer in Bozeman, Montana, before divorcing and relocating to Tennessee. That whole *brother-in-arms*, crossing the *thin blue line* sort of thing.

She'd initially thought they *wouldn't* protect him. After all, he'd had some kind of dustup at his job and had been forced to resign from law enforcement. But even knowing that Bethany was a freelance investigative journalist didn't seem to make them wonder whether Lynch had killed her to stop whatever story she was working on.

Without any family to press for justice for Bethany, Hayley felt she had no choice but to start her own investigation. To drum up local interest, she'd created a website and posted blogs about the case.

She'd expected immediate outrage from the citizens of Gatlinburg once they read her posts. After all, Bethany was a local, and her bullet-riddled body had been found here, on Lynch's property. And there was plenty of circumstantial evidence pointing to him as the killer. But the reception had been mixed. There were even a handful of cyberspace crazies who'd treated her words like a manifesto, ready to go vigilante after Lynch.

It had galled her to publish a post defending him in an effort to calm them down. But it was the right thing to do. She'd turned over the metadata from her site to the police so they could investigate the worst of the threats. Then she'd erased the rants from her page and turned off the comment feature altogether. But she still posted at least once a week, trying to keep Bethany's case from being forgotten. She'd just toned down her rhetoric.

Another burst of frigid rain shook her from her thoughts and pushed her faster, desperate for shelter. When she finally stepped onto the fieldstone walkway, she drew a ragged breath. Soon she'd be inside, hopefully gathering a mother lode of evidence that the police couldn't ignore.

If he stuck to his routine, he wouldn't be home until dinner time. That was hours from now, but she wasn't taking unnecessary chances. She'd spend no more than one hour inside.

Struggling against water-logged jeans tugging against her legs, she climbed the steps to his porch. She drew a few more deep breaths, then peered into the front windows. Since she'd seen Lynch leave for work earlier, no one should be inside. But she wanted to double-check.

The room that she was looking into was the main living area. Stairs hugged the right wall, a kitchen was to the left, and there was an opening to a hallway in the back wall. But other than her own bedraggled reflection in the glass, she didn't see anyone, certainly not Lynch.

She tried to imagine his appearance after trudging through an acre of mud and freezing rain as she'd just done. No doubt he'd look fantastic under any circumstances. That was one of the reasons it was so hard to convince anyone that he was a killer. The man was gorgeous.

The black trench coat he typically wore and that black Stetson that she'd never seen him without would have looked ridiculous on anyone else in this part of the country where baseball caps were the norm. But on him they looked really, *really* good. Even though, to Hayley's way of thinking, the black coat and hat marked him as the bad guy, like in those old Spaghetti Westerns.

He'd been wearing that coat, that hat, this morning as he'd climbed up into his truck. The coat had stretched across his broad shoulders, flipping back in the wind to reveal his long legs. Other women turned into ogling fools when they caught sight of his muscular body, his chiseled features. And Hayley admitted, only to herself, that his carefully groomed stubble and barely-there mustache sometimes made her fingers itch to trace them. Which only went to prove what was obvious to her, and what everyone else missed.

Dalton Lynch was dangerous.

He was the quintessential fallen angel; his physical beauty and easy, sexy smile were the perfect weapons that disarmed those around him. At least, everyone except Hayley. She was immune to his charm. And she was going to bring him down.

She took a quick look around. The rain had eased considerably. The wind was no longer howling. It was as if the storm's sole purpose had been to hinder her efforts. Now that she'd reached the house, the angry weather system was moving on to harass someone else farther down the mountain.

Stupid, fickle storm.

The chances that Lynch might decide to go home for lunch, maybe to check his property for wind damage, had just gone up exponentially.

Plan A, taking an hour to search this place, was no longer viable. Plan B was to search for thirty minutes, at the most. Even that was pushing her luck since his work was about fifteen minutes away. But she'd come too far, worked too hard, to leave without at least trying to find something incriminating. She was going to pray that if he did decide to leave work, he'd be delayed a few minutes before he could head home. She needed every one of those thirty minutes.

She took out the picklock set that she'd bought from one of the spy shops in Pigeon Forge. Intended as a novelty store for tourists, they had a limited inventory of equipment that could actually be used for surveillance. And without being an experienced investigator, she wasn't sure what was worth getting. Grabbing the picklock set had been an impulse decision at the register. Now she was grateful she had it.

Tutorial videos on the internet and weeks of practicing on the locks at the cabin that she'd been renting for several months had her feeling confident that she could handle any lock Lynch might have.

A frustrating few minutes later, she realized she shouldn't have been so confident. The dead bolt had proven impervious to her novice attempts.

She checked her phone. *Twenty-five minutes left. Now what?*

She eyed the front window. Could she get into the house that way? It was a lattice of small glass squares that she couldn't climb through even if she broke every one of them. The spring locks visible behind the glass would have to both be pulled back at opposite ends of the window, at the same time, in order to lift it. Lynch, no doubt, could do it. But she wasn't a runway model and had the short arms and legs to prove it. There was no way she was getting this window open.

But there was more than one way into a castle.

After trudging through the mud again to the back of the house, she tried her luck with the kitchen door. The pick-lock made short work of the doorknob lock. But this door had a deadbolt too. And it proved just as ornery as the other one. It refused to budge.

There was another way to get the door open, though. Like the front window, this door had little glass panes. All she had to do was break one of them and reach in to flip the lock.

Guilt had her hesitating. It wasn't like she'd ever broken into someone's house before, or purposely damaged their property. *Bethany. Do it for Bethany.* Quickly, before her guilt could wear her down, she raised the butt of her pistol, then slammed it against one of the panes.

The glass shattered, raining shards all over the hard wood floor. After carefully flipping the dead bolt, she rushed inside. Thunder rumbled in the distance, as if in warning. She checked her phone.

*Twenty minutes.*

Adrenaline gave her tired limbs renewed strength to race through the kitchen. She ran past the built-ins in the living room and zipped down the back hall. Even though Lynch lived alone, she'd watched him through her binoculars enough to know that he sometimes had friends or co-workers over. If he had anything incriminating, it would be hidden in a private office, or a bedroom, not left in a kitchen drawer or on his coffee table for others to see.

The back hall led to a half bath and a laundry room. No office, at least not downstairs. She sprinted to the staircase, belatedly realizing she was leaving a muddy trail through his otherwise pristine home. Another flash of guilt shot through her, but she ruthlessly tamped it down.

She ran up the stairs as fast as she could go. At the top, she checked her phone again.

*Seventeen minutes.*

Good grief. How was she supposed to search this big place that quickly? The turrets alone would take a while, once she figured out where their entrances were. She shoved her phone into her pocket and yanked out her gun, just in case her calculations—or wishful thinking—were off and he came in unexpectedly.

First door, top of stairs. A bedroom with an attached bath. Not the office, not the master. She checked the next few doors. Closet, bedroom, closet. Another bath was at the far end. Then she tried the last door.

The master bedroom.

A quick glance told her there was a closet and bathroom off to the right. Both doors were open but she didn't bother to check inside. She didn't need to. She'd found what she was looking for. The entire left wall of the bedroom was a home office. A large black desk was flanked by two enormous bookshelves and a row of cabinets mounted above it. The desk had three drawers on each side, and stacks of papers on top.

Jackpot.

This was where he did his work at home, whatever work he did. That was one of the mysteries she'd yet to figure out, exactly what he did for a living. All she knew was that he drove up the mountain to an enormous cabin every day, parked in the paved parking lot out front that often had close to a dozen vehicles, then came home every evening. Perhaps today she'd get the answer to where his money came from and what a disgraced former cop actually did to earn a paycheck.

She raced to the desk and plopped down on the rolling chair. Her mental clock told her she was almost out of time, so she didn't waste the few precious seconds it would take to check her phone. Instead, she discarded the pistol on top of one of the piles of papers. Then she yanked open the nearest drawer, and froze.

Behind her there'd been a solid thump, as if something heavy had echoed against the floor. A killer's shoe?

She glanced longingly at the pistol. Why had she set it so far away?

Why wasn't Lynch yelling at her?

*Click, tap, click.*

Very slowly, she looked over her shoulder. It wasn't Lynch who was staring at her. An enormous grayish-white wolf-dog stood ten feet away.

Growling, it took a menacing step toward her, its long claws scraping against the floor. *Click, tap, click.* A low growl rumbled in its throat. Ice-blue eyes watched her as it lifted its snout, testing the air.

She inched her hands toward the pistol. "G-good dog. It's okay. Good dog."

The growls grew louder. Hackles raised. Muscles bunched.

Hayley lunged for her gun.

The dog launched itself at her like a missile.

# Chapter Two

Hayley crooned soothing words to the wolf-dog and gently massaged its ears to distract it as the veterinarian felt for more injuries.

"Is he going to be okay?" she asked again, guilt riding her hard. It wasn't this gorgeous, sweet, senior dog's fault that his owner was a murderer. He'd been protecting his domain, or trying to. But when he'd leaped at her, she'd jerked to the side and he'd knocked himself silly on the desk. She'd realized a split second before she was about to shoot him that his blue eyes were cloudy and there were no teeth in that growling muzzle. Thank God she hadn't pulled the trigger.

The white-haired vet glanced up, peering at her over the top of his glasses. "You seem awfully worried about a dog you found wandering on the side of the road."

The suspicious tone of his voice was impossible to miss. But there was no help for that. All she could do was ensure that this magnificent animal was taken care of before she made her escape. She certainly couldn't admit that she'd broken into the owner's home and the dog got hurt while she was ransacking the place.

It whined and snuffled its head against her hand. She rubbed the velvety muzzle and pressed a kiss against its fur. When she realized the vet was still waiting for her response, she shrugged. "He was covered in blood and stumbling all over the place. Anyone would have stopped."

Thank goodness she'd found the remote to open Lynch's gate at the end of his driveway. Without being able to pull her Blazer right up to the house, she'd never have managed to get the massive dog to the vet's office. She certainly couldn't have coaxed him over the fence like she'd coaxed him into her vehicle, not as frail as he was.

The vet grunted noncommittally. "Head wounds bleed a lot, makes it look worse than it is. It was smart of you to tie that pillowcase around his head to keep pressure on the wound until you got him here. But those stitches I put in should do the trick. He won't even need a cone of shame to keep him from licking them. They're too high up."

"What about his unbalanced gait? He could barely stand. Could he have a concussion or something?"

This time the doctor smiled. "He's blind and old. That's the way he walks."

A spark of panic shot through her. "You know this dog?"

He blinked. "What?"

"You said that's the way he walks."

"I did? Oh." He scratched his chin. "I meant that I'd expect him to walk that way, given his age and condition. In case you hadn't noticed, he doesn't have any teeth. He's already well past his expiration date but too stubborn to head over the rainbow bridge just yet." He ran his hands over the dog's shoulders and ribs, then gently patted its neck before straightening. "Are you sure you don't want me to take another look at that cut on *your* head? Or have one of my assistants drive you to the hospital? You need to get that taken care of."

She self-consciously touched the bandage he'd insisted on taping over her left temple when she'd first arrived. "I'm okay, really. Like you said, head wounds bleed a lot. Looks worse than it is." She grimaced at the cuffs of her shirt which were spotted with both the dog's blood and hers. Her coat was even worse. She'd left it in her Blazer rather than drip blood in the office.

It had taken all her strength to roll the dazed animal into some bedsheets in Lynch's bedroom. Then she'd half dragged, half carried him down the inside stairs and then the porch steps. By the time she'd jogged to her SUV and drove it back to Lynch's house to get the injured animal, her legs were like jelly. She'd opened her door, stepped out, and did a face-plant beside the driveway.

He gave her a skeptical look. "You still should get that checked. It might need stitches. It's definitely going to bruise."

"Thank you, I will," she lied. She had no intention of going to the hospital today, or ever. Even if she was at death's door, she didn't think she could stomach a hospital visit. She'd seen enough doctors and experienced enough needle-sticks to last a lifetime. A repeat of that experience wasn't on her bucket list.

"What kind of dog is he?" she asked. "He looks like a wolf hybrid."

He chuckled. "To most people, a Siberian husky looks like a wolf."

"He's a husky?" She couldn't help the skepticism that crept into her voice. The dog was huge, much larger than any she'd ever seen—with the exception of the rest of Lynch's pack.

"A mix, probably husky and something like an Irish wolfhound. That would explain the blue eyes and size." He waved toward his patient. "He's probably got a good headache building if he doesn't have one already. I'll write a script for pain pills. We can fill them here. You okay with that?"

"Oh. Of course." He was subtly asking if she was willing to cover the costs even though it wasn't her dog. She would, somehow. Money was tight since she'd run out of paid vacation and was now on unpaid leave, living off her savings and the occasional side job updating websites. But the dog's injuries were her fault.

"Can I pay now and board him here overnight? I'll pick him up in the morning and try to find his owner." Actually, she'd anonymously let Lynch know that he needed to pick up his pet at the vet's office.

"Sure," he said as he crossed to the door that led to a back hallway and the inner workings of the office. A cacophony of dogs barking and the occasional howl of a cat never seemed to stop. Hayley imagined he was used to the noise and barely noticed it. "But can you wait a few minutes until I get an assistant in here? We're, ah, a little full right now. We'll have to get a kennel ready."

The dog whimpered beneath her hand and she realized she was clutching him too tightly. She eased her grip and feathered her fingers down his neck until he settled back onto the table. "I really do need to leave. Will it be quick?"

"I'll get someone in here as soon as possible."

Was that a yes or a no?

He held out his hand. "Thank you, Miss Nelson."

Her face heated at the fake name that she'd given him as she shook his hand. "Thank you, Dr. Cord. I appreciate you working him in so quickly."

He nodded and left, closing the door behind him with a sharp click.

Hayley regretted the lie. But she couldn't risk someone recognizing her name from her social media attacks against Lynch or the one TV interview she'd snagged when she'd first tried to get the public interested in her friend's case. She wasn't exactly famous, but no point in taking any more risks than she already had.

She continued to pet the sweet animal, which was settling down into a gentle snore on top of the stainless steel table. The old-fashioned round clock on one wall had her inhaling sharply. Over an hour had passed since she'd run into the lobby asking for help.

This had been the closest vet's office to Lynch's home. Looking back, she probably should have gone somewhere else, just in case he used this place. But the assistants who'd carried the dog into the examination room didn't say anything about recognizing him. And neither had the vet. She'd been lucky. But she wasn't counting on her luck holding much longer.

She really needed to get out of here before Lynch got home and found the disaster she'd left for him: broken glass and mud downstairs, blood all over his desk and bedroom floor upstairs, sheets missing off his bed and the comforter piled on a nearby chair. She belatedly realized she should have worn gloves. But her fingerprints weren't on file anywhere, so it shouldn't really matter even if he did file a police report. As long as she stuck to her story and didn't admit she'd been inside his house, they couldn't compel her to provide fingerprints. Could they?

She blinked and pressed a hand to her throat. Good grief. Was she really rationalizing how to avoid being arrested? Unbelievable. Before today, the worst crime she'd ever committed was speeding. Now she could actually go to jail, or worse, if caught.

When she'd planned her little escapade, she'd assumed she'd be able to pick the lock, take some pictures of some documents, and leave with no one the wiser. It had never occurred to her how quickly things could escalate out of control. She shouldn't have broken that glass pane in the kitchen door.

She shouldn't have gone over there to start with.

Somehow she needed to reset, get back on track and look at the investigation with fresh eyes. Crossing to the dark side, becoming a criminal in order to catch one, wasn't who she was, and she couldn't stomach doing anything like this ever again.

She glanced at the clock again and frowned. Surely it didn't take this long to get a kennel ready. Or send in a vet tech. She crossed to the door where Dr. Cord had disappeared. But when she tried the knob, it wouldn't turn. It was locked.

Her pulse leaped in her throat. She drew a shaky breath and told herself not to panic. It made sense that the doctor wouldn't want clients going into the private back areas, probably an insurance liability thing. She'd just use the door to the lobby. Then she'd ask someone at the front desk to watch the dog while she paid for its treatment.

She started toward the other door just as it began to open. Her relief quickly turned to alarm. It wasn't a vet tech stepping into the room.

It was Dalton Lynch.

# Chapter Three

Six foot three inches of intimidating male stepped into the room, then shut the door behind him, signature Stetson and trench coat in place. Lynch seemed surprised, and not at all pleased to see her. But instead of confronting her, he crossed to the examining room table and bent over the dog.

He stroked its fur, making soothing sounds with his deep voice, as if to reassure the animal even in its sleep. When he gently traced the area of shaved fur over the dog's eye, just above the small row of stitches, his mouth thinned into a tight line.

Hayley moved past him to leave. But he straightened and grabbed her arm.

"You aren't going anywhere until you explain how you ended up at a vet's office with Denali, *Miss Nelson*."

Panic had her throat tightening. She frantically pushed at his hand on her arm. "Let go of me," she choked out.

His eyes widened in surprise and he immediately released her. But when she would have grabbed the doorknob, he used his body to block her way.

She scrambled back, putting the table and the dog between them. Spots swam in her vision. A strange buzzing sounded in her ears. Her chest hurt, as if someone was standing on it. Good grief, what was happening?

"Breathe, Hayley," he ordered. "You're hyperventilating." He took a step toward her.

She slammed back against the wall, hands outstretched to ward him off.

He swore and yanked open the door, then disappeared into the lobby.

Hayley gasped like a fish, desperately trying to suck in air, but nothing was happening. Her lungs were empty. The room swirled around her, going dark.

"It's okay." The kindly voice of Dr. Cord sounded beside her. "Sit down, Miss Nelson." Gentle hands guided her to a chair.

The wicker seat creaked as she slumped into it, still gasping. The doctor held something over her mouth, spoke calmly, giving her instructions. And finally, blessed air flowed into her oxygen starved lungs. A few moments later, her vision cleared.

The first thing she saw was Dalton Lynch kneeling by the door, his handsome face lined with worry as he watched her. Beside him, the dog, Denali, whimpered and scratched the floor as if he was trying to reach her, his nose in the air, testing the scents.

The doctor smiled and patted Hayley's hand. "Denali is worried about you, young lady."

She drew another ragged breath, then gave him a shaky smile. "Thank you, Dr. Cord. Thank you for helping me."

"Thank Mr. Lynch. He yanked me out of another patient's room and insisted I come in here." He patted her shoulder and wadded up what she now realized was a paper bag that he'd held over her mouth. "I'll come back to check on you in a few minutes. There's an irate pregnant poodle and her disgruntled human waiting for me to finish my exam next door." He chuckled.

Before she could fully grasp what was going on, he was closing the door behind him, cocooning her in with Lynch.

The dog whimpered, almost knocking him over in its attempts to get to her.

"If you don't mind," he said, "can I let Denali check on you? He's been frantic hearing you struggling for breath. Since he's blind, he relies heavily on scent and touch."

In answer, she slid to the floor and held out her arms.

He let go of the collar and Denali lunged forward, nearly knocking her over in his enthusiasm. He licked her face and excitedly wriggled his body like a puppy, desperately trying to get closer to her.

"Denali. Back," he ordered. "You're going to hurt her."

She wrapped her arms around the dog's neck. "No. It's okay." She buried her face in his fur, enjoying the hug as much as Denali. Once he finally settled down, she reluctantly let go and turned him back toward his owner. "I'm okay now, sweetie. Go on."

The dog gave her a last lick, then hurried to Lynch and rubbed its muzzle on his leg. He attached a leash to its collar and nodded at her. "Thank you. He was inconsolable while you were hyperventilating."

"He…he's a great dog. Thanks for sharing him. I needed that hug." She smoothed her hands down her jeans, then pushed herself up into the chair. "I can't believe I almost passed out. I've never done that before."

"Understandable, given the circumstances." He gave her a tight smile, silently acknowledging the elephant in the room, that she thought him a killer.

Would a killer insist that a doctor help someone who'd been waging a war against them, trying to put them in jail? Or show affection for his dog, wanting it to be comforted by touch since it was blind and confused over what was going on? The last few moments had thrown her off-kilter. Her thoughts and long-held convictions were all a huge jumble.

"That bandage on the side of your head," he indicated, "did Denali do that?"

"What? Oh. No, no. I fell. It wasn't his fault."

He nodded, looking relieved. "He can be overzealous,

as you saw. Could you please tell me how you ended up with him? And how he got hurt?"

"I…" She coughed, her throat so dry she could barely speak, probably from gasping for breath moments earlier.

He pulled the other chair to him and sat across from her, but kept the chair pushed against the wall. Was he trying to help her not feel intimidated by giving her space and not towering over her? The answer to that seemed to be yes, when he also cracked the door a few inches. Not enough for Denali to get out or another animal from the lobby to slip in, but enough so that she didn't feel trapped.

"There's some water over there." He waved toward the sink behind her. "I think I see some disposable cups in the corner. I'd get you one, but I don't want to frighten you."

She clasped the arms of the chair. "Why are you being so considerate, so nice?"

He let out a deep sigh. "I'm treating you the way I would anyone else. Look, we both know what you think of me. And I'm not going to waste either of our time trying to convince you otherwise. Just get some water, and then tell me what happened. Okay?"

She coughed again, then pushed out of her chair and got a cup of water as he'd suggested. A few gulps and the tightness in her throat began to ease. She took another sip, then tossed the cup in the waste can before resuming her seat. "How…how did you know I was here? That your dog—Denali—was here?"

"Dr. Cord called me. Denali's microchipped. All my dogs are."

She fisted her hands beside her. Of course they were. And naturally the vet hadn't told her. She didn't remember anyone checking for a microchip. But then again, the doctor had insisted on bandaging her own wound while a vet tech got Denali ready for his exam. That must have been when they scanned for the microchip.

No wonder he'd taken so long with the dog and talking to her. He'd wanted to figure out what was going on, and then he must have stepped into the back hall to call Lynch. He'd been stalling ever since, waiting for Denali's owner to get here. Thankfully, Lynch must not yet realize that she'd broken into his home. If he did, he'd have led with that rather than ask how she'd ended up with Denali.

"Hayley, how did you—"

"I prefer that we use our last names." Keeping some sort of formality between them was an act of desperation at this point. She was having a hard enough time keeping her guard up and reminding herself that he was a bad man. Thinking of him as Dalton, and hearing his kind-sounding, deep voice say *Hayley* was shredding her defensive shields. So much for thinking she was immune to his charm.

He gave her a sad smile. "I prefer that you call me Dalton, but do what makes you comfortable. About Denali—"

"He was weaving around on the side of the road and I brought him here. That's all I know." The lie had her face turning warm. Which was ridiculous, of course, considering who she was lying to. Somehow she needed to turn this around, regain her equilibrium. She'd never expected to actually *like* Dalton Lynch if she ever got face-to-face with him. And yet, that's exactly what was happening.

*He's dangerous. Remember that. Keep your guard up.*

His gaze dropped to her flushed cheeks. "He was inside my house. How did he get out?" His voice was matter of fact, without a hint of judgment. But his piercing blue eyes told her he wasn't necessarily buying her claims.

She shrugged. "How should I know?"

"Right." A world of disappointment was loaded in that one little word. "Where exactly did you find him?"

"The road that runs past your house." She arched a brow. "And mine. It's no secret that I live ten minutes down the same road. Or that I perform surveillance on you. I was driving by and saw him and brought him here."

"Surveillance isn't what I'd call it. More like harassment." He sounded more weary than aggravated. He petted the dog sitting at his feet. "But if Denali did manage to slip out when I was leaving this morning and you really did find him, thank you for bringing him here to get taken care of." He ruffled the dog's fur. "He's a feeble old guy and spends most of his days sleeping in my master bedroom closet on a therapeutic bed to relieve his joint pain. I'm surprised he was able to get downstairs on his own. I usually have to carry him outside for bathroom breaks and what little exercise he can handle."

He seemed so kind, and so darn nice, as if he really did have an emotional attachment to his dog.

Then again, didn't serial killer Ted Bundy have a dog once?

He stood, towering over her again. Then he moved to the far right, away from the door, leading the dog with him and ordering him to sit. "Again, thanks for taking such good care of him. I appreciate it."

She shoved to her feet and hurried to the door. But at the opening, she hesitated. "You're letting me go? Just like that?"

He frowned. "Did you think I was going to kidnap you?"

She swallowed hard, not sure what to say.

An expression of annoyance flashed across his ruggedly handsome face. "Have you ever considered that I might not be the bad guy that you think I am? I'm like everyone else. I just want to live my life, go to work, make a positive difference in the world, maybe do something fun with my friends during my free time."

He seemed to be waiting for her reply, but she didn't know how to respond.

He shook his head. "It would also be nice not to have

someone following me and reporting my life's details on the internet. Some day in the future, once your friend's case is resolved, you'll realize I'm not your enemy. When you do, I'll be happy to accept your apology."

She blinked. "That's never going to happen."

He opened his mouth as if to argue, but gave her a crisp nod instead. "Before you go home, you might want to see a doctor, if you haven't already. That cut on your temple is starting to bleed through your bandage."

She instinctively reached up and pressed the bandage, then winced at the stab of pain.

He watched her, but didn't say anything else. Instead, he waited, acting the gentleman, letting her leave first and keeping his distance.

This whole episode was destroying her preconceived notions of how he would react in a given situation. He'd reacted...normally, like any other kind person might. Actually, he'd been more than kind, more than generous and incredibly understanding. It didn't make sense, given who he was. It had her doubting herself for the first time. Not that she'd judged him guilty on a whim. She had evidence that told her he was the one responsible for her friend's death. The facts were the facts. Nothing he'd done today changed the truth. Dalton Lynch was a killer.

Then why didn't he seem like one?

His dog whined and scratched the floor.

Lynch patted his head. "He needs to go out. If you aren't leaving yet, I'll—"

"I'm going." She ran out the door, not caring what he or anyone in the outer office might think. Once she was inside her Blazer, she locked the doors and collapsed against the seat. In spite of her urgency to leave, she couldn't drive like this. She had to calm down first. It was one thing to perform surveillance, to look at pictures, to read journal entries about a killer. It was quite another to be in a confined room just a few feet away from him, and suddenly doubt everything she thought she knew.

She let out another shuddering breath, then carefully backed out and headed down the rural two-lane road that would eventually lead past his home to hers. It wasn't a long drive, but it was enough for her panic and fear to recede. Her unexpected doubts were still there. But all it would take was a review of her documentation and her world would tilt back on its axis again.

Hopefully.

When she rounded a curve in the road and his home came into view, her stomach jumped. Two police cars sat in the long driveway, lights flashing. Another car was parked closer to the house, a black Mercedes—exactly like the one she often saw parked at Lynch's workplace. And she recognized the tall, dark-haired man in a business suit standing on the front porch speaking to one of the policemen as one of Lynch's coworkers. His head turned toward her as she drove past. Had he recognized her, or her Blazer?

Her pulse rushed in her ears. The earlier panic washed over her, nearly drowning her. She had to force herself not to slam her foot on the accelerator. Instead, she drove the speed limit, until she rounded the next curve. Then she floored it.

She'd just topped the last hill before her cabin when sirens sounded behind her. She stiffened and looked in the rearview mirror. Two police cars were coming up fast. The same ones that were in Lynch's driveway?

*Please, God, no. Please let them pass me.*

She pulled to the side of the road, praying that they'd drive by.

The first one did.

The second one didn't.

The car that had passed her skidded to a halt in front of her Blazer, as if to keep her from pulling back onto the road. The other one sandwiched her in from behind, so close to her bumper that there was no way she could back up and pull out, even if she'd been foolish enough to try.

Her hands ached where she was clutching the steering wheel.

*Deep breaths. Deep breaths. No one saw me break into Lynch's house. It will be okay.*

A knock sounded on her window.

She jumped, then flushed hot with guilt as she looked into the face of a Gatlinburg police officer. He motioned for her to roll down her window.

As she did, the sound of a roaring engine coming up fast had both her and the policeman looking back. The Mercedes that had been parked in front of the house pulled to a stop behind the second police car. And behind it, a familiar dark blue Chevy pickup truck jerked to a halt.

Lynch hopped out of the truck just as the man in the Mercedes emerged from his car. Together, they strode toward Hayley like two avenging angels, or a couple of really well-dressed hitmen ready to end this charade once and for all.

*Breathe. Breathe.* Black dots swam in her vision. *Get a grip, Hayley. Not again. Focus. Breathe. Air in, air out. Air in, air out.* The dots faded. Her breathing evened. She shuddered in relief.

"Ma'am," the officer said, drawing her attention again. "You need to step out of the vehicle."

She flinched at the sound of boots pounding against the pavement as Lynch and the other man approached.

"Was I speeding, officer?" She desperately tried for an innocent-looking smile.

Lynch stopped beside the policeman, his gaze riveted on her. "You didn't know about my security cameras, did you? Or that my boss offered to check on my house when the vet called about Denali? You should have told me the truth, Hayley."

"It's Miss Nash," she informed him, forcing another false smile, even as dread coiled in her belly, all because of one phrase: *security cameras.*

His deep blue eyes flashed with disappointment again, sparking an answering wave of shame inside her. Then he walked away, as if she wasn't even worth his scorn. His opinion of her shouldn't matter. But for some reason, it stung.

"That's her. Hayley Nash," the other man, his boss, told the policeman. "She's the one in the video."

The officer put his hand on the butt of his holstered gun. "Get out of the car."

She started shaking so hard that she could barely push open the door. She managed to stand without collapsing, then let out a surprised yelp when the policeman whirled her around and shoved her against the side of the Blazer.

"You're under arrest for breaking and entering."

# Chapter Four

Hayley smoothed her hands down her scratchy orange jail-issued jumpsuit, the color ridiculously cheerful and bright for this early in the morning. She leaned against the wall, while her police escort filled out some paperwork at a counter a few feet away.

The officer's wake-up call telling her she had a visitor hadn't actually woken her up. She'd never fallen asleep.

All night she'd been sitting on her bunk, if a concrete shelf with a paper thin mattress could be called a bunk, trying not to gag at the smell of urine and vomit that permeated the jail. At least she was alone in her cell. It had bunks to accommodate four people. But even alone, she couldn't stomach the smell, or the sounds of hopelessness drifting in from other prisoners down the hall, or the bland, practically unidentifiable food that had been shoved through a security drawer. If she hadn't regretted breaking into Lynch's home before, she sorely regretted it now.

Her life of crime was definitely over.

Her wrists still ached from the handcuffs, even though the officer had only put them on for the few minutes that it took to escort her from her cell to this hallway. But she'd worn them for so long yesterday after her arrest that she could still feel their cold burn, like the ache of a phantom limb.

Footsteps echoed on the terrazzo floor and she looked up to see the officer coming toward her.

"This way, Miss Nash." The policewoman led her to a sunny yellow door, making Hayley wonder if the bright colors were someone's sick sense of humor in this depressing place.

"Remember what I told you," the officer said, and proceeded to remind her of the rules. "You have to use the phone to communicate with your visitor. Otherwise, they can't hear you through the glass. When the meeting's over, you come back to the door and press the button on the wall to let me know you're done. Thirty minutes is the max per visit, unless you put in a special request ahead of time and it's approved. If your thirty minutes expires and you're still on the phone, the line shuts off. You're to hang up the phone and come back to this door where I'll cuff you again and return you to your cell. Understood?"

"Can we skip the return-me-to-my-cell part?" Hayley smiled.

The officer didn't.

"Thirty minutes." She yanked open the door and ushered Hayley inside.

When Hayley saw the long row of chairs and dividers between each one, she turned to ask the officer where her visitor was. But the door shut in her face, an electronic buzz announcing that it was locked.

Great. How was she supposed to figure out which little cubby she was supposed to use to meet with her public defender? Hopefully they knew what she looked like and would flag her down as she walked by.

Half an hour didn't seem like nearly enough time to meet a lawyer and figure out strategy for her case, or even to determine how she could get out of here on bail. She was about out of money and needed to do more freelance computer programming to get an influx of cash. Did she even have enough money to make bail? She had no idea.

She only passed three inmates talking through their phones to people on the other side of the glass. They were too engrossed in their conversations to look her way, which was fine by her. She was three chairs from the end of the row when she saw someone sitting on the other side of one of the partitions.

No. It couldn't be.

Dalton Lynch lifted a hand in greeting and smiled. She strode to the next chair, then the next. But no one was waiting there to talk to her. The police officer who'd told her she had a visitor hadn't said who it was. Hayley had assumed it would be her public defender, the one she'd asked for after being arrested but so far hadn't seen. If she'd realized Lynch was waiting for her, she'd have stayed in her cell.

She straightened her shoulders and marched down the row toward the exit. Something yellow flashed off to her left as she started to pass Lynch. She kept going. Then stopped. Cursing her curiosity, she backed up and leaned past the partition to see what had caught her attention.

He was pressing a piece of yellow legal paper against the glass with one word written on it in bold black ink: CHICKEN.

She whirled around and headed toward the exit.

# Chapter Five

Hayley let out a startled cry and jerked upright, blinking in the early morning light as she tried to bring everything into focus.

A chuckle had her turning. The same policewoman who'd brought her to the visitation area yesterday stood in the open door of her cell, dangling a pair of handcuffs.

Hayley slumped against the wall and tugged her blanket up around her, despair and frustration nearly swamping her. "What do you want?" she grumbled, eying the handcuffs.

"You don't want a break from this place to see who came to visit you, that's fine by me." She turned around.

"Wait, please." Hayley jumped off her bunk and padded in her socks to the door.

The officer turned and put her hand out to stop her. "Stand back so I can close the door."

"No, please." She stifled a yawn, then cleared her throat. "I'm sorry. You woke me up and I was…confused. Who's here to see me? Is it my lawyer, finally?"

"Lady, I'm not a cruise director or your maidservant. I don't know and don't care who's here to see you. I just come get the prisoners and move them wherever they're supposed to go. If you want to see for yourself, I'll give you two minutes to go to the bathroom or whatever you need to do. Otherwise, I have other prisoners to see to."

Hayley hesitated. Lynch wouldn't try to see her again, would he?

"One and a half."

"Okay, okay. I'll hurry."

Five minutes later, they were at the bright yellow door.

"You know the drill," the officer said. But just like yesterday, she proceeded to recite the visitation rules. Then the door buzzed, and she shoved Hayley inside.

She quickly finger-combed her hair, which was a tangled mess that hung almost to her waist. She hadn't had time to brush it out or tame it in a ponytail or braid. When she realized she was primping, she forced her hands down and straightened her shoulders, then moved down the long row.

*Please be my lawyer. Please be my lawyer.*

Again, there were only a few people there. And when she reached almost the very end, a familiar silhouette sat sprawled sideways in one of the chairs, his gray suit jacket open, his long legs out in front of him, boot tips shining in the fluorescent overhead lights.

He straightened to face her and smiled in greeting.

She continued to the end of the aisle, even though she didn't expected she'd find anyone else. Certainly not her taxpayer-appointed lawyer. Apparently "free" lawyers weren't in any kind of hurry to help the clients they'd been forced to represent.

She sagged against the wall, blinking against the burn of unshed tears that wanted to cascade down her face. Two days and two nights in this awful place and the only person willing to visit her was Dalton Lynch. How could the universe be this cruel?

She pressed her hands to her eyes and breathed deeply until the urge to cry passed. Then she went to the partition where Lynch was waiting. But she didn't sit.

As he picked up the receiver on the other side of the glass, she automatically reached for the phone on her side, then stopped. No. This wasn't happening. She wasn't tired enough or hungry enough to listen to him gloat about her being in here. There wasn't much in her control right now, but whether she spoke to him or not was.

She headed for the exit.

She slammed her hand against the buzzer to let the officer know that she was ready to leave. Then waited.

The feeling that someone was watching her kept increasing until she finally glanced over her shoulder. Lynch was standing in front of the first glass partition. He held up a piece of paper as he'd done yesterday, but this one had a different message.

I CAN GET YOU OUT OF HERE.

She blinked. What did he mean by that? Was he going to drop the charges?

The door opened behind her.

He flipped the paper over.

WE NEED TO TALK FIRST.

"Let's go." The officer motioned for her to step into the hallway.

Hayley hesitated, then motioned toward Lynch. "But I didn't get to—"

"Now." The officer yanked her out of the room and shut the door.

# Chapter Six

Dalton waited two days before returning to the jail as part of his plan to get Hayley to cooperate. As exhausted and bedraggled as she'd looked the last time he'd seen her, he hoped that giving her more time to experience the questionable accommodations of Gatlinburg PD would make her more amenable to the deal that he wanted to offer. Unfortunately, he didn't have Denali with him to soften her up or make her more willing to talk. But he did have other ways of at least making her hunger to get out of here, *hunger* being the operative word.

He stood a few chairs from the end of the row in the visitation room and started unloading the contents of a bag onto the table space in front of the glass partition. When he was done, a hearty breakfast of scrambled eggs with cheese, crispy bacon, hash browns and a stack of three fluffy pancakes sat in front of him. He slathered butter and syrup on the pancakes. Then he took out the last piece of his arsenal, a thermos of steaming hot coffee. He filled the cup, then placed it right next to the glass so that the steam caused some condensation. He arranged his napkin, fork and knife, then settled down in the chair to wait.

He didn't have to wonder whether she'd like the food he'd set out. He knew this was her favorite breakfast, from her favorite café in town. Because while she'd been performing surveillance on him, his coworkers had done the same to her.

And while she *suspected* him guilty of one murder, he *knew* that she was guilty of something else—helping a network of criminals conduct their crimes beneath law enforcement's radar, including killing anyone who got in their way. The only real question was whether she knew that her website work was facilitating those crimes, or whether she was an innocent pawn. For his boss, Mason Ford, the verdict was in. Guilty. Dalton still had his doubts.

He checked his watch. Right on time, Hayley marched past him. Once again, she'd find the last two seats were empty. His bribes to the other visitors had ensured that they had this end to themselves.

As she'd done last time, she marched back to stand in front of him, arms crossed, her mouth in a tight line. He couldn't help but smile at the mutinous look she was giving him, and the stubborn set to her jaw. Good grief, the woman was beautiful, even after four days in jail, with no makeup, and her glorious dark brown hair a riot of tangled curls. Too bad they hadn't met under different circumstances. She was exactly the type of woman who set his blood on fire. Sexy and sassy, and smart as a whip.

Perfect.

Her gaze dropped to the table, and he could almost see her salivate as she looked at the food. He'd been a cop for seven years. He knew the taxpayers didn't allocate enough money to jails to afford great-tasting meals. They focused on nutrition. His spies behind these walls had told him that Hayley was mostly turning her nose up at the jailhouse culinary delights, barely eating enough to survive. From the pained expression on her face, his volley had hit the target.

She eyed the phone on the wall, obviously debating whether or not to pick it up.

To help her decide, he held up his sign again.

I CAN GET YOU OUT OF HERE.

She chewed her lower lip in indecision. Then she grabbed the phone and motioned toward his.

He picked up the receiver, but before he could say anything, she did.

"My court-appointed attorney keeps putting me off. I've yet to talk to him. I don't suppose you have something to do with that?"

He made a point of glancing around the room before responding. "Everything we say in here is recorded."

"Meaning yes? But you won't admit it because that would be illegal?"

He smiled. "How's the food in here, Hayley? I've heard it's not very good." He scooped up a forkful of eggs and slid it into his mouth, closing his eyes as he chewed. "Mm. Those are so good."

She glared at him.

He wiped his mouth with a napkin and set it down. "Talk to me and I can see about making a deal to get you out. I'll even take you to a fancy dinner, or breakfast if you prefer. On me."

She arched a brow. "Asking me out on a date, *Dalton dear*?"

He grinned. "Jail hasn't gotten rid of your spunkiness, has it?"

"It hasn't made me forget my principles either. I don't date murderers."

He leaned back in his chair. "Strike one. New rules. You quit calling me a murderer or I'm out of here."

She rolled her eyes. "What's this deal you mentioned?"

"Not here. Like I said, everything's being recorded. I need to speak to you in private. Actually, my boss—Mason Ford—and I need to speak to you."

"Then get me out of jail and we'll talk. I assume you can drop all charges against me, or at least arrange bail? Then we'll meet somewhere neutral, with someone else there to protect me, like a police officer."

He shook his head. "What I need to say requires privacy. And it has to happen before you're released, while I have leverage. If I drop charges, and you're released, there's no incentive for you to meet with me. If you agree, we'll go to an interview room. No cameras. No cops."

She cocked her head. "No cops? Weren't you a police officer in Montana? You say that word as if you're on opposite sides from law enforcement. What happened back there? Did you kill someone else?"

He smiled tightly. "Strike two. What's it going to be? Will you agree to meet with Mason and me?"

"Alone?"

"Yes."

"Why alone? So you can kill me like you did Bethany?"

"Strike three." He hung up the phone.

Her eyes widened.

He swept the food into the bag. Then he poured the coffee back into the thermos, all while she waved her hands on the other side of the glass, frantically trying to get his attention. Without acknowledging that he even saw her, he shoved back his chair and walked out.

# Chapter Seven

Hayley paced back and forth in her cell on the seventh morning of her incarceration, hoping and praying for an officer to announce that she had a visitor. When they brought breakfast, she asked whether they'd forgotten to tell her that she had someone waiting in the visitation room. But she was told that no one had inquired about her. Just as they hadn't yesterday. Or the day before.

At this point, she'd jump at the chance to speak to anyone, including Dalton Lynch. Especially Dalton, because he'd offered to get her out of here. Whatever he wanted in exchange, she very likely might say yes—if he ever gave her the chance.

Would she die in here, alone, before a judge or prosecutor even remembered that she was here? Every time she asked to speak to a lawyer, the officers said they'd passed along her requests but that the court was backed up right now. It didn't make sense. People didn't go this long without a hearing, did they?

Later, when lunch arrived, she plopped down onto her bunk, forced to admit defeat. No one was coming to see her today. Ignoring the nauseating food, she drew her knees up and tried to make sense out of what was going on.

No lawyer.

No hearing.

No bail.

And a man she'd accused of murder was the only one who'd bothered to visit her, until her insults had driven him away. Remembering how considerate and concerned he'd been at the vet's office, she felt bad for having thrown those accusations at him. But she couldn't seem to help herself. She'd thought of him as a murderer for so long, it was difficult to sit there talking to him as if he was innocent.

Even though she was beginning to hope that he was.

It would mean she'd been wrong, had nearly exhausted her savings and run up her credit cards to pursue an investigation against someone who didn't deserve to be treated that way. But it would also mean these insane doubts were justified. And that she wasn't going crazy. Because ever since she'd seen him sitting in that visitation room without that Stetson and dark trench coat, she'd been thinking of him in ways she'd never thought she would.

The way a woman thought about a man she was wildly attracted to.

It was her bitter cross to bear that he consumed her thoughts, day and night. Ever since he'd run out of a room to get a doctor to help her, and feathered his large hands so gently across the fur of a wounded animal, he'd become *human* to her. And then, when she'd seen his sandy blond hair glinting in the overhead fluorescent lights and realized for the first time that it wasn't dark brown or even black, as comical as that seemed, it made her think of him as less threatening, less of a villain.

She shook her head then rested her chin on her knees. The problem was that she *wanted* him to be innocent. He seemed so nice, so darn sweet, that she desperately wanted to believe she'd been wrong about him.

But if she was, then who'd killed Bethany?

And why had Dalton come to visit her in jail after what she'd done to his home?

What could he, and his boss, possibly have to speak to her about? And why the need for secrecy?

So many questions without any answers.

A buzzing sound had her jerking her head up. Two policewomen shoved two prisoners dressed in orange jumpsuits into her cell, then shut the door behind them.

"Be nice, Molly," one of the officers called out. "You're in enough trouble as it is. Don't add another assault charge to your rap sheet." She headed down the hallway with the other policewoman.

Hayley blinked at the one she assumed was Molly, an Amazonian-size woman with gooey red lipstick and purple fingernails that resembled curved talons as she shoved her frizzy platinum-blond curls back from her face.

Beside her, a skinny girl with dark oily-looking hair offered Hayley a nearly toothless smile and giggled. "You think she's got some smokes to share with us, Molly?"

Molly offered her own smile, revealing a surprisingly perfect-looking, bright white set of teeth. "I sure hope so, Tabby. For her sake."

They both started toward Hayley.

# *Chapter Eight*

Hayley slammed the pay phone down onto the receiver. Every attempt she'd made to reach her pro-bono lawyer was met with some kind of excuse.

"Lady, you done had your turn. It's the rest of us's turns now." The woman behind her shoved Hayley out of the way and grabbed the phone.

Hayley would have shoved back but she didn't know if the other prisoners waiting in line would jump on her. All semblance of civilization and manners seemed to evaporate the moment most of these repeat offenders were placed behind bars. She had the bruises to prove it. But, thankfully, so did Molly and Tabby. After they'd attacked her and she fought back like a banshee, pouring all her anger and frustration into every punch, every yank of their hair, they'd left her alone. But she didn't know how much longer that would last. Did she have to become a hardened criminal too, just to avoid being beaten up?

She *really* needed to get out of here.

"Miss Nash?"

She glanced around to see one of the policewomen who'd shoved Molly and her pal into her cell, not particularly worried that they really might harm her.

"What do you want?" Hayley snapped.

She arched a brow. "You have a visitor. But if you'd rather go back to your cell—"

"No, no. Sorry. Please. Yes, I want to see whoever is here."

"You know the routine? The rules?"

"Yes, officer." Hayley nodded enthusiastically and held out her wrists to be handcuffed.

# *Chapter Nine*

When Dalton saw Hayley's condition as she sat behind the glass partition and picked up the phone, it took every ounce of self-control that he had not to curse and walk out right then, demanding to see the chief of police about his shameful treatment of prisoners.

She looked like she'd been through the apocalypse.

But his reckoning with the chief would have to wait. When she saw him, her bruised face had lit up like an eager child's on Christmas morning, eager to see the gifts under the tree. He'd given her several days to stew, to adjust her attitude. He'd wanted her eager to help him, so he could get her to agree to their terms, but he hadn't wanted it like *this*.

She motioned toward his phone and actually smiled at him. Which had him feeling even more like a jerk. He had to remind himself why he was here, what was on the line. Lives. People's lives. He had a feeling he'd have to remind himself about that a dozen times before this discussion was over.

He forced an answering smile and picked up his receiver. "Hi, Hayley."

She clutched her phone with both hands. "I'm really sorry about being so mean when you were here last time. I won't do that again."

He really hated himself in that moment. "Don't worry

about it." He motioned toward a light bruise on her cheek. "What happened? Did you fall?"

She rolled her eyes. "Yeah. Into Molly's fist. But I got her back." She raised her hand and displayed reddened knuckles with scabs across them. "Hurt like crazy, but she hasn't tried to jump me since then. Or Tabby either."

"Jump you?" He fisted a hand beneath the table. "What exactly happened?"

She waved a hand. "Nothing I can't handle. Let's talk about something else. Like getting me out of here. I'm totally willing to meet with you and your boss, alone. Like you said."

Shock rippled through him at her words. He hadn't expected her to give in on the being alone point, not yet anyway. What had this Molly and Tabby done to make her so willing to forget everything she'd fought for? "Have you changed your mind about me being a killer?"

She squeezed her eyes shut for a moment, before meeting his gaze again. "Let's just say, I'm trying to have an open mind. And, you know, be nicer. Follow your rules." She pressed a hand against the glass, her eyes imploring him, begging him. "Convince me, Dalton. Convince me that you're innocent. I'm willing to listen now. I really am."

Her words hit him like a sucker punch and had him feeling lower than pond scum. She was desperate enough to throw out her deeply held beliefs about his guilt all because of her prolonged incarceration—on a first offense for a nonviolent charge.

And he was the reason she'd been locked up so long.

It had taken some less than savory means, promises of favors and help in future cases, to do it, things he'd never have considered when he'd been an actual officer of the law. He'd done it for the best of reasons, but that didn't make him feel any less guilty. Perhaps giving her a few answers of her own, truthful answers, might assuage his guilt just a little bit. It was the least he could do.

Mindful of the cameras and recorders in the room, he carefully worded his reply. "I have an alibi. It's ironclad. But I can't share it with you, because it involves an investigation that's ongoing, one where other peoples' lives are at stake. I swear to you that you'll get the answers you need, soon, about me, about your friend. But I can't give them to you right now."

Her eyes grew wide with shock as he spoke. Her hands shook on the receiver. A full minute passed before she slowly nodded.

"Okay," she said. "We're making progress. Sort of. Maybe you could tell me about Montana. Tell me what happened to make you resign from the police force. The media was oddly quiet on the reasons, as if someone pressured them not to say what really happened. I'm guessing your new boss, Mr. Ford, had something to do with that."

"Your guess would be correct."

"Will you tell me what happened?"

He sighed and sat back in his chair. "Knowing the truth won't make you feel any better about me."

"Why not? You didn't…hurt anyone, right? It was some kind of procedural issue, you broke some rules? That's what the local news reports said, without specifics."

He laughed harshly. "Yeah, well. Mason threatened them with a libel lawsuit if they said otherwise. It's a long story, Hayley. And not one I want to talk about here. If you really are willing to talk to Mason and me, then I'll work on making it happen."

She pressed her hand to the glass. "You'll arrange for that talk you wanted, soon? And then get me out of here right after?"

"As soon as possible. I'll start working on it right now." He shoved back his chair to leave.

A look of panic crossed her features. "I still have time, another fifteen minutes or so. Can't we talk about something else until they take me back to my cell?"

He wanted to curse himself, and his boss right now for breaking her like this. He scooted his chair closer to the partition. "Sure. What do you want to talk about?"

"I don't know." She chewed her bottom lip, looking so nervous, so worried about the prospect of going back to jail that it nearly broke *him*.

"How about Denali?" he offered. "Would you like to hear how I rescued him as a stud dog from a puppy mill? How I got all my other dogs as half-starved puppies from that same mill, after breaking it up as part of an investigation in Montana?"

She nodded vigorously, a look of relief crossing her features. "I'd like that very much. Maybe we can even get the policewoman to let us talk more than the thirty-minute deadline."

"Maybe," he said, knowing it wouldn't happen. He needed to get her out of here as promised, before any more damage was done.

He proceeded to regale her with stories about Denali and his other dogs, focusing on how well they'd done after being rescued, rather than on how miserable their lives had been before that. He told her about the frustrating but often hilarious hijinks of transporting eight dogs halfway across the country, and how overjoyed they'd been when released on his land, finally being allowed to stretch their legs and truly experience freedom for the first time. He even spoke about his parents, telling her about some of the many funny times they'd had together after they retired to Florida. He loved the way her face relaxed and how happy she seemed talking about them. But the cruel world intruded far too soon.

She tried to keep a brave face as she was led away. But he could see the fear in her eyes as she waved goodbye.

And he was darn well going to do something about it.

He strode out of the visitor room, went through the required paperwork and delays it took to get out of the police department. Then he sat in his truck and made two calls.

The first was to the chief of police.

The second was to his boss.

"Mason," he said, without waiting for his boss's greeting when he picked up the phone. "She's agreed to talk. I want to make this happen and then get her out of here. Yesterday wouldn't be soon enough."

## Chapter Ten

The metal loop bolted to the tabletop in the interview room made Hayley shudder. Thank goodness she wasn't wearing handcuffs right now and that she wasn't chained to that loop. But her orange jumpsuit was a daunting reminder that she wasn't free yet.

She straightened as the door opened. Dalton and Mason entered, setting off a spark of panic inside her. She hadn't expected that. After seeing Dalton at the vet's office, and then listening to him tell her stories about his dogs and family, she'd begun to think of him almost as a friend, or at least someone she was no longer afraid of.

But she'd been exhausted and hungry during his jailhouse visits. Last night the dinner that had been served had been unexpectedly appetizing. She'd eaten every bite and had slept soundly for the first time since being locked up. Breakfast this morning had been equally savory, most likely due to pressure exerted by Dalton. She was feeling almost like her old self again. Her brain was firing on all synapses, which had her fears coming back to haunt her and make her second-guess…everything.

Could she trust him? Was he guilty or innocent in Bethany's murder?

Even if he hadn't made her feel uneasy today, his boss, Mason, did. He was just as tall and muscular as his employee, but where Dalton's eyes were kind and compelled her to *want* to believe him, Mason's were frosty enough to make her shiver.

A detective she'd never met before, Olson, followed them inside. The gun holstered to his belt seemed like a joke when the other men dwarfed him in both height and bulk. What were the chances he'd be able to use that gun before they could overpower him in this tiny room?

She drew a shaky breath and pressed back against her chair. Doubting Dalton, after essentially bonding with him, seemed like a form of betrayal, especially since he'd promised to get her out of jail. But she couldn't stop the swirl of images in her head, the memories of what she'd read in her friend's journals, the pictures she carried in her purse everywhere she went since beginning her research into Bethany's death.

Dalton dipped his head in greeting, once again minus his Stetson. Did the police make him take it off whenever he came here? Or was it part of his plan to make him seem more approachable? She hated that she was having these doubts.

"Good to see you again, Hayley." He offered her a friendly smile and took the seat directly across from her. The detective sat to his left and his boss sat to his right. "I don't think you've ever been formally introduced to my boss even though you've seen each other before. Meet Mason Ford."

His indirect reference to their little arrest party on the side of the road had her face flushing hot. That was a memory she'd love to forget.

"Ma'am." Mason set a thick manila folder on the table in front of him and rested one hand on top of it. His muddy-brown eyes mirrored suspicion and distrust, where Dalton's seemed full of empathy.

Rubbing her sweaty palms on her orange jumpsuit, she tried to smile but was pretty sure that she'd failed when

Dalton's brows drew down in concern. "I ate like a queen yesterday afternoon, and slept really well for the first time since coming here. I'm pretty sure I have you to thank, Dalton. My roommates were mysteriously moved to a new cell after you left. And the quality of the food went way up."

"I'm sure I don't know what you're talking about. I don't have any kind of influence in this place." He winked.

Her smile was genuine this time. But when she noted the detective frowning at them, she sobered. Whatever Dalton had done, he'd done it to help her. And she didn't want him or whoever he'd bribed or cajoled to get in trouble over it.

"I understand that once we talk, you'll drop all charges." She ran her hands up and down her arms. "I'll get to go home. Today, right?"

"That's the deal. As to whether you can go home today, Detective Olson, what do you think?"

"If you drop the charges, there's no reason to hold her. After we leave here, I can take her to booking, get her personal belongings back, let her change clothes. She can leave after filling out some paperwork."

His declaration should have made her ecstatic. But her newly refreshed mind was wondering what Dalton and his boss had to gain by letting her go. The case against her was open and shut. Even if she had a great lawyer, *or any lawyer at all*, she'd be found guilty and go to prison. There was no fighting the video. Or her fingerprints. Or her blood if she'd left any spots on the driveway after cutting her head. Perhaps a lenient judge might sentence her to probation since it was her first offense. But having been in jail—which was probably like a trip to an exclusive resort compared to an actual prison—she didn't want to even *risk* the possibility of going to prison. It would destroy her. So she'd agreed to talk. But there had to be something more, something for them to gain, to agree to this deal. What was in it for them?

Her gaze went to the thick folder on the table. Maybe the answer was inside. "What's in the folder?"

He glanced at the detective before answering. "It contains information from our investigation into the events surrounding Bethany Miller's death. We're willing to share it with you, in exchange for you answering our questions."

"Your investigation?" She glanced from Mason to Dalton. "You're private investigators?"

"Not exactly." He motioned to Mason, who pulled a piece of paper from the folder and set it down along with a pen. "Before we go any further, you need to sign that. It's a binding contract with the terms of our discussion."

"Terms?"

"Conditions. Two of them."

Disappointment was a sharp twist in her gut. "I knew it was too good to be true. This is a trick."

"No trick. That's an NDA, a nondisclosure agreement. In exchange for me dropping all charges, you agree not to reveal anything that we discuss during our meeting without incurring substantial punitive damages. If you break the agreement, the charges against you will immediately be reinstated."

"I'd go back to jail."

"Yes."

She didn't want to go back to her cell. She *really* didn't want to go to prison. But what could they possibly have to discuss that required a nondisclosure agreement? It was all so odd.

"You said there were two conditions. What's the second one?"

He motioned toward the detective. "The second one you already agreed to the last time we spoke. Detective Olson will step outside the room. This has to be a private discussion."

His clear blue eyes seemed friendly, his expression open

and honest, as if she could trust him with her life. Which was exactly what she'd be doing if she met his conditions. A week ago, she'd have been terrified to be this close to him. Yesterday she would have agreed to anything just for the chance of getting out of jail. Today, rested and fed, she was back to thinking the way she had before, with a heavy dose of suspicion. Was it possible that he was being *too* nice? Too nice to trust?

She'd heard the joy in his voice as he spoke about his dogs, laughed with him at funny anecdotes about his parents, former ranchers struggling to adjust to the land of gators and golf. He'd drawn her in, like an old friend, making her feel comfortable.

Was that his plan all along?

Had he seen the breaking-and-entering charges as an opportunity to bend her to his will? Fear and anxiety over her future weren't the best foundations for forming opinions or making important decisions. Could she trust herself, the decisions that she'd made while under duress?

And how much of this feeling of camaraderie with him was due to her physical attraction to him? Even now, part of her yearned to be held in his arms, to believe that he was a man she could rely on and count on to help her, instead of the villain she'd painted him to be for so long.

Risking her life because of hormones or duress was foolish. And she didn't think of herself as a fool.

She gave him an apologetic look. "I'm sorry, Dalton. I really am. But I've changed my mind on that point, on being alone with you and Mason. I have to ensure my safety. I do want this deal, even though I don't see how anything I could possibly say could help you in any way. But I won't bet my life that my judgment of your character, even though it's changed drastically over the past few days, can be trusted. Can we come up with some kind of compromise?" She motioned toward the metal loop in the center of the table. "Perhaps you could be shackled—"

"Forget that." Mason snatched the folder from the table and stood.

Dalton stopped him with a hand on his sleeve. "It's okay, Mason. If it makes Hayley feel safe, Detective Olson can chain me to the table."

"No," Mason snarled, his face reddening. "Not happening. I won't allow one of my employees, let alone a friend, to be treated like a criminal. It goes against everything I stand for, everything my business stands for. I refuse to let that happen, again, ever, to someone I know is innocent. Forget it. We'll find another way to get what we…" He clamped his jaw shut, as if realizing he'd said too much.

"Another way to get what we…what?" Hayley asked, feeling as if she was on the verge of discovering the real reason that they wanted to talk to her.

Mason aimed a scathing glance her way but didn't answer. He didn't sit either. There was no doubt that he considered their potential deal a no-go.

Panic reared its ugly head, making her want to agree to anything. But her self-preservation instincts were strong. So instead of agreeing to their conditions, she squelched her pride and resorted to pleading. "I really don't want to go back to jail." She put her hand on Dalton's. "Please."

He stared at her hand on his for a long moment, then cleared his throat and glanced at his boss.

Mason shook his head. *"No."*

"Mr. Lynch, Mr. Ford." Olson's tone was placating. "It's just a simple precaution that would make Miss Nash feel safe. It won't even be that uncomfortable. I could—"

"Absolutely not." Mason adjusted his suit jacket and tucked the folder beneath his arm. "Forget the deal, Dalton. You're pressing charges against Miss Nash. And I'll get my lawyers to push the district attorney to file harassment charges against her like I've wanted to all along. Your misdirected sympathy isn't going to keep me from legally pursuing her anymore. She wants to lock you up. You get that part, right?" He aimed another scathing look at Hayley. "We're done here." He flung open the door, then motioned for Dalton to join him.

Hayley pulled her hand back and clasped them both together on top of the table. What his boss had just said had her feeling awful for not trusting Dalton. All this time, Mason had wanted her arrested. But Dalton had refused. He'd given her the benefit of the doubt, patience, respect for her views even though he didn't agree with them. She was having a harder and harder time believing he could ever do something as violent and ugly as hurt her friend, let alone kill her.

But if that was so, then why had Bethany written all those things about him in her journal? And what did those pictures mean?

From the sympathetic look that Dalton was giving his boss, he must have understood why Mason was so angry at the prospect of Dalton being handcuffed. Something horrible had obviously happened in Mason's past. And because of it, he wasn't budging on this issue.

And, apparently, now Dalton wasn't either. He pushed his chair back and stood.

Desperate to keep her chance from slipping away, she grabbed the NDA and signed it, then tossed the pen on top. "There. I'm ready to talk. All I want is for you to ensure my safety. It's not like I'm asking for something impossible or even that difficult. There has to be a way to make this happen."

"Gentlemen," Olson said. "I have an idea."

# Chapter Eleven

Detective Olson had apologized profusely to Hayley for the dust and spiderwebs in this lineup room when he'd brought in the flimsy table and chair. He'd explained that most lineups were conducted digitally these days and that this room was rarely used anymore.

A few feet in front of her, taking up most of the wall, was a rectangular two-way mirror. Or was it called a *one*-way mirror? She could see her reflection, while in the booth on the other side of the glass, Dalton and Mason could see her. It made her self-conscious, knowing they could be watching right now, hearing every little whisper of fabric when she shifted positions or crossed her legs. She shivered and ran her hands up and down her arms.

The speaker above the glass crackled. "Is the room too cold?" Dalton asked. "Do you need a sweater?"

Point proven. "No, I'm, ah, fine. Thanks."

Another burst of static sounded. It was Detective Olson's voice this time. "I'm getting all the recording equipment shut down right now. We're almost ready. As agreed, I'll step out of the booth and stand outside the room you're in. Your conversation with Mr. Lynch and Mr. Ford will be completely confidential. When your meeting is over, I'll come into the lineup room with a policewoman who will escort you up front to change and be processed out. Understood?"

She understood *processed out*.

"Yes. Thank you."

"Okay. The interview will begin in just a few more minutes."

She clasped her hands on the table, already thinking about what she'd do once she finally got home. A long shower was at the top of her list. Maybe two. Then she'd catch up on some website updates that she did on the side. Rent was due soon, and she didn't think she had enough available on her credit cards to pay it.

Building custom websites had started out as a way to get extra money to help pay off her daunting student loans. And since her corporate employer didn't allow freelancing on the side, calling it a conflict of interest, she was forced to keep quiet about her little venture and couldn't advertise it openly anywhere.

Bethany had inadvertently helped her get her first client. She'd been sitting on Hayley's couch with her laptop, showing Hayley a boutique gift website that Hayley had never heard of before. But rather than be impressed with the novelties for sale, Hayley had laughed about the amateurish quality of the company's website. She'd declared that she could out-design whoever had created it. Bethany had dared her to prove it.

The very next day, Hayley had approached the company about upgrading their system, offering them a ridiculously low fee to see if she could tempt them to hire her without references. She'd confided that she designed websites for a corporation during the day, and had showed them some of that work. They were so impressed that they'd jumped at her offer. Her little secret side-career was off and running.

She could still remember the joy of putting that ghost icon on the bottom of each web page, a nod to the nickname she'd been given in college for completely non-computer reasons. She should have trademarked the ghost image, and likely would eventually. But she didn't want her corporate employer to know that she was moonlighting, so she couldn't risk it. But to her, it was like a signature, declaring the website as her creation. She couldn't be more proud.

And when that same client had later asked her to create a series of proprietary website pages unviewable by the public, she'd brainstormed how to do what they wanted. They were too small to have their own programmers. So she needed to set up a way for them to access the secret pages but also to have the flexibility of searching the internet, per their request, without anyone seeing their trail. They needed to be able to ensure the security of their information, and keep proprietary data from being found by any search engines.

What she'd come up with was a series of web pages that weren't linked to any other web pages, not even the original site. The client would have to key the exact internet addresses in order to access them, which was a bit of a chore. But she created an algorithm to help them remember the addresses.

Then the client had asked her to set up an interface using the TOR browser, because they'd heard it had been designed with cybersecurity and anonymity as its primary goals. She did it and they were thrilled. And she was more than thrilled with the bonus they gave her. That first client had referred her to others with similar needs, and her business had taken off.

The high cost of medical insurance and the awesome 401(k) plan at her corporate job had her debating whether to risk going solo, or keep her day job. But before she could make that decision, the worst had happened.

Bethany had disappeared.

A few days later her body was found on Dalton's property. Hayley's ensuing investigation had adversely impacted both her corporate job and her side job. She really needed to do some updates for her clients to bring in an influx of cash. Yet another reason to hurry and get this interview over with.

The speaker crackled again, then another voice came through, Dalton's deep, incredibly compelling tone. Instead of the easy familiarity of their most recent conversations, he spoke with a polite formality. Was that because his boss was with him? Even more surprising was that he opened the conversation asking her basic, general questions about herself that seemed inconsequential and unnecessary. She relaxed in her chair and answered his banal questions about what she'd studied in college.

He asked about her job as a computer programmer in nearby Pigeon Forge, and why she'd decided to rent a cabin in Gatlinburg when she'd been living much closer to her office before this. Again, not exactly a shocker that it was because of her friend's death, and the fact that police were getting nowhere with the investigation. She'd wanted to be close enough to go to the police station every day to prod them. And she'd wanted to keep an eye on Dalton.

What did surprise her was that he asked about her work outside of her official one. When she asked how he knew about her one-person company, he couldn't recall where he'd heard about it. One of her clients must have mentioned it to him. But how would he have met them? Did his work involve small retail companies? She still didn't really know what kind of work he did.

She answered his questions as best she could, without revealing any of the details about her secret web pages. Her clients wanted those behind-the-scenes proprietary pages kept secret and she had no reason to reveal anything about them.

As they volleyed back and forth, she wondered what the point of his questions were. Other than the ones about her company, everything else that he was asking was common knowledge. Most of the answers could be found through a simple internet search. Her life wasn't exactly a mystery. She wasn't one of those people who worried about what they put on social media, even though she probably should.

He was good at interviewing people, putting them at ease. Was it his background as a cop? Or some kind of strategy?

Instead of answering his latest question, she asked one of her own. "What do *you* do for a living? You said you weren't exactly a private detective. But you're not a cop either. So why do you have an investigation file on Bethany?"

The speaker went silent.

"Dalton? Are you still there?"

Static sounded. "Still here. I guess you could think of me as a PI, sort of. I'm more a jack-of-all-trades—investigator, problem solver, bodyguard when necessary."

Bodyguard? She could see that. He definitely had the physique for it. And she could see how her website could interfere with that work. He probably needed his identity kept secret so people wouldn't zero in on him as a bodyguard when he was with clients. Guilt rode her hard again. "But you work for Mason."

"He's my employer. Regarding your website business, you—"

"Is he a bodyguard, too?"

Low murmurs indicated they were having a side conversation in the booth. But she couldn't make out what they were saying.

A moment later, another voice sounded. Mason's. "I run a company called the Justice Seekers." Where Dalton's voice was patient and soothing, Mason's was gruff and borderline hostile. "My team is a diverse group of men and women with all kinds of strengths and talents. We do whatever it takes to get justice for our clients. The actual work we do varies depending on their needs. And I'm adding five minutes onto our half hour since you're asking questions instead of answering ours."

She blinked. "You can't do that."

"Did you read the fine print in the agreement you signed? I can, and will, if we need the extra time."

She crossed her arms, frowning at the mirror. "Let me guess. One of *your* talents is that you're a lawyer. They're really good with fine print."

"Actually, no." His voice sounded ridiculously cheerful compared to his earlier gruffness. "But I do have a lawyer on staff. He's the one who put together that NDA."

"Of course he did," she grumbled. "I've never heard of these Justice Seekers. They didn't come up when I was looking into the ownership of the building where Dalton goes to work every day. I gave up on that, by the way. Never could figure out who owned it."

"I prefer to keep my company off most peoples' radar so I've set up a few hurdles that you obviously ran into during your investigation," Mason said. "We prefer to get our clients through word of mouth rather than through any traditional advertising. Plenty of people know about the work we do, or we wouldn't risk telling you about it, NDA or not. But we like to keep it as quiet as possible for a variety of reasons."

"Such as?"

"Such as the fact that everyone I hire is either former law enforcement or worked very closely with them, and they were each double-crossed or set up in some way that destroyed their careers. For that reason, most of the law enforcement people that we work with on behalf of our clients don't trust us. But the few who do, and realize how much value we can provide them on their cases in exchange for helping us with ours, do it secretly in order to protect their own careers. That's the main reason that we try not to advertise what we do. To protect those who risk everything to work with us."

"Sounds admirable, actually. Giving wronged people a second chance," she said. "I certainly wouldn't want to jeopardize any police officers' careers by blabbing about your company. But you said that's the *main* reason you want secrecy. What's another?"

"It's an extension of the first reason, Miss Nash. In order to do their jobs effectively, my employees need to be as anonymous as possible. Undercover work, for example, is common. When someone broadcasts information about them, like you do with your blog posts, it shines a spotlight and makes undercover work almost impossible."

She curled her fingers against her palms, hating that he was once again making her feel guilty. "Okay, I get the need for secrecy. But what do you want from me?"

"Taking down your website against Dalton would be a great start," Mason said, his voice laced with anger again.

Dalton chimed in as if to head off an argument. "Did you know that your freelance journalist friend, Miss Miller, hired the Justice Seekers to help with the last news investigation she was working on before she died?"

She grew still. "What are you talking about?"

"That thick folder that Mason brought into the interview room is our file on Miss Miller. She was doing a freelance investigation, hoping to sell it as an exposé to one of the national TV news programs. But things started getting dicey and she was worried she might be in over her head. She shared what she had with us, and we'd just started our own deep dive into what she was uncovering when she was killed. The fact that her body was discovered on my property is no coincidence. We believe the killer was sending a message, to me and the rest of the Justice Seekers, that if we didn't stop digging, we'd meet the same fate."

What he'd said actually made sense. Bethany had journaled that she'd reached out to a group to help her nail down her story and get more hard evidence before she could take it to a news network. But she'd never mentioned them beyond that one entry. And the name Justice Seekers was never mentioned. But Dalton's name was, over and over.

"Dalton, are you saying that you were working with her? You specifically? Not one of the other Seekers?" She clutched her hands together on top of the table, waiting for his answer.

"Yes. I was. I worked undercover, meeting the contacts she'd made in the underworld, trying to get them to trust me so I could figure out who was running the show. Unfortunately, she was killed before I got very far."

"Were you ever in a bar with her? As part of that work?"

He laughed. "Are you kidding? Most of our meetings were in bars. I meet lots of clients that way. It's an easy cover, just a couple of people drinking and talking in a roomful of other people who are drinking and talking. No reason to think there's anything important being discussed. It's an easy cover for a lot of things."

She stood and crossed to the mirror. "Bethany gushed about you in her journals. She talked about how, ah, hot you were. She said you were an item, that you two were dating."

A cough sounded, then he cleared his throat. "That's news to me. I assure you, our relationship is, was, always professional. I certainly never did anything to give her the impression that it was anything more, not intentionally at least. Is that why you think I killed her? Because of some journal entries?"

She squeezed her eyes shut a moment, then let out a shuddering breath. "You'd have to read her journals to understand. They're quite convincing, especially if you combine them with the pictures and the lack of other suspects. And that she never mentioned that you were helping her. I thought you were an ex-cop on the take, working with bad guys, and that you double-crossed her. That's how the journals read. All along, I wanted the police to do a thorough investigation, and became more and more convinced that you were the one who killed her. Now, I don't know what to think."

Static crackled. "You still have these journals? And pictures?" Dalton asked.

She hesitated. "You don't sound angry."

"Why would I be angry? Nothing I've heard makes me think you're arbitrarily being vindictive. On the contrary. You're listening to me and doing everything you can to solve the murder of your friend. I'm not angry. But I'd like to hear more, especially about the pictures."

She thought about the stack of photographs in her purse, the purse that was currently in lockup with her other personal effects. Dare she mention that they were in this very building? They were her ace in the hole, the one thing she took with her everywhere she went, just in case she found a witness who might recognize some of the people Bethany had photographed. Not that it had done her any good so far. The police hadn't been interested in either the journals or the pictures when she'd first complained that their investigation into Dalton hadn't been extensive enough. Her hope had always been to find more evidence, then try again.

Maybe this was the perfect time. She could at least show the photos to Detective Olson, since they were in the building.

He'd been nice and helpful. He might actually do something, unlike the other detective she'd spoken to. If she could hand off this investigation to someone who'd actually pursue it, she could move on with her life. She'd be more than happy to take down her website and go back home, as long as someone figured out who killed her friend—and brought them to justice.

"Hayley?" Dalton asked. "You still have the pictures?"

She stepped back from the mirror. "I do. They're in my purse, with my other personal effects. Right here at the station."

Another hesitation, then, "Are there date and time stamps on them?"

"Bethany was an investigative journalist. Of course there are dates and times on them. Not that the police seemed to care," she grumbled.

"What do you mean? You showed them to the police?"

She didn't see the point in lying. "The detective I spoke with wasn't impressed. She said anyone can Photoshop things these days, and that without corroborating evidence, the photos were worthless. I told her about Bethany's letters and journal entries and she still wasn't interested. That's why I've been trying so hard to both protect the public from you and get you to break, maybe even confess."

"Did she get copies of the pictures from you?" he asked.

She shook her head. "No. She thought I was crazy. Barely glanced at them and said they didn't prove anything."

Again, one of those aggravating silences. She could imagine them muting their side of the speaker and having side conversations about her.

She rubbed her hands up and down her arms again. She was a jumble of nerves, the effects of this past week making her ramble all over the place, accusing Dalton one moment and regretting it the next. Getting out of this place couldn't happen fast enough. "Is the half hour up?"

"Just a few more questions," Dalton said. "Do you remember the name of the detective you spoke to, the one you showed the pictures?"

"Simpson, or Sampson. Something like that. She told

me I didn't have any proof of any wrongdoing and that I should just let it go."

"You mentioned they were in your purse here at the station?"

"Yes. But I'm not turning them over to you. I'm not ready to give them up just yet. I have some thinking to do."

"If I get Detective Olson to bring you your purse, will you at least hold the pictures up to the glass so we can view them? And grant us more time in the interview to allow for some follow-up questions, if needed?"

She shrugged. "I don't see the harm in that. As long as it's not that much longer."

A few minutes later, she was standing in front of the mirror, holding each photo up one at a time while they looked at them. Since there were over fifty pictures, it took a while, especially since they asked questions between them, and often would have her hold a specific one up longer than the rest while they obviously conferred with each other in the booth.

She didn't have to turn the pictures around to know what they showed—known criminals, Bethany in some shots with Dalton, then Dalton in many of the others without her. There was no denying the exchanges of cash for what appeared to be kilos of cocaine or some other illegal drug. But if he really was undercover, playing a role, that could explain everything.

"Can you put that last one up again?" Dalton's voice sounded oddly strained.

She fanned out the ones in her hand. "This one?"

"Yes. Please."

A few minutes later he asked, "How did you get the pictures, and the journals you've mentioned, if they belonged to Miss Miller?"

She set the stack on the table beside her purse. "They were in a storage unit she kept outside of town. I remembered her mentioning she had one and I went around to every storage company around here until I found one under her maiden name. It was prepaid for a year, but I showed them the local news article about her death. And the owner went ahead and let me get into the unit. I may have claimed to be her sister and that I didn't want to wait for the courts to go through probate." Her face turned warm. "I told him I just wanted something to remember her by. It was a treasure trove of information on her investigation."

She leaned back against the table, but it wobbled so she straightened. "She wrote about you, a lot. She described your truck, down to that huge toolbox or whatever it is that you keep in the back, even wrote down the license plate number on some of her notes that I found later. It was easy to believe she had a thing for you, and that it was mutual."

"I'm sorry it looked that way to you, Hayley. I assure you those pictures that you just showed us are from after she hired the Justice Seekers. Mason can vouch for that, based on the date and time stamps. I'm not a drug runner, or a gun runner."

She smiled sadly. "Yeah, I kind of don't believe that either. Not anymore."

"Thank you for that, at least," he said, sounding tired.

"I'm sorry, Dalton. I still need some time to come around on the whole murder thing. I have to—"

"Think on it. I know. Thanks for your honesty. And your time. I'll tell Olson to come get you."

"Remember the NDA that you signed." Mason's voice crackled through the speaker. "It covers any physical evidence shown by either party to the other during the discussion. Originally, that was intended so that you could review our folder—if you'd agreed to sit with us face-to-face. Which you didn't. But that clause also extends to the pictures you have. If you show them to Olson, or anyone else, our agreement is null and void. You go back to jail. And we press charges. I assure you, I will pursue you to the fullest extent of the law, even if I can't convince Dalton to do the same. Even if your harassment doesn't rise to the legal level of stalking, I imagine my contacts in the FBI would be interested in pursuing a case of cyberbullying against you. I suggest that you think really hard about that before you do anything else to harm Dalton, or any other of my company's employees."

"Mason, stop it," Dalton said. "She doesn't deserve to be treated—"

"Oh yes, she does," Mason continued. "And frankly, Miss Nash, I don't care one whit whether you believe that Dalton is innocent. Your defamation against him ends today. And if you doubt for one second that I'll follow through, I suggest you perform an internet search on my name and Beauchamp, Louisiana, a little town in Sabine parish. That will tell you just how far I'll go when someone wrongs the people I care about."

She stared at the mirror, her pulse rushing in her ears. "Are you threatening me, Mr. Ford?"

Silence met her question.

"Hello? Are…are you still there?"

A knock sounded on the door, making her whirl around in surprise. It opened to reveal Detective Olson and a female uniformed officer.

Olson smiled. "Ready to go to Processing?"

So that was it. After Mason tossed out those threats, the Justice Seekers were gone. And now she had a choice to make. She glanced at the stack of pictures, considering her options. Above all, the most important thing, the only thing that would allow her to sleep well at night and face herself in the mirror, was to get justice. For her friend. But also for Dalton. So what was the best way to make that happen?

"Miss Nash?"

"Coming." Decision made, she grabbed her purse, then the stack of pictures, and started toward him.

# Chapter Twelve

Dalton pressed his palm against the panel to the right of the door frame. A split second later, after his prints were scanned and authenticated, the massive steel door swung open on silent hinges. He strode across the stone floor of the massive room that he and the other Justice Seekers affectionately called the great hall. Most of the team was already there, sitting at the giant round stone table with a computer tablet sitting in front of each of them.

Mason gave him an aggravated look as Dalton took his seat. "Nice of you to join the rest of us."

Since Mason was already nodding at one of the other Justice Seekers to continue what she was saying, Dalton didn't bother to explain why he'd been late. His boss would find out soon enough.

"Go on, Kira," Mason said. "You were giving us the rundown about the photographs."

She gave her report as she tapped a pen on her yellow legal pad, which she tended to favor over her computer tablet. A habit that Dalton often took up as well. It came in handy, like when he was in a visitation room at the local jail where they wouldn't allow electronics. But Kira favored it because of her previous occupation as a prosecutor, and the need to be able to take notes during courtroom testimony without the noise that a keyboard might make.

"Our contacts at Gatlinburg PD indicated that Miss Nash

has adhered to the NDA," Kira continued. "She didn't disclose the pictures to Olson, or anyone else that we're aware of."

"That we're aware of," Mason repeated, not sounding pleased.

Kira shrugged. "Tapping into their security camera feeds would be risky, at best. I don't recommend trying, especially since she could show the pictures to someone else even after leaving the station. We'd have to keep her under 24/7 surveillance to be positive that she's keeping her word. Even then, if she has electronic copies, she could email them."

Mason nodded. "Understood. The benefits of viewing the police video don't warrant the risk at this time. Even involving our contacts to legally hunt down that information might not be necessary. As damaged as Dalton's reputation already is around here, I'm not sure the pictures would make much difference. Not that it's your fault, Dalton."

"Thanks for that," Dalton said dryly.

Mason smiled, his demeanor much improved now that he was back in the huge cabin that served as their office building and not sitting in a police station. Of all the Seekers, their leader was the one with the most to resent when it came to his past life in law enforcement. Any time he had to make the trek downtown to deal with police, or other officials, his mood turned sour.

"Bishop," Mason said to one of the others at the table. "How are you making out with the murder list? Figured out any patterns? Can you make any predictions?"

Dalton knew the answers before Bishop spoke. It was obvious by his haunted expression that he hadn't made any real progress. After he finished speaking, his bleak gaze spoke volumes. He was growing just as disheartened as the rest of them.

"What about you, Diaz?" Mason motioned toward the

man a few seats to Dalton's left. "What's our former Marine MP got to report on the Miller case today?"

Jaxon Diaz, third-generation Cuban-American, recently dishonorably discharged from his job as an MP in the Marines for refusing to follow orders—even though those orders would have resulted in the deaths of half his unit—sat forward in his seat and provided an update on the research he'd been conducting.

Dalton listened to Jaxon, then Brielle, then LeMarcus as they each took turns giving reports. Unfortunately, they all had one thing in common—none of them were making much headway.

The sound of footsteps echoing through the room had all of them turning to see former FBI profiler Bryson Anton coming through the same door that Dalton had recently entered.

Bryson gave Dalton a subtle nod, before taking his seat to Mason's left.

Never one to miss anything, Mason's eyes narrowed as he looked from Bryson to Dalton. But he was savvy enough not to say anything right now, and motioned for another Seeker to provide updates on their work on the Miller case.

Normally, they each worked on separate cases or teamed up in twos or threes as needed. Not this time. They were all working the same investigation and would be until the bitter end. Because this wasn't just about justice for those who'd already died and preventing the deaths of more to come. It was about justice for one of their own, the man who would normally be sitting in the only empty chair at the table—Seth Knox, also known among their team as the Rancher.

The same man who'd been in the last photograph that Hayley had pressed against the glass earlier today.

"Are you ready with your report?" Mason asked, indicating Dalton.

In response, Dalton tapped on the computer tablet in

front of him. There was a collective gasp in the room when the picture he'd taken with his phone in the lineup booth appeared on the bank of large screens behind the round table, as well as their individual screens.

"When was this taken?" Kira demanded.

"Where?" another asked.

Mason held up his hand. "Everyone, settle. Let Dalton explain what you're seeing."

Dalton motioned toward the former prosecutor. "Kira told you about the photographs that Miss Nash has. You all know that Mason and I interviewed her today at Gatlinburg PD and that she signed a nondisclosure agreement to keep confidential the pictures she showed us. The picture on the screen is one that she had. I took a snapshot of it on my phone."

He tapped a few more keys, making the frame zoom in on the bottom right, where the date and time stamp were displayed. "This may be the last known photograph taken of Seth."

He zoomed back out and pressed his finger against the screen, drawing a red circle around a person in the background. "That's Bethany Miller. This picture was taken in one of the bars where she frequently met with contacts during her investigation into the drug-and gunrunning that she was hoping to reveal during a prime-time news special. I'm sure you all recognize some of the men she's talking to. Many have already been arrested, partly due to our help. And notice where Seth is looking. Right at them. I don't think that's a coincidence, or the timing, or the fact that this was with other photographs from Miller's cameras she hid and used to record her meetings."

Jaxon tapped his screen. "You think Seth might have stumbled onto this ring even before Miller officially brought us onboard? And some of the thugs killed him?"

"Possibly. We've never found a thread of anything to

explain why he disappeared, even after we found his body. I think he could have stumbled across something that he wasn't supposed to see or hear, and whatever that is could be related to our case. I don't believe in this big of a co-incidence, that the same people we're investigating are in the picture with him and he's killed after that picture was taken. We need to switch gears, reanalyze his daily routine and figure out where this bar comes into play. Why was he there that particular night? We need to go back several more weeks and build a new timeline, figure out what made him go there."

Mason sat in silence a moment, then spoke to the man on his immediate right. "Caleb, I think our special friend may know something about Seth's disappearance, or at least what led up to it. I want answers."

"Yes, sir." He typed on the keyboard in front of him, probably sending a copy of the picture to his phone.

"Go now and take Kira with you," Mason added. "Given her prosecutorial background, that might make the questioning go more smoothly."

Kira looked eager to get started as she shoved back from the table.

Dalton stopped her. "Check the emergency car, see whether it's been driven anywhere. Maybe check the hood for warmth, the gas gauge. It was full last time I checked."

"Not my first rodeo, cowboy." She winked and headed for the door.

Mason motioned toward their former Gatlinburg police officer. "Brielle, you put together the original timeline around the weeks before Seth's disappearance. You've spoken to his friends, already have a rapport with his family. Can you get started on the new, expanded timeline?"

"You bet. I'll need help though. That's a lot of ground to cover and we'll need the timeline ASAP to assign out more interviews to the rest of the team. I'll start at the bar where that picture was taken. Bryson, can you assist?"

Bryson glanced at Dalton. But before either of them could say anything, Mason interjected, his gaze directed at Dalton even though he was still talking to Brielle. "Take Jaxon. He's younger and might fit in at a bar better than our profiler. Besides, I need to speak privately to Bryson and Dalton for a few minutes. Everyone, thank you, as always. I'll see you back here in the morning. Hopefully we'll have made some progress by then."

There was a collective look of surprise at the abrupt end to the meeting. But the room soon emptied, leaving Mason, Dalton and Bryson alone.

Mason tapped the virtual keyboard on his computer and all of the tablets went dark. He leaned back, gently rocking his leather chair as he steepled his fingers in front of him.

"Okay, gentlemen. What's going on? Why were both of you late to an emergency meeting? And what's with the secretive looks you kept exchanging? Spill it."

Dalton rested his forearms on the table. "Mason, although you're inclined to think Hayley's in this as deeply as the criminals she works for, up to and including that she could even be The Ghost, I'm still skeptical. We did enough surveillance on her early on to know she doesn't go out much, other than to follow me. And there's nothing in her background to indicate relationships with mastermind criminals."

"Other than her creating websites for many of the criminals coming up in this investigation, and using a ghost icon to mark her work?" Mason arched a brow. "Seems awfully coincidental since we're looking for a criminal who calls himself The Ghost." He held up his hand to stop Dalton's reply. "But I do agree, she doesn't fit the profile of our serial killer. Our very own profiler has said as much." He motioned to Bryson, who nodded his agreement. "So I am open to other possibilities. Just not as open as you are."

Dalton didn't appreciate that gibe. Mason had already mentioned after their interview at the jail that Dalton seemed too considerate of her, as if his emotions were involved. His denials had fallen flat, probably because he was beginning to wonder himself if he was losing his objectivity around her.

"Go on," Mason urged. "You were going to explain what you and Bryson are up to."

Dalton exchanged a quick look with Bryson, then continued. "I've always been skeptical that tricking Hayley into revealing her personal little corner of the dark web will lead us to The Ghost. But if there's any chance it will, it's become even more critical with the discovery that Seth's death may be related to our case. Somehow, we have to accelerate this and get her on board. The Ghost has never waited this long between kills before. Another victim's going to die soon if we don't figure out the killer's identity and stop him. Hayley's side job could be the key, even if she's not aware of it."

"Agreed," Mason said. "I take it you have a plan, something you and Bryson cooked up together?"

They both nodded.

"But you're not going to like it," Dalton said. "I know I don't."

"Why is that?"

Bryson cleared his throat. "It means sharing far more information with Miss Nash than we ever intended. Though, not the whole truth, of course. But the worst part is that you'll have to cash in one of those hard-won favors the bureau owes you, along with our main Gatlinburg PD contact." He started to say something else, then hesitated.

"Go on." Mason frowned. "Finish it."

Bryson cleared his throat. "You, ah, might have to

grovel to make this happen. And, honestly, I'm not even sure they'll agree if you do."

Mason grimaced at the mention of groveling. "I'm already being way nicer to our insiders on this case than I'm comfortable with. And I've never made a particularly good lapdog for the official agencies, even when it was part of my job as chief of police in Louisiana." He idly tapped the table. "Is what we want them to do legal?"

Dalton nodded. "Technically, yes. It involves lying to Hayley, even more than we already have. We all know that law enforcement is allowed to lie in order to trick criminals." He rubbed his stomach, wondering if he was starting to get an ulcer because of what he was doing to her. It would serve him right. "The real danger is if she tries to call the FBI or the police to double-check the lies. It could get our friends in trouble."

"What's the worst that could happen to them?" Mason asked.

"They could lose their jobs."

Mason nodded, looking somber. "Make sure they know the risks. But also let them know that if they do get fired, I'll make sure they're generously compensated financially. That's the best I can offer. I'm not hiring more Seekers." He glanced at Seth's empty spot at the table. "Not yet." He sat forward in his chair. "Tell me what you need me to do."

# Chapter Thirteen

Even with a fire roaring in her tiny rental's fireplace, and a thick blanket wrapped around her as she sat cross-legged on the couch, Hayley couldn't quite shake the bone-deep chill that had settled inside her at the police station earlier today. Another shiver had her sighing heavily and tossing aside the blanket. She stuffed her feet into her fuzzy yellow slippers before padding across the scarred hardwood floor to throw another log onto the fire.

There weren't that many logs left. Her remaining stash wouldn't last more than a few days. Soon, she'd be forced to buy another cord of wood. Thankfully, she'd just finished making some of those overdue website updates that her clients had wanted. So she'd have money wired to her bank account tonight.

More shivers had her tightening her robe and staring with longing at the thermostat near the fireplace. As if on its own free will, her right hand inched up toward the lever to turn on the heater. *No.* She jerked her hand down. The last time she'd run the central heat, she'd ended up with an energy bill that she was still trying to pay off. What little insulation the cabin had was enough to keep the pipes from freezing, but that was it. The heater would run nonstop once it was on, just trying to keep up.

Instead, she plodded into the kitchen to make a second cup of hot chocolate. As she mixed the ingredients, her thoughts once again wandered back to the harrowing day that she'd had. She still wasn't sure what to think of Dalton. Which was why she'd changed her mind about giving those pictures to Detective Olson.

And then she'd come home and searched the internet for information on Mason Ford in Beauchamp, Louisiana, as he'd told her to do. And came away with a whole new respect for him. And, surprisingly, a healthy dose of sympathy as well.

The man had been an island in a swamp of unethical, backstabbing hypocrites. When he uncovered the illegal schemes going on in his own police department, his brother had paid the price, being framed for murder and sent to prison. Mason had secretly brought in the FBI to help, but it was too late for his brother. He'd been murdered in prison. The town paid a hefty price for their deeds, with many of the deputies and town leaders going to prison, and their insurance policy paying millions to Mason in a civil lawsuit. He'd used that money to move hundreds of miles away and start over, forming his group he called the Justice Seekers.

Of course, that last part, about the Justice Seekers, wasn't on the internet. She'd filled in that gap based on what she'd been told today at the police station.

The microwave dinged, startling her. She took out the cup of hot chocolate. A deep whiff of the sweet confection helped ground her in the present, and ward off thoughts of Seekers and crooked towns and the worst week of her life.

But not all of it was bad.

Dalton had turned out to be the bright spot. She wanted to dig back into her investigation not to prove his guilt anymore, but to hopefully prove his innocence. Knowing his alibi would help. But since he wouldn't share it, she'd have to keep digging.

And if she really could prove his innocence, what then? If he was innocent, then what she'd done to him was unforgiveable. For now, until she could be sure, she had to push that potential guilt aside.

She sipped the delicious liquid, not even caring that it scalded her throat. Then she returned to the couch to continue her perusal of the pictures spread across the coffee table that Dalton and his boss had been so interested in at the jail.

Especially the last one she'd pressed against the glass.

Dalton's voice had sounded so thick, so…odd…when he'd asked her to put that picture back up so he could see it again. She picked up the picture now, wondering what he'd seen that had him ending the interview just a few minutes later.

Was there something in the photo that had surprised him? Upset him? Angered him?

She tilted it to catch what little light shined down from the outdated, one-bulb fixture above her. It was one of several dozen pictures taken by a hidden camera that Bethany had used, showing a bunch of thugs in a bar. And Bethany, talking to them, doing her best to infiltrate their inner circle and get them to open up about their criminal enterprises and the bosses they worked for.

The group of men around her were familiar because Hayley had spent a considerable effort in identifying everyone she could in these photographs. Most had records and were already back in jail for one reason or another. Some of the same men appeared in many of the photographs and even videos that Bethany had collected, and Hayley still didn't know who they were. But this picture didn't seem any different than the others. So why had Dalton fixated on it?

She set the picture down and sorted through the others, separating them by date and time stamps. When that didn't provide any aha moments, she re-sorted them based on the people in each photograph. The ones where she'd identified everyone went in one pile. The rest, where at least one of the main people around Bethany was someone she didn't recognize, she put in another pile. Little by little, she whittled down the stacks until she ended up with one lone picture that showed a man that wasn't in *any* of the others.

The photograph that Dalton was most interested in.

Excitement flashed through her, warming her enough that her shivers finally stopped. She grabbed the photo. According to Bethany's notes, her hidden camera took still shots every fifteen seconds. Pretty much everyone in that bar was in three or four pictures, at least. Except this guy. Had he realized he'd stumbled onto something and quickly hid? Was that why he didn't appear in any other shots? Or did someone else realize he didn't belong, and did something to him? Or was there another explanation?

"Who are you?" she murmured, staring down at him.

She dissected his appearance into a laundry list of attributes: deeply tanned, as if he spent a lot of time outdoors; average height since he didn't tower over anyone else in the bar, and no one else towered over him; dark brown hair in a military-style cut, light-colored eyes, although she couldn't tell in the dim light exactly what color they were. He didn't wear a hat and was clean-shaven. His clothes were simple: jeans, a dark button-down shirt and a waist-length jacket. Inexpensive, everyday clothes that blended in with pretty much everyone else in the place. Nothing about him stood out.

A knock sounded on the front door.

She straightened and turned around, not that it did any good. The door was solid, without any glass to reveal whoever was on the other side. And no peephole either. She jerked back toward the fireplace and the boxy TV sitting on a rickety table beside it. The digital clock on the old-fashioned DVD player on top of the TV showed that it was just past nine thirty. Not exactly late by most people's standards. But it was an odd time to stop by a remote cabin halfway up the mountain. The rare landlord visits out here occurred during the day. And he always called ahead so he didn't drive all the way out only to find her gone.

Had anyone ever just…stopped by?

No. Not once. *Never.*

The knock sounded again. Alarm skittered up her spine. Was a burglar trying to find out whether anyone was home before breaking in? Her gun. Where was her gun? In her purse, the one she'd had in jail. She'd bagged it with her clothes that had developed a definite jailhouse funk from sitting in the evidence lockup for so long and had left them on the back porch. She'd intended on going through the bag tomorrow. It hadn't occurred to her to take the gun out of the purse first.

*Stupid, stupid, stupid.*

"Miss Nash?" a woman's voice called out. "I'm Detective Sampson, with the Gatlinburg police. We met once before, remember? Would you please open the door?"

Sampson? That was the detective who hadn't cared about her story when she'd tried to tell her about Bethany's notes and pictures. Wait, the police. Had Mason or Dalton decided to press charges after all? She couldn't go back to jail. She just couldn't. She *wouldn't.*

Instead of going to the front door to let Sampson inside, she dashed through the kitchen to the back door and flung it open.

She let out a squeak of surprise and cartwheeled her arms to regain her balance so she wouldn't fall against the man in a business suit standing on her porch. Blocking her exit.

"Whoa, ma'am. Didn't mean to frighten you."

Her flight reflex deserted her, leaving her trembling and frozen in place, unable to do anything but stare like a rabbit watching the snake about to devour it.

So much for her being a badass.

"Ma'am," he repeated, slowly reaching into his suit jacket pocket as if to keep from scaring another ten years off her life. "I'm Special Agent Jaylen Holland with the FBI. The person knocking on your front door is Gatlinburg Police Detective Erin Sampson. We'd appreciate it if we could have a few minutes of your time." He held up his identification, which should have made her happy that he wasn't a serial killer bent on murdering her. But instead, all she could seem to focus on were the three letters on the seal: FBI.

Oh, dear God, help her. What did they think she'd done?

"Miss Nash? May I come in?"

She swallowed hard and managed to make her shaking fingers pull the edges of her robe more tightly together. "Do I have a choice?" she whispered, barely able to force the words through her tight throat.

He smiled sympathetically. "My apologies for worrying you by coming out here unannounced. But, after what you went through at Gatlinburg PD, Detective Sampson and I were concerned that you'd try to avoid us if you knew we wanted to talk to you."

Her face heated as the truth of his words hung in the air between them. After all, instead of opening her front door for a police officer, she'd run to the back door and would have kept on running if he hadn't been there.

She frowned. "Wait. You know about my arrest?"

He nodded.

"What else do you know?"

"That you're looking for answers." He held up a briefcase that she hadn't noticed before. "And I'm here to give them to you. Some of them at least."

Her hand tightened on her robe. "You're here about my friend's murder?"

The knocking sounded again from the front of the house.

He arched a brow. "Perhaps we can continue our discussion inside. It's pretty chilly out here."

In spite of her fears, she couldn't help smiling at his assumption that the cabin would be a lot warmer than her porch. She stepped back to let him inside.

# Chapter Fourteen

Dalton bolted up out of bed and swiped his pistol off his nightstand. He swept it out in front of him as he peered into the dark recesses of his bedroom, all while listening to the cacophony of howls and barking outside his second-story window. Denali, who'd been sleeping in the closet, lumbered to his feet, softly growling as he began a circuit around the room to figure out what had Dalton so alarmed.

Dalton moved to the window and flipped the plantation shutters so he could look down into the front field. All of his dogs should have been enjoying a warm bed inside the barn. Instead, they were circling something, hackles raised, their deep-throated barks and growls filling the air.

Fang, the alpha of the pack, hop-skipped forward, barking ferociously. The terrified scream of a cornered animal had Dalton swearing and reaching for his discarded jeans and shirt from the chair by the bed. He quickly dressed and then shoved his pistol into his pocket in case he was going to have to put some poor wounded animal out of its misery.

He ran down the hallway, taking the stairs two at a time. After grabbing his trench coat from a hook by the front door, he ran outside and raced down the front steps.

"Fang, Sheba, back," he yelled as he rushed toward the pack of yipping dogs. "Down. Guard."

Thankfully the two leaders were well trained. They backed up several feet, yipping and growling but no longer taunting the terrified creature in front of them. The rest of the dogs followed their lead, and Dalton was finally able to get his first good look at what they'd caught.

Sitting on the cold, hard ground, her arms wrapped around her legs as she rocked back and forth, was his nemesis. He didn't think he'd ever seen someone look so pitiful as she jerked her head back and stared at him, wide-eyed, her face a white sheet.

He slowly bent down so as not to scare her even more, not even sure that she recognized him. "Hayley? It's Dalton. It's okay. You're safe now."

She blinked, her eyes glazed and unfocused.

"What happened to you?" he asked. "Why are you here?" He swore again. "And why in the world don't you have a coat on? It must be thirty degrees, if that."

He shucked out of his trench coat and then draped it around her shoulders. She shivered so hard her teeth chattered together, but at least she didn't fight him and he was able to fasten the top few buttons. Of course the reason she didn't fight him was probably that her terrified mind hadn't even registered who he was.

The sound of a low growl had him ordering the dogs back again. "Fang, retreat. Retreat. Go home."

The dog whined in disappointment but backed up as ordered. He yelped his own command and the pack trotted after him toward the barn.

Dalton gave Hayley a quick perusal, worried that his dogs may have become overzealous in their guard duties and actually hurt her. That wasn't their training, or he wouldn't allow them to roam freely on the property. But for her to be this shaken, it seemed she must have been hurt. He didn't see any scratches or blood to indicate that she'd been bitten. Had something else happened?

"Hayley, it's Dalton. Are you hurt?"

Again she didn't answer. Instead, she stared past him, toward the dogs.

He glanced over his shoulder at the driveway, then at the road a few hundred yards away. But he didn't see her Blazer. "How did you get here?"

She blinked again, then seemed to finally focus. "D-Dalton?"

He looked past her toward the woods that bordered his property to the south, in the direction of her house. "Did someone break into your home? And you ran all the way here for help?"

Fresh tears glistened in her eyes, then spilled down her cheeks. "I w-w-was wrong. A-bout y-you. Came to a-pologize. I'm s-s-sor-ry," she whispered between clicks of her chattering teeth.

He stared at her in shock as her stuttered words clicked in his mind. "You ran through the woods in the middle of winter, in the middle of the night, to apologize to me?"

She blinked several more times, frowning. Then shook her head. "Didn't…r-run. Car. Broke d-down." She waved toward the road as if to show him. "O-over th-the hill." She suddenly grabbed one of his hands, making him start from her icy cold touch. "I'm s-so sorry. Y-you have to for-g-give me."

It dawned on him that Sampson and Holland must have made their planned visit. But he'd never expected it to have this severe an impact. Good grief, what had he done by agreeing to the plan?

Guilt and anger had his face flushing hot. "Come on. Let's get you inside before you get frostbite." He straightened and pulled her to standing in front of him. But she was shaking so hard she started to fall over. He caught her, then lifted her in his arms and cradled her against his chest to carry her into the house.

Once inside, he leaned down to sit her on the couch, but

her arms tightened around his neck. He stood in indecision. She was shaking and he didn't know if it was because she was so dang cold or because she was still scared. Whispering soothing words, he tried again to put her down. She shifted against him, mumbling something incoherent.

The shock of her cold lips against his neck made up his mind. He cradled her with one arm to work his trench coat off her with the other. Then he shifted her and let the coat fall to the floor. He grabbed the throw from the back of the couch, sat down with her still clutched against his chest and tucked the throw around both of them.

A short time later, her breathing changed and she softened against him. He sighed and settled more comfortably against the couch and waited. And tried not to think about how amazing it felt to actually, finally hold her.

About twenty minutes later, she let out a sound of alarm and suddenly stiffened.

"It's okay, Hayley. You're—oof!" A flailing arm caught him in the stomach. The edge of the blanket smacked him in the face as she tried to get off his lap. "Just hold it a second. Let me get the blanket before you—"

She shoved against him and fell to the floor with a solid thump.

"Before you fall," he finished. He couldn't help smiling at the curses coming from her. But it was too dark to see much. He flipped on the table lamp beside him, then froze.

The muzzle of a pistol was pointed directly at his chest, just a few feet away, cradled between her hands.

With lightning speed, he knocked her arm up and yanked the pistol away from her. She was so startled, all she did was stare at him, mouth open.

"If you feel threatened enough to pull a gun on someone," he gritted out, "you'd better have your finger on the trigger and not give them a chance to take it from you. If I was truly a threat, you'd be dead right now." He ejected the magazine, then swore as he ejected the chambered round as well. If her finger had been on the trigger, she'd probably have shot him whether she meant to or not because of how badly she was shaking.

As if only just realizing what she'd done, she pressed a hand to her throat. "I'm so sorry. I didn't realize—"

"Stop apologizing. How about explaining to me why you're here at…" he glanced at the digital clock on the equipment below the TV "…eleven thirty at night, skulking across my property without a coat. And don't give me those lies you did earlier about your car breaking down as you were driving over. I don't believe that story after you pulled a loaded gun from your pocket. Did you park around the curve in the road, hoping to sneak up on me for some nefarious reason like when you broke in? And you assumed the dogs were locked up?"

Her eyes widened. Then she vigorously shook her head as she shoved to her feet. "No, no, no. That's not what I was doing."

He kept his seat on the couch and crossed his arms. "I'm waiting."

She blew out a deep breath, then sat beside him, facing him. "The gun… I'm sorry—"

"Just tell me what you're doing. You realize my dogs could have hurt you, or worse? They're trained to guard, to protect me and my property. You're lucky I came down when I did. If they'd seen your gun, they would have attacked. That's part of their training."

The blood drained from her face, leaving her deathly pale. "I didn't realize…" She swallowed. "My Blazer really did break down. I couldn't sleep, so many things running through my mind. And the house was so cold, I decided to drive to your office building, or cabin, whatever. I was going to leave a package for you there. But since I'm here now, and I've already woken you up, I could give it to you now."

"What are you talking about? And why is your house so cold? Is the heater broken?"

"Never mind about the heater. I've got something in my car for you. I don't suppose I could convince you to drive me to it, could I?"

## Chapter Fifteen

When Dalton pulled up beside her Blazer, he hopped down from the truck and jogged to the passenger side to help her, in spite of her insistence that she could manage it on her own. She was over a foot shorter than him and there was no way she could climb up into his elevated truck without help, let alone hop out without risking falling on her face.

She murmured her thanks, seeming embarrassed to accept his help. But at least she didn't fight him, and didn't accuse him of trying to kill her. That was nice, for a change.

While she rummaged in her SUV, he quickly checked it out in case whatever was wrong was a simple fix. It was. Hayley's face was bright red when he pointed out that she'd run out of gas. He opened the massive storage box that ran the width of his truck bed just behind the back window and took out his emergency gas can to fill her tank.

A few minutes later she parked in her driveway and he pulled in behind her to wait until she was safely inside. But instead of going into the house, she crossed to the passenger side of his truck with the satchel she'd retrieved and opened the door.

Her face turned a lovely shade of pink as she smiled at him. "I need to talk to you about this satchel. It's warmer in your truck than my cabin, so would you mind—"

"Of course."

After helping her into the truck and getting back in, he

turned in his seat to face her. "Why is your cabin cold? Do you need me to—"

She put her hand on his, sending a tingle of awareness straight to his groin. It was so unexpected that he forgot whatever he was about to say. Had he ever noticed before that she had blue eyes? Not dark, like his, but lighter, reflected in the light from the dashboard and her porch light.

She smiled again.

He cleared his throat. Twice. "You wanted to tell me something about that satchel?"

"I do." She picked it up and ran her fingers almost lovingly over the leather, as if saying goodbye to an old friend. "In here are the photographs I had at the police station. And other pictures and journals and flash drives with my research, as well as Bethany's. There are—"

"Hold it. Wait. Why are you telling me this?"

"Because it's yours. I'm giving it to you. Everything I have on my investigation into Bethany's death, including her own journals and what she left behind on her investigation into the drug dealing and gunrunning. I want you to have it."

He stared at her, stunned. "You're turning over everything you've been collecting for the past few months, plus everything your friend compiled?"

She nodded. "And that's not all. If you check my website, the one I created to try to get a following to pressure the police to investigate you, you'll find it's been taken down. I won't harass you anymore. You don't have to worry about me causing you problems in the future. I'm really sorry about everything I did. You can't imagine how sorry."

Her words were more alarming than reassuring. It seemed as if he finally had part of what he wanted—for her to take down her poisonous website. He'd never expected her to give him her notes or the pictures. None of this made sense.

Was she tricking him? Had she figured out that he'd been less than honest and his goal was to get information from her?

"Why?" he asked, letting that one simple word hang in the air between them.

She stared through the windshield at her cabin. "Because I got a visit tonight, from an FBI agent and a detective from the Gatlinburg police department." She swallowed hard, her hands fluttering in her lap. "They made me promise not to share any of the information that they revealed to me. But I don't see the harm in sharing it with you, since it's about you and you're working with them."

He sat quietly as she explained about Detective Sampson and Special Agent Holland's visit earlier in the evening. She explained how they'd sworn her to secrecy and had shared the information on the case that they were working on with a secret task force, the one that Dalton was part of. She'd been shown reports, pictures, affidavits, so much information, and all of it proving that Dalton hadn't killed Bethany Miller. Dalton had been undercover at the time, and they had dates and time stamps proving it, along with a list of all the other agents and police who'd been working that particular night with him to close a drug ring and get illegal guns off the street.

She wiped tears from her cheeks and let out a shuddering breath. "I didn't know that you were telling me the truth all along. You really were working with Bethany, helping her on her investigation. You brought in other agencies to bring down the same criminals that she was trying to bring down, even before her death. Half of those criminals in the pictures have already been arrested and put behind bars because of you. All this time, my website, my efforts to get justice, were just making your job harder. They told me you were forced to back off on your role, that you couldn't work undercover anymore because of me. Instead, you're investigating in an administrative capacity now. Again, because of me."

He fisted his hands against his thighs to keep from reaching for her. She looked so vulnerable, so shaken, so ridiculously contrite that he wanted to haul her onto his lap and tell her everything was going to be okay.

Even though he knew it wasn't.

"I'll never be able to fix this," she said. "I wish there was something I could do. But other than giving you all my notes and taking down my website, I don't know of anything else that I can—"

"You can help us."

She blinked. "Help you? What do you mean?"

He forced a nonchalant look, even managed a smile as he took the plunge, misleading her yet again. But the groundwork had been laid. He'd be insane not to take advantage of it. They were so close to getting what they really needed. He had to go for it.

"I appreciate that you're finally realizing that I'm not the bad guy you thought I was. And this—" he patted the satchel "—will be much appreciated by the, ah, task force. But there's something else you might be able to do that would help even more. Provide us your expertise on websites."

She straightened in her chair. "My expertise? You want me to help with your investigation?"

He nodded. "This task force is consuming resources left and right. And, as you said, I'm more behind the scenes now rather than on the frontline." Yeah, right. Like he'd ever agree to that. "One of the things I'm trying to do is break into some suspects' websites, for a variety of reasons that I can explain later. But the team is spread thin and I don't have anyone besides me who can really assist on the computer side at the moment. You're a computer programmer, and you've done a lot of web work, so, well, it would be a huge favor if you could show me what I'm doing wrong. Might give me a break in the case."

She slowly nodded. "Sure. Of course. I can try. You think this will help you catch the bad guys at the top of the food chain?"

"Yes." It definitely would. And it might catch Hayley, too. Sometimes, like right now, he really hated his job.

"And catch Bethany's real killer?"

He hesitated, then nodded. "Yes." Another lie.

She smiled, finally looking more like the Hayley he remembered. Was that a good thing? Or a bad thing?

"Happy to help," she said. "Especially now that I know your Stetson's color is wrong."

He frowned. "My Stetson?"

She waved a hand in the air. "Never mind. Do you want me to come to your workplace tomorrow morning?" She flushed. "I mean, this morning? Like maybe around nine?"

"Nine would be perfect."

Her smile widened. "Thanks, Dalton. Helping in some way, and knowing that I'm not hurting anyone this time, will really help my conscience."

It was killing his, using her guilt as a weapon against her. Handing her the rope to hang herself. "Like I said, I appreciate your assistance."

After helping her out of the truck and waiting until she was safely inside the cabin, he sped down the road. After the first curve, he jerked the truck to the shoulder. He sat there several minutes, thinking about the crazy twists and turns of the past week, and the unbelievable conversation he'd just had with Hayley. When he felt he could speak without yelling, he took out his cell phone and pressed the speaker button. Then laid it on the seat beside the satchel.

It took three rings before Mason's groggy voice came through the speaker. "This had better be important to wake me at this hour."

"Task force, Mason? Affidavits? Photos? What did you do?"

"She bought it?" Mason's voice immediately changed. He sounded downright cheerful.

"Yes. She bought it. She's coming to the office this morning to help me with the online part of the investigation."

"Excellent. Then the plan worked."

"No, the plan didn't work," Dalton said. "The *plan* was to get a few of our law enforcement allies to provide me an alibi for Bethany's murder. Then they would threaten her with prosecution if she didn't stop interfering in our work. The plan wasn't to make up lies about an official task force that doesn't even exist. The Justice Seekers aren't working with anyone on this case, not officially. What happens if she goes to the FBI or Gatlinburg PD to ask about the task force? Won't they be surprised since there isn't one?"

"I may have gotten creative but I don't see it being a problem. After her recent experience in jail, I don't see her walking into the police station to double-check our story. Why are you so upset?"

"You changed the plan without warning me. She threw me for a loop when she mentioned the task force. It's a good thing I was able to keep a straight face while I let her talk, so I could figure out how to play along when I didn't even know what she'd been told. You can't expect me to play a role when I don't know you've changed the script."

When Mason didn't say anything, Dalton continued, "She thinks I'm going to help her investigate the murder of her friend in exchange for consulting with us about websites. If she thinks I'm on a task force working with the local PD, how long before you think she asks me to show her the medical examiner's report on Miss Miller's death? How do you expect me to navigate all the questions *that* will raise?"

A reluctant-sounding Mason finally answered. "I can see how that might be…awkward. Challenging."

"It would be a disaster."

"Look." Irritation tinged Mason's tone again, though he sounded much more conciliatory than he had when he'd first answered the phone. "We got what we wanted, what we needed—her backing off and voluntarily agreeing to help us. We need to find The Ghost. If she's the criminal I believe her to be, she could be our key, as you agreed earlier. If not, my apologies. But I don't think I'll have to say I'm sorry any time soon."

"What if nothing goes as planned?" Dalton asked. "What if she realizes that she's being tricked?"

"Maybe she'll have to disappear, just like her friend."

He fisted his hand on the steering wheel. "That's your solution? Make her disappear?"

"If necessary, yes."

HAYLEY DROPPED HER headphones onto the floor and drew her knees up on the couch. She didn't know what had possessed her to throw that listening device into the satchel before giving it to Dalton. A last remaining niggling doubt perhaps? Her subconscious telling her something was off about the late-night visit by a police officer and a special agent? Either way, she hadn't expected anything when she'd put on her headphones.

Boy, had she been wrong.

She swiped at the tears running down her cheeks. Dalton had worked his way past her defenses and convinced her he was a good guy. And even though her mind was telling her that it was a good thing she'd learned the truth, her breaking heart wished she'd never found out.

And how stupid was that?

If she hadn't found out, she wouldn't know that Dalton

and Mason had plotted to murder Bethany. And that they were willing to do the same to her if necessary.

There was also that confusing discussion with Mason talking as if she was a criminal. Was that because of her breaking into Dalton's home to find proof about what he'd done? Or something more sinister? He'd mentioned a ghost, or had he said *The Ghost*? Was he fixated on her because he was trying to find someone who called themselves The Ghost, and she happened to use a ghost icon in her work? What was that all about? And why had he zeroed in on her as someone to even suspect?

She had to think, really think. And she only had until nine in the morning to come up with a plan.

She swiped at her tears and put her foolish hopes and dreams about Dalton away. He was her enemy, once again. And she'd do well to remember it.

The cabin was too cold for her to focus, so she rebelliously clicked the heater on. She'd deal with the outrageous energy bill later. Right now, she needed to get warm and get her brain firing again. She made another steaming mug of hot chocolate, stoked the fire and added another precious log to get the flames roaring. Then she sat on the couch considering every option she could think of.

What it seemed to boil down to was that the police couldn't be trusted any more than she could trust the Justice Seekers. After all, an actual policeman and FBI agent had gone along with Mason's plan and provided her with false information to get her to take down her website. She briefly considered putting it back up again, but that would invite questions from Mason and Dalton and she wasn't ready to go down that road and admit that she'd been listening in on their conversation.

Who could she trust? That was the real question. And there was only one person she could think of. Herself. She had to go on the offensive again and get some real information, hard facts, to figure out what was going on. So where was the information? After her break-in attempt at Dalton's home, she couldn't imagine that he would risk keeping anything there. If it had been there before, he would have moved it. But where?

*The Seekers' headquarters.*

It was the only place that made sense. She needed to get inside that building and get whatever they were hiding. The police, other than Sampson this time, would have to pay attention to her if she brought them hard facts. And if they didn't, she'd go to the press. A little national attention would put Gatlinburg PD under a microscope. They'd have to look into her claims, once and for all.

So how could she get inside? Her brief breaking-and-entering career was a dismal failure.

She straightened in her chair. Of course. It was so obvious. She already had an invitation. All she had to do was meet Dalton at the Seekers' cabin, and he'd open the door for her. He'd said he needed her help with computers. She could use that as her ruse to get inside.

But how could she get out with the data that she needed? She doubted their computer security would allow her to save anything to a flash drive without sending a security alert to Mason and the others. And she couldn't simply walk out the front door carrying a box of folders if she found anything incriminating in some physical files. She had to find another way to save and store that information.

This part of the problem had an equally easy answer. She hadn't been performing surveillance for months without learning a few tricks.

She jumped up and got her gun, the one that Dalton had returned to her after she'd pointed it at him. She shoved a loaded magazine into it and set it on the end table beside her. Then she headed into her bedroom.

After grabbing a button-up blouse, a needle and thread,

and a very special, very expensive button, she sat on the couch and drew her feet up. Then she bent over the shirt to sew on the new button that looked almost exactly like the others. Except that this button had the ability to bring down the Justice Seekers.

Too bad it didn't have the power to heal the damage to her breaking heart.

## Chapter Sixteen

Hayley peered through her Blazer's windshield from the back of the parking lot, past the other vehicles parked closer to the massive cabin where Dalton worked. Trees surrounded the place, framing the building against the backdrop of the beautiful Smoky Mountains. It all seemed so natural, normal, without a hint of the illegal things no doubt going on inside. The only thing here that seemed nefarious was her, and the little camera posing as a button on her blouse.

She glanced down, assuring herself the ridiculously expensive camera was still there. It wasn't like those clumsy old-fashioned wired ones that criminals in TV shows used. This one would transmit recordings via Bluetooth to the receiver in her Blazer.

The sound of a familiar powerful engine had her straightening. A jacked-up, blue Chevy pickup pulled into the lot. Dalton had arrived. Right on time. He parked a few rows in front of her in his aptly named Silverado. Perfect for a man who spent his life in boots and a cowboy hat. Then again, he'd moved here from Montana where he'd owned a ranch, so she assumed his choice of headwear and footwear came honestly. He really was a cowboy.

Too bad the color of his Stetson had turned out to be accurate after all.

He hopped out of the truck effortlessly, not bothering to use the running board to step down. To her surprise, he wasn't wearing his usual business suit. Instead, he was dressed casually in blue jeans visible beneath the hem of his dark trench coat.

He headed straight for her Blazer, obviously having seen her when he'd driven into the lot.

She fidgeted with her camera button, then took a deep, bracing breath before pushing open her door.

He held out his hand to help her. She wanted to ignore his offer, but that would seem suspicious after they'd left on such good terms last night. When she placed her hand in his, she felt the warmth and gentleness of that touch zing straight to her belly. Why was she cursed to crave this man, knowing he could never be hers? Knowing he and his boss had discussed making her go "missing"? She'd replayed that conversation over and over in her mind as she'd tossed and turned last night. All it had done was confuse her. He'd seemed to be defending her, and yet in the end, hadn't he agreed to whatever Mason had proposed?

"Hayley? You look flushed. Is everything okay?"

She jerked her hand back and tried to cover her telling action by smoothing down her jacket. "Must have had the heater going too high in my car. I'm fine."

A flash of disappointment crossed his achingly handsome face, as if he wished she hadn't pulled back her hand. "I have to admit I'm surprised you showed up. I figured after a good night's sleep, you'd go back to suspecting me again."

*If he only knew.*

She tightened her hands on the strap of her purse hanging off her shoulder. "Of course not. I'm glad to be here, to have a chance to actually make a difference."

His searching gaze had her wondering if he saw through her act. "Good. I don't want you to feel nervous or uncomfortable."

She was so uncomfortable that part of her wanted to

run screaming into the woods. But the pistol snugged into the back of her jeans beneath her jacket gave her the confidence to stay instead of getting the heck out of Dodge. "You could have asked me to come here when we were at the police station yesterday."

"I needed to get the okay from the team before moving forward. We don't grant access to this place to just anyone. Even clients have to be researched before being allowed here. Many of them never see the inside."

She glanced toward the structure. It really was huge, and gorgeous. It appeared to be only one-story but she imagined there was probably a lower level, maybe even a basement below that on a grid of stilts anchoring it to the side of the mountain, like most cabins around here. Land like this with a view was too expensive not to build as big as possible in each lot, which often meant building high instead of wide. This one, however, was definitely wide.

The building stretched from one end of the parking lot to the other and then some. A-frame gables extended out on both ends, shading an elevated front porch that would have looked inviting if there were any rocking chairs. But it was completely devoid of furniture, as if no one ever bothered to sit outside. Seemed a waste for such a beautiful place.

"I'm surprised there's no sign out front. I guess that goes along with your word of mouth way of getting clients, like Mason mentioned at the police station."

He cocked his head. "Just like with your website business. You get your clients through word of mouth instead of blatant advertising. Right?"

She hesitated, then nodded. "Right. Exactly."

He led her toward the building.

"How many people are on your team?"

His jaw tightened, for just a moment. If she hadn't been watching him, she'd have missed it. "Normally, twelve.

Plus Mason makes thirteen. We're a man down right now. But we'll staff up again. Eventually."

"A man down?"

He stopped at the bottom of the porch steps. "One of our Seekers, Seth Knox, died several months ago. Not long after your friend was killed."

His words, laced with obvious grief, had her placing her hand on his arm in solidarity without even thinking about it. "I'm sorry for your loss. Losing a friend is tough. Was it unexpected?"

His gaze dropped to her hand on his arm before he looked her in the eyes. "He was murdered. Stabbed."

She drew a sharp breath. "Oh my gosh. Was he mugged or something?"

He watched her for a long moment, then shook his head. "How did we get on such a morbid topic? Let's head inside and I'll give you the fifty-cent tour before introducing you to the team."

He led her up the stairs. There was an electronic keypad by the door, which looked as if it could easily keep out the occasional curious bear, or even a group of determined criminals if they wanted to break in. But rather than press any buttons, he pressed his hand beneath it. There must have been a biometric reader that validated his palm print, because a buzz sounded and the door popped open. He stepped back and waved her inside. "Welcome to the Justice Seekers' home base."

She'd barely gotten past the threshold when she stopped in surprise. The inside was absolutely nothing like the outside, which was a shame. There was no hint of the log cabin exterior in here. The beautiful golden logs had been covered with drywall and painted a pale gray. The room they were in was probably forty feet wide and just as deep, with black metal desks in two rows of six, separated by a network of glass walls framed in black metal. The floor was carpeted, a low-pile industrial-looking gray that matched the walls. Everything looked sleek, modern, industrial— the exact opposite of a typical mountain cabin.

"You don't like it. Let me guess, too modern? Doesn't match the outside, right?"

"Well, it looks cool, like a city loft or a converted ware-house, I suppose. It's just not what I expected. Seems a shame to cover up the natural beauty of the logs."

"That's Mason's doing. He has his reasons. Here, follow me and I'll show you the rest."

She motioned toward the empty desks as he led her past them. "Where is everyone?"

"Conference room. Morning meeting, strategizing what we're working on."

He put his hand on the small of her back. She jerked away, worried he'd feel the bump of her gun. "What are you doing?"

His brows raised. "Sorry. Didn't mean to offend you. Just wanted to guide you away from those steps before you took a tumble."

She glanced down, surprised to see she'd been about to put her foot on some steps that seemed to come out of no-where, curving down to the right. The level part of the floor took a wonky curve to the left before continuing straight. "Wow. I didn't see that. Thanks."

"You have to watch yourself in here. The floors slope and turn unexpectedly. Stay close and you'll be okay."

When he guided her around yet another seemingly random change in the flooring, she shook her head. "Why is the cabin built this way? Seems dangerous."

"It is. On purpose. We all know every inch of the build-ing, all the hidden doorways and secret rooms." He winked and she wasn't sure whether or not he was kidding. "Even if we lost the lights, we'd be able to walk it in the dark with-out a problem. Anyone else, not so much. It's a safety feature for us. Kind of like all the quirks of an old castle in medieval times. It gives the advantage to the inhabitants instead of the intruders. But if things ever got really bad, there are metal shutters that will come down on the front part of the building, sealing it shut. There's no reason for shutters on the back of the castle since it hangs off the cliff. It's inaccessible."

"Castle? I'd expect that at your house, since it looks like one. But this is just a log cabin, right?"

He smiled. "Right." He stopped at the left end of the room. But instead of leading her to the right along the back wall, he pressed his hand beneath another keypad. A panel slid back, revealing a hallway that continued straight toward the back of the cabin.

He hadn't been kidding about hidden doorways.

As they stepped through, everything changed. Gone was the mix of drywall and glass and metal. This section of the cabin was exactly as she'd envisioned the place from the outside. Golden, chunky logs formed the hallway. Wooden planks lined the ceiling. And at the end was a railing that was more like a work of art. Each supporting baluster was a tree branch that appeared to be hand hewn to reveal the beauty of the wood beneath the bark.

She joined him near the railing but kept back a good two feet.

He looked at her in question. "Don't you want to see the living area below? This gallery gives a great view downstairs and the valley far below if you look out those windows."

"No, no. I'm good right here." She forced a smile. "I can see it all just fine. Gorgeous two-story fireplace. Love the stacked stone. Most people do river rock. I'm not a fan."

"You're really pale."

"Am I?" She took another step back. "Is the tour over?"

"Heights. That's it, isn't it? You're afraid of heights?"

Feeling silly, she forced a laugh. "I know it sounds dumb to someone who isn't scared of, well, anything, I imagine. But when I was little, about ten years old, I went hiking with a club of other kids and, of course, chaperones and guides. The trail we were on had been damaged from recent rains but we didn't realize it until it collapsed." She pressed her hand to her throat, remembering. "I fell fifty feet. The only reason I survived was because I hit enough tree branches on the way down to slow my fall. It took five hours to get a helicopter positioned where the rescuers could rappel down to get me."

He took her hand in his before she realized what he was going to do. But instead of feeling afraid, she felt…comforted. She clung to his hand as the images from her near fatal disaster threatened to overwhelm her.

"I broke three ribs, my left arm, both my ankles. And those were just the bone injuries. I spent months in a hospital, rehab after that. That started my fear of heights, and cemented a phobia of hospitals, too. I'd have to be on death's door to walk into one of those places ever again."

"I'm sorry you went through that." He pulled her against him and hugged her tight. The logical part of her screamed for her to push him away. But her heart and body craved his touch like air and told her that she had to have misunderstood that conversation he'd had with Mason. There had to be another explanation. Because he'd never, not once, been anything but kind and gentle and achingly sweet to her.

Cursing her misgivings, she allowed herself to sink against him and wrap her arms around his waist. She was pathetic. She knew it. But she couldn't have refused his hug for anything.

It was over all too soon and he was gently pushing her back to look down at her.

"Better?" He gently feathered her hair back from her face. She slowly nodded. "Better." Because she truly was.

Being held by him was like magic. It had chased away the awful memories of the past. Too bad it couldn't protect her from the future. He wasn't her friend, or a prospective lover, no matter how badly she might wish he was. She had to keep reminding herself of that.

It was her uneasiness, and the height scare, that had her thinking and feeling this way. Somehow she had to get her head out of the clouds and her feet firmly planted on the ground again. She needed to get back to her self-appointed mission of finding evidence.

"There's a lot more to see back here," he said. "If you ever want the full tour, just say the word."

"Castle stuff? Bolt-holes and secret chambers?"

He grinned. "You know about castles?"

"I've seen *Braveheart* and *The Three Musketeers*. Oh, and *Robin Hood*—the one with Kevin Costner. Does that count?"

"Definitely not. We'll have to work on getting you a more proper castle education some other time. For now, let's head back to the conference room and I'll introduce you to the team." He squeezed her hand before letting go. "Follow me. Careful where you step. I'll take you back a different way. It will bring us out the other side of the main room, closer to the conference room."

"Sounds good." She turned with him and headed down another hallway. This one had paintings and pictures on both walls. She admired one of the paintings as she passed it, and idly glanced at one of the photographs. Then she stumbled to a halt. She backed up and stared at the picture—of one of her website clients, except the name beneath the photograph was wrong.

He came back and stopped beside her. "Someone you know? I don't recall the exact reason he hired us. It's been a while." He motioned to the name beneath the picture. Buster Thomas.

She frowned and leaned in closer.

"Do you recognize him?" he asked.

The air seemed to thicken around them with tension, as if her answer was important. Why was he staring at her so intently? And why would he expect that the name Buster Thomas might mean something to her? It didn't. Because the man in that picture wasn't Buster Thomas. His name was Todd Bartholomew and she'd been working for him for the past two years.

Something was off again. Going with her instincts this time, she shook her head. "Can't say that I do. Should I?"

He stared at her another moment, then shrugged. "Not necessarily. It just seemed like you did there, for a few seconds anyway."

He led her down the gallery, pointing out the paintings, talking about the local artists. But it wasn't the paintings that held her attention. It was the photographs, allegedly of clients of the Seekers. But far too many were *her* clients. And the names beneath each and every one of them was *wrong*.

What did it all mean?

He leaned past her to push something on the wall and a panel slid back, revealing that they were at the main room, but on the other side. They hurried down the walkway, stepping right when it sloped to the left, or left when it sloped to the right. She definitely would have fallen if she wasn't watching his every move.

He stopped beside a closed door. "Conference room. They're ready to see you now."

She nervously eyed the door. "How do you know they're ready?"

He smiled and tapped on the door, then pushed it open.

The conference room was nearly full, with men and women sitting on both sides of a long rectangular table.

One of them, a dark-skinned young woman with gorgeous, curly black hair that hung to her waist, flashed a bright white smile at Hayley when she saw her. Hayley watched in confusion as the woman shoved out of her chair and jogged across the room.

"You must be Hayley Nash. It's so good to finally meet you. I'm Brielle Walker."

Hayley awkwardly stepped forward and allowed the other woman to hug her.

Brielle stepped back and linked her arm in Hayley's. "Come on. Mason and Dalton said you were going to meet the team."

Feeling as if she was in the middle of a nightmare, she was relentlessly drawn into the conference room.

# Chapter Seventeen

When Hayley entered the conference room, it went quiet. She counted eleven men and women, including Brielle and Dalton somewhere behind her. Brielle gave her a quick squeeze and whispered, "It will be okay," before resuming her seat farther down the table.

A hand reached past her, making her jump in surprise. Dalton pulled out a chair for her.

"Didn't mean to startle you," he said. "Would you like to sit while I introduce the team?"

"I, ah, really don't see the need to meet everyone. No offense intended. I just want to help you with your computer problems and…" She stared in shock at yet another picture of one of her clients on the wall behind Brielle. How many did that make? Six? Seven? What was going on?

She continued to stare at the picture, at the name beneath it. The wrong name. Was this a test? They were a team, after all. They worked together. Did all of the Seekers think she was the bad guy? That she was the one who'd done something wrong? Was it possible that her supposed clients had given her aliases instead of their real names? And it was their real names under these photographs? Or was it the other way around?

"Are you okay?" His brow furrowed in concern.

She pointed. "Who's in that picture on the wall behind Brielle?"

Brielle glanced over her shoulder. "Timothy Hawkins. Why?"

*No. It wasn't Timothy Hawkins.* She clenched her fingers against her palms, digging into her flesh.

Another picture caught her attention. This one was larger, a group picture. Mason Ford was standing in the middle, as usual unsmiling. To his right were six of the people in this room, including Brielle and Dalton, and four of the men at the table. To Mason's left were six more, including one woman who looked vaguely familiar in her business suit with long blond hair slicked back into a ponytail. Didn't she used to be a prosecutor and she'd resigned in disgrace a few years ago?

But that wasn't what had Hayley's stomach dropping. It was a man in the photograph who wasn't at the table. A man she recognized.

"Who…" Her voice came out a gritty croak. She cleared her throat and pointed at the picture. "That picture, the man on the far right. Who is he?"

"The Seeker I told you about," Dalton said. "The one who died—Seth Knox."

She looked up at him accusingly. "He was in that picture I showed you at the police station. The last one I put up against the glass before you ended the interview."

He slowly nodded. "Yes. He was. Have you seen him before?"

She scrambled for her gun and jerked back, holding it with both hands out in front of her. "Nobody move. Don't you dare come near me. Any of you."

Dalton took a step forward.

She jerked the gun toward him, aiming for his chest. "Don't. I swear I'll shoot."

"What's wrong, Hayley? This is a friendly meeting. Why are you pointing a gun at me?"

She nearly choked, then cleared her throat again. They were all in on this, whatever it was, against her. It was the only explanation that made sense. Otherwise, she was losing her mind.

"Friendly? Who *are* you people? Really? Not my friends. And you sure aren't the good guys. One of you, this Seth guy, is in a photograph that I have showing known gun runners and drug dealers. I'm supposed to believe he's another Justice Seeker undercover, right?" She snorted. "Great way to cover up your own crimes, pretend you're trying to bring criminals down when you're actually in cahoots with them."

Dalton's eyes widened. "That's what you think?"

She motioned with her head toward the picture that she'd asked Brielle about. "That man, in that other photograph, another one of your clients, right?"

He slowly nodded.

"And yet, I built a website for him and his company this past year. His name isn't what Brielle said it was. His name is Frank Johnson." The gun started to shake and she had to concentrate hard to steady it. "You're all in on this, whatever this is. Some kind of massive conspiracy or something. You're all in on it together aren't you?"

"What are you talking about?" he asked. "What conspiracy?"

"The pictures, in here, in the gallery. One picture, maybe even two, could be a coincidence. But six? Seven? No way. Something is going on and I don't want any part of it."

"I don't understand," he insisted. "What pictures are you talking about?"

Everyone was staring intently at her. She felt as if she was a bird staring back at snakes waiting to strike. She moved another step back.

"The names are all wrong," she said. "And they can't be your clients. They're mine! None of this makes sense. You're playing some kind of twisted game with me."

"Calm down," Dalton urged. "Let's talk this out. Put the gun down and—"

She scoffed. "So you can make me go missing like you did to Bethany? That's what you and Mason said last night, isn't it? When you discussed me in your truck?"

His eyes widened. "The satchel. You put a listening device in there."

"Thank God I did. Now I know the truth, or part of it. I was right all along about Bethany, about you." A tear rolled down her cheek and she bit her lip to keep from giving in to her grief. "I trusted you, Dalton. Even after hearing that conversation last night, I was hoping that somehow I'd misunderstood, that you were the good guy my heart wants to believe you are."

"Trust your heart," he said. "I can explain all of this. Put the gun down."

She shook her head, tears flowing freely. A noise sounded behind her. She whirled around, just as Mason stepped into the room. A hand reached over her shoulder and plucked the gun from her hands. She whirled back the other way to see Dalton handing the gun to one of the men seated at the table.

"No!" She lunged for her weapon.

Every single person at the table drew their own guns and aimed them at her.

She froze. Dalton didn't. He stepped in front of her, facing the others.

"Put them away," he ordered, his voice harsh and loud in the room. "She's not armed and the gun she had wasn't even loaded."

After some hesitation, they slowly put their weapons away. Hayley stared at him in confusion as he faced her again.

"My gun *was* loaded. After last night, I didn't dare go somewhere with you without it being loaded. I checked it several times this morning."

"The gun you had when you walked into the cabin was loaded. I switched it out. For your safety and ours."

Her mouth dropped open. "When you put your hand on my back, in the hallway? You switched guns?"

He nodded.

"How did you know?"

"I saw the bulge beneath your coat when I helped you out of your Blazer."

She cursed viciously. "What are you going to do now? Kill me?"

He sighed heavily and looked past her at Mason, who still hadn't said anything.

"She told the truth," Dalton said. "She admitted they all hired her to build websites and that their names were different than the fake names that we listed beneath the pictures. She pointed out Seth in the team photo. If she was in on this, she never would have admitted any of that. She'd have bluffed her way through."

Dalton was defending her?

His gaze was riveted on Mason, as if her fate hung in the balance. Did it?

Mason looked as morose and cold as always, but he nodded, as if agreeing to some secret pact. "Let's do it."

"Do what?" she demanded. "Please. Someone explain what's happening."

Dalton's gaze filled with sympathy. "You'll have all of your answers in a few minutes. And you're safe, I promise. There's no reason to be scared."

"I want out of here." She stepped toward the door. Mason blocked her way.

She wrapped her arms around her waist.

Dalton's jaw tightened. "Everyone out."

Hayley backed against the wall, feeling as if she was in another dimension as everyone filed out of the room, everyone except her and Dalton.

"What do you want from me?" she whispered, unable to force anything louder through her chattering teeth.

"I want what you want," he said. "I want the truth."

"What are you talking about?"

"Seth Knox. I told you he died. He was murdered, and mutilated, with both his hands cut off. His body was burned beyond recognition. Only DNA proved it was him. We're still trying to figure out who killed him. The first real clue was that picture you have from the bar. Seeing that told us his death is likely related to the drug-and-gunrunning case that we've been working on."

He seemed so sincere. But how could she trust him again? "How do I fit into all of this? You and Mason talked as if I was a criminal in your truck after you left my cabin."

"That part's complicated. The criminal enterprise that we're trying to bring down is run by someone who's killing off people and gloating over it, leaving their calling card at every murder. We're desperate to figure out who he is and stop him before someone else is killed. One of the threads we've been trying to follow has to do with hidden website pages. Like the ones you build for your clients."

Her gaze flew to the pictures on the wall, then back to him. "My clients. They're connected to this killer?"

"We believe so, yes. With every member of the drug-and-gunrunning network that we bring down, we try to figure out who they ultimately report to. The ones we've traced all had one thing in common. Every single one of them. Their websites were designed by the same person. That person is you, Hayley. That's why Mason and the others are suspicious. Some of them believe you're pulling the strings, that you're deeply involved in their criminal network as a willing participant."

She violently shook her head. "No. No, I would never do that."

"I believe you."

"What?"

"I believe you. But I have to be able to prove that you're innocent so the rest of the team comes on board."

Hysterical laughter bubbled up in her throat. "This is rich. I've been performing surveillance on you for months, trying to prove you're guilty. And now you're telling me that all the Seekers think I'm guilty, and you're trying to prove I'm not? Is that what you're saying?"

"It is. All along, you've been our target as much as I've been yours. We've been trying to find out what you know and how involved you are in the criminal network."

She drew a shaky breath. "This, the pictures on the wall, they were, what, some kind of test?"

He nodded. "Juvenile, I know. But there's a lot at stake. Mason didn't want to risk allowing you on our computer system until the team met you and we agreed whether or not to trust you. Come on. Follow me. All of your questions are about to be answered. And I promise, no one is going to hurt you." He held out his hand.

She shrank back. "Mason wants to make me disappear."

His jaw tightened. "I can explain that, too. I couldn't before. But I've grown weary of all this subterfuge and we're running out of time. We need to start working together, instead of against each other." He strode to the other end of the room, to a solid wall.

She wasn't even surprised when he pressed his hand on the wall and a panel slid open. But rather than follow him, she ran to the conference room door that she'd come through earlier. It was locked. No special keypad or place to put her hand that she saw. Just an old-fashioned knob, locked from the other side. And wasn't that weird? What did they do, lock unruly clients in here?

She could kick it, maybe. If it was a hollow interior door, it wouldn't be that strong. It should open fairly easily.

A glance over her shoulder told her that would be pointless. He'd stop her. Her shoulders slumped. For now, she gave in and followed him down what appeared to be a tunnel.

All the while, she silently berated herself for being so stupid, for coming here assuming she'd be able to protect herself. Would they find her body in a ditch tomorrow, like they'd found Bethany's?

At the end of the hallway, another panel opened. She followed him into the next room, then froze. Apparently Dalton wasn't the only one into castles. This massive room wasn't like the ultra-modern glass and metal main room. It wasn't like the log-cabin portion on the back. It was every bit a medieval castle, from the stone floors to the stone walls and flickering sconces.

But it was the middle of the room that had her stunned. It boasted a huge round table, also built of stone, with elaborate carvings all over the top. A semi-circle of computer monitors along the back wall faced the table. And there were people sitting there, all of them looking at her. The team, from the conference room, including Mason.

The carvings in the table spread out like the spokes of a wagon wheel, or slices of a pie. Each person had a triangle carved in front of them, cordoning off their section of the table, with what appeared to be a name. Their names?

Dalton left her standing there and took one of the seats, leaving only one empty. For her?

She wanted to run away, but she was too intrigued. She wanted, needed, to know what this place was. Forcing herself forward on shaky legs, she didn't stop until she was close enough to read what was carved into the top of the table in front of the empty chair.

*Seth Knox.*

Underneath his name was a phrase: *The Rancher.*

She slowly circled the table. No one made a move to stop her. She read each name, each phrase carved beneath it.

*Dalton Lynch, The Cowboy.*

*Brielle Walker, The Cop.*

*Bryson Anton, The Profiler.*

*Han Li, The Special Agent.*

More names, more…monikers? Describing, what, their main function as a Seeker? Or their background before they joined the team?

*The Tracker.*

*The Detective.*

*The Prosecutor.*

*The Marine.*

*The Lawyer.*

*The Bodyguard.*

*The Judge.*

One enormous round table. Twelve slots, thirteen if she counted their leader.

She read the elaborate script carved in front of Mason. Below his name was carved *The Chief.* But it was the second title below the first that had her convinced that she'd truly dropped down a rabbit hole.

*King Arthur.*

She swung back toward Dalton, asking the question, even though she feared that she already knew the answer. "What *is* this place?"

The corner of his mouth tilted up. "Hayley Nash, welcome to Camelot."

She bolted toward the door.

# Chapter Eighteen

Dalton blew out a deep sigh as Hayley disappeared down the tunnel.

"We've got a runner." Brielle's wide grin flashed his way.

"You don't have to sound so dang cheerful about it," he grumbled as he pressed the table in front of him and his computer tablet flipped up. He typed some commands and the cameras on the inside of the building filled his computer screen.

"Where is she?" Bryson asked, scooting his chair close to Dalton's.

"Trying to bust down the conference room door."

Mason tapped the tablet in front of him. "Is Sampson ready with the video?"

"She is."

"Let Miss Nash go, for now. We have work to do."

Bryson exchanged a look of disappointment with Dalton, then slid his chair back in place.

Dalton typed some commands, then watched the screen as Hayley ran out of the conference room to the front door. She tried it several times before he was able to get it unlocked.

Her surprise was palpable, as was her suspicion as she glanced behind her, then up at the ceiling as if looking for the cameras. But she didn't wait around. She took off running again, leaping off the porch and scrabbling across the grass to the parking lot. Soon, she was in her Blazer, tires screeching as she wheeled around then sped down the road.

All in all, Mason's plan in bringing her here had gone like clockwork. Except for the part where she'd been terrified and took off. In hindsight, he should have given her more time in the conference room, explained things before taking her to the great hall. After her earlier comments about the castle, he'd thought her excitement over seeing the round table and stonework would have been enough to keep her there long enough for him to bring up information on the computer monitors to explain everything else. Instead, he'd scared her half to death. He glanced at the door to the tunnel and debated going after her.

"Dalton? Sitrep," Mason called out.

He sighed and turned back to his screen. "As we theorized would happen if things didn't go well, Hayley just passed her house and is heading toward town." He brought up the street map that showed a blip from the tracker that Bryson had placed on Hayley's Blazer after she'd entered their building. "She's heading toward Gatlinburg PD now. I've texted Sampson. She's ready."

"Check back later. Jaxon, you're up first. Give us an update."

It was late afternoon before Dalton was able to wrap up his business with the others, get an update from Detective Sampson at Gatlinburg PD and go to Hayley's place. As he pulled his truck to a stop out front, he studied the sad, run-down facade of the small rental cabin. The location was remote, isolated. He didn't like that she was out here all by herself, vulnerable.

He hopped out of the truck and headed toward the front door, unsurprised when it opened before he reached it. His truck's engine wasn't exactly quiet, which was why he never drove it when he worked undercover. What did surprise him was that she wasn't holding a knife, or even a fireplace poker to bash him over the head since he'd taken her gun. Instead, she leaned a hip against the doorframe, a bottle of whiskey dangling in one hand, a shot glass full of the amber liquid in the other. Her bloodshot eyes told him this wasn't her first glass.

She gestured toward him. "Which one are you? Lancelot? Sir Galahad? That was the whole point, right? The knights of the round table. Camelot. Wait, I bet you're the infamous black knight, with no true allegiances, wicked, the bad boy. A rebel knight, with a Stetson." She snickered and tossed back the entire shot in one gulp, then wiped her mouth with her sleeve.

"How did you do it, Sir Knight?" she slurred. "How did you erase my recordings of the inside of your office building?"

He braced a hand above the doorway, wondering if he'd have to catch her before she crashed to the floor. She looked about ready to pass out.

"Well?" she demanded. "Go on, Dalton. You can tell me." She held up her whiskey bottle. "And good old Jack Daniels here." She chuckled. "How'd you do it?"

Without giving him a chance to respond, she said, "Imagine my surprise when I caused a ruckus at the police station and pulled out my recorder to prove my claims, and all it showed was snow. You know, electronic snow, like when your recorder records absolutely nothin'. Enlighten me, Sir Knight. What trick did you pull to make that happen?"

He winced as she poured and then tossed another shot of whiskey back. "The office portion of our building, basically the front part, not the living quarters in back and below, is a Faraday cage, taken up several notches."

She wobbled on her feet. "A fair a what?"

"Faraday cage. The concept is to build a cage, a box, or in our case, most of the top floor of the cabin, so that no electronic signals can get in or out. But we took it to a new level. We built it so that any electronics inside are useless, at least, in the traditional sense. They don't work unless they're hardwired to underground lines with special shielding. Cell phones, little spy cameras, don't work in Camelot. Even the computer tablets that we use in the great hall don't run wirelessly. You may not have noticed the tiny filaments that attach to the back of each tablet and thread through pin-sized holes in the round table. That connects them to the main computer system." He gestured toward the interior. "Wouldn't you rather sit down to continue our conversation?"

"The drywall," she said, ignoring his suggestion. "That's why the top floor is so industrial-looking. You've covered up all the layers that jam signals. That's why your boss covered those gorgeous logs. Son of a gun."

"Not nearly as attractive. But effective."

"And my little camera? Did you know I had it?"

"Yes. There are electronic scanners at the front door. Brielle signaled me when you weren't looking."

She shook her head. "Dang. She sure seemed like a nice person. Can't judge a book, or a knight of the round table, by their smile, can you?" She shook her head again, then started to tip over.

He grabbed her waist to steady her. She slapped at his hand and he pulled it back only after he was reasonably certain she wasn't going to fall.

"Brielle would probably be insulted if she heard you call her nice. That might damage the mean reputation she works so hard to project." He smiled. "But she does care about people or she wouldn't work there. She was just doing her job, protecting all of us."

She rolled her eyes. "Whatever. With that cage thingy

you've got up on the mountain, I can see why you didn't chase after me to stop me from leaving. You knew if I went to the police, I'd have nothing to show for it. They'd listen to my wild story and think I was crazy. That was your plan, wasn't it? You wanted to discredit me."

He waved toward the living room behind her. "Shouldn't we go—"

"Detective Sampson," she said, gesturing with her whiskey bottle. "Now she was the icing on the cake, the final straw that tipped it all in your favor. Remember her? You and your boss sent her to my house to lie to me about the so-called task force and your alibi. She heard the commotion in the lobby when I was trying to get the desk sergeant to go up the mountain and arrest you for kidnapping and whatever other charges we could come up with. First, she denied that she'd met me before today, treating me like I was a total lunatic when I said she'd come to my house. Then she insisted there was no way I could have been up on the mountain with you since you'd left her office five minutes ago. She even had a video to prove it. Your doing?"

He stepped back to avoid the whiskey she sloshed onto the porch. "My idea, yes. But Jaxon's the one who set it up. He's the ex-Marine, worked in security and has a knack for anything video related."

Her shoulders slumped. "Well, of course you have a video expert, and a cop on the take."

"Sampson isn't on the take. She's one of our allies at the police department and helps us out when red tape and lifetime politicians get in the way of doing what's right. And we don't compensate her for it. She refuses to take any money, even to cover her expenses when she incurs them helping us. She doesn't want it to seem like we're buying favors."

"Sounds like splitting hairs to me."

He shrugged.

"You keep saying *us*. You mean the knights of the round table? Right?"

He cocked his head, noting how green her complexion was turning. "You do know that whole Camelot thing is for fun, right? We don't take it seriously, other than using castle tricks to secure the place."

"You don't take it seriously? Your house has turrets! Two of them."

He didn't bother to explain that he'd bought the house from Mason because he loved the land it was sitting on. His boss was the one with the castle fascination. He was the one who'd built the turrets and covered the outside in stone.

"Looked serious to me," she continued. "A real expensive stone table, for sure. And only twelve chairs, not counting Arthur of course."

"That's our own joke on him, carving the name Arthur in the table. He doesn't like that, prefers to be called Mason. Can we go inside now and get out of the cold? Your lips are turning blue and I'm pretty sure you're about to lose all that whiskey you've been drinking."

"Who was in on it?" she pressed. "All of Camelot?"

He braced both arms on the door frame, hoping he wasn't about to get thrown up on. But he was more worried that she was going to pitch forward onto the floor and he wanted to be ready to catch her. "Mason, Detective Sampson, a few others. Look, I'm sorry about all of this, Hayley. I truly am. But since so many clues point to your involvement in our case, we've had to cover ourselves, be prepared to discredit you if you ended up going to the authorities—which you did."

She sloshed more whiskey into her shot glass, but most of it dribbled down her blouse and jeans. She wiped at her shirt, then drew several deep breaths. "I don't feel so good."

"Can't see how you would."

She gestured with the whiskey bottle again. "You know

what, Dalton? You're the handsomest serial killer I think I've ever met."

"Not exactly a compliment. Here, let me take that bottle for you." He reached for it but she jerked it away. Her momentum carried her backward, but she somehow kept her balance.

"Don't touch Jack. He and I aren't finished yet. Come on inside, pretty boy. It's cold out there." She giggled. "Not that it's ever warm in here."

Dalton stood undecided in the doorway as she weaved her way toward what he assumed was the hall that led to bedrooms and bathrooms. If he left her alone, would she be okay? As drunk as she was, coming inside didn't seem like a good idea.

"Hurry up and close the door behind you," she called out without turning around. She disappeared through the opening.

Dalton straightened, but instead of going in, he reached for the doorknob to pull it shut. He'd come back when she was sober and try to talk to her again.

"Well, dang," he heard her slurring from whatever room she was in. "Why is the floor moving?"

A loud thump sounded, followed by the unmistakable sound of glass shattering and pinging across the floor.

"Jack! Oh, no. Jack. Wait, where did all that blood come from?"

Dalton swore and ran inside.

## Chapter Nineteen

Dalton shifted on the couch, holding Hayley's legs across his lap as she squirmed and tried to sit up. The thick, sharp shards of the broken whiskey bottle had sliced her left thigh through the jeans that she'd been wearing earlier. He'd had to cut them off and put some shorts on her so he could tend to her wound. But trying to keep pressure on the bandage he'd fashioned from a first-aid kit he found in her bathroom was proving nearly impossible. She wouldn't be still long enough for him to secure it.

He reached for the roll of first-aid tape on the cushion beside him. Once again, she swiped it away, giggling as she grabbed his arm to haul herself up to sitting.

"You're an awesome doctor, Sir Knight. So gentle and sweet." She winked and shifted sideways, trying to see her leg. "Whoa. The room's moving again."

He swore and grabbed her arm, jerking her toward him to keep her from hitting the coffee table. "Lie down and be still so I can finish securing your bandage. And quit grabbing the tape." He yanked it from her grasp.

She plopped down and crossed her arms. "You're no fun."

"Yeah, well, I tend to be a serious kind of fellow when someone's bleeding to death."

Her eyes widened. "Someone's bleeding?" She jerked upright, her breasts flattened against his arm.

He gritted his teeth and shoved her down, not as gently this time. "Stay."

She gasped. "I'm not a dog!"

"Obviously not. My dogs mind much better than you." He rushed to secure the bandage while she was lying down, knowing his reprieve wouldn't last.

She giggled, her outrage forgotten. Then her eyes widened in dismay. "Oh, no!"

He blew out a breath. "What is it this time? Did you remember you're out of whiskey?"

She frowned. "What? I am? Did you drink it?"

He rolled his eyes. "Your floor did, when you dropped the bottle in the hall, then fell onto the glass." He pressed another piece of tape on the gauze. Fresh blood was already staining it. He grabbed the hand towel on the cushion beside him and pressed it against the bandage. "You have to be still, Hayley, or the bleeding isn't going to stop." He shook his head. "You probably need stitches. I should take you to the hospital and—"

She grabbed his arm. "I told you, no hospitals."

"I understand your fear but—"

She crossed her arms indignantly. "I'm not afraid of anything." She frowned. "Why are you here? Where's Jack?" Her eyes widened. "Why are my legs on your lap? And why are you holding onto me?"

Her outrage would have been funny if they hadn't already had this same conversation. Twice. Drunk Hayley couldn't hold a thought for more than a few minutes.

He started over, explaining her fall in the hallway and that he was trying to help her. But she kept squirming.

"Good grief, Hayley. If you can't be still so I can stop the bleeding, I'll have to call an ambulance whether you want me to or not."

She gasped and flattened herself against the couch, giving him a hurt look. "You don't play fair."

"I'm not playing. If I can't stop this bleeding, we *are* going to a hospital. Now don't move."

She grew still, her eyes suddenly bright with unshed tears. "I'm not the only one that fell that day, when I was a little girl. Some of my friends fell too." She started to tremble and clutched his arm. "But I'm the only one who lived. Don't send me to the hospital, Dalton. Please. I don't want to die."

"Oh, Hayley. Why didn't you tell me about your friends? Don't worry. I won't take you to the hospital. But you have to be still. And stop talking about dying. No one's dying on my watch."

The bereft look in her eyes tugged at his heart.

"Are you going to make me disappear, Dalton? I don't want to disappear."

He winced and hung his head, regretting that conversation in his truck a thousand times over.

"Dalton? You didn't answer me."

"No, sweetheart. I won't make you disappear. And neither will Mason."

"Promise?"

"Promise."

"Dalton?"

"Yes?"

"Did you call me sweetheart?"

"You're drunk, Hayley. I'm sure you heard me wrong. Just be still. I think the bleeding has almost stopped."

A few minutes later, he carefully lifted his hand to check the bandage. The blood that had seeped through was dark now, and drying. Finally. The bleeding had stopped.

He was about to reassure her that they wouldn't have to go to the hospital. But it wasn't necessary. She was sound asleep.

And looked like an angel.

Her thick dark hair puddled around an oval face that

was delicate, almost fragile-looking when relaxed in sleep. Plump pink lips softly parted on each indrawn breath, as if beckoning him closer, daring him to see if she tasted as delicious as she looked. When she was angry and hurling accusations, it wasn't hard to ignore her physical attributes. But asleep, her legs across his lap, looking so feminine and sweet, it was pure torture.

He wanted her. Really, desperately wanted her.

But when he tried to imagine a scenario where she'd want him, too, where the two of them could even be friends, his mind went blank. It didn't seem possible. There were too many unanswered questions between them. Too many suspicions. And until those were resolved, he wasn't even sure what the future held for her, or him. Nothing was a certainty, regardless of who had right on their side.

The feel of her warm, smooth skin beneath his fingers made him realize he'd been stroking her calf. Cursing, he yanked his hand back. Then he stretched both arms along the back of the couch and rested his head against the cushions.

# *Chapter Twenty*

Dalton woke to the sun coming through the blinds. He tried to raise his hand to shield his eyes, but he couldn't move. Something warm and soft was on top of his arm, and on top of him. His eyes flew open.

Good grief. He was flat on his back on the couch, and Hayley was sprawled out on top of him. Sometime during the night, one of them had pulled his trench coat over them like a blanket. But even with that, and her luscious curves plastered against his hard angles, he was freezing. He could see his breath in the air. Inside the cabin.

Had the heater broken? It had seemed chilly when he'd arrived last night, but he'd been so busy keeping her from bleeding to death that he forgot about checking the heater.

She mumbled something, her soft lips moving against his neck. He shivered but not from the cold. In spite of the chill in the room, he started sweating. And when she shifted her leg against him, his lower half stood at attention.

He swore and curled his fingers against the couch to keep from sliding them around her. It was just his luck that the first time, maybe the only time, that he'd ever managed to get Hayley in his arms, it was by accident. And she was asleep.

Holding her, without sinking his hands in her hair, tasting every inch of her the way he craved, was a delicious form of torture. Where she touched him, he burned. And he was just selfish enough to lie there a few more minutes, soaking in every curve, every slide of her skin against his. He'd wondered what it would be like to have her pressed to him, her breasts flattened against his chest. It felt like heaven. A forbidden heaven. And if he didn't wake her soon, he was surely going to hell.

She shivered and snuggled closer. He gritted his teeth and gently tightened his arms around her, slowly rising to sitting. He had to get the heat on. And he didn't want her to wake and find herself on top of him and be embarrassed. It had been a gift she'd given him without even realizing it. And he didn't want it to become something she regretted.

When he finally had her sitting against the other end of the couch, he let out a relieved breath, then went off in search of a blanket. He found one in her hall closet and covered her with it. Then he took care of his needs in the bathroom, before scrubbing his teeth with a finger and some toothpaste. He clicked the heat on, surprised to see it had been turned off. Then, to get it toasty as quickly as possible, he put the last few remaining logs on the fire and stoked the coals. He'd have to see about getting her some more firewood later today. And find out what was going on with her heater.

"Dalton? Is that you?" Her sleepy voice had him turning around. Her hair was a riotous tumble of tousled curls, falling nearly to her waist. Her eyes seemed glazed and confused as she stared at him, pulling his trench coat around her. He didn't think he'd ever seen a more beautiful creature.

"Morning, sleepy head."

She blinked and shoved her hair back, then stumbled over the end of his coat. "Why am I wearing your coat? And why are you here so early?" She squinted at the clock beside the fireplace. "Good grief. I never get up this early."

She smacked her lips and made a face. "My mouth tastes like cotton."

He stood and wiped his hands on his jeans. "That's probably what's left of Jack Daniels from last night."

She blinked again, then pressed her hand to her mouth. "Oh no. That really happened? I thought it was a dream."

"It really happened. Um, what do you remember?"

She took off his coat and tossed it on the couch before crossing to stand in front of the fireplace. "Not much. Except..." She glanced down, frowning. "Why am I wearing shorts in the middle of winter? And why is there a bandage on my leg?"

He sighed and turned her toward the bathroom. "Your jeans were a bloody mess and I had to take them off to bandage some cuts from the broken bottle of whiskey. I found some shorts in your dresser and put those on after seeing to your injuries. Go do whatever you need to do when you first wake up and then I'll do my best to explain. I assume you have coffee around here?"

"Kitchen. Duh." She motioned toward the other side of the cabin and hurried into the bathroom.

After calling Bryson and asking him to take Denali outside and to feed his dogs, Dalton put the coffee on to perk. He'd just finished pouring both of them a cup when she stopped in the doorway, dressed in a fresh pair of jeans and a dark blue blouse. Her face was pink from a recent scrubbing and her hair cascaded in shiny waves that had his fingers itching to touch them. But it was the serious look on her face that had regret curling in his stomach.

"You remember everything now, don't you? Including what happened at Camelot, and the police station?"

She nodded, then grimaced. "I need aspirin. And I want my gun back."

"I'll call and tell you where I hid your gun after I leave. I'd rather not get shot this early in the morning. The bottle of aspirin is over there, on the counter." He waved toward the coffee. "Cream? Sugar?"

"Black." She shook out two aspirin, then took the coffee cup that he held out to her. She swallowed down the pills, then cupped her hands around the mug as if to warm them. "Good call on the gun. You're a smart guy."

He set his own mug down and leaned back against the counter. "You've been through a lot, much of that because of me. I'm sorry about that. But this thing is bigger than both of us, and sometimes people caught in the middle get hurt."

"Is that what's going on?" she asked. "I'm caught in the middle? And I get no say in what happens?"

He straightened and walked toward her, slowly, so as not to frighten her. He took it as a good sign that she let him, without backing up or trying to kick him.

"I came here last night to level with you, to tell you everything. I'm as tired of all these secrets as you are. And I've seen enough to believe that Mason is just plain wrong. You're innocent. And I'm convinced that you can be trusted."

"You're referring to my computer programming that you and Mason talked about in your truck?"

He nodded. "Ask me anything. I promise not to lie. You've earned the truth. You deserve the truth."

"Just like that?"

"Just like that."

She set her mug on the counter and wrapped her arms around her middle. "Did Bethany really hire the Justice Seekers to help with her investigation?"

"She did."

"Did you kill her?"

He took a step closer, then tilted her chin up so he could make sure she looked at him when he answered. "No. I didn't kill her."

She shuddered, then touched his hand on her chin, stroking his skin instead of knocking his hand away. A war of emotions gathered in her eyes—confusion, anger, and if he wasn't wrong, something else. Desire. "Should I be afraid of you?" she breathed.

He feathered his hands down the sides of her face and leaned down until his mouth was just inches from hers, until he could see the silver specks of color around the blue in her eyes. "Don't ever fear me. I would never, ever hurt you."

He wanted to kiss her, craved the feel of her lips beneath his. But there was a flash of uncertainty in her gaze. He sighed, then took a step back to give both of them some room.

"Why didn't you kiss me?" she whispered.

"Because you still don't trust me. Not completely. I want you in my arms, in my bed. But I want you willing, and just as eager for me as I am for you. And above all, I don't want you frightened or unsure."

She looked away, confirming that he'd made the right decision. "I have so many questions."

"I know. I'm still here. Ask them."

She scrunched up her mouth, as if thinking really hard. "Okay. Tough one first. Why do you wear a Stetson? Did you wear it all the time in Montana? Is that a thing there?"

"That's the tough question, huh?" He grinned and raked his hands through his hair, just then realizing he'd left his hat on an end table in the other room. "I could count on one hand the number of native Montanans who wear cowboy hats on a regular basis, unless they're acting for the tourists." He shrugged. "I grew up on a working ranch outside of Bozeman that catered to tourists every summer as a dude ranch. Visitors expect cowboys to wear cowboy hats instead of ball caps, so that's what we wore. As a kid,

I saw a Stetson in a souvenir shop downtown and fell in love. I've been wearing them ever since."

She smiled. "I can imagine you as a little boy, running around with your big hat."

"Was that the end of your burning questions?"

She sobered. "No. I have another one. But you'll get mad."

"Even if I do, I won't yell or do anything to hurt you. Go ahead. Ask."

She met his gaze again. This time, her jaw was set at a mutinous angle.

"What happened in Montana? Why did you get a divorce and quit the police force? Are the two connected?"

He grimaced and picked up his coffee. "Can we sit down for that one?"

She carried her cup into the main room. Disappointment shot through him when she sat in the chair instead of the couch. But the fact that they were finally talking to each other without one of them drawing a gun or running off was progress.

She swiped his Stetson off the table and examined it. "I like the way it looks on you." She plopped it on her head, and it slid to her nose. She laughed and took it off. "Guess you won't have to worry about me wearing your hat."

"Maybe when this is over, I can pick up one more your size."

Her gaze shot to his. "Maybe." She licked her lips. "You had a family ranch in Montana, that much I found out online. How big was it?"

"Close to forty thousand acres."

"Is that a lot?"

He shrugged. "Most ranches there are closer to two thousand acres."

"Wow. I guess it really was big. You raised cattle?"

"Mostly. Angus and Hereford."

"Angus I've heard of. What are Herefords?"

"Beef cattle, just like Angus. Bigger, though. Hardier. You've probably seen them and didn't know the name. They're red and white, brownish-red really, more like rust. We raised horses, too, quarter horses. At any one time we could have a thousand head of cattle and a couple hundred horses."

"How fun."

"I liked it. Didn't *love* it the way my parents did. I guess when you grow up with something, you tend to take it for granted and want something else. That's why I became a police officer. Shortly after that, my parents retired to Florida and left me the ranch. I think it was my father's way of forcing me to give up the cop life and get back to basics. He knew I couldn't do both. So I figured I'd prove him wrong, by hiring a foreman to manage the ranch so I could go downtown to the police station every day. Worked pretty well. Until it didn't."

"I'm sorry, about what happened. I don't know the details, of course, but I did research. I know there was some kind of dustup with your wife and that she got the ranch in the divorce. In spite of you saying you didn't love the ranch, your voice says otherwise. You sound wistful when you talk about it."

"It is what it is. Cindy and I were high school sweethearts who never should have gotten married. We were too different, fought half the time we were together, even back in high school. The attraction was more physical than anything else, and we were too naive to realize that would wear off. Turns out it wore off a lot quicker for her. Two years into the marriage, she decided she preferred my foreman over me."

"How is that even possible?" Her eyes widened and her face turned a delightful pink. "I mean, wow. I'm sorry that she did that to you."

He smiled at her obvious discomfort. She was so cute when she blushed. "Don't be. We're better off apart."

"What happened? I mean, not in your marriage, but to make you quit being a policeman and become a Seeker?"

He rested his arm across the back of the couch. "She didn't want me, but she did want the ranch. Since it had been in my family for generations, there was zero chance she'd end up with it in the divorce. So she came up with another strategy. She had my foreman beat her up and then she went to my boss claiming I was the one who'd hurt her."

Her eyes grew big and round. "What a horrible woman."

He smiled. "Yes and no. I think she was manipulated by her lover more than anything. She regretted it later, apologized. Then again, that might have been because the private investigator that I hired was able to get her and my foreman on a recording talking about their plan and how they were using the fake spousal abuse allegations to get the ranch and get me fired so I'd leave town."

"But…you did get fired, or you quit. And you left town."

"I quit, yes. Even after being proven innocent of all charges, I had no desire to work with people who'd turned against me and believed the worst. And I didn't see the point in staying when I wouldn't be able to do what I wanted, help people. So, even though I won, and the ranch was kept by me in the divorce, I decided it no longer mattered. I didn't want it. I signed the deed over to my ex and moved here six months ago."

She shook her head. "I don't know many people who would have done that. None, actually. You had to have lost a ton of money."

"I'm no saint in that deal. Far from it. I deeded it in exchange for an initial lump sum and monthly payments for the next five years. She did get it at a tremendously reduced price. But a ranch that large isn't something many people want to manage. It's a ton of work and can lose money in a second if you aren't on top of things. Selling it would have meant waiting for years for the right buyer to come along. Or, if I got desperate for money, I'd have had to sell off all the livestock and pieced it out in smaller chunks, maybe even to developers. I loved the ranch too much to do that, so it was a compromise."

"What about your parents? Were they okay with that?"

"Surprisingly, yes. I mean, my dad was disappointed at first. But after finding out what had happened, he was soured on the whole thing and was just glad I got out of there and was able to get a fresh start with a good chunk of change in my pocket. He was even happier when I moved here and bought a few hundred acres to start my own legacy. Eventually I'll start raising horses. I just haven't had the time yet. For now, I enjoy the beauty of the land, and all that elbow room."

"Your father knows you're a Seeker?"

"He knows I help people, without really understanding exactly what a Seeker is all about. I prefer to keep it that way. We don't always follow the letter of the law in getting justice for folks. It's what gives us an advantage over our law enforcement counterparts. That's not something everyone can come to terms with, or get behind. I'd rather not burden my dad, or my mom, with that knowledge."

She rested her cheek in her palm. "It is hard to understand how a former police officer would make such a switch and would be willing to break the law. And be okay with that."

He considered how to respond. "It's not like any of us are in this to break the law. We respect the law, for the most part. And having been a police officer, I know better than most just how hard it is trying to enforce those laws and keep people safe. To this day, I'm extremely grateful for their service, and that they risk their lives for people they've never even met. But their hands are tied when they shouldn't be, like when they have to call off pursuit of a dangerous suspect because he's outside their jurisdiction. It's not right that the guy gets away and then hurts someone else. Being a Seeker means I can do what's morally right, even if it's not legally allowed. It's a risk, since I could get arrested if caught. But it's a risk I'm willing to take."

"Wow. That was quite some speech."

He cleared his throat. "Yeah, well, I guess you pressed one of my buttons."

She surprised him by moving to the couch and lacing her fingers with his across the back of the cushion. "I still don't understand everything you do. But I get that you help people, no matter what it takes, or the cost to yourself. And I think that's wonderful." She pulled their joined hands to her lips and pressed a whisper soft kiss against the back of his hand.

That innocent touch sent a jolt of heat through his body. He wanted so badly to kiss her lips, to pull her close. But he remembered the doubt in her eyes earlier and didn't want to pressure her. If the day came that she could look at him without any doubts or secrets remaining between them, he'd kiss her and likely never stop.

"My turn to ask questions," he said.

"Who said you get a turn?"

He shrugged. "I was hoping."

"Okay. You can ask. No promise about whether I'll answer."

"Feisty as always." He grinned. "One of the things I admire about you."

Her eyes widened. "Really? That's usually what guys like the least about me."

"Idiots."

She laughed. "What do you want to ask me?"

"How did you meet Bethany?"

"Oh. Gosh. Seems like I've known her forever, but I guess it was my freshman year. No, we were sophomores."

"College?"

"High school. She'd lost her only family in a car accident and ended up in foster care. I guess I was her lifeline back then, and she became mine off and on when bad things happened in my life. We both went to Tennessee State together too. But I was focused more on studies and she was focused on partying. We grew apart for a while. Never did quite get as close as we once had been. I don't suppose the whole Chandler thing helped. It made things awkward."

"Chandler?"

"Chandler Harding. Bethany hung out with this close-knit group of three guys and a girl at college. Chandler was one of them. They invited me to some parties and I ended up dating him for a little while. But he got too serious way too fast. I wanted to focus on school, not a relationship. So I broke it off. Later he starting dating Bethany. That's the awkward part, especially since they ended up getting engaged. My relationship with her wasn't quite the same after that."

"Chandler Harding. Sounds familiar."

"I can't imagine why. He died several years ago, before you moved to Gatlinburg. It was a tragedy, really. He got mixed up in the drug scene. One day he was arrested, and the next I heard he'd been killed on the way to the courthouse. Traffic accident. Bethany took it pretty hard, as you can imagine, especially since she'd lost her parents the same way. But she wanted space to grieve on her own. I eventually landed in Pigeon Forge to start my computer programming career. She moved to Gatlinburg, pursuing her passion for photography by selling pictures to all kinds of businesses around here to promote their wares to tourists. It didn't pay the bills very well so she freelanced doing investigations on the side, figuring the combination of pictures and a story would work to her advantage. It did. She sold stories to all kinds of news outlets."

"You said you went your separate ways. You weren't friends anymore?"

"We were still friends. I mean, if I needed something, I always knew I could call her. And vice versa. It just wasn't as easy as it used to be. We admittedly drifted apart. It had been months since we'd last spoken when she called me out of the blue one day to meet her for dinner, to catch up. A month later, she was gone. You know the rest."

"So you're looking for her killer because of guilt? You thought you'd let her down, because you weren't as close as you once were?"

"I never thought of it that way. But I suppose that's part of it. She had no one else, not really. I can't help feeling that I could have done something to prevent her death."

"You couldn't. Trust me."

"Why do you say that?"

"I just don't think you should feel guilty about her. Whatever happened, it's not your fault, or your responsibility."

She cleared her throat. "Thank you. That's nice of you to say." She twisted her hands together in her lap, a thoughtful expression on her face.

"Uh-oh," he said. "I know that look. More questions for me?"

"Just one." She paused as if gathering herself, her knuckles turning white because she was clasping her hands so tightly. "If you didn't kill her, why do you think it would be a disaster if I ask to see the medical examiner's report?"

"What are you talking about?"

"The bug I put in the satchel. You and Mason discussed it that night."

"Good grief. I didn't remember that he and I had talked about the ME's report."

He scrubbed his face with his hands. This wasn't a question he'd expected to come up. And he wasn't sure how to proceed. Mason wouldn't want him to tell her anything. But he'd crossed that line the moment he told Hayley that he trusted her, and that he'd answer any question that she had. He wasn't playing by Mason's rules anymore. He was following his own conscience.

"Dalton?"

He pulled his hands down. "It's complicated."

"I'm sure you can explain it so that I understand it."

"That's not what I mean. It's complicated because it's tied up with the ongoing investigation." He drew a deep breath, prepared to lay it all out on the line. To finally tell her the whole story. "After Bethany hired us to help her bust the crime ring, we realized—"

His phone buzzed in his pocket. "Sorry. Let me see who's calling." He pulled it out, then sighed heavily. "It's Mason, and he added the 911 code, which means it's urgent. I have to take this. Give me a minute."

She gave him a tight smile as he headed into the kitchen.

He kept his voice low, hoping it wouldn't carry. "Hey, Mason. What's going on?"

When his boss finished updating him, a sick feeling settled in his stomach. "Got it." He checked his watch. "You think Sampson can get us access to the scene that fast? It happened two hours ago? All right. I'll meet you there."

He ended the call and slid the phone into his pocket.

"That sounded dire. What's going on?" She stood in the doorway, making no apologies for her obvious eavesdropping.

"Not something that I can discuss. I need to go." He motioned toward her leg. "How's the cut this morning? It's not bleeding again, is it?"

"It wasn't when I got dressed. I had a good doctor last night."

He smiled and squeezed past her. "Gotta go."

"You said you'd be honest with me," she called out.

He stopped at the door, then turned around. "I am being honest. I need to leave."

"What's going on?"

"A new development in the investigation."

"Into Bethany's murder?"

He hesitated.

"Dalton. Tell me. Please." She swiped his Stetson from the end table and handed it to him.

He set it on top of his head. "There's been a murder, and Detective Sampson is going to let us take a look at the scene as soon as the medical examiner releases it."

"A murder. You think the killer is the one who killed Bethany?"

"No."

"Then why are you going to the scene?" She put her hands on her hips. "You think it's this Ghost again? The one that has killed other people?"

"We know it is."

"How?"

"It's…"

"Complicated?"

"Yes. I really have to go, Hayley."

"Take me with you. I'll stay in your truck until you're ready to leave. Then you can take me to Camelot and I'll do whatever you need me to do with your computer. My life is a wreck right now. So is yours. We need this case closed."

"You're right about that," he said.

"If my running out of your office building yesterday is the reason that someone else has died, if I could have prevented their death—"

He crossed to her and took her hands in his. "The body, the person who was murdered, they've been dead for some time. You couldn't have prevented it."

She turned her hands over and laced their fingers together. "What about the next one? Or the one after that? Let me help you. I'll do whatever you need. I want to find this killer as much as you do and prevent any more deaths. And if I can prove that I'm innocent along the way, bonus."

He wished he'd had more time to answer her earlier questions. Then she would have understood better what she was up against. What they were all up against. He stood in indecision, then sighed. "How soon can you be ready to leave?"

# *Chapter Twenty-One*

As parks in Gatlinburg went, Hayley didn't think this one was much to brag about. It was off the beaten path, halfway up a mountain, nowhere near any of the hundreds of gorgeous waterfalls that made other parks popular tourist destinations. This one was rarely used, except for an occasional jogger who might stumble across it.

Which was probably why the body had lain here undiscovered for some time.

She waited in the passenger seat of Dalton's truck, as promised, while he joined Mason and a handful of his fellow Seekers, along with two uniformed officers beside one of the strands of yellow tape roping off a section of the park. Behind them, two members of the crime scene unit were setting numbered yellow markers under trees and along the jogging path while a third snapped pictures. The medical examiner and his assistants were currently hunched over something just inside the tree line, likely the victim.

A gray sedan pulled up on the driver's side of the truck. The driver got out of the car, and for a moment her gaze locked with hers. Hayley stiffened as she recognized Sampson. The detective's eyes widened, then she whirled around without nodding or acknowledging her in any way and headed toward the others. That puzzled Hayley. After all, it was she who should be upset that Sampson had lied. Not the other way around.

The group greeted the detective when she reached them. She spoke briefly to the uniformed officers, who then nodded and walked off toward the CSI team. Sampson must have been updating the team about whatever had been found, because they all seemed to be listening intently. At one point, Dalton glanced over the top of Sampson's head toward Hayley and nodded. She wasn't sure if the nod was meant for her or Sampson, so she didn't motion back.

A few moments later, everyone turned toward the jogging path to their right. The ME and his team were rolling a gurney toward the parking lot with a black body bag strapped on top. The CSI team had stopped their work and were standing, respectfully watching the procession. The two uniformed officers watched as well, their hats over their hearts. Hayley glanced at Dalton to judge his reaction. He'd taken his hat off, too, and held the Stetson politely by his side, his expression somber. Everyone's was.

But it was Sampson who seemed the most affected. She had her hand over her heart and seemed to be shaking, just enough for Hayley to notice. Dalton must have noticed, too. He subtly moved closer to her, as if to offer his support.

As the ME's van drove out of the lot, Sampson turned to Dalton and he hugged her. The others closed rank, their hands on each other's shoulders to form an unbroken circle in a show of solidarity. And then Hayley knew: the victim must have been a police officer.

When the group broke up, they each went their separate ways, getting into the various cars and SUVs in the parking lot. After one last hug, Dalton kissed Sampson on the cheek and walked her to her car. He stood watching her drive away.

Hayley dropped her gaze, feeling like she was intruding on a private moment. When the driver's side door opened, she started, then blew out a shaky breath as Dalton looked at her with concern.

"Did I startle you?" His voice was regretful, gentle, kind.

How had she ever thought him capable of hurting anyone?

He shut his door but didn't start the engine yet.

"I'm sorry about your friend, the police officer who died."

"What makes you think he was a police officer?"

"I assumed...because the other police stood at attention, and your friend, Detective Sampson, was so upset."

He considered her answer a moment, but didn't look at her. Instead, he stared through the windshield. "He wasn't a police officer or this park would have been crawling with cops. He was an attorney, a defense attorney who worked a lot with Sampson, and with it being a small town, a lot of the police knew him too."

"Did you?"

He shook his head. "No. The other Seekers knew him. It's hitting them hard."

"He was another victim of The Ghost?"

"Yes. The drug dealing and gunrunning rings that have popped up on our radar around here, we believe those are connected to the killer. But we aren't sure how. Either he's one of the criminals in those networks and he's killing those negatively impacting his business, or he's killing people for another reason and planting evidence about criminal networks to keep the police too busy to exclusively focus on his murders. We're still trying to figure out the specific link between victims, other than that they're all either in law enforcement or work closely with them."

"That sounds like the people who work as Seekers."

"Don't think we haven't thought of that. Seth was a Seeker, and we're beginning to believe he was one of The Ghost's victims. But he's not on the murder list."

"Murder list? There's an actual list?"

"Yes. Why do you use a ghost as an icon on the websites that you design?"

His question couldn't have caught her more off guard. "Why? I just… I mean, it was my nickname in college and—"

"It's your nickname?"

"Well, it was. The other kids resented that I barely showed up for classes and still managed to pass with flying colors. They called me a ghost since they never saw me. At first, it hurt my feelings. But after a while, I sort of liked it, wore it like a badge of honor. Even started signing my assignments with a hand-drawn image of a ghost. Why are you asking that? Please tell me you aren't trying to call me a murderer because some serial killer calls himself The Ghost." She smiled, expecting him to smile back.

He didn't.

"And your websites? Why put the ghost icon there? That's fairly unusual."

"It's my signature. My way of signing each website that I create. I know it's not commonly done, not in the business world. But I don't have any other way to claim my work since I'm keeping my company secret. It makes me smile. Pride in my work. None of my clients ever said anything about it. If they had, I'd have taken it off."

"Why isn't it trademarked? We checked and you haven't registered it. You were trying to keep it a secret that you were the one who'd designed those websites."

"Well, sure. I work for an IT company as a programmer. Developing websites on the side is a conflict of interest. They'd fire me if they found out. I'm no murderer. This ghost stuff is a coincidence."

"And it's a coincidence that several of your clients are criminals?"

She tightened her fists beside her. "Yes. It is. I never

knew they were criminals until yesterday, assuming that wasn't another lie on your part. Why are you—"

"The murder list. The killer leaves a piece of paper attached to each victim. It didn't make sense at first, because that first victim had their own name written down on the paper, then crossed off. But when the second victim was found with their name and the name of the first victim crossed off, the connection was made. The list grows with each victim. But we haven't been able to get ahead of it and figure out his next planned kill in time to save the person's life. That's what most of the team is working on, desperately trying to get ahead of the killer so we can prevent the next murder instead of playing catch-up."

His gaze locked on hers with the intensity of a laser. "We call the killer The Ghost because that's how he signs each murder list. But this time, it was different. This time, he included a hand-drawn picture."

He held up the phone. It showed a piece of yellow legal pad paper with five names. The first one was Bethany Miller. It was crossed out with a red streak that could have been ink or blood. Each of the others were crossed out the same way. And at the bottom was a picture. Of a ghost.

She pressed her hand to her throat. "That picture, it… it's—"

"Exactly like the icon you use on your websites. *Exactly*." He started the engine, then punched the gas.

## Chapter Twenty-Two

Hayley sat in the conference room at Camelot, the same one she'd been in the day before. But this time the only person with her was Dalton. As if to reassure her that she wasn't a prisoner, he'd left the door open.

But the way he was badgering her with questions, interrogating her, made it seem like they'd lost all the ground they'd gained between them. Had he completely changed his mind about her and now believed she was guilty of… something? At best, helping criminals? At worst, he thought she was a killer? The tables had definitely turned. And she didn't like it one bit. It was so exasperating and infuriating that she was either going to start crying soon or grab his gun and shoot him.

She motioned toward the website on the laptop's computer screen. "I already told you that I built that website. And I gave you my client list. How was I supposed to know they weren't legit?"

"Don't you vet your clients, research them, before taking them on?"

"Oh, please. I'm not a cop or a private investigator. Before I started looking into my friend's murder, the best I could do in that arena was an online search. Even now, I'm not much more skilled than that. And I assure you, if you perform a search on my clients' companies, they pass the smell test, nothing fishy at all. Why would I expect anything else? Obviously if I'd known they were criminals, I wouldn't have done business with them. But that's not anything that ever occurred to me."

"What about the secret web pages you create for them? You don't connect them to the main websites. And you set up each client to use Tor when using the hidden pages. Why would you do that?"

"They wanted the access through Tor because it helps ensure privacy and security for things they didn't want the public to see, proprietary things. I created the hidden pages so web crawlers couldn't discover them, set them up with Tor, end of story. If they're doing something else after I set up their websites, it's nothing I know about."

"You didn't think they were using Tor and your hidden pages for something illegal?"

"Why would I? There's a ton of legal stuff that goes through Tor. It makes it easy for international companies to use Bitcoins to purchase goods. Even some banks use Tor and Bitcoin. These questions might make sense to ask now, given the ghost thing, and that you're telling me my clients are using my websites for nefarious purposes. But none of that was on my radar when I was struggling to pay my student loans. I just thought the secret pages were something different and neat. A new challenge for my programming muscles."

He turned the laptop and typed a few keystrokes, then turned it back to face her. "What do you see?"

She lifted her hands in a helpless gesture. "My ghost icon on one of my websites. And before you ask, no, I have no idea how it ended up on that so-called murder list today. Why are you treating me like this? If you think I'm the killer, have the police put me in jail and be done with it. Don't keep hurting me like this."

He glanced at her, and she could have sworn she saw

a flicker of regret. But then he motioned toward the computer. "Show me these secret web pages."

Every command, every sick insinuation, was cracking her heart just a little more. But it was also making her angry enough to spit. She'd give him whatever information she could just in case it could save a life. But not a second more than that.

A moment later, she waved to the screen. "There. See the title? And the pictures down the side? It's clearly internal company policies and things like that. Boring stuff outside clients have no desire or business seeing."

"That's just the main hidden page for that particular client. There are more. Bring them up."

She blinked. "What? Why? Those are private. I can't just show them to you."

"You said that you'd do whatever it took to try to help."

"Revealing my clients' private information is unethical."

His jaw tightened as he punched some keys on the keyboard. "I figured out your algorithm for how you named your hidden pages for this one particular client. So I was able to find a lot of their secret pages. I'll bring one of them up right now." He punched a few more keys then turned the screen around to face her. "Tell me, Hayley. What exactly is ethical about this?"

She looked at the screen, then sucked in a sharp breath. "What is that?" Her voice was so tight she could barely speak.

"Seems pretty clear to me. One of your secret web pages, filled with crime scene photos from this morning's murder. Notice your ghost icon on the page, clearly marking it as your work? And that—" he pointed to the yellow image on the right side "—is the murder list. You do this kind of work for all your clients?"

She stared at him in horror. "You think I did this? Posted these…these…" She gestured toward the screen, then snapped the laptop closed. "I didn't do that, Dalton. I swear."

"Who else would do it? You said your clients don't have their own programmers."

"I don't know. But I didn't do this. How could I? I've been with you for most of the past few days. Even if I wanted to modify that page to put those images on it, I wouldn't have had the opportunity."

"Those pictures were from when the crime scene was fresh, before the body started to decompose."

She swallowed hard, trying not to gag. Then she shoved back her chair. "I'm leaving."

He grabbed the laptop and punched more keys, then turned it toward her as she rounded the table. "What about that one?"

She stiffened but hesitated at the open doorway. In the outer office, Brielle stared at her from over her computer screen, an accusing look on her face. Behind her, at another desk, one of the others—Bryson maybe, the former FBI profiler, if she could believe what had been carved into that round table—gave her the same suspicious, decidedly unfriendly look.

"We're not done, Hayley," Dalton called out. "I haven't figured out the algorithms to bring up the addresses for your other clients' pages. Are you going to show them to me? Or are you afraid I'll see what else you've been doing for the criminals that you work for?"

She slowly turned around. The anger vibrating in his voice had her chest tightening. This was the Dalton Lynch she'd expected when she was following him around. But after seeing how kind he really was, instead of the monster she'd envisioned, and the way she'd thought their relationship had changed these past few days, it was crushing to see him like this. She'd thought he genuinely cared about her. God knew she cared about him, even now, even though he was ripping her heart out.

"I told you that I didn't know that any of them were criminals."

"And yet, every single one of them is exactly that, a criminal. That's not looking too good for you."

She drew a deep breath before she could trust herself to speak. "After that first website, my client referred me to the next client. And so on. I had the bad fortune of my first client being a criminal, so it makes sense that anyone he referred to me was also a criminal. There. That's probably how so many of my clients are bad guys, okay?"

"You expect me to believe that? Ghost?"

She sucked in a breath at his cruelty. Unshed tears burned at the backs of her eyes, making her hate herself for letting him hurt her this way. She fought to keep them from falling, and stepped to the laptop. Then she punched in a web page address for one of her other client's hidden pages, determined to prove that the rest of them were simply boring proprietary data.

Except that wasn't what came up on the screen.

She stared in horror at the graphic pictures of yet another murder victim, a murder list on a yellow legal pad and the ghost icon. Her ghost icon.

Her hand shook as she pulled out a chair and sank down into it. "I didn't do this. I swear."

He said nothing. He simply sat there with the same judgmental look that the other Seekers had when she'd stood in the doorway.

Pulling the laptop closer, she brought up every hidden page that she'd ever created. Ugly photographs of various murders showed up on several of them.

"God help me," she whispered, before shutting the lid on the computer. "I never go to those pages. There's no reason for me to do that. And even if I did, why would I post those awful pictures? Why would my clients post them? It makes no sense."

"Proof of death. You post them on specified pages as you do the dirty work for each client so they'll know the job is done. They probably wire your fee for your real work to an unnumbered account you have offshore."

"Are you kidding me? You think I'm some kind of killer for hire?"

"Are you?"

She blinked back the burn of angry tears that wanted to fall. No way would she let him see her cry. "When Bethany was killed, I was in Pigeon Forge at my day job. The police verified my alibi a long time ago."

He shrugged. "Maybe the medical examiner was wrong about time of death."

She tightened her hands on the arms of the chair. "When was the second victim killed?"

He told her, and she checked her phone's calendar. Thankfully she had a verifiable alibi for that date and time, too. They volleyed back and forth until she'd dispelled, at least in her opinion, any possibility that she could have killed these people.

She shoved back her chair and slapped her palms on the table. "I don't know why someone hacked into my client websites and left those awful photos. Or whether my clients really did hire some killer and that person put those pictures out there. Or why a killer would use my ghost icon on his murder list. Maybe I'm being framed. I don't know. I leave that to you *professionals* to figure out. I hope you enjoyed this little interrogation. Because it's the last time you and I will ever speak. I'm done."

He looked past her and arched his brows. "She has an alibi for every murder. Was that good enough to convince you once and for all that she's innocent?"

Hayley whirled around. In the doorway, Detective Sampson stood with handcuffs dangling from one hand, her other resting on the butt of her holstered pistol. Behind her were four uniformed officers.

Sampson slid the handcuffs in her back pocket, then gave Dalton a crisp nod. "Good enough. I'll cancel the arrest warrant, update the chief. Keep me posted on any new evidence or theories, Dalton."

"You bet."

She gave Hayley a tight smile. "If what you said is true, then I hope you can forgive me, and Dalton. I was ready to arrest you at the park. I had a warrant already, based on the murder list and the ghost icon matching your websites. But Dalton convinced me to wait, so he could try to prove you were innocent." She motioned to the uniformed officers. They all headed toward the front door.

Hayley slowly turned around. "She was here with a warrant, to arrest me?"

"Yes. I'm sorry I was so rough, that I put you through this. But I didn't want you going back to jail. I told Sampson that you had nothing to do with any of the murders. That someone's trying to set you up, as you just said. But she wasn't buying it."

"So…you did this…showed me those awful pictures, accused me of horrible things, because she was watching?"

Again, he nodded. "She got here right after you and I did. Mason convinced her to wait in his office." He waved at the camera in the corner of the ceiling. "She watched the whole thing. Thankfully, you're organized enough to know what you were doing when each murder occurred. I'm sure she was searching the internet and making calls at the same time, verifying as much as she could or she wouldn't have left without you in cuffs. And she'll do more, to be absolutely sure your stories check out."

She started shaking. "I was almost arrested for murder. Oh my God." Her voice broke and she covered her face with her hands, no longer able to hold back the tears of anger and fear and frustration.

He swore and pulled her into his arms.

A knock sounded on the open door behind them, but she buried her face against Dalton's chest. She didn't care who it was. She couldn't take any more. Not yet.

"Dalton." It was Sampson's voice. "You mentioned at the park that you wanted me to see whether Chandler Harding had a record, that his name rang some kind of bell. I asked one of the admins to run it down. They emailed it to me and I just had Brielle print it out." She tossed a thin manila folder on top of the desk. "He's got a rap sheet longer than my two arms put together. But he died years ago. What's that have to do with our current situation?"

"Probably nothing. I don't know. Just another thread to pull."

"Well, enjoy pulling. I don't have time to read ancient history. I've got to update the chief. And make plans to attend yet another funeral."

The door clicked closed.

Hayley pushed herself back and wiped at her eyes. But she couldn't quite look at him. She was too bruised, too hurt, even though he had an explanation for the brutal way he'd treated her.

Suddenly her world tilted and she was in his arms, which had her tears flowing all over again. He sat down and drew her against him, gently rocking while talking to her and rubbing his hand up and down her back.

She shouldn't have liked being held by him after what just happened, and her earlier disastrous meeting here, too. But then again, she'd treated him terribly for months. And yet he'd set up this little drama to save her. It dawned on her that in spite of everything, he believed in her. He'd stood up for her when no one else had. He was in her corner, protecting her, helping her, keeping her safe. She couldn't remember anyone ever doing that before.

When she was finally able to stop crying, she pushed back and stared up at him. "I've soaked your shirt."

He smiled and gently pushed her hair out of her eyes. "You can soak my shirt any time if it makes you feel better."

"Why?"

"Why what?"

"Why did you help me, with Detective Sampson? And why did you hold me, just now?"

"Don't you get it, Hayley? I'm falling for you. Not just because you're mind-blowingly sexy. I'm falling for you because you're whip smart and sassy, and you care as much about justice as I do. That's rare. And it's why I realized you were innocent even before you had those alibis. I already told Mason that I was going to fight for you, hire a lawyer, whatever it took if you didn't have any alibis. You're a special woman. And I'm in your corner now. We'll get through this, and then maybe we can have a first date like other couples. Something without blood or hospital threats or the police involved."

"Or Jack Daniels?" she teased.

"Well, now. Drunk Hayley is adorable. Don't be too hasty."

She laughed.

His smile faded and he cupped her face in his hands. "There's one other thing I need to tell you. I want to explain that comment you asked about, regarding the medical examiner and your friend's death."

"No." She pressed her hands against his. "I can't take any more revelations today. The only thing I want you to do right now is kiss me. Will you do that? Please?"

In answer, he cupped the back of her head and pulled her against him, then pressed his lips to hers.

She'd been kissed before, but never like *this*. His kiss

was exquisite, magical, perfect. It wrapped around her heart and warmed her soul, giving her all the goose-bumpy feels and drugging her with desire. But more than that, it transformed her, made her feel safe, cherished, loved. He melted away her fears, soothed her hurts, and then he melted her.

By the time he ended the kiss, they were both gasping for breath and staring at each other in wonder.

His hands shook as he cupped her face again and stared into her eyes. "Hayley." His voice was husky with desire. "That was… I don't even know what that was. Just…wow."

She laughed and hugged him, feeling happier in that moment than she ever had. "It was worth all the bad. More than worth it."

He held her tight. "Hopefully all the bad will be over soon. I'm so sorry for what I've put you through."

She pulled back and pressed her finger to his lips. "Don't. Don't spoil the glow."

His brows arched. "Glow?"

"The magic. Don't spoil it. Not yet. We deserve a moment. Or two."

He gently kissed her, a tantalizing taste of more to come. "It's been a long, tough day and it's barely past the lunch hour. Unfortunately, I've got a lot more work to do if we're going to catch this killer. How about I take you home? Then I'll stop back by when I'm done here and take you somewhere for a decent meal. You can't have had time to go to the grocery store since getting out of jail."

She sighed and reluctantly hopped off his lap. "You're right. I haven't. Dinner with you sounds great. Thanks."

"My pleasure." He stood and fished his keys from his pants pocket. He started toward the door, then turned back and grabbed the manila folder from the table. "Let's go."

Brielle looked up as they exited the conference room. She ran around her desk and surprised Hayley with a quick hug.

"I'm sorry, Miss Nash. After seeing that picture on the murder list today, I was just as convinced as Erin—Detective Sampson—that you were The Ghost we've been looking for. I'm sorry you had to go through all this to get to the truth."

"Th-thank you. I appreciate that."

The others in the office lined up to apologize as well, and assure her that they'd find whoever was behind this.

Once in Dalton's truck, Hayley sniffed, fighting back tears again.

"You okay?" he asked.

"They were so nice. And I've been so horrible to you and—"

"I think it's time we both let go of the past. How about we make a pact to be nice to each other going forward and figure out the rest later, okay? No more apologies or guilt."

"Sounds good to me."

Once they reached her cabin, he walked her to her door. She smiled up at him on the porch, ready to thank him, but he wasn't looking at her. He was looking past her.

And reaching for his gun.

## *Chapter Twenty-Three*

Hayley stood frozen in indecision, staring at the open front door of her house where Dalton had just disappeared. She'd locked the door. Hadn't she? They'd left together, in his truck, to go to the park. Of course she'd locked it. She remembered him waiting while she did, then helping her into the truck. So why was her door ajar when they'd gotten here?

Her exhausted mind couldn't seem to process what was happening. Someone had broken into her home. And Dalton had gone inside to check it out.

She took a step forward. What if whoever had broken in was still there? What if Dalton was hurt and needed help?

He was taking far too long. He hadn't let her take her gun with her to the park. Now she regretted not insisting that she bring it. Well, she might not have a gun. But she could call 911. She yanked out her cell phone.

"Don't."

He stepped onto the porch and grabbed her phone, then dropped it. She stared in horror as he stomped on it, grinding his boot heel and leaving a twisted, worthless mess.

"Why did you..." She watched in shock as he threw the ruined phone across the road into the woods. "Dalton? What's going on?"

"We can't risk someone tracing your phone."

She noted the white pillowcase tossed over one of his

shoulders. Something was inside. She had no idea what. And he wasn't looking at her. He was scanning the road, left and right, as if looking for something. Or someone.

Goose bumps covered her arms. "Dalton?"

"We're leaving. Now."

She glanced toward the doorway. "Is someone inside the house?"

"They were, but they left before we got here." He grabbed her arm and pulled her with him toward the truck.

"If no one else is here, then why do we have to leave? If the place is trashed, shouldn't we call the police?"

His jaw tightened. "Nobody trashed your house."

After yanking open the passenger door, he practically tossed her inside, then threw the pillowcase in the middle of the bench seat. She'd barely gotten her seat belt clicked into place before he was tearing off down the road.

The faint sound of a siren had him looking in the rear-view mirror. But he didn't seem surprised. If anything, he seemed to have expected it.

She turned around to see faint red and blue lights down in the valley, racing up the mountain.

"The police are coming," she said. "Did you call them from my house, before we left?"

"No."

She waited. Again, he offered no further explanations.

"Hold on," he ordered.

She grabbed the armrest just as he jerked the wheel. The truck skidded around a curve, then shot down a narrow side road so concealed by overgrown bushes and trees that she'd never noticed it before. It was barely wide enough for the truck.

She clutched the handle above her to keep from being tossed against the door each time he swerved for one of the sharp curves. It was only about two in the afternoon and yet it was nearly pitch-dark because of the thick tree canopy, blotting out the sun. His headlights cut a swath through the darkness.

The sound of the sirens faded, then disappeared. Ahead of them, the road finally straightened and he punched the gas, making the truck jump forward, throwing her back against the seat.

"Dalton, please, would you tell me what's going on before we die in a fiery crash? What happened at my house? Where are we going?"

He braked, then turned down yet another road. She gave up asking him any questions. Another twenty or thirty minutes passed with him driving like a madman before he finally slowed. A few more turns and the headlights illuminated a log cabin even smaller than hers.

He pulled to the far left side of the gravel driveway and parked.

"Where—"

He hopped out of the truck and slammed his door shut.

She groaned in frustration and released her seat belt. Once again, he was yanking open her door, then lifting her out before she could even try opening it herself. He set her on her feet and slammed the door shut. Then, with a quick look around as if to ensure they were alone in this remote wilderness on the edge of the earth, he grabbed the pillowcase and the manila folder, then pulled her with him to the front porch.

Once inside, he flipped on the lights, turned on the central heat, then strode into the eat-in kitchen where he set the pillowcase and folder on the table.

She rubbed her arms against the chill and noted the small living room visible from the front entrance that ran along the back, then hesitantly followed him into the kitchen. "What is this place?"

"A last resort that few people know about." He hung his truck keys on a peg beside the window. "If something happens to me, you grab those keys and get out of here. Go to Camelot and press 911 on the keypad. One of the Seekers will help you."

"Why are you telling me this?"

"Backup plan. I want you safe. I don't want you risking your life trying to help me. I mean that."

She stared at him. "I could never leave you if you were hurt or needed me."

His face softened and he pressed an achingly sweet kiss against her lips. "Let's hope it never comes to that." He turned away and worked on the knot in the pillowcase.

"Why are you so worried all of a sudden? Why did we have to leave my cabin and hide out here?" She rubbed her temples, then winced when she hit one of the healing bruises from her recent exploits. From hitting her head on Dalton's driveway, to her fight in jail, to losing the battle with Jack Daniels, she felt like she'd been through a war. Unfortunately, the war wasn't over. "All this James Bond, clandestine spy stuff is driving me crazy. I'm just an ordinary person who's really tired and I want to understand why you—"

"This is why." *Thump. Thump. Thump.*

She stared at the items he was dumping out of the pillowcase onto the table.

A baseball bat with red smears across it and, oh dear Lord no, strands of hair stuck to the wood.

A pistol that she'd never seen before.

A pill bottle that rattled and rolled across the table before coming to a rest against the bat.

There were also some bloody-looking clothes. Hers. She recognized the outfit. Of course it hadn't been saturated with blood the last time she'd worn it.

He tossed the still half-full-looking pillowcase to the floor, then motioned toward the items on the table. "I found this. All of it. In your house. It wasn't sitting out in the open.

But while searching for an intruder, I found that bloody bat behind a door. That sent me on a different kind of search, looking in places where people typically hide proof of their crimes."

He motioned toward the gun. "That was under your mattress. It's consistent with the type of weapon we believe was used to kill The Ghost's first and second victims." He waved toward the bottle of pills. "Although there isn't a label, I'm guessing that's a highly lethal toxin, the same one used on the murder victim The Ghost killed several weeks ago. They were in a cabinet in your kitchen, beside some over-the-counter medicines. Those clothes were at the bottom of your laundry basket. I imagine the blood matches one of our murder victims. There's more of the same in the pillowcase, evidence of The Ghost's crimes."

She frantically shook her head. "I swear to you. None of this is mine. I mean, the clothes are mine but not the blood, the pills. I don't even own a bat. I had nothing to do with the murders. You have to believe me."

He frowned. "Hayley, I didn't—"

"I swear I'm not a murderer."

He swore and tossed his Stetson on the counter, before stalking toward her.

She backed up against the wall, spread her hands in front of her. "Whatever you think I did, you have to believe me. I'm innocent."

He shook his head. "Don't you think I know that? If I had any doubts, any at all, I'd have left you back there in your cabin for the police."

She slowly lowered her arms and he stopped right in front of her. "Then…the reason you took that stuff, and drove us here is because…?"

"Because, having been on the receiving end, I know a frame-up when I see one. You either have a powerful enemy setting you up, or you're just a convenient fall guy to get someone off the hook for their crimes. Either way, they're doing everything they can to destroy you. Gatlinburg PD is in your cabin right now, searching your place. Did I find all the evidence your enemy left? I hope so. But probably not. I knew with everything I did find that someone would have already called the police with an anonymous tip and we couldn't risk hanging around for a more thorough search."

"Wait. You're saying that someone broke into my cabin and left all that stuff to make it look like I'm the killer?"

"Worse. I don't think it's just anyone. It's The Ghost that we've been trying to hunt down. He hacked your web pages and posted the pictures from the murder scenes. He's killed four people so far—a police officer, a defense attorney, a former prosecutor, a retired detective."

"Five."

He looked at her in question.

"Bethany. She counts, too, doesn't she?"

"Right. Five. If Seth was murdered by The Ghost too, that brings the count to six. The killer left blood, hair, DNA all over your home to frame you. We have to figure out who wants you locked up, and why."

"I can't believe this is happening."

"Believe it. We have to get ahead of this thing and get your life back. We have to figure out who the real killer is, fast. He expected you to go to jail tonight. Since you aren't, he'll have to change his plan."

"Dalton?"

"Yes?"

"If it's not too much to ask, could you please give me a hug? I could really use one right now."

He pulled her into his arms and cradled her against his chest.

# *Chapter Twenty-Four*

Dalton stood in the kitchen, holding Hayley in his arms. She wasn't crying this time. But she was shaking so hard he wanted to pummel whoever was doing this to her. She was a dynamo, a little firecracker, smart and sensitive. And she'd given up so much to pursue what she felt was right. He admired her for that, even though her pursuit had made it difficult for him.

Holding her now was like a balm to his battered soul. The anger and tension from moments ago seemed to melt away with her snuggled against him. He could stand here forever and be happy, just holding her.

The real world intruded all too soon when his cell phone buzzed in his pocket.

She pushed out of his arms and cleared her throat, her eyes mirroring such a sense of dread that he almost wished he hadn't brought his phone. He wanted to reassure her. But what could he say? He'd do everything he could to keep her safe. But it was hard to protect someone without knowing where the next blow was coming from.

The phone buzzed again. He checked the screen, then leaned back against the counter to take the call.

"What's going on?" Mason demanded as soon as he answered. "Sampson said the cops are crawling all over Miss Nash's cabin, that they've found evidence that she's The Ghost after all, but she's missing. I sent Bryson to your house to look for you, and you're obviously not there. Where are you?"

"She's not The Ghost, Mason. You were there today, at the office. You heard her provide an alibi for every murder."

"Sampson's going to bend and twist those alibis every which way until they break. She found compelling evidence that only the real killer would have at Nash's cabin, pending DNA tests. But it's not looking good."

"Yeah, well, so did I. Like a bottle of pills that I believe contains the poison one of The Ghost's victims was given. Only that bottle wasn't in the cabinet earlier today when I took a bottle of aspirin out of that same cabinet. And those bloody clothes weren't in the laundry basket when I put other clothes there earlier while tending to Hayley's cuts when she fell on some broken glass at her cabin. She's been with me every second since then. Someone is setting her up. You know even better than I do what that's like. She deserves our support and protection, not our doubts. And no more stunts like we've pulled on her at Camelot, twice. If that's a problem for you, fire me. I'm done with those bullying tactics."

A deep sigh sounded into the phone. "No one's quitting or getting fired. Are you sure about those pills? And the clothes? They weren't there earlier? You couldn't have missed them?"

"I'm sure."

"All right. Then I agree that someone is trying to make her look guilty. But you should have called me and told me what was going on before Sampson went on the warpath and hit me out of left field. She's convinced Miss Nash is involved, even if just as a co-conspirator. And since you aren't home, she's demanding to know where you're hiding her."

"What makes you think she's with me?"

She lifted her head from studying the apparently fascinating wood designs on the tabletop.

He smiled, trying to reassure her.

"I'm not stupid, Dalton. You just said she hasn't been out of your sight. Besides that, everyone at Camelot noticed you were wearing the same clothes two days in a row, and how disheveled Miss Nash was. Doesn't take much to connect those dots."

He shifted against the counter. "Okay. Here's the sitrep. When we left her cabin to go to the crime scene at the park, the front door was locked. I'm sure of it. When I brought her back, it wasn't. I went in to clear it, expecting to find a burglar. Instead, I found a bloody bat, bloody clothes and other items that weren't there when we left. Since she was with me the whole time, obviously someone else went inside to stage the scene. I grabbed what I saw and took it with me. But I knew, with the scene staged like that, that whoever did it was likely to have called the cops. So we couldn't hang around. Sure enough, sirens sounded right as we were leaving. She was set up, Mason. Feel free to let Sampson know. Like I said, I was with her the whole time. Someone else left those items in her cabin."

"The Ghost."

"Exactly. I'm thinking that Bryson might be the person to talk to Sampson, make her see reason. They've been friends a long time, even before he joined the Seekers. Then get Sampson to tell Bryson what all's going on. She needs to pull videos from the businesses along the major routes to the mountain and see if any vehicles or drivers stand out as ones who could have planted that evidence. It's not a busy road. It shouldn't be that hard. There's a good chance our killer is caught on film. If so, maybe one of the Seekers can try to get a copy."

"I'll put someone on it. Where are you now?"

"My cabin, the place where I lived before I bought the house."

"You kept it? I figured you sold it."

"Since it's so remote, I thought it would make a great hiding place if I ever needed one."

"Looks like you need it now." He sighed heavily.

He shifted the phone to his other ear. "Hayley needs clothes, toiletries—"

"What about you?" Mason interrupted, always putting his Seekers first. "What do you need?"

"Just for Bryson to take care of my dogs, especially Denali. He watches them when I'm out of town so they know him. I've got clothes and stuff here for me. I'll be fine. But Hayley needs pretty much everything. Her cabin's a crime scene. And knowing Sampson, she's got a few uniforms watching Hayley's house in Pigeon Forge, so that's off-limits, too. Maybe Brielle can pick up stuff at a store and bring it here?" Hayley gave him a grateful smile. "I'll text her a shopping list after this call."

He spoke to Mason a few more minutes, discussing strategies and what to do next. "When Brielle comes with Hayley's things, can you have her bring dinner? There's nothing to eat here."

He ended the call and worked with Hayley on the list of what she needed. After texting it to Brielle, he put his phone away.

"This is really happening, isn't it?" Hayley asked.

He crossed to her and held out his hand. "Come on. We've done all we can for now. The other Justice Seekers will handle it from here. Let me take you on the grand tour of my little two-bedroom, two-bath hideaway. Then we can veg out in front of the TV and break out my video collection of old movies. There's no cable or internet. It's the best I can offer."

She took his hand. "Sounds like a perfect first date to me."

He grinned. "First date, huh? How many bases do I get to round on the first date?"

"That's for you to find out, I suppose."

"Then let's get this tour over with and get to the finding out part." He winked and tugged her down the hall.

# Chapter Twenty-Five

The cabin tour was even shorter than Dalton had anticipated. After showing her the master bedroom off the back
corner of the house and heading back into the hallway, Hayley let him know, through glances, smiles, and the unsub-
tle trailing of her fingers down his arm, that a tour wasn't
what she wanted right now.

She wanted him.

All the tension, fear, and emotional turmoil had caught
up with both of them. They shared a heated kiss, two starv-
ing souls, wanting and needing the connection they both
shared but had been trying to deny for so long.

By the time they stumbled their way to the main room
again, they were wrapped up in each other's arms, sharing passionate kisses and frenzied caresses like a couple of
horny teenagers. As things got more heated, he frantically
began working on the buttons of her blouse, craving the
touch of skin on skin. She worked just as enthusiastically
at his belt buckle, making him suck in a sharp breath when
her warm hands bumped against the hard ridge in his jeans.

Brielle. He needed to stall her, tell her to take her time
before coming to the cabin. But just as the thought occurred to him, the sound of an engine and tires crunching
on gravel out front told him it was too late.

He groaned with disappointment and broke their kiss.

Sitting up, he pulled her with him, then went to work re-fastening his buckle.

Her swollen lips and passion-glazed eyes had him grinning with male satisfaction. "You are so ridiculously beautiful, you know that?"

Her lips curved in a sexy smile. "You haven't seen my best attributes yet." She slid a hand down her generous half-exposed breasts, barely contained behind her sagging blouse.

He groaned again. "You're killing me."

Her smile grew.

Three rapid knocks on the door were followed by, "Hurry up, cowboy. This stuff is heavy."

She gasped and jumped up, her fingers flying across the buttons on her shirt.

He gave her another quick kiss, then stood, grimacing at the tightness of his pants. "Unfortunately I have to let Brielle in or she'll probably shoot me."

Her eyes widened. She started finger-combing her hair.

He laughed at her adorable efforts to compose herself and strode to the door. When he opened it, Brielle shoved a huge brown paper sack into his arms.

"Make yourself useful for a change."

He stepped back to let her in. "Nice to see you, too."

"Yeah, whatever. Got me runnin' around town bein' a gopher of all things when I could be out looking for bad guys." She stopped when she saw Hayley, then smiled. "Not that I mind, for you, girl." She jabbed her thumb toward Dalton. "I just don't like doing him any favors."

He rolled his eyes and set the bag on the table. "Smells great. Barbecue?"

"Food of the gods. Chow down, my friends. I got a little of everything—baby back ribs, pulled pork, fried okra, you name it." She handed the other bag that she was carrying to Hayley as she joined them in the kitchen. "If there's something you want that I didn't get, then you don't need it. I even threw some makeup in there." She looked Hayley up and down. "Then again, maybe make *out* is the operative word of the day. Tell me something, hon. Is that shoe-size thing accurate in a man as big as Dalton? I always wondered."

Hayley's face flushed a delightful pink.

"Brielle, leave her alone." He gave Hayley an apologetic look as he continued unloading the bag of food onto the table. "Don't mind her, Hayley."

"Fine way to treat someone who brought you food and clothes." Brielle waved toward the bag. "Seriously, honey. You got what you wanted in there? You need anything else?"

Hayley seemed overwhelmed beneath the force of Brielle's personality. She glanced uncertainly at Dalton.

He gave her a reassuring smile and she peered inside the bag. "You thought of everything," Hayley noted. "Thanks. I really appreciate it. I'll pay you back when I can."

Brielle shook her head. "That's all courtesy of the Justice Seekers' petty cash fund. No worries there."

"Well, thanks again. And the food looks wonderful. But I'd rather have a quick shower first, if that's okay. Murder scenes and bloody baseball bats have me feeling icky. I wish I could wash all of this awful stuff out of my mind too."

"It'll be okay. Promise," Dalton told her. "Towels and anything you might need are in the linen closets in each bathroom. Feel free to use the master. The shower in there is a lot bigger."

The sound of another car pulling up out front had him peering through the plantation shutters. "Mason's here."

Brielle pulled out her phone and checked the screen. "Looks like he wants us to come outside. Kira sent him a video feed from a gas station at the bottom of the mountain. It's coming up on that fancy car computer of his right now." She headed to the door.

Dalton looked back at Hayley. "I'll be back in a few minutes."

"Take your time. I'm fine." She clutched the bag of clothes and toiletries.

He smiled and headed outside.

Mason's black Mercedes pulled to a stop beside Brielle's SUV. He'd had the car fully customized with expensive gadgets that law enforcement would drool over, including a state-of-the-art computer that was far more powerful than any police officer would have. It was attached to a metal arm that angled out over the middle console. He motioned for Brielle and Dalton to join him.

Brielle hopped into the front passenger seat while Dalton crouched in the open doorway to watch the video feed playing out on the computer screen.

Mason motioned toward the feed. "Kira said there were seven vehicles that went up the mountain from the time you and Miss Nash went to the park until the time you left Camelot to take her back to her cabin. She didn't recognize any of them. And the video quality is too poor to see much detail as far as the occupants of the vehicles. But she's sending a copy to Jaxon to try to get it enhanced."

He punched a few keys, and the video sped up, then stopped with a red pickup in the still frame. "This is the first one. She texted me the time stamps so I can fast-forward to where each vehicle comes into view. Either of you see anything familiar about that truck?"

"Not me," Brielle said. "Looks like a legit business truck though. There are vegetables in the back. He's probably heading up to Crawford's market at the top of the mountain."

"Agreed," Dalton said. "I'm pretty sure I've seen that

same truck at Crawford's before. And there look to be two little kids in the back seat."

Brielle leaned toward the screen. "You're right. That's probably not our guy."

"Next one." Mason punched some more keys, stopping the frame to show a white Cadillac. Then a blue Toyota. Another pickup, this one green and so rust-riddled it was amazing it even ran. When he punched up the fifth vehicle, Brielle let out a gasp of surprise.

Dalton stiffened, his hand tightening around the door. "That little traitor."

Mason looked from one to the other. "Traitor? I can't see the driver. You recognize the vehicle?"

"You bet we do," Dalton said. "That's the emergency car that I left for our guest, just in case there was a wildfire or some other unexpected event so they could get out safely."

"Wait," Mason said. "I thought we had a bodyguard up there twenty-four seven. How would our guest manage to leave and him not know?"

Brielle was already shaking her head. "At first, Dalton had us taking turns once a day to drop off supplies and make sure everything was okay. Remember, we had no reason to think anyone knew they were there. But after you two saw that picture of Seth at the police station, Kira and Caleb went up to check on things."

"And I hired a bodyguard that same day," Dalton added. "Because things seemed suspicious. The bodyguard was supposedly there for protection. In reality, his job was to let us know if anything odd was going on."

"Like a joy ride in the emergency car to plant evidence." Mason's face was grim. "Someone needs to check on our bodyguard."

Brielle tapped her phone. Dalton hadn't even realized she'd taken it out. "I just texted him. He's not answering."

Dalton swore.

Mason snapped the computer closed. "Dalton, you'd better let Sampson know what's going on. Tell her we know the identity of our Ghost and get a BOLO out on the emergency vehicle. Tell the Seekers to be on the lookout for it, too. Brielle, you've got EMT training. Follow me to the safe house. I have a feeling it's too late to help our bodyguard, but we have to try."

"On it."

Dalton straightened so she could hop out of the car and run to her SUV. "What do you want me to do, Mason?"

"After you bring Sampson up to speed, just hang out here with Miss Nash. No one but the Seekers knows she's here. If The Ghost realizes their setup isn't working and that we know their identity, then it's obvious who the next victim will be."

"Hayley."

Mason nodded. "Keep her safe. I'll text you an update as soon as I have one."

Brielle's tires kicked up gravel as she zipped down the road. Mason followed suit, leaving Dalton standing out front.

He yanked out his phone and punched in Sampson's number.

## *Chapter Twenty-Six*

After the heartache, fear and tension of the past few months, especially these harrowing last two weeks, Hayley was finally glimpsing something she'd worried that she'd never see again. Hope.

Her emotions had been tamped down so hard for so long she was ready to explode. And when she'd walked through the cabin with Dalton, knowing he finally believed her, and that she believed him, and they were going to face this thing together, she'd been overcome. Everything she'd bottled up inside, all the longing and desire, had been impossible to contain even one more second. And to her amazement, he'd felt the same way.

Kissing him, holding him, had been magic, magic she'd never wanted to end. But the cruel world had intruded all too soon. She needed to hurry and find out the latest news, see what the next hurdle would be. But at least this time she knew she'd have Dalton with her to jump that hurdle.

She quickly dressed, then towel-dried her hair as best she could. Unfortunately, she couldn't find a blow-dryer. She hadn't asked Brielle to bring one since she'd assumed there would be one here. Her long, thick hair would probably be damp the rest of the day, but it couldn't be helped. At least she wasn't planning on going outside in the cold.

She fashioned her hair into a thick braid that fell down the middle of her back. Then she shoved her dirty clothes into the bathroom hamper. After one last look in the mirror to make sure her makeup looked okay, she headed into the master bedroom. She was almost to the hall door when a knock sounded.

At the window.

She whirled around. A face stared back at her through the glass, a face that couldn't possibly be there. She started shaking so hard her teeth chattered. She squeezed her eyes shut, convinced she was seeing a ghost.

The knock sounded again.

"Hayley, it's me. Open up."

She opened her eyes. That wasn't a ghost. Bethany was really here. Alive. She sobbed and ran to the window and tried to open it.

Bethany pointed to the lock on one side.

Hayley flipped it back and slid the window up. She pressed her hand against the screen. "Bethany? Is that really you? I thought—"

"That I was dead?" She grinned and pressed her hand against Hayley's.

"I thought you were a ghost."

Her brows shot up, and she let out a laugh. "Imagine that." She chuckled again. "Well, I'm not dead. I'm flesh and blood. Freezing my ass off, but still flesh and blood. Can you open the back door? We need to talk." She dropped her hand from the screen.

Hayley clasped the windowsill, her greedy gaze drinking in every detail. "It really is you. I can't believe… I don't understand what's going on. I saw the article in the paper about the police finding your body. I took a leave of absence so I could focus on getting you justice, finding the killer. How are you here, alive?"

Bethany glanced around before answering. "Brielle, you've met her right? One of the Seekers?"

Hayley nodded. Even though she was seeing her friend with her own eyes, just inches away, her mind couldn't seem to accept that she was real. Was this what Dalton had wanted to tell her when she'd asked about the medical examiner's report? That Bethany wasn't dead? That he and his allies in the police station had set up a fake murder? Why? Why would they do that? He said he was going to answer all of her questions, but then they'd had to flee her cabin. She hadn't thought to ask him those questions again since arriving here. Now she wished she had.

She shook her head, realizing that Bethany was trying to tell her something. "I'm… I'm sorry. I think I'm still in shock. You were explaining something about Brielle?"

Her friend sighed heavily. "Short version, the Seekers faked my death to keep me safe because some really bad people were after me once they figured out I was doing an exposé on them. I've been in a safe house, a cabin like this one, while they tried to put all the bad guys away who might do me harm. But the main guy has been killing people, putting out some kind of murder list. So the Seekers figured they could save resources by bringing me here—protect two people at once. Two birds with one stone kind of thing. Brielle brought me here."

The fog in her mind was starting to lift. And her joy at seeing her friend was fading beneath a mountain of questions. And doubt. "Brielle didn't mention you when she came inside."

"No? Well, she did say that she wanted to break it to Dalton in private, about combining safe houses. They're talking out front right now. But I got tired of waiting so I sneaked out of her car and headed around back. Gosh, Hayley. It's so good to finally see you again. I've missed you so much." She rubbed her hands up and down her coat sleeves, then shoved them in her pockets. "Did I mention it's freezing out here? Can you open the back door? I'll answer all your questions, explain everything. I promise. Just hurry, okay?"

Hayley stared at her as various images, snatches of conversations and research flitted through her mind like a checklist.

The frustrating meetings with the police. Their refusals to give Dalton a serious look as a potential suspect in Bethany's death. Because they knew she wasn't dead? Were they helping the Seekers fake her death while they brought down the crime ring? Dalton had said they weren't officially working with the police, no task force. Did Sampson fake the death then, to help the Seekers? Maybe she told her bosses the fake death story in the paper was part of some case she was working, so they didn't ask questions when there wasn't a body in the morgue. That would explain Dalton's concern about her asking for a medical examiner's report.

He'd also sworn that he had an airtight alibi, but that he couldn't share it without jeopardizing the case. Because he couldn't tell her that Bethany was alive? She was still their client?

More puzzle pieces floated around. Like Dalton asking her how she'd met Bethany. Her telling him about Chandler Harding, the guy she'd once dated, the man who later became Bethany's fiancé. Dalton said the name sounded familiar. It had bothered him enough to ask Sampson to look him up. And he had a rap sheet, a history of criminal activity. When Sampson had asked him why he wanted the information and whether it was related to the current case, he'd said it probably wasn't, but it was another thread to pull.

Bethany had just told her that Brielle had left her in her vehicle out front. Did that even make sense? Wouldn't Brielle bring her inside where it was warm and have her share the food she'd brought?

Something had been niggling at Hayley ever since Dalton had questioned her about her old nickname, Ghost. The killer was using the same moniker. Was that really a coincidence? It didn't seem like it, since the killer was also hacking into her websites to point the blame at her for the murders. She'd told Dalton that her college friends had come up with that nickname. But looking back, it was one friend in particular. Bethany.

Perhaps the most worrisome issue was that if Brielle was busy talking to Dalton and Mason out front, couldn't Bethany just have told them she was going inside to get out of the cold and see her old friend again? Why wouldn't she use the front door? The only reason to use the back door was if she didn't want to be seen by the Seekers. And there was only one reason Hayley could think of for Bethany not to want them to know she was here.

Bethany was The Ghost.

*Oh dear Lord.* She had to get to Dalton.

"O-okay. Sorry. Still so shocked to see you that I'm not thinking straight. I didn't mean to leave you out there in the cold." She forced a smile. "I'll, ah, go open the back door right now." She turned around.

"Hold it."

The unmistakable sound of a round being chambered had Hayley stiffening.

"Turn around."

She slowly turned.

Bethany had the barrel of a pistol pressed against the screen. "You never were good at hiding your emotions. I can tell you aren't buying my story. Looks like we're going to do this the hard way." She raised her other hand, revealing a wicked-looking knife.

Hayley drew a sharp breath.

Bethany rolled her eyes. "I'm not planning on stabbing you. Not yet anyway." She slashed the screen from corner to corner, making an X, then put her knife away. "Climb out the window. Make any noise, scream, do anything to alert your lover and I'll blow your stupid head off. Then, when he runs in here to rescue you, I'll shoot him too. Got it?"

Hayley nodded.

"Do it. Now."

## Chapter Twenty-Seven

Dalton sat on the front porch steps, holding the phone away from his ear so that Sampson's yelling wouldn't destroy his hearing. While she ranted about him not leveling with her and keeping her in the loop, and mucking up her crime scene at Hayley's cabin, he practiced trying to blow out his breath like smoke rings in the freezing cold air.

His toes were starting to lose feeling inside his boots. But no way was he going inside the warm cabin until this conversation was over. Hayley had already been through so much. He didn't want to clue her in about her friend being The Ghost until this was over and there was no more danger to her or anyone else. She'd earned a reprieve from worry and stress. He was going to do everything he could to let her enjoy this break for as long as possible.

Something Sampson said caught his attention. He put the phone back to his ear. "Wait, what did you just say? About the car on the gas station's video?"

"Are you even listening to me?" she accused.

"Partly. Tell me about the car."

She cursed him up and down, then sighed loudly, as if she'd finally run out of thunder. "I said your people don't need to search for the car anymore. We found it in the woods behind Miss Nash's rental cabin. And you're in luck. There are shoe prints leading from the car to the back door. And tool marks on the door. That lends credence to your theory that someone else is involved and planted the evidence."

"It's not a theory. It's a fact. I told you—"

"Hayley's innocent, yeah, yeah. I'll go with hard facts to come to my conclusions. But it's leaning in your favor, especially since I can corroborate that she was with you at the park, then after that at Camelot without an opportunity to put those items in the cabin herself. Plus, having met her, and knowing her history with badgering my former fellow Gatlinburg officers over finding her friend's alleged killer, that sure doesn't jibe with her being the killer. So, yes, I agree with you that she's likely not the suspect we should be after. But that doesn't mean I don't want to talk to her. She's not in the clear just yet."

He made a circling motion with his hand. "Hold it. Rewind. If Bethany arrived in that car and parked it in the woods, then broke in and planted evidence, why is her car still there?"

"Good question, Sherlock. One we've been asking ourselves as well. So I sent the CSI team to scour the yard, the woods, the driveway, you name it, looking for evidence that there was another vehicle. My theory was that she has a partner, someone helping her. But there's nothing to indicate any other vehicles were parked here except for that huge truck of yours. I sent a guy up to your house to find tire tracks on your driveway and compare them to the ones at Miss Nash's. They match. I don't suppose you gave the perp a ride in your truck when you and Miss Nash left out of there in such a hurry, did you?" She chuckled.

Dalton wasn't laughing. He was staring at his truck, parked in the gravel at the end of the house. And the toolbox that ran the width of the bed. A toolbox plenty big enough for someone to hide in.

"I'll call you back."

He shoved the phone in his pocket and yanked out his

pistol. A few seconds later, he was looking down into the toolbox at a pile of blankets, blankets that he hadn't put there. Blankets that would have kept someone warm and cushioned from bumps during the long drive to the cabin, and while waiting for an opportunity to climb out and go inside. When no one else was on guard.

*Oh dear God, please, no!*

He tore off toward the house, taking the steps two at a time. Having seen the autopsy photos of The Ghost's victims, knowing how Bethany liked to inflict as much pain as she could before finally killing them—a detail that he hadn't shared with Hayley—he didn't follow his training. He didn't wait for backup or slowly clear the cabin. Instead, he swept his pistol out in front of him, running from room to room. Even before he reached the master, the tomblike silence had fear curling through his gut.

He burst inside, then stumbled to a halt. Cold, bitter air blew in through the open window. The slashed screen fluttered in the breeze.

The sound of a loud engine starting up had him whirling around and sprinting for the front door. He leaped off the porch and tore down the driveway after the fleeing taillights of his truck. Hayley was driving, and Bethany was sitting beside her, pointing a pistol at her.

He dropped to his knees and fired at the left rear tire. But the truck turned out of the driveway a split second before he squeezed the trigger. He ran across the front lawn, firing two more shots at the tires before the truck disappeared around a curve.

He let out a guttural yell, then grabbed his phone and punched Mason's number.

When Mason answered, Dalton gritted out, "She's gone, Mason. God help me, The Ghost has Hayley. Use that fancy computer of yours and get the team, the police, hell, everyone looking for my truck. She's holding a gun on Hayley and Hayley's the one driving. Tell everyone that. I don't want her hurt."

"I just pulled over and I'm sending out the notification right now. What's your license plate number?"

Dalton rattled off the information.

"Okay, message sent. I'm heading to the cabin now. Tell me exactly what happened."

He paced back and forth across the lawn, unable to stand still with the frustration and rage boiling through him. He told Mason about the car that Sampson had found, about his toolbox, the blankets.

"Our supposed guest must have been in the car in the woods when I was at Hayley's cabin. She was planning on planting evidence when she could get into the house. But when I took Hayley with me to the crime scene at the park, she realized her plan might not work, that I'd tell the police Hayley couldn't have left those things since she was with me the whole time. She changed plans, got some blankets and waited for me to bring Hayley back home. She probably hid in the bushes by the garage, then purposely left the front door ajar to get me into the house. That's when she climbed in the back of my truck and hid in the toolbox."

He stopped pacing, and scrubbed the stubble on his face. "You know what this means, don't you? She's been using Hayley as her fall guy all along, probably hired us as a front, too, because everyone was getting too close in the drug-and gunrunning investigations and she needed an excuse for why some of the bad guys might mention her as one of their cohorts. She used her job as a freelance reporter as her cover. She needed everyone to believe she was re-searching a story and the bad guys had found out and she needed protection.

"We've been used, Mason. Used like crazy. And she's been laughing at us this entire time. But it's falling apart on her, so she's changing the game plan. She doesn't care anymore if we know she's The Ghost. What's her next step, Mason? What's her new plan? Tell me why she took Hayley if she knew we were on to her? We didn't believe that Hayley was The Ghost. What was the point of taking her?"

"I'm almost there. We'll figure it out together. We'll find her. Don't worry."

"Just hurry." He hung up and jogged back toward the cabin. Only then did he see what was waiting for him. A yellow piece of legal paper fluttering in the breeze, pinned to the front door with a knife. Somehow Bethany had brazenly snuck the door open and left that note while he was talking to Sampson. He yanked the paper free and scanned its contents. It was another murder list, just like the others. Except The Ghost had added Seth's name at the top, as if to brag that he was the first victim, and the Seekers had never figured it out. But there was another new name on the list, at the bottom.

Hayley Nash.

He fell to his knees and shouted his rage to the branches and skies overhead.

# Chapter Twenty-Eight

"Take a left," Bethany ordered once they finally reached the main road.

Hayley hesitated. A left would take them past Dalton's home toward Camelot, which was likely empty if everyone was out searching for The Ghost. But a right would take them past her rental cabin. Were the police still there, processing the scene? Maybe she could honk or swerve as she drove by and get the police to go after them.

The cold barrel of the pistol pressed against her cheek. "Left. And don't drive crazy if we pass any other vehicles. I go down, you go down. Remember that."

Hayley turned left.

They were just starting to pass Dalton's house when an older blue sedan barreled out of the driveway straight toward them. She screamed as the car rammed into the back side of Dalton's Silverado, spinning it around. Trees and sky seemed to whirl in circles.

"The ditch, the ditch," Bethany yelled.

Hayley frantically fought for control but the truck skidded off the shoulder, hopped across the ditch and slammed sideways against a stand of trees. Dirt flew up in a cloud around them and rained down onto the windshield.

Bethany smacked the gun against Hayley's shoulder. Haley retaliated with a fist against Bethany's jaw, sending her crashing against the far door. She drew back her fist again, then stopped. The gun was pointing at her again, inches from her nose. She slowly lowered her hand.

"Get out," Bethany snarled, waggling her jaw as if to see whether it was broken. "Hurry. Before I decide to shoot you right now."

Hayley pushed open the door and carefully lowered herself, trying to reach the running board without falling. A hard shove sent her tumbling out, banging her shins against the truck as she fell to the ground. She rolled sideways, cursing at her friend. Former friend.

"You're pathetic, Hayley. I don't know what Chandler ever saw in you. I truly don't. Get up."

Adrenaline and anger gave her the strength to stagger to her feet. Blood dribbled from a gash on her right knee. Yet another pair of jeans was ripped clean through. She glared at Bethany. "Some way to treat a friend. What now?"

"Yes, well. Business is business."

"Business?"

"Later. Do be a dear and check on the other *accident* victim, won't you? And hurry up." She raised her pistol, her cold eyes letting Hayley know she wouldn't hesitate to use it.

The blue car had ended up on the shoulder, as if it had been purposely parked there. But glass all over the road told another story. Both of the front side windows had blown out. And the windshield was a spiderweb of cracks, with a smear of blood across it. A man was slumped over the steering wheel. He must have hit his head on the windshield. There wasn't any sign of an air bag, probably because it was an older vehicle, one of those classic cars people collected.

They reached the driver's door and to Hayley's relief the man groaned. He was still alive. Then she realized who he was—one of the Seekers, the former profiler. Bryson.

"Get him out of there," Bethany ordered. "We need his car."

"He's injured. We have to help him."

Bethany fired a shot through the door. "Not anymore."

Hayley covered her mouth in horror. Bryson had fallen to the right side of the bench seat. The only thing holding him in place was the seat belt. His eyes were closed. Blood matted his hair and ran down the side of his face. There was a small hole in the left side of his suit jacket, near the lower part of his rib cage, marking the entrance wound. Hayley couldn't see the exit wound.

"Get in." Bethany motioned with her gun.

Not wanting to give Bethany another excuse to shoot him, just in case he was still alive, she opened the door and unbuckled him. She threaded the belt around his arm until he was freed. Then she ran around the car to the passenger side.

"What the heck are you doing? Get back here. Just shove him in the floorboard."

She wasn't about to leave an injured man in the car to die, if he wasn't dead already. He'd have a better chance on the side of the road. Hopefully someone would drive by and help him.

She yanked open the passenger door and used all her strength to pull Bryson out as gently as she could and roll him onto the grass away from the tires.

"Stop messing with the dead guy. Get in the driver's seat."

"Coming," she yelled. She gasped in surprise when Bryson opened his eyes and blinked at her.

He groaned.

"Shh," she warned, pressing her finger against his lips. "Close your eyes. Play dead." She yanked his tie off over his head and wadded it against what must have been the exit wound, his right hip area where he was bleeding the worst. Then she grabbed his right hand and shoved it against his tie. "Hold that tight. No matter what, don't let go. That's all I can do for you right now. I'm so sorry. Hold it tight. Someone will come along. Just hold on."

"G-gun," he whispered, his voice faint. "Take...my gun."

"What are you doing?" Bethany shouted. "Reading his last rites? Get over here."

She bit her lip, then flipped back his jacket, looking for his gun. He was wearing a holster, but it was empty. Disappointment slammed through her.

The sound of shoes on pavement told her Bethany had lost what little patience she had.

"Close your eyes," she whispered again. "Please."

A bubble of bright red blood dribbled out of his lips. His eyes closed.

She whispered a frantic prayer, hoping she hadn't just witnessed his last moments. She shoved herself up. But her knee protested, sending her stumbling against the car. Bethany had just reached the front bumper, but stopped and followed her to the driver's door.

She held up another gun. "Was this what you were looking for on the dead guy? Lucky for me, it fell out when you were so gently pulling him out of the car." She laughed and got into the front seat, pointing the gun at Hayley the whole time. She tossed Bryson's gun in the back seat and slid all the way over.

Hayley sat behind the wheel and shut the door, dismayed to see Bryson's blood all over her hands. *Please let him be okay.* "Where to now?"

"To Camelot, my lady. Drive."

She started the engine and pulled out onto the road.

# *Chapter Twenty-Nine*

As Dalton drove the Mercedes down the long narrow road from the cabin, Mason checked in with the Seekers and then Detective Sampson to get updates. When he hung up, his face was grim.

"Tell me," Dalton gritted out. "Is she—" He choked, then cleared his throat. "Have they found Hayley?"

"No." Mason squeezed his shoulder. "They haven't found her yet. Don't give up hope."

"You saw what that witch did to the others."

"There's a reason that Bethany didn't just kill Hayley outright. She went to a lot of risk, a lot of trouble, taking her as a hostage. That reason, whatever it is, is keeping her alive. Have faith."

"I'm trying, believe me. What's everyone doing to find her?"

"Everything that can be done. Brielle and Kira are coordinating with Sampson. Most of the others are out driving the roads, looking for your truck. You and I can set up the command post at Camelot and see what's been searched and what hasn't. Roadblocks are up. She's not getting off this mountain. It's just a matter of pounding the pavement, finding every cabin and business out this way. This isn't one of the more populated mountains in the area. We've got enough manpower to make this happen."

"You said *most* of the others. Has everyone called in?"

"Everyone except Bryson. Last I heard he was going to your house to check on your dogs. He should be calling in soon for an assignment."

A sharp curve up ahead had him slamming the brakes. Mason swore as papers went flying into the floorboard.

"My truck's brakes aren't as touchy as yours."

Mason rolled his eyes and retrieved the papers and folders.

"Wait." Dalton motioned toward one of the folders. "That's the rap sheet on Chandler Harding. Open it."

"Chandler who?"

"Harding. He was Hayley's boyfriend in college. After she broke up with him, Bethany dated him and got engaged. He was killed a few years later."

"A love triangle, sort of. Maybe Bethany resents Hayley because of it." Mason flipped open the folder.

"Enough to frame her as a criminal mastermind and a serial murderer?"

Mason shrugged. "I've heard crazier stories in my time."

"Just tell me what's in there."

"Looks like he was a career criminal. Good thing Hayley dumped him."

Dalton grunted noncommittally and edged around another sharp curve.

"Wow. He was into drug-and gunrunning way back when. The Feds finally caught up to him and looks like they had a really strong case. Then he ended up getting killed in a hit-and-run in a caravan on the way to the prosecutor's office. Destroyed their case. Most of the people in their net had to be let go for lack of evidence after that. I'll bet Bethany took over after his death. She's not just a killer doing hits for the crime rings. She's the leader of the crime rings."

"Makes sense. All the pieces fit that explanation." He

leaned over, trying to read some of the pages that Mason was flipping through.

"Hey, hey, eyes on the road."

Dalton swore and swerved around a branch that had come down in his lane. When they entered the last straight-away that would lead to the main road, he motioned toward the folder. "Back up a few pages. I saw a list of names. What was that?"

A minute later, Mason let out a low whistle. "We've got our murder list. These are the people our Ghost has been executing—half are already dead, even more than we knew about. She must have started framing Hayley after the first series of murders and didn't want to draw our attention to the early ones since she couldn't frame Hayley for those. Get this. The victims were all involved in the court case against Chandler, from his arrest through the planned prosecution. This is a witness list, part of Discovery. Sampson didn't notice this?"

"She said she didn't have time to read an ancient rap sheet."

Mason shook his head. "Bethany's killing everyone associated with the last case against her fiancé." He frowned. "Why would Hayley be on that list?"

Dalton shrugged. "We've already established that she was using Hayley as her fall guy when her crimes started coming to light and the criminal network started coming apart. She knew Hayley had computer expertise, so she could lure her into her network without her knowing. Hayley was an easy target, someone who trusted Bethany, a scapegoat. What if Bethany's plan was to kill people associated with her fiancé as another way to tie Hayley into the crimes, because of her past connection with him? It really all boils down to Bethany trying to save herself in whatever way she could. Why not get a little revenge along the way, like say if her fiancé ever said anything about Hayley to make Bethany feel threatened."

"Huh," Mason said as he flipped through the folder some more. "Looks like Chandler was going to make a deal with the prosecutor, give up names. How much you want to bet that our Ghost was already ensconced in the criminal enterprise with Chandler and was worried he was going to give her name to the prosecutor? That hit-and-run could be her handiwork."

"She killed her own fiancé."

"I'd bet on it."

"Her parents died in a car accident too."

"Maybe we should tell the police to re-open that investigation."

"Maybe." Dalton pulled to a stop on the main road, then turned toward Camelot. "This explains why The Ghost did what she did. But it's not giving us any clue about where she might take Hayley. Or even why."

A moment later, he slammed the brakes again, almost making the Mercedes slide off the side of the road.

"What the heck, Dalton? You need me to teach you how to drive?"

Dalton pulled to the shoulder. "My truck's off in the trees. And Bryson's lying over there, in the ditch." He grabbed his gun and jumped out of the car.

Behind him he heard Mason on the phone calling 911, then his shoes crunching on glass as he ran to catch up.

Dalton squatted down and pressed his fingers against Bryson's carotid, checking for a pulse, all while keeping his pistol trained on his ruined truck about twenty feet away.

"I've got the truck," Mason told him as he ran past, pistol sweeping out in front of him.

Dalton pitched his gun on the ground and leaned over his friend, who was lying on his back, eyes closed. He had a pulse, but it was alarmingly weak. Dalton lifted his eyelids, checking his pupils. Then he pressed a hand against his chest to see if he was breathing. He sent up a silent prayer when he felt the slight rise and fall. Bryson was holding on, barely.

He winced when he checked the gash on Bryson's head. But the blood looked like it was clotting. He gently felt for other injuries, trying to see where all the blood was coming from.

Mason skidded to a halt on the glass-littered shoulder, then dropped down on his knees in the grass beside them. "The truck's empty. There are skid marks on the road, and tire tracks along the shoulder. Two vehicles were involved in the accident. My guess is Bryson saw your truck and tried a PIT maneuver to stop it. He must have hit his head pretty hard, got knocked out or something. They dumped him out and took his car."

"I can't figure out where all the blood is…" Dalton lifted Bryson's jacket and saw the small hole underneath his arm. "He's been shot."

Mason swore a blue streak.

Dalton lifted Bryson's right hand, looking for the exit wound. "Smart guy. He was able to take off his tie and press it partially into the wound to staunch the bleeding. Probably saved his life."

"Hayley," Bryson whispered.

Mason and Dalton looked at each other in surprise.

Dalton leaned down close to Bryson. "Don't try to talk. An ambulance will be here soon."

As if to prove it, a siren sounded from down the mountain.

"Probably five minutes out," Mason said. "Hold on. Just hold on, buddy."

He whispered again, struggling to form words. Dalton put his ear next to his lips. When Bryson stopped talking, he leaned back. "Hayley pulled him out of the car, then used his tie to staunch the bleeding. She told him to play dead."

"She saved his life."

"Don't sound so surprised. I've been telling you she's a good person, Mason."

"I'm finally starting to believe you."

The siren was closer now. Bryson's lips moved again and he seemed agitated, his hands fluttering at his sides.

This time it was Mason who leaned down to listen. He glanced up. "Camelot. He said Camelot. Bryson, is that where Bethany was taking Hayley?" He grabbed Bryson's hand. "Squeeze my fingers if that's what you meant." He looked up again. "He squeezed my hand."

The ambulance pulled up behind the Mercedes, lights flashing.

"Go," Mason urged. "I'll stay with Bryson. Go save Hayley."

Dalton looked from the ambulance, to his friend, torn over the idea of leaving him.

"You're not abandoning him," Mason said. "I've got this. And you're not alone. Remember, we're a team. I'll send the other Seekers to help. Now, go."

Bryson's pain-glazed eyes fluttered open and he looked at Dalton. "Go."

Dalton squeezed Bryson's shoulder, then sprinted for the car.

# Chapter Thirty

Hayley's teeth chattered as she gripped the railing, fighting through the pain in her knee to climb the steps of Camelot's front porch. It wasn't a simple cut. Something had torn when she'd fallen out of the truck.

"Ah, poor baby," Bethany gloated. "You're shivering. Guess I should have let you grab your coat at the cabin. No worries. We'll be nice and toasty in just a minute." She kept her pistol trained on Hayley until she made it to the top of the porch, then she motioned toward the door. "Hustle, hustle. I want to be inside before any of those pesky Justice Seekers show up. It was nice of them to all go looking for you and leave the place empty for us, don't you think?" She glanced at her watch, as she'd done several times since they'd left Bryson lying beside the road.

"You can't get inside," Hayley said as she rested against the log wall by the front door and rubbed her aching knee. "That's a biometric reader. I can't imagine anyone gave you a special code to get in."

"You always did underestimate me, Ghost. Always the overachiever in school, especially in college. Never showing up for class but still making straight A's while the rest of us struggled. I resented the hell out of you for that. Well, this is where I excel. Breaking rules and making others play right into my hands. Give it a minute. You'll see."

"Is that what this is about? You resent me? For making good grades?"

"That's only one of the many reasons that I resent you."

"I've been your friend for years. Did that not mean anything to you? Was any of that real?"

She seemed to consider that a moment, but before she could answer, engines whined behind them. Hayley whirled around. Two red four-wheelers burst from the cover of the woods off to the left and raced across the parking lot. They stopped in front of the steps, and three men climbed off each one, their body armor and the weapons strapped on their jackets marking them for what they were. Muscle for hire. Mercenaries.

"Right on time." Bethany held her hand out toward one of them. "The glove. Hurry."

The man looked like he would tower even over Dalton. He jogged up the steps ahead of the others and handed a large glove to Bethany. As she fit it over her right hand, she arched a brow at Hayley. "Biometric reader you said? I'm guessing it's programmed to read the palm prints of the Justice Seekers. How many are there? Let me think—the twelve knights of the round table, plus their fearless leader, King Arthur. Or Mason. Or whatever. That's thirteen. Oh, wait, my bad. They're one man down. Seth Knox. I wonder if they felt the need to remove his biometrics yet from the computer. What do you think? Let's try it out." She grinned as she pressed the glove against the panel.

The door buzzed and popped open.

Hayley gasped in shock.

Bethany chuckled. "I figured they'd be too sentimental to remove his prints. That's the reason I killed him, you know. He was one of their computer experts and I needed someone to break into their computer system for me. I lured him to a bar to get him drunk and get the information that I needed. Let's just say, he wasn't cooperative. But he ended up being my key to get inside anyway." She wiggled her fingers in the glove. "Hint. This isn't leather."

Hayley turned around and threw up.

Laughter echoed as Bethany headed inside. Two of the men grabbed Hayley by the arms and carried her into the main room. The others rushed in after them and shut the door.

Suddenly all business, Bethany pointed toward the conference room. "In there, then go through the panel on the left like I showed you on the diagram." She tossed the glove to one of the men. "Get those account numbers. Tell me when the money's been transferred."

The men all disappeared into the conference room that Hayley remembered would lead to the great hall. Was that their destination? They planned on using the computers there?

"This way." Bethany motioned her forward, the same way that Dalton had once led her on his guided tour.

Hayley limped forward, careful to watch where she was stepping. She kept expecting Bethany to stumble or fall, but she maneuvered with no difficulty, shoving the gun in Hayley's back whenever she was too slow. They didn't stop until they were standing at the two-story railing overlooking the great room below.

Hayley quickly stepped back, sweat breaking out on her brow at the long drop below.

"Oh, that's right. Your fear of heights. Actually, let's be honest, I haven't forgotten that little heartbreaking story you told me about when you were little. As a matter of fact, I was counting on it. Move, to your right until we reach that hall over there, then go in the first door to the left."

Hayley stumbled to a halt. "Left?"

"That's correct. A room with a view. I'm sure you'll enjoy looking out the rear window at the sheer drop below. What is it? Fifty, sixty feet to the valley floor?" She pressed her lips next to Hayley's ear. "But no trees to break your fall this time."

Hayley shuddered.

Bethany laughed and shoved her forward.

Once inside the room, Hayley turned her back to the wall of windows. Bethany had followed her and was pointing the pistol at her from a foot away. Whatever her former friend had planned, this appeared to be the end of the line for Hayley.

"I don't understand." She stalled for time, scrubbing her face with her hands as she'd seen Dalton do, but using the gesture to hide her eyes so she could glance around for something to use as a weapon. But the only things in the room were a bed and a wooden chair at a desk. Could she hit Bethany with the chair? It didn't look all that heavy. But could she grab it fast enough and swing it around before being shot?

"Understand what?"

Hayley motioned around the room. "This. The murders. You trying to frame me. Why? What did those people ever do to you to deserve to die? What did I ever do to you?"

Bethany shrugged. "You're more irritating than you think, so perky and pretty and sickeningly perfect. The rest of us mere mortals struggle for everything we have but it all comes easy for you." She shook her head. "But it really boils down to business. You made an easy fall guy. At least until you found my storage unit and raised such a ruckus with your website. The Seekers worried that people might come here to harass Dalton and would see me by accident. Oh, you didn't know they kept me here initially, to protect me, did you? That's how I knew about those stupid uneven floors and stairs that come from out of nowhere."

She waved her hands. "This was my room. Lovely view. You really should check it out. But once they curtailed me sitting on the porch and going outside—again because of the crazies you stirred up on the internet—they moved me to a cabin way out in the middle of the sticks." She grimaced. "Hated it. Regardless, like I said, it wasn't personal. It's just that, well, how I choose to make my living has gotten a bit dangerous. I only hired the Seekers as a cover, to make the police think I was innocent and in danger when they found out about my drug-and gunrunning activities. I needed a ruse, so they wouldn't suspect me. So I used my journalist angle."

She curled her hand into a fist. "I was going to take the money and run. But before I could, they'd frozen most of my companies' assets. That's *my* money. Millions, Hayley. I have millions from Chandler after I took over the business from him and built that into even more millions. All frozen. That's why I'm doing this. It boils down to money, as crass as that seems. But it hasn't worked out the way I'd planned. So I had to come up with another plan. Which brings us to today's venture. I brought the best hacker that money could buy with me to Camelot. He's in the great hall right now, moving my money to an offshore untraceable account. Then I'm out of here."

A voice came through an intercom in the ceiling that Hayley hadn't noticed earlier.

"Miss Miller, one of the Seekers is here."

Bethany frowned, her knuckles tightening around the gun. "That was faster than I expected. Show me." She tapped the wall and a panel flipped down, revealing a video screen. It blinked, then displayed an image of the front porch and the parking lot beyond, and a very tall man in a black Stetson and trench coat vaulting up the steps.

"Well, look at that," Bethany smirked. "Your Prince Charming is here to rescue his lover. This, I have to say, wasn't part of the plan. But it's just too delicious an opportunity to pass up. After all, Chandler always pined over you. I had to kill him because of it. I can tell you've grown quite fond of your knight. What poetic justice to have your heart ripped out as I destroy him." She pressed a key below the screen. "Let him in. Then lock it down."

Everything happened so fast. Dalton ran inside, gun drawn, then metal shutters slammed down from the ceiling with a loud whoosh and banged shut. Dalton had told her about those shutters. Every window and door on the front side of the cabin was now sealed. He'd also told her the back part was inaccessible from the outside. He was trapped and no one would be able to get inside to help him.

"Keep hacking that computer," Bethany said through the speaker. "The rest of you, kill our intruder."

"No!" Hayley grabbed the wooden chair and swung it toward Bethany.

Bethany threw up her hands to protect her head. The chair smashed against her arm, knocking the gun loose. It flew across the room and hit the far wall, then fell to the floor beneath the bank of windows.

They both dove for the gun at the same time. Bethany reached it first, but Hayley jumped on top of her and sank her teeth into her wrist.

"Ow!" Bethany yelled, dropping the gun again.

Hayley scrambled after it, hands outstretched.

A boot slammed against her injured knee. She cried out in agony. Another kick slammed into her stomach, knocking the breath out of her. She gasped, tears of anger and pain streaming down her face.

Bethany swiped the gun off the floor and ran out the door, slamming it closed behind her.

Hayley flipped onto her stomach. The blinding-hot pain from her knee had her arching off the floor, but being on her stomach eased the tightness in her diaphragm. She gulped in blessed air, whispering a prayer of thanks to her kickboxing teacher in college who'd taught her that trick. A painful army crawl got her to the door.

She pushed herself to sitting and reached for the knob. Locked. She swore and slid backward to get better leverage to try to stand and kick it open. Then she noticed the chipped paint at the bottom of the door, and the steel shining through. This was no hollow interior door. It was solid steel. Kicking it wouldn't do any good.

She curled up in a fetal position. She wanted to give up. She wanted to lie there and cry and pound the floor until her anger and fear and pain were spent. But she couldn't. She didn't have the luxury of being selfish, of giving up, when the man she now realized she was in love with was about to be ambushed. He had no idea there were six men locked inside Camelot with him, armed to the teeth, with body armor that would make it even harder to defend himself. Somehow she had to help him.

Which meant she had to get out of this room.

The computer screen beside the door was still on. The view showed the main room, from another angle. Dalton was pressing his hand against the pad that should have opened the panel to the hallway that led back here, where she was. But the wall didn't open. He sprinted across the room to the other side, where they'd both come through on their way to the conference room days earlier. It wouldn't open either. No matter what he tried, he was stuck. Leaving only one door to try. The conference room. Which would lead to the great hall, and all those mercenaries waiting to kill him.

A sob burst from her as she watched him go into the conference room.

She looked back at the video screen. Other camera angles popped up, as if someone was scrolling through each one, searching for threats. A view of the parking lot showed that help had arrived, not that it would do any good with the steel shutters sealing the place. The Seekers were on the porch, trying the door, using tire irons to pry on the steel shutters, desperately trying to find a way in. But nothing was working.

Unwelcome tears tracked down her face as she watched their futile efforts. She had to let them inside, somehow, to help Dalton. But how?

She slowly turned and looked at the windows. Maybe the stone wall beneath them wasn't as sheer-faced as Bethany had said. Using the end of the bed to push herself to standing, she limped across the room and peered through the glass. Her pulse thudded in her ears. Nausea coiled in her stomach. She clutched the windowsill like a lifeline as she strained to see the rock wall supporting this side of the cabin. She couldn't see it.

Drawing a shaky breath, she shoved the window up, then, before she could lose her nerve, she pushed out the screen. She didn't hear it hit the ground. She swallowed, drew a few more deep breaths, then poked her head out the window. The building was on the edge of a jagged, rocky mountainside that seemed to drop almost straight down before reaching the pine tree filled valley far below.

She very carefully angled her hand out the side of the window and ran it across the stone. It was more like concrete block than real stone, probably painted a faux rock finish. But there were crevices between the blocks. Enough for a fingerhold? Or a foothold, if someone was truly desperate?

Spots swam in her vision at the thought of trying to somehow lower herself out the window to reach the one she'd seen directly below this one. Even if she could somehow do that, which didn't seem possible, how could she open the other window? She'd have to kick it in. How could she cling to those tiny crevices while kicking in a window? She couldn't. It was impossible. Then what could she do? There had to be another way to get help for Dalton.

She turned around. The screen showed more views,

each one popping up for a few seconds, revealing different hallways, rooms, tunnels. Why? Was Bethany scrolling through the camera views trying to find Dalton? Did that mean he hadn't fallen for her trap and had managed to go down some hidden passageway? Even if he had, it was only a matter of time before her hired killers found him. Six against one, five if one of them was busy trying to hack into the computers.

*Hack into the computers.*

She straightened and limped to the screen. Not just a screen, a connection, hardwired to Camelot's security system. If she could activate the onscreen virtual keyboard function, since it was already logged into the security system, she might be able to access the controls for those metal shutters that were keeping the Seekers from helping Dalton.

She popped the screen off its base, revealing the tiny motherboard and wires that connected it to the main computer and got to work.

## Chapter Thirty-One

Dalton dodged left, then right, carefully counting steps as he made his way through the pitch-black tunnel, following the map in his mind so he wouldn't fall victim to any of Camelot's defenses. One of the mercenaries that The Ghost had brought with her hadn't known about the traps. As he'd followed Dalton into the tunnel, a quick jab to his throat and a violent twist of his arm had him slamming to the floor and hitting the right side of the wall. A trapdoor had popped open and the man's screams of terror ended with a sickening thud two stories below on solid bedrock.

"One down. Hold on, Hayley. I'm coming. Just hold on." He shoved his pistol into his holster and gingerly ran his hand along the wall to his left. There, two bumps. He pressed them. Then he slid his hand to the right two inches, found the next set of bumps, and pressed again, hard.

Lights popped on in the tunnel overhead.

"Finally." He looked at the floor, then very carefully skirted around another trapdoor before pressing another spot on the wall. The wood paneling popped out, then flipped over to reveal a screen with a keyboard attached to the bottom. He blew dust off the glass, then typed a command. Nothing. He frowned and typed it again. Still nothing. Whoever was helping Bethany by triggering the steel shutters must be mucking with other controls. He'd hoped to activate communications with the rest of his team, and open the shutters. But that wasn't happening.

Not from this tunnel anyway.

He needed to manually override the mechanical systems. And the only place he knew of where he could do that was on the opposite end of the castle. Past the great hall where he'd counted three people—including Bethany—sitting at the round table when he'd punched up a computer screen in the conference room. He'd debated taking them on, then a bullet had whizzed past his head, making the decision for him.

He typed a command on the screen, then breathed a sigh of relief when the wall slid back, revealing another tunnel to his right, with dim lights on overhead. He took off running, knowing this tunnel didn't have any hidden traps. There were precious few of those, by design. But they gave him the opportunity to get somewhere fast, which was what he needed right now.

A few minutes later, he skidded to a halt, swearing as he dropped and rolled, firing his pistol at the towering shadow up ahead. Bullets whizzed past him, pinging off the rock walls. He fired two more times, then lunged for a door on his right. He slammed it closed, then sprinted across the long, narrow room.

Breathing heavily, he listened to the sound of footsteps running through the hall on the other side. He was just about to open the door when a shuffling sound had him whirling around, taking the difficult head shot because of the guy's body armor. His aim was true. The mercenary dropped to the floor, dead.

"Like a pack of rats. How many more of you suckers are there?" He ran to the fallen man and took a pistol and three magazines from his pockets.

The sound of more footsteps running toward him had him jumping up and tearing down the hall in the opposite direction. Then he ducked into an alcove and waited. He regulated his breathing, listening carefully for the sounds of pursuit. But the footsteps had stopped. He waited patiently for his prey to pass him by.

A whoosh of air had him jerking around to see the panel behind him sliding into the wall. He dropped to his knees, firing into the dark void over and over. Finally, he stopped, and waited.

A groan sounded, followed by a dull thud.

Dalton felt along the wall to his left for one of the castle's mechanical levers, then remembered they were always on the right in this section. He found the lever and pulled.

Lights flickered on, revealing another mercenary lying in a pool of blood in front of him. Good grief, that one had been close.

Another whisper of sound had him whirling around. A flash of metal, a knife driving down toward him. He jerked to block it but the blade sank deep into his arm. He gritted his teeth at the sizzle of pain and jerked back, freeing himself from the blade. He brought his gun up to shoot, but the man who'd stabbed him ducked around the corner. Dalton slammed the lever down and the panel slid shut.

He sank to the floor, cursing himself for relaxing his guard even for a second. He couldn't help Hayley if he bled to death. He scooted to the dead man and rummaged through his jacket pockets. As expected, a man in his line of business had a first-aid kit. Not a doctor-approved kind by any means. The kind to be used only as a last resort, to stay alive. The way blood was pouring from Dalton's arm was the definition of last resort. He pulled out the staple gun, pressed it to his flesh and squeezed.

THIS WAS IT, the most important test she'd ever taken in her entire life. Hayley bit her bottom lip, then pressed Enter.

Electronic snow sizzled across the screen. Her heart rose

in her throat. No, no, no. What had she done wrong? She slammed her palm against the wall and shouted her frustration. The screen blinked, then came back on. She drew in a sharp breath, then laughed. The camera view showed the main room in the front of the building, and sunlight was pouring through the windows once again. She'd done it. She'd raised the shutters.

The front door slammed open and Seekers ran inside, weapons drawn.

Hayley's fingers practically flew across the virtual keyboard on the screen as she put phase two of her plan into motion. She pressed two function keys and then Enter. The monitors in the main room started flashing. One of the Seekers, Jaxon she believed, ran to one, then motioned toward the others. They read the screen, then as a whole looked up, and gave a thumbs-up to the camera.

She grinned so hard her face hurt. They'd gotten her message. They knew what they were up against and that Dalton needed help. They rushed into the conference room and disappeared.

She slumped to the floor, her pulse rushing in her ears. "Take that, Bethany Miller. Straight A's trump criminals any day of the week." She giggled like a child, wrapping her arms around her middle. She'd saved the day. Little Hayley Nash had triumphed over evil. It was only a matter of time before the Seekers routed all the bad guys and Bethany, and saved Dalton. Then her knight in shining armor would come get her. She'd listed her location in the message for the Seekers. They knew she was here. All she had to do was wait.

She closed her eyes and massaged her hurt knee. It was bruised and lumpy and had blood caked all over it. A cut tendon maybe? That gave her pause. Something that serious might require a trip to a hospital. She clenched her fists. Well, maybe if Dalton was with her, she could handle it.

Yes, with Dalton, she could handle anything. She dragged in another deep breath, then started coughing. Her eyes flew open.

The room was filling with smoke.

## Chapter Thirty-Two

Dalton braced his good arm against the wall, relief settling through him as he watched his fellow Seekers on the computer screen, marching out the bad guys they'd vanquished from the great hall. They'd even caught the guy who'd knifed him when he'd come racing back through a tunnel to the front room. He'd been shocked to see the others and had immediately surrendered.

Dalton pressed a button, activating the transmitter to talk to Mason who was in the main room at the front of the building. "You said Hayley hacked in and raised the shutters?" Mason had already told him that Bryson was in the hospital and was going to make it. And that Hayley had helped them catch the bad guys.

Mason nodded to the camera. "She did. She made the monitors flash to alert us once we were inside. And she sent messages warning us, giving us the logistics of how many bad guys we had to worry about and telling us to hurry and help you."

He grinned. "That's my girl. Feisty as always. Where is she? Did you take her out already?"

"She said she was in one of the rooms off the back hallway, to the right of the gallery. Now that we've secured the place, I'm going to send Bishop and LeMarcus up there to get both of you. An ambulance is on the way for that arm of yours."

"Sounds good. I'll head down the back hall. I'll probably reach her before anyone else does. I'm just a few tunnels away. Hey, I didn't see anyone march Bethany outside. I'm guessing she fought to the end and wouldn't surrender?"

He frowned. "I got here after most of the fun since I was with Bryson. Hang on." He turned away from the camera and spoke to someone offscreen. When he turned back, his frown had deepened. "We haven't found her yet. Brielle and a few others chased her down some tunnels. A panel came up between them and jammed. They're trying to get it open now. It won't be long."

Dalton swore. "Get the whole team back here. She may be going after Hayley." He jerked open the nearest door and took off running. He zipped down a tunnel, then another, turning onto the back hallway. He coughed and dropped to the floor beneath a wall of black smoke. Orange flames flickered from the far end of the hall, slowing eating up the balcony and coming toward him. He scrambled forward, ignoring the jolts of pain every time he used his injured arm. He checked each door as he passed it, throwing it open. There was only one more door, ten more feet. The flames were getting close, too close.

"Hayley!" he called. "Hayley, it's Dalton. Get out of there."

"Dalton!" Her voice sounded muffled behind the door. "Help me!"

"The door's locked, lover. She can't open it."

He jerked to the side and rolled. Bullets blasted at him from somewhere near the balcony, just missing him. He grabbed his pistol and brought it up. Bethany's guttural yell had the hairs sticking up on the back of his neck as she charged toward him through the flames.

"Oh my God," he whispered. Her hair was on fire, flickering around her head. Her clothes were charred. She must have gotten caught in the fire after starting it. "Drop and roll," he yelled. "Drop and roll."

She ran toward him, flames flickering, the acrid odor of charred flesh filling the hall. She raised her gun.

Dalton squeezed the trigger over and over until she finally dropped to the floor. He swore and yanked off his trench coat, using it to smother the flames. But when he pulled it back, he knew it no longer mattered. Her sightless eyes stared up at the ceiling.

"Dalton!" Hayley's voice, screaming for help.

"I'm coming!" He scrambled toward her door.

The fire on the balcony hit an area rug and greedily raced across it to the door before he could reach it, engulfing it in a wall of flames. It became an inferno in a matter of seconds, driving him back.

"Hayley!"

He didn't know if she heard him. The fire was too loud, too hot, driving him back even farther. He turned around. More flames were greedily licking the hardwood floor from the opposite end of the hall, leaving him stuck between two fires with nowhere to go. Bethany had laid her trap well. He couldn't count on any help from his fellow Seekers. There was no way they could reach them. But how was he going to reach Hayley?

He pictured all the schematics that Mason had made him memorize when he'd first started working here, the layout of this section of the castle. He sorted through the various possibilities and arrived at only one chance. And he wasn't even sure if it would work. But he had to try.

He jumped up and ran down the hall, toward the second wall of flames, away from Hayley's door. Just before he reached the fire, he slammed his hand on the wall. A hidden escape hatch opened. He dove inside.

TEARS WERE STREAMING down Hayley's face. She could barely hold her eyes open because of the smoke. But some of those tears were from grief, not smoke. Grief so bone deep that she could barely function. Dalton's voice had called out to her from the hallway. But then the she-devil's voice had answered, and a hail of gunshots later, all Hayley could hear was the roar of flames outside her door.

Trapped. She was good and trapped. And she didn't even know if Dalton had made it out. She was terrified that he hadn't and that Bethany had finally gotten her ultimate revenge.

"Hayley! Hayley, open the window!"

Dalton? She crawled to the window, coughing black soot into her hands. She tried to peer out, but the smoke was too thick to see.

"Hayley, it's Dalton. Please, open the window, love. Hurry!"

Her hands shook as she shoved the window up once again. A brittle cracking sounded behind her. She looked over her shoulder, squinting through the smoke. The door. It was bowing inward, as if the hungry flames were seeking out the fresh air. She jerked back toward the window and stuck her head outside, breathing in precious oxygen. She wiped her streaming eyes. "Dalton?"

He was leaning out the window directly below her, a sheet tied around his waist, anchoring him.

"The fire's going to break through that door any second," he yelled. "You have to jump, Hayley. Jump to me. I'll catch you."

The door cracked again behind her. There were shouts, in the distance, the other Seekers maybe? And sirens. But they were faint, far away. No one could reach the back of this castle. It was a cliff, with a sheer drop below. No trees close enough to break her fall. No way for anyone to save her this time.

She shook her head violently back and forth. "I can't. I can't, Dalton. Go on. Get out while you still can."

"If you don't jump, I'll burn. I swear I will, Hayley. I'm

not leaving the castle without my princess. Don't stop to think. Turn around, climb out the window and flatten yourself against the wall. You can even close your eyes. All you have to do is let go."

A sob burst from her lips. Images of laughing children surrounded her, running down a trail, horrible screams as it collapsed beneath them. Her screams, the crack of bone, tear of flesh as she slammed against tree branches on the way down. Then, hours of lying there, in unimaginable agony waiting to be rescued. She couldn't do it. She couldn't. She laid her head on the windowsill and shut her eyes.

"Hayley, I understand your fears," he called out from below, his voice gentle, sweet, soothing. "It's okay. Just know that I love you. I want to make sure you know that, all right? I love you, Hayley Nash. I want to make love to you, make babies with you, watch your hair turn gray and rock on a front porch with you sassing at me the whole time. But if all we have is these last few minutes, I understand. We'll face the end together. We'll die together. I'm here for you. It's okay."

She jerked her head up. He'd die for her? Forget that. She wanted him to live.

The door burst open behind her with a thundering boom. Flames roiled over her head, reaching for the air outside.

She scrambled out the window, biting her lip to not cry out from the pain of her knee bumping against it.

"That's it, Hayley," he called out. "That's it, sweetheart. You're doing great."

She clung to the windowsill above her, flattening her body against the rock wall. Her hands ached. Her arm muscles burned. Her whole body started shaking.

"I love you," he called out. "Trust me. Just let go."

"I love you, Dalton!" She let go.

## Chapter Thirty-Three

Hayley shielded her eyes from the sun overhead, watching as the workers fastened the last of the black metal fire escapes onto the back of the new castle. Most of the Justice Seekers roamed around the enormous patio, drinking and eating, laughing at each other's outlandish stories as music piped in through the outdoor speakers. Beside Hayley, Dalton stood watching the workers as well, his arm wrapped around her waist. Everyone was there, even still-recovering Bryson in his wheelchair, marking this very special occasion: the completion of Camelot. A newer, better, far safer Camelot than the previous one.

Mason had been shaken to the core after Dalton and Hayley had come so close to perishing in the flames. He'd razed the entire thing to the ground and built this new building in a completely different location. It was still perched in the gorgeous Smoky Mountains, with incredible views. But it was on a long piece of flat land that had cost a fortune to have carved out this high up.

The patio extended twenty yards past the base of the building in all directions. And there were trees, right up close to the building, with different levels of branches in case anyone needed to break their fall. Not that they should have to with balconies and fire escapes clinging to the stone facade.

"You might want to wipe that look of distaste off your

face before Mason notices how much you hate his new castle," Dalton teased.

Her face grew warm. "I'm sorry. It's just so—"

"Ugly?"

She laughed. "Safety before beauty. At least the front is beautiful. It must have cost him a fortune."

"Not really."

She glanced up in question.

"Let's just say that Bethany might have bequeathed him the money as her penance for what she did."

"Wait. I thought the millions she was trying to get transferred to an untraceable account went through. The money's lost forever."

"It's untraceable. I agree with that." He winked.

She shook her head. "Some things I just shouldn't ask about." She tilted her head, hoping a different angle would make the fire escape ladders look better. Nope. Still hideous. "I think the fire traumatized Mason more than it did us. He went a bit overboard."

"No. He didn't." He gently turned her to face him. "Anything that helps ensure your safety is a good thing." He grinned. "Even if it's ugly."

She shook her head in wonder and smoothed her hands up his suit, delighting at the way her engagement ring winked in the sunlight. "I love you more than you'll ever know, Dalton. You saved me, in every way that a person can be saved."

He stared down at her in wonder and slowly shook his head. "No, Hayley, my love. I didn't save you. You saved me."

She smiled up at him through yet another waterfall of tears, then kissed her sweet knight.

And they lived happily-ever-after.

\* \* \* \* \*

# MOUNTAIN OF EVIDENCE

CINDI MYERS

For Gay and Reed

# *Chapter One*

## Missing Man: Presumed Dangerous
## $25,000 Reward!

The bold announcement on the poster tacked to the post office bulletin board was enough to catch the attention of almost every patron who waited in line, but it was the photo beneath the words that made Eve Shea's stomach sink. The dark-haired man with the chiseled features of an outdoorsman and determined blue eyes looked out from what was probably a company ID photo, but in the context of the poster looked more like a mug shot.

**Wanted: Dane Trask**
**43, 6'2", 180 lb.**
**Blue eyes, dark brown hair**
**Armed and dangerous**
**If you know anything about the whereabouts of**
**this man, call the number below.**

*Dane, where are you, and what have you done?*
Eve thought as she stared at the picture of her former lover—the man she had once dreamed of marrying. Though she and Dane had agreed to stop seeing each

other six months ago, Eve couldn't help but feel for him. He hadn't been the man she needed, but she had believed he was a good man, and now the news reports were saying that he had done terrible things—embezzled money from his employer, and even committed acts of terrorism. Could she really have loved a terrorist?

"Ma'am? It's your turn." The man behind her in line got Eve's attention and nodded toward the front counter, where a clerk waited, deep frown lines furrowing her brow.

"Oh! Sorry." Eve hurried to the counter and handed over her parcel to be weighed.

Dane was still on her mind as she exited the building a few moments later and started the short walk to the flower shop she owned on Main Street in Montrose, Colorado. The last time she had heard from him had been two months ago, when he had texted to wish her a happy birthday. It was just like him to remember and acknowledge the date. "I understand we can't be lovers," he had said when they ended their three-year relationship. "But I'll always be your friend."

A knot formed in her throat at the memory. In some ways, the split might have been easier if he had been a jerk about it, but that just wasn't Dane. He wasn't the type to act out of anger or spite. Looking back, she could say that was one of the reasons things hadn't worked out between them—Dane was always so controlled. She had wanted passion, romance, an undying commitment.

She had wanted a baby. And Dane had been adamant that he had no desire to be a father again. He adored his daughter, Audra, but she was twenty-three and he had no interest in raising another child. It was the one big difference they simply couldn't get past.

She pushed open the door to Eve's Garden and an electronic chime announced her entry. She breathed in the scents of fresh roses and carnations and some of the tension in her shoulders eased. A trio of fountains burbled in the corner and a pyramid of ivy, ferns and other green plants basked in the light streaming through the front display window. Fresh flower arrangements awaited buyers from a bank of lighted coolers, and racks of greeting cards and shelves of small gift items invited browsing. Everything about this place was peaceful and beautiful, the product of her inspiration and hard work.

"Good morning." Sarah Maclean, a tall fortysomething woman who wore her blond hair in a pixie cut, emerged from the shop's back room. Eve had hired Sarah as her first full-time employee two years ago. She hadn't been looking to take on any help but Sarah, who had experience as a floral designer and a desire to go back to work once her youngest child entered high school, had persuaded Eve that she would be an asset to the business. Which, indeed, she was. "I've got the arrangements for the Women's Club luncheon ready to go, and I just sent Manuel out with the orders for First Bank and Hightower Financial," Sarah said.

"Thanks," Eve said, passing through to behind the front counter. "I'd say you're far too energetic this early in the morning, but I'd be a fool to complain."

"I never can sleep past six and I like to keep busy," Sarah said. "Oh, and I stopped by the post office on my way in and collected the mail from our box. It's on your desk."

Eve had been so shaken by Dane's wanted poster

she had forgotten to even check the post office box. "I'll go through the mail, then start working on the order for the Salazar wedding and reception," she said. The wedding and subsequent banquet would require an extra shipment of roses, lilies, stephanotis, and trailing ivy for the bride's bouquet, six bridesmaids' bouquets, boutonnieres for the groom, father of the bride, attendants and ushers, corsages for the mothers of the bride and groom, a hair wreath for the flower girl, four large arrangements for the front of the church, and ten table arrangements for the reception, plus small swags for the buffet tables. It could easily be Eve's largest commission of the year.

"All right, but first I want to know how your date went on Friday night." Sarah picked up her coffee cup and leaned back against the counter, as if in anticipation of a long chat. "Was he as good-looking as his picture online? Did the two of you hit it off?"

Eve had to think a moment to recall what Sarah was talking about. Friday already seemed so long ago. She shrugged. "He was okay, but I doubt I'll see him again."

Sarah's shoulders and face sagged with disappointment. "What happened? Why wouldn't he want to see you again? You're so nice, and funny, and is he blind, because honestly, you're gorgeous."

Eve laughed. "You might be a little bit biased." In addition to running the shop with the organization only a mother of four could bring, Sarah was intent on whipping Eve's life into shape. She wasn't overly pushy, just Eve's number one champion and cheerleader. "Nothing happened. Not really." That was part of the problem. Doug Howard had been a well-mannered, good-looking, friendly guy who owned a local pest control company.

He was divorced with two boys, and seemed like a good father and a very nice man. But Eve had felt zero attraction to him and by the end of the evening was counting the minutes until she could politely say good-night.

"No sparks, huh?" Sarah looked sympathetic. "Don't you worry, hon. You keep putting yourself out there and you'll find the right man."

Eve nodded. "I won't stop trying, I promise." After her split with Dane, she and Sarah had devised what they called "the plan." Eve had registered for two online dating sites, and discreetly put the word out to friends that she was interested in meeting eligible men who were ready to settle down and start a family. She reasoned that the more candidates for "the one" she auditioned, the more likely she was to meet her Mr. Right. It was a little like interviewing a candidate for a job—the most important job she could imagine—her life partner and the father of her children.

But in six months of going out at least once and often twice a week, she hadn't even come up with one possible finalist for the position.

"What about Saturday?" Sarah asked. "Did you go out Saturday night?"

"Saturday I stayed home." She had binge-watched romantic movies, eaten ice cream and, frankly, felt sorry for herself.

"All this stuff with Dane has you upset, doesn't it?" Sarah asked. She knew the whole story of Dane and Eve's ill-fated relationship. Eve sometimes thought her friend mourned the break-up harder than Eve had. Now Sarah's expressive features twisted into a look of horror and pity. "The news stories are just horrible, but you have to ignore them. Dane isn't part of your life any-more. You have to move on."

"Dane will always be part of my life," she said. "A part that's in the past, but I can't just ignore the fact that he's missing and no one knows whether he's dead or alive. And that he's been accused of horrible things. That isn't like the man I know at all."

"I saw a notice at the post office this morning," Sarah said. "Offering a $25,000 reward for information about Dane's whereabouts. The poster said he's dangerous. Do you think that's true?"

Was Dane dangerous? He certainly hadn't been to her. But he had been an army ranger, and he was ath-letic and fit, and knew how to handle a gun. For some unknown reason, he had left his job almost a month ago, saying he was headed for a hike in Black Canyon of the Gunnison National Park. And he hadn't been heard from since. Park rangers found his black Ford pickup at the bottom of the canyon, but they hadn't found his body or his backpack, which led some people to believe Dane had tried to fake his own death.

But why?

"You're not answering me," Sarah said. "Does that mean you think Dane *is* dangerous?"

"No!" Eve protested. "I just…" She shrugged. "Be-fore all this, I would have said I knew Dane pretty well. Now, I don't know what to think."

"I always liked him," Sarah said. "Even if I did think he took you for granted. And I never understood why he was so reluctant to have more children. I mean, he and Audra get along great. You'd think he would want to repeat the experience."

It was an old argument, one Eve no longer wanted

to hear. "I can't worry about Dane now. I have to get to work."

She moved to the tiny kitchen off the workspace and poured a cup of coffee from the pot Sarah had started earlier, then carried it to her desk in the equally tiny office. There was just enough room in there for a desk, a filing cabinet and a desk chair. Any visitors to the office had to stand in the doorway to speak to her.

She switched on her computer, then began sorting the pile of mail on the desk blotter. A floral supply catalog, two flyers from printing companies, an announcement about a florists' convention, a reminder about a seasonal sale from one of her suppliers, a bill from a wholesaler and a small pile of ads and come-ons she transferred straight to the recycling bin under the desk.

At the bottom of the pile was a nine-by-twelve manila envelope. When she turned it over to read the address on the front, she stopped breathing for a moment. The envelope didn't have a return address, but the handwriting for her name and PO box was familiar to her from birthday and Valentine's cards over the past few years.

Hand trembling, she picked up the silver letter opener embossed with the name of a floral wholesaler—a trade show freebie from last year—and slit open the envelope. She slid out a single sheet of paper.

### FOR IMMEDIATE RELEASE
### *TDC Enterprises Falsifies Reports in*
### *Major Environmental Fraud*

The press release that followed charged TDC with lying about contaminant levels at a mine site they had contracted to clean up as part of the federal government's Superfund cleanup program. TDC had been awarded a hefty chunk of taxpayer money to return the contaminated Mary Lee Mine to an environmentally safe condition, free of arsenic, mercury, sulfuric acid and other hazardous chemicals that had leached into soil and water on or near the site over the years.

Instead of using the government funds to remove contaminants from the site, this press release charged TDC with adding even more contaminants, and then lying about everything in official reports.

Eve read through the release twice, her wariness growing. Unlike the traditional press releases that had crossed her desk in the three years she had worked for the *Montrose Daily Press* prior to opening this shop, this one contained no contact information, or sources for these allegations.

She picked up the envelope again and examined it. Something hard lay inside. She upended the envelope and a brass key landed on the desk with a *thunk*. Pain squeezed her heart as she stared at the key. She had one just like it, tucked away in the jewelry box on top of her dresser at home. Dane had given her that key. Why was he sending her its mate now?

# *Chapter Two*

"Dane Trask is becoming a huge pain in the keister." Ranger Brigade Commander Grant Sanderlin would have preferred to use stronger language to describe the current focus of his force's efforts, but he had given up swearing for Lent and, after a lecture from his ex-wife about watching his mouth around their daughters, he was trying to keep up the practice. Dane Trask's efforts to frustrate his pursuers at every turn were making that more of a challenge.

"Trask is annoying," Lieutenant Randall Knightbridge agreed from his position at the conference table to Grant's right. Knightbridge's full-sleeve tattoos peeking beneath the cuffs of his uniform shirt reminded Grant of the skateboarders his oldest daughter used to date. But in Grant's first month in command of the Ranger Brigade, he had learned that Knightbridge's deep-set dark eyes didn't miss a thing. "But Terrell, Davis and Compton are just as bad."

Yes, TDC Enterprises, Trask's employer and the chief source of the allegations against him, had managed to insert themselves into the investigation in ways that grated. Their insistence on offering a $25,000 reward for Trask's apprehension, and then bypassing law enforcement altogether and setting up their own information hotline, meant the Rangers weren't privy to any information TDC received about Trask unless the company decided to share it. And more recently, two killers who may or may not have been TDC employees had tried to murder one of Grant's officers and the woman who was now, apparently, that officer's fiancée.

"We're still trying to find out more about the men who attacked Officer Beck and Cara Mead," Officer Carmen Redhorse, on Grant's left, said. Grant thought of the sharp and fearless Redhorse, a native Ute, as the most tenacious of the officers under his new command. She wouldn't stop searching until she had discovered all there was to know about the two killers. "TDC isn't being very cooperative, and a judge refused to grant us a warrant for their employment records," Redhorse continued.

"Keep talking to everyone who had contact with Walter George and Anthony Durrell at TDC," Grant said. "Someone knows if TDC was as ignorant of the men's histories as they say, or if they hired them as killers." He looked around the table. "What else have we got?"

"The latest test results from the Mary Lee Mine show contamination with radioactive material." Jason Beck, a new member of the team who had been assigned to the Ranger Brigade from the US Park Police, spoke up. Tall, with close-cropped brown hair, Beck looked younger than his twenty-nine years. "There are no radioactive elements occurring naturally in that area, so it's possible TDC brought them in—either knowingly or unknowingly—in all the waste rock that's been dumped there."

"TDC contends that those reports are evidence Trask

stored illegal nuclear material at the mine." Lieutenant Michael Dance, muscular and intense, spoke from the other end of the conference table.

"But as yet they haven't offered any explanation of how or where he obtained this mysterious material," Beck said. "Or how they would know about it."

"It's an interesting puzzle," Grant said. "But the Montrose County Sheriff's Department and Homeland Security are involved in investigating the terrorism allegations against Trask. Our focus is on finding the missing man, since he disappeared from our jurisdiction and the few suspicious sightings we've had seem to indicate he's still here."

"Here" was over 130,000 acres of public land that included the National Park, Curecanti National Recreation Area and Gunnison Gorge National Conservation Area. A lot of very empty country, much of it without roads, where the former army ranger might be camping out.

"It could explain why Trask disappeared in the first place," Beck said. "Though Montrose hasn't been very forthcoming with any information they might have, and Homeland Security sure isn't going to share whatever they have."

"That is about to change, at least on the Montrose side of things," Grant said. He strode to the door and opened it. "Deputy Martin, you can join us now."

Montrose County Sheriff's Deputy Faith Martin, a few brown curls escaping her tight bun, surveyed her new colleagues warily. Grant imagined the petite, feminine officer had had to prove herself over and over again in what had been, as far as the reports he received indicated, an unblemished career as a law enforcement officer. "Deputy Martin is our new liaison with the sheriff's department," Grant said. "Deputy Martin, please report on the department's progress in their investigation into the charges against Dane Trask."

Martin nodded, took the empty chair beside Knightbridge, and proceeded to speak without notes, in a calm contralto voice. "TDC has shared security footage they attest shows Trask smuggling uranium ore from another site they're in the process of mitigating," she said. "One near Uravan, Colorado, an area of active uranium mining in the forties and fifties."

"Attest?" Beck asked.

Martin shrugged. "He's carrying a rock. The video is poor quality, so we can't tell if it's really uranium ore. Someone suggested it might be waste rock Trask was testing as part of his job duties, but someone has convinced Homeland Security that is not the case."

"Even if Trask did take old uranium ore from a defunct mine, it wouldn't be high enough quality to make anything useful to a terrorist," Dance said. "It's one reason those mines played out."

"Maybe the terrorist doesn't know that," Mark "Hud" Hudson said. Another new recruit, he was the team's tech expert, though his muscular build and fondness for sports belied the usual geek image. "Maybe Trask is pulling a fast one on them."

"TDC has pulled back their allegations against Trask's admin, Cara Mead, at least for the time being," Martin said. "Apparently whatever evidence they had against her was circumstantial, at best."

Jason Beck, Cara Mead's fiancé, mumbled something under his breath. Grant sent him a warning look and he sat up straighter in his chair. "Thank you, Deputy Martin," Grant said.

Grant consulted his meeting notes. He was about to dismiss the group when a knock on the door interrupted. "Come in," he called.

One of the three civilians who served as administrative support for the team—Sylvia—peered around the door. "I'm sorry to interrupt, but there's a woman here who says she needs to speak to whoever is in charge of the Dane Trask case. She says it's urgent."

The energy level in the room immediately rose. Grant knew better than to hope they might be a little closer to getting Dane Trask out of their hair, but sometimes you did get lucky. "Put her in my office," he said. "I'll be right there."

All of his officers were working on this case, but if this woman wanted to speak to the person in charge, that would be him. Dane Trask might be a pain in the keister, but he was Grant's pain.

# Chapter Three

Striking. It wasn't a word Grant had used to describe a woman before, but it fit Eve Shea perfectly. She had thick, honey-colored hair that flowed past her shoulders, and was mussed by the wind, not so much styled as somewhat tamed by the tortoise shell clips that held it back on each side of her face. And what a face—dark, thick brows above wide-set hazel eyes and a nose that was maybe larger than considered conventionally beautiful, and a sharp chin. The strong features suited her. He estimated she was in her middle thirties—young, but not too young. She wasn't a large woman, but she carried herself with the air of woman who was prepared at any moment to kick butt and take names.

"I'm Commander Grant Sanderlin," he said after Sylvia had introduced his visitor and left.

Ms. Shea shook his hand with a firm grip. He released her hand reluctantly, her skin smooth and cool against his own. He motioned for her to sit and took his own chair. "What can I do for you, Ms. Shea?"

"If you're investigating this case, you already know Dane Trask and I dated for three years. We split up six months ago."

Grant felt the sensation of something clicking into

place in his mind. He'd been so distracted by this woman's presence that he had failed to register the significance of her name. One of his officers—Hudson, he thought—had interviewed her shortly after Trask was reported missing. "Do you have some new information for us?" Grant asked. "Has Trask contacted you?"

The sudden tightness around her mouth made him think his words had touched a nerve. She opened the large leather satchel slung over one shoulder and withdrew a manila envelope. "I received this in the mail this morning," she said, handing the envelope across the desk. "The handwriting on the envelope is Dane's—or a very good forgery."

Grant slipped on his reading glasses—the fact that he had to use them in the past few months still grated. He took a pair of nitrile gloves from his desk drawer and slipped them on before he slid the single sheet of paper onto the desk and studied it. "What is this?" he asked after a moment.

"It's a press release," she said. "Or, at least, it's in the style of a press release. I used to work as a reporter for the *Montrose Daily Press* and I probably had hundreds of these come across my desk in my time there. Though they usually include contact information to allow the reporter to follow up on the story. This one doesn't."

Grant skimmed the document again. "Why do you think Trask sent this to you?"

"I don't know. Maybe he wants me to take it to my former employer and ask them to publish it. But I can't do that."

He looked at her, one eyebrow raised in silent question.

"It would be totally irresponsible to print something this inflammatory," she said. "Especially without any proof."

"Maybe he's expecting you to find the proof," Grant said. "Or he thinks you already have it."

"I own a flower shop. I haven't worked as a reporter for quite a while, and I don't have a connection to TDC."

"Then I have to ask again—why did Trask send this to you?"

The tightness around her mouth became a frown. She reached into her purse again. "This was in the envelope, too."

He took the small brass key. "It looks like the key to a safe deposit box," he said.

"Yes." She let out a long breath. "I have one like it in my jewelry box at home. I'd forgotten all about it until I received this one."

"What's the significance of the key?" Grant asked. "You said you and Trask had broken up—yet you still had the key to a joint safe deposit box?"

"Not a joint box—this belonged to Dane. And the only reason I still have a key is that he gave it to me so long ago I think we both forgot all about it. Or at least, I did."

"Go on. Why did he give you the key in the first place?"

"It was after we had been seeing each other for about a year, when it felt like things were serious between us. He asked me if I would mind being a signatory on his safe deposit box. That would allow me to access the box in the event something happened to him. He said the box contained his will and some other legal documents and that he could count on me to handle everything properly for him."

"Was he anticipating something happening?" Grant asked. "Was he ill, or had he mentioned threats from someone?"

"Nothing like that. That was just how Dane was—how he *is*. He's prepared for any eventuality, and he's usually thinking two steps ahead of everyone else."

"You agreed to be responsible for his affairs if something happened to him?"

"Yes. He didn't think his daughter, Audra, was old enough to deal with those things. She was barely twenty at the time." She shrugged. "And I thought he was the man I'd marry. The request to do this for him wasn't unreasonable."

"If things were so serious between the two of you, why did you end the relationship?" Did Trask have another woman in his life they should question? Or a secret vice that might have led him to abandon his everyday life?

"He didn't feel the same way about marriage and family as I did," she said. "We parted amicably and remained friends." She nodded toward the envelope on the desk in front of Grant. "Maybe that's why he sent that to me. He needed help and turned to a friend."

Grant examined the key more closely. "Did you ever see the contents of the box?" he asked.

She shook her head. "We went to the bank and I signed some papers and got the key, but I never opened the box. I really had forgotten all about it."

"When you received this key this morning, did you go to the bank and open the box?"

"No. I came straight here."

Smart woman—if she was telling the truth, and that

should be easy enough to verify. Banks recorded everything. "Which bank?"

"Community United," she said.

He made note of the name, then studied her for a long moment. She pretended not to notice his scrutiny, instead focusing on the photograph on the credenza behind him, of him with both his daughters. "Are those your children?" she asked.

"Yes." He could have left it there, but added, "Beth is seventeen and Janie is fifteen. They live with their mother in DC." *And I don't see nearly enough of them.*

"They're very pretty girls."

He would have liked to talk with this woman about his daughters, one of his favorite topics, especially now that he lived so far from them, but he forced himself to focus on the task at hand. "What kind of a relationship did you have with Trask?" he asked.

"Pardon me?" A hint of frost tinged her voice.

"I'm trying to get into this man's head, to think like he thinks. To try to figure out his next move. At one time not that long ago you were closer to him than probably anyone else. Maybe you can help me understand him more fully."

Some of the tension eased from her body. "Dane is very intelligent, very capable. He's the kind of person who excels at everything he does. He makes everything look easy. He's very calm and dependable. He's not one to fly into rages or act impulsively." She leaned forward. "Disappearing like this—it's not like him. When Dane does something, he's thought about it a long time and come up with a plan. He doesn't act rashly."

"He sounds perfect." Grant couldn't keep the note

of derision from his voice. "Who initiated the break-up between the two of you?"

"How is that pertinent?"

"You said he was the type to plan things. Maybe breaking up with you was part of his preparations to disappear."

"Our splitting up wasn't his idea, it was mine. But I don't think Dane was surprised when I told him I couldn't date him anymore."

"Was he upset about it? Did he try to talk you into reconsidering?"

"No."

*And that hurt, didn't it?* Grant thought. If you were with someone for three years, he ought to at least protest a little. "Dane wasn't one to argue with a decision," she said, as if to defend Trask. "He could see I'd made up my mind and he respected that."

"Did you keep in touch?"

"A couple of times after that I ran into him in town. And I got a text from him on my birthday."

"When was that?"

"January 10."

"Do you know if Trask dated anyone after the two of you split?"

"Your officer asked me that and the answer is, I don't know. I didn't keep up with his personal life."

She was giving him another "that is none of your business" stare, but he had to get past people's barriers to the information they possessed that would help him do his job. "What was your first thought when you saw the envelope?" he asked.

"I was afraid."

The answer surprised him. Eve Shea didn't strike

him as a woman who frightened easily. "Why was that? Did you feel Trask was a threat to you? Has he ever threatened you before, or tried to harm you?" He could taste the anger at the thought at the back of his throat, and inhaled deeply to beat it back. He was interviewing a potential witness, not defending a crime victim.

"Dane would never hurt me!" Her shock at the idea rang clear in the words.

"Yet you were afraid when you saw the envelope, addressed to you in Trask's handwriting."

"I'd seen a poster at the post office shortly before. It said Dane was dangerous and offered a $25,000 reward for information on his whereabouts. The idea that someone believes he's dangerous, and is offering that kind of money to track him down..." Her words trailed away and she shook her head. "I was frightened for Dane—knowing he had people hunting him like that. And I thought..." She paused and wet her lips. "I thought if he was getting in touch with me, he must be really desperate."

"You still care about him," Grant said, keeping his voice very even, with no hint of emotion.

"Of course I care about him. He's a friend and he's out there somewhere, alone, unable to defend himself against all these accusations."

"You don't believe the charges against him."

"Dane Trask is the last person in the world who would be a terrorist or have anything to do with terrorists," she said. "He was a soldier, a real patriot. He wasn't cynical or snide about it, either. Dane really does love his country. As for the embezzlement claims—it's ridiculous. Dane had money. He wasn't in debt. I never heard him wish for more money or talk about getting rich or anything like that. And he loved his work. He would never steal, and he certainly wouldn't steal from an employer."

"So you think TDC is making up the story?"

"I don't know what to think, but Dane didn't steal from them. He just wouldn't."

Grant slid the letter into the envelope once more, then stripped off the gloves. "We'll look into this. Thank you for bringing it to our attention."

"I'd like to be with you when you open the deposit box," she said.

"I thought you didn't want to know what was in it," he said. "That's why you were turning this over to us."

"I didn't want to be by myself when I found out the contents," she said. "But of course I want to know."

"I don't see the need to involve you any further," he said.

She stood, and he thought she would leave. Instead, she met his gaze, her expression all determination. "In order to open that box, you'll need a warrant," she said. "That takes time. As a signatory on the account, I can open the box for you," she said. "Won't that make things quicker?"

He could have countered her argument with one of his own—that obtaining a warrant shouldn't be difficult, since Dane was a crime suspect and a missing person. Instead, he nodded, intrigued. "All right," he said. "You can come with me to open the box." He suddenly had a desire to take a very personal interest in this case—and in Ms. Eve Shea.

EVE WATCHED THE man in the driver's seat of the Ranger Brigade cruiser out of the corner of her eye. Slender but muscular, about six feet tall, his sandy brown hair glinting silver at the temples, a few lines fanning out from his blue eyes, Commander Grant Sanderlin made her think of the sea captains she'd seen in paintings. All he needed was a peaked cap and a pipe clenched between his teeth. It was a strong, capable and yes, sexy image.

She closed her eyes and silently cursed fate or whatever had decided that now—after dozens of uninspiring dates—she met a man who lit a spark in her and he was about as unsuitable as they came. After Dane, she had sworn off dating older men. His reference to his daughters' mother alluded to divorce, but that didn't mean he hadn't remarried. And he had not one but two almost-grown daughters.

"I want to stop by your house and retrieve your safety deposit box key," he said, interrupting her thoughts. "I want to see if it really is a match to this one."

She shifted toward him in the seat. "Is that why you insisted I ride to the bank with you?"

He didn't answer, only asked, "Where do you live?"

She could have refused to tell him, but what would be the point? She had no use for that key, and the sooner this was over with, the better. She gave him the address, a rural area on the south side of town. He smiled and nodded, and her heart beat a little faster. He was a handsome man, but the fact that she was thinking about that at a time like this made her uncomfortable.

"You mentioned you used to work for the newspaper," he said. "But you own a flower shop now?"

"Yes. Eve's Garden—on Main Street."

"Am I keeping you from your work?"

Would it make a difference if she said yes? "I have an assistant who's there now." Weekday mornings were usually not particularly busy times, and Sarah was more than capable of handling anything customers were likely to need.

"You'll have to give me directions to your home," he said. "I only moved here a little over a month ago and I'm still learning my way around."

"Oh? Where did you move from?" she asked.

"Washington, DC. You might already know that the Ranger Brigade is a task force of officers from many branches of law enforcement. I'm with the FBI."

He said it the way another man might say "I'm with the post office." Or "I'm with the school district." Just another government job, though this one required him to carry a gun and arrest people.

Her gaze swept over him once more. He probably wore a shoulder holster under the suit jacket that emphasized his broad shoulders and muscular arms. He had to be at least Dane's age, but like Dane, he kept himself in shape. She supposed it was a requirement of the job.

She pulled her attention away from his body as they passed through the town of Montrose. "Turn left at the third traffic light," she said.

Her little bungalow sat in a grove of trees near the river, a rustic construction of stone and weathered metal that looked both modern and decades old. "Nice," he said, as if he meant it, as he stopped the cruiser in the driveway.

"It was built by a sculptor," she said. "I got it for a good price because it only has one bedroom and one bathroom." She took out her keys, and he followed her to the front door and waited while she unlocked it and stepped inside.

Light from the large windows spilled onto the polished wood floors and dappled the leaves of the dozens of houseplants that filled the wide windowsills. More plants, along with vases of fresh flowers, adorned the kitchen island and several side tables. "I see you like to bring your work home," the commander commented.

"I like living things in the house," she said. "And having plants is very healthy."

She stopped in the kitchen, feeling awkward. All those dates, and she hadn't invited any of those men inside her home. No one since Dane.

"The key?" he prompted.

"Oh, of course. It's back here." She indicated the short hallway that led to the bedroom, and he motioned for her to precede him.

She was acutely aware that she hadn't bothered making the bed that morning, the sheets half trailing along the floor on her side of the bed, the comforter a rumpled pile at the foot of the bed. The pajamas she'd worn— pink fleece with cartoons of sheep all over them—were draped over a white-upholstered armchair in the corner.

Aware of the man beside her taking this all in, she hurried to the dresser, and the wooden chest that served as her jewelry box. The box, of juniper wood with an inlaid marquetry hummingbird, was the work of a local artist and had been a gift from Dane their first Christmas together. That had been in the early days, when she believed they would marry and have children together.

She opened the box and lifted out the top tray, then rummaged in the loose collection of single earrings, broken bracelets, a watch that needed a battery and costume jewelry she no longer wore. "It's in here somewhere," she said.

Sanderlin came to stand beside her, the bulk and

warmth of him feeling intimate in this small room, with the unmade bed just behind them. "Are you sure that's where you put it?" he asked.

"I'm positive. It was the first thing I ever put in here." She continued to rummage through the contents. "Dane gave me the box on Christmas Eve and asked me that same day to go to the bank with him to fill out the paperwork and get the key. Afterwards, we went ice skating, then had dinner and came back here and I made a point of putting the key in this box." Frustrated, she spilled the contents of the box onto the dresser. A couple of beads and some loose change spun like tops amid the tangle of necklaces, bracelets and earrings.

Sanderlin leaned closer, their shoulders rubbing, and helped her comb through the piles. "It's not here," she said.

"Are you sure you didn't give it back to Trask when you split up?" Sanderlin asked. "Maybe with a bunch of other things, and you just forgot."

"I didn't give it back," she said. "He never mentioned it, and I truly had forgotten. But I know it was here." She had a sensory memory of her fingers brushing over the toothed edge of the key as she searched for a pin to fasten a shawl only a few weeks before.

"Is anything else missing?" Sanderlin asked.

She stared at the jumble of jewelry on the dresser top, dismay growing. "Nothing. Just the key."

"Is it possible someone came in and took it?"

"You mean—broke in?" Nausea rose at the idea.

"Have you noticed anyone strange hanging around? Has anything happened to make you feel uneasy, especially in the last few days?"

"No." Could someone really have come into her home without her knowing about it?

Sanderlin glanced around the room, as if assessing the situation. "For now, let's go to the bank," he said. "We don't need your key to access the box."

Numb, she followed him out of the room. She studied the rest of the house with new eyes. Had some stranger really come in without her knowledge and stolen that key?

That was ridiculous.

"Maybe the key fell out when you were looking for something else and you didn't notice," Sanderlin said.

She nodded. "That must be it." But the skin at the back of her neck prickled. Something felt very wrong about this.

They left the house, and ten minutes later the commander pulled into the bank parking lot and followed Eve into the building. A slim young woman with jet-black hair looked up from a desk near the door. "Good morning," she said. "May I help you?"

"We need to open a safe deposit box." Sanderlin handed the woman, whose name tag identified her as Liz, the key.

Liz stood. "I'll need your identification and the box number."

"Two eight two," Eve said, and opened her wallet to her driver's license.

"You remembered," Sanderlin murmured as they followed the woman through a vault door and into a room lined on both sides with safety deposit boxes.

Was he implying she had visited the box more recently than she had told him? "Numbers tend to stick in my head," she said. She could have told him she still remembered her high school locker combination, though really, why should he care?

Liz took the key and Eve's identification to a computer terminal in one corner and began typing in information. A few seconds later, she beckoned them to her. "I'll need you to sign here, showing the date and time you're accessing the box," she said.

Eve signed the electronic keypad and Liz returned her driver's license. "I'll retrieve the box for you, and replace it when you're done."

The box felt very light when Liz handed it to Eve. "When you're ready to leave, press that button and I'll come let you out," she said, indicating a button on the wall by the vault door.

Eve waited until she and Sanderlin were alone in the vault before she carried it to the counter that ran the length of the middle of the room and lifted the top.

They both stared into the box. "It's empty," Eve said, stating the obvious. "Why would Dane send me that key when there's nothing there?"

# Chapter Four

Grant pushed the button to summon a bank employee. Eve continued to examine the safety deposit box, as if she expected to find something they had missed. Her shock over finding the box empty appeared genuine, as had her consternation over being unable to find her copy of the box's key.

Liz returned. "Well, that didn't take long," she said, but her smile faded when Grant showed her his badge and identification. "I need to know who last accessed this box and when," he said.

Liz glanced from the badge to his face to the empty box. "I'll have to ask my supervisor," he said. "I believe that information is confidential."

"I have permission to access this box," Eve said. "Surely you can tell me who else has opened it."

"I'll have to ask my supervisor," Liz said again, and fled.

"Do you get that kind of reaction often?" Eve asked when they were alone again. "She acted as if she'd seen a ghost. Or maybe an ax murderer."

"The badge can catch people off guard," he said.

"Must make it tough to pick up women," she said.

"I haven't had much of a problem with that."

She turned away, but not before he caught the hint of a smile. Was she flirting with him? Because she was nervous and trying to break the tension? Or because she felt the same attraction he did?

The door to the vault opened again and a short man in a dark suit that appeared to be too large for him entered, followed by Liz. "I'm Dwight Lawson," he said. "What seems to be the problem?"

Grant displayed his badge again. "I need to know who last accessed this deposit box, and when."

"I came here today to retrieve something from the box and the box is empty," Eve said. "I want to know who else has been in here."

Lawson walked to the computer terminal and began typing. A moment later he said, "The box was opened yesterday at 4:30 p.m. by the owner, Dane Trask."

Behind Grant, Eve gasped. He reached back and squeezed her hand, a warning to let him do the talking. "Who escorted Mr. Trask into the vault?" he asked.

Lawson consulted the screen again. "Ms. Emerson is one of our senior employees," he said.

"I need to speak with her," Grant said.

"She just returned to her desk," Liz said.

"Bring her here please," Lawson said.

While Liz went to fetch her coworker, Lawson turned to Grant. "What is this about?" he asked. "I heard the news reports about Dane Trask."

"We're trying to find Mr. Trask," Grant said.

Liz returned with an attractive black woman Grant judged to be in her fifties. Her name tag identified her as Felice. She glanced at Grant and Eve, then addressed her boss. "Liz said you wanted to see me."

"You admitted a man to the vault yesterday about

4:30," Lawson said. "A Mr. Dane Trask, for box number 282."

"Yes, sir. I remember because we were going to close the lobby soon."

"What did this man look like?" Grant asked.

"Not to be rude, but who are you?" Felice asked. "I can't talk about our clients to just anyone."

"Special Agent Grant Sanderlin, with the Ranger Brigade." He showed her his badge. "We're looking for Mr. Trask."

"Don't you watch the news?" Lawson asked. "There's a $25,000 reward for information leading to Dane Trask's apprehension. The man is a suspected terrorist."

Felice's eyes widened at this, but she held her ground. "I help my daughter with my two grandsons in the evenings," she said. "The only TV I see these days is *Daniel Tiger* and *Dinosaur Train*."

"You're not in any trouble," Grant reassured her. "I just need you to describe this man for me."

She pursed her lips, considering. "He was tall," she said. "Maybe six-two. A white man, with short dark hair and brown eyes. Handsome. And very charming." She flushed, looking years younger.

Except for the eyes, that could describe Dane Trask. Or any number of other men. "You verified his identity?" he asked.

"Of course."

"What kind of identification was it?" Grant asked. "A driver's license?"

The lines on her forehead deepened. "Not a driver's license." She moved to the computer terminal and consulted the display. Her face cleared. "It was a military

ID. I remember now that I thanked him for his service and he said he was happy to serve."

"I'll need to see the security feed for this area for yesterday afternoon," Grant told Lawson.

"I'll need a warrant to show you that," Lawson said.

"I can get one," Grant said.

"And while he's doing that, Dane is getting farther and farther away from us," Eve said.

Lawson looked startled, as if he had forgotten she was in the room. He turned back to Felice Emerson. "Was there anyone else in the vault area at the same time as Mr. Trask?" he asked.

"No, sir."

"Then I can show you the security footage," Lawson said. "We'll need to go into the back offices, if you're done in here."

He led the way back through the lobby, past the tellers' counter, through a door that blended in with the wall. He tapped a code on a keypad beside the door, then escorted them in, to a room where a row of wall-mounted monitors displayed black-and-white images of various areas of the bank. In the vault they had just left, Liz and Felice stood with their heads together, talking. Lawson frowned up at the image, then moved to a desk where a young man looked up from yet another monitor. "Special Agent Sanderlin is with the FBI, and he needs to see the security footage for the vault area for yesterday afternoon at 4:30."

If the man was surprised at the request, he didn't show it. His expression didn't change as he began typing, then scrolling.

"I can't believe that man was here and no one noticed," Lawson said. "That story has been all over the news."

Grant didn't answer. Eve stood at his side, silent, but practically humming with tension. He wanted to take her hand again, to steady her, but didn't think it would be appropriate.

"Here you go," the young man, who wore no name tag, said. He angled the screen toward them and they all leaned in to view a tall, dark-haired man follow Felice into the vault. He said something that made her laugh and she left him. As soon as she was gone, he opened the box, dumped the contents into the satchel he had slung over one shoulder, then summoned Felice to escort him out. The entire sequence took less than five minutes.

"He kept his head down, and angled so you can't really see his face," the young man said. "The cameras are placed to catch faces, so you'd have to make a real effort to avoid them."

The man in the video had been making an effort, even putting his hand up to shield his face at one point.

"Run it again," Grant said.

"That isn't Dane," Eve said when they had watched the clip a second time.

"I need a copy of that," Grant said. Maybe Hud could enhance the image to get a better ID.

"I don't see how you could tell who it is," Lawson said. "But Felice checked his ID. She wouldn't lie about something like that."

"IDs can be faked," Grant said.

They waited for the copy of the security feed, Grant thanked Lawson, and they left. Eve remained silent until they reached the cruiser. "That wasn't Dane," she said again.

"How can you be sure?" Grant opened the passenger

door and held it for her, admiring her legs as she slid in, while trying to appear not to do so. She had very nice legs, shapely with good muscle tone.

"I just know it wasn't him." She looked pained. "We were lovers for three years. I know how he walked, how he carried himself. The person in that video—there were similarities, similar height, similar build, but that wasn't Dane."

Grant was inclined to believe her. Dane Trask's face was on posters all over town, online and on TV. The odds of him strolling into a bank at that time of day and not being recognized by anyone were slim to none.

"The shoes weren't right," Eve said.

"What do you mean?" He put the cruiser in gear and backed out of the parking space.

"The man in the photograph was wearing athletic shoes. Dane didn't even own a pair. If he needed casual shoes, he wore hiking boots or leather sandals. I used to tease him about it." Her expression was triumphant. "It definitely wasn't Dane."

"I believe you," Grant said.

"He didn't even look at the contents of the deposit box," Eve said. "He just dumped everything in that satchel."

"He was in a hurry," Grant said.

"Or maybe he didn't know exactly what he was looking for, so he took everything."

This struck Grant as particularly insightful. "That's a very good observation. Who knew Dane had given you that deposit box key?"

"No one. At least, I didn't tell anyone. And why does that matter?"

He waited, and saw when the answer came to her.

Her face paled, but she held steady. "You think the person who got into that box did so with my key."

"We have Trask's key. Yours is missing."

"Someone stole the key from my house? When? And how did they know it was there?"

"A jewelry box on the bedroom dresser isn't exactly a devious hiding place," Grant said. "Experienced thieves know to check places like that."

"But again—why would anyone want to steal that key, or the contents of Dane's deposit box?"

"Maybe for the same reason Dane sent you the key. Because there was something in there he wanted the public to know about."

"Maybe whatever it was proved he isn't guilty of the crimes he's being accused of. Or maybe he put a letter in there, explaining why he disappeared." Eve hugged her arms around her middle. "How are you going to find out who's doing this and stop them?"

He couldn't decide if the question was evidence of her faith in him and his team—or an accusation. "I'll start by getting a crime scene team to go over your house. Maybe they'll find some sign of a break-in that we missed. I'll have my tech experts look at the bank security cam footage. Maybe they can enhance the image to make identifying the man in the picture easier."

"I could talk to Audra, and maybe Dane's coworkers," Eve said. "Maybe one of them knows something."

"No." He didn't wait for her reaction, merely closed the space between them and took her hand. "Whoever did this, they could be dangerous. You need to go about your regular life and let me handle this. If anyone is watching you, let them believe you don't even know the key is missing. Don't get involved."

"What do you mean, if someone is watching me?" Instead of pulling away, she leaned into him. "If you're saying that just to frighten me, it's working."

He forced himself to release his hold on her. It was either that or pull her close and kiss that terrified look away. But that kind of he-man behavior had never been his style, so he took a step back, and kept his expression neutral and professional. He slid a business card from his pocket and handed it to her. "If you see anyone suspicious, or if anything happens to make you feel uncomfortable or uneasy, you call me. Anytime, day or night."

She stared at the card. "Do you think I'm in danger?"

He wanted to reassure her that she would be fine, that he would never let anyone harm her, and there was no need for her to worry. But he respected her too much to lie to her. "You're probably fine," he said. "But I like to exercise what we call an abundance of caution. You don't have to change anything you're doing now, just be aware and report anything suspicious."

She compressed her lips together and nodded, then tucked his card into her purse. "Does this mean I'm going to see you again?" she asked.

The question caught him off guard. For a flash of an instant, his all-business demeanor slipped and he stared at her. "Would you like that?"

She very deliberately looked him up and down, that ghost of a smile playing about her full lips again. "If I am in danger, you look like a handy man to have around, that's all."

He knew a challenge when he heard one—and he was more than ready to meet this one. "I plan on sticking close," he said. He'd leave it up to her how close he could get, but the next few weeks—or months, or maybe even years—with her could prove very interesting.

# Chapter Five

"There you are. I was beginning to think you'd been arrested." Sarah greeted Eve from behind the wire frame of an archway she was filling with greenery and fresh flowers when Eve returned to the flower shop that afternoon.

"Sorry I was gone so long." Eve stashed her purse under the counter and moved in to help trim the rosebuds, baby's breath and tree fern Sarah was inserting into test tube vases and wiring to the arch.

"What happened?" Sarah asked. She didn't stop working, but she fixed Eve with an expectant gaze.

"I ended up speaking to the Ranger Brigade commander." Sarah clipped a broken stem from a branch of baby's breath, then began separating the branch into smaller pieces.

"Oh? What was he like?"

"He was…nice." Less prickly and much kinder than she had expected. She had thought he would view Dane as a criminal and her as bad by association, and possibly even an accomplice. Instead, he'd been sympathetic. Even understanding, if a little too nosy for her comfort.

"Nice?" Sarah set aside the coil of florist's wire and

turned to face Eve, hands on hips. "Nice how? Nice charming? Nice looking?"

"Both, I guess." Eve poked a stem of fern into one of the test tubes and added a rosebud. *Powerful. Sexy.*

"You're blushing!" Sarah chuckled. "Oh, this has got to be good. Tell me everything. Are you going to go out with him?"

"What? No!" She gave up on the flowers and set them aside. "I went there to turn over the stuff Dane sent me, not to get a date." But she'd flirted with him. She hadn't been able to stop herself.

"You're clearly attracted to this guy. I haven't seen you blush over anyone in months. And the plan was you would go out with anyone eligible." Sarah's smile faded. "Or is he not eligible?"

"He's even older than Dane and he has two teenage daughters."

"So he's married."

"Divorced. But he's older, with older children. Like Dane."

"So you're attracted to more mature men." Sarah elbowed her. "Nothing wrong with that."

"Sarah, I'm not going to date this man. I mean, he could end up arresting Dane, and that would be…" She let her voice trail away.

"Yeah, awkward." Sarah picked up the wire and clippers once more. "So what happened?"

"I gave him the letter and he insisted on driving me to my house to retrieve the safety deposit box key Dane gave me that first year we were dating."

"I guess he wanted to see if it was a match," Sarah said.

"I think he didn't want me opening the box and taking out anything incriminating before he had a chance to see it."

"You wouldn't do that," Sarah said. "Would you?"

"Of course I wouldn't."

"Not in your right mind, of course, but love messes with people's minds."

"I'm not in love with Dane anymore." That was true. She had cared deeply about him at one time, but over the last six months of their relationship, and in the six months since they had broken up, she had come to see him in a different light. He was a good man, but he kept his emotions too tightly controlled. She needed a man who was able to show her love more, the kind of man who could be silly with a child or sentimental with her. He didn't have to be just like her, he merely had to be willing to meet her halfway when it came to expressing his feelings.

"Okay, so you got the key from your house," Sarah said. "Then what?"

"We didn't get the key. It wasn't there."

"You mean you couldn't find it. Couldn't you remember where you put it?"

"I knew I put it in the jewelry box on my dresser. But it wasn't there."

"Maybe you just forgot, or—"

"I didn't forget. The commander thinks someone broke into my place and took it."

"Someone broke into your place? When?" Sarah put an arm around Eve's shoulders. "Oh honey, that's so awful. What else did they take?"

"They didn't take anything else, except the key. And they didn't do any damage. I wouldn't have suspected anything if not for that missing key."

"But—"

"Don't interrupt, just listen."

Sarah covered her lips with one hand and nodded, eyes wide.

Eve told her about going to the bank and discovering someone had been there before them—someone who claimed to be Dane Trask. "I watched the security camera footage," Eve said. "The man was similar to Dane, but it wasn't Dane. And he had a key to get into the deposit box. I have Dane's key, so this impersonator must have had mine."

"Or he obtained another key somehow."

"The bank only issues two. If you lose one, you have to pay a couple hundred dollars to have the lock drilled out and replaced."

"Huh." Sarah clipped a foot-long length of wire and wrapped one end twice around the neck of a flower-filled test tube. "If it wasn't Dane, who was it?"

"I don't know. That's what the commander and his officers are trying to find out." She picked up the clippers again and snipped at a cluster of miniature roses. The tension of the day had drained her. All she wanted to do was go home, take a hot shower and go to bed. Alone.

*Liar*, her conscience whispered. She wanted to go home to a man who loved her, one who would hold her and comfort her and declare his intention to slay dragons if need be to console her.

"Oh, I almost forgot." Sarah patted Eve's shoulder. "A man stopped by to see you just before lunch. A really good-looking guy. Early thirties, nice suit, no wedding ring." Sarah ticked off these points like a bird-watcher listing the identifying features of a rare avian find. Eve knew the genus and species of this particular rarity by heart. Where she was concerned, at least, hominid eligible—the eligible man—was a rare find indeed.

"What was his name?" Eve asked. "Did he say why he wanted to see me?" Maybe one of the men she had met online decided to come meet her in person—a scary thought, given that information about where she lived and worked was supposed to be kept confidential.

"He just said he had been hoping to meet you. He asked if he could leave his card on your desk. I was busy putting this thing together." Sarah indicated the arch. "So I said yes. Then I forgot about it until just now."

Eve squeezed around Sarah and headed for her office. She spotted the business card while she was still in the hall, a small rectangle of white card stock in the center of her desk blotter. Her mysterious visitor hadn't tossed the card onto the desk. He had place it precisely in the center of the desktop.

"So, who was he?" Sarah crowded into the doorway beside Eve. "Did he say what he wanted?"

Eve leaned forward and plucked the card from the blotter. "Toby Masterson," she read. Her heart beat harder as the smaller print under his name registered. "He's an accountant with TDC Enterprises." The company Dane had worked for.

The company that had accused him of serious crimes.

"Is there a note?" Sarah asked.

Eve flipped the card over. This side was blank. "Did he say anything else you haven't told me?" she asked.

"No, I swear." Sarah actually crossed herself. "But he seemed really nice. Very friendly."

Sarah made friends with everyone. She had a knack for getting a smile or at least a pleasant word out of the surliest customers. But just because Mr. Masterson succumbed to Sarah's charm didn't mean he was a nice person. "Did he say anything else?" she asked.

"Only that he'd stop by again some time." Sarah's smile broadened. "Just think, you might have two handsome men pursuing you. Wouldn't that be a nice change?"

"I don't want to be pursued." Especially by a man she'd never met who sought her out. She frowned at his card again. Was it possible she had met him, and had forgotten? She shook her head and tucked the card in her desk drawer. She didn't have time to fret over Mr. Masterson. She had work to do. "You can go home as soon as you're done with that arch," she told Sarah. "I'll close up the shop. I'll probably stay late, working on the order for the Salazar wedding."

"Thanks. I was going to ask if I could leave early. Robby is having a mini meltdown over having to pick out a tux for prom at the end of next month. I promised I'd help him out."

Eve tried to imagine Sarah's youngest child, who at sixteen was already six-foot-four-inches and probably weighed all of 120 pounds, in a tuxedo, and failed. Did they even make formal wear with legs that long? "Good luck," she said. "If you need to leave now, I can finish the arch."

"I'm almost done. Manuel promised he'd be by a little before five to pick it up to deliver to the Elks Hall for some kind of ceremony they're having tonight."

Eve settled in to work and was soon absorbed in planning arrangements, calculating flower totals and filling out order forms. Sarah left and Manuel came and went. At six o'clock she switched off the lights in the front room, locked the door and turned the sign to Closed, then returned to her desk. She was on her way back to her desk when her cell phone rang, with a call from Cara Mead, Dane's administrative assistant.

"Cara! What is it? Have you heard something about Dane?" Eve answered.

"Not a thing," Cara said. "When he does surface again, I'm going to give him what-for for worrying us all so much."

Eve pictured the petite brown-haired Cara standing on tiptoe to grab the six-two Dane by the ear to pull him down to her level. "I suppose you've seen those horrible reward posters around town," she said. "When I spotted one in the post office this morning, I felt a little sick. I just can't believe Dane would do the things he's accused of."

"I don't believe it either," Cara said. "I think someone is trying to cover up something and making Dane the scapegoat. That's sort of why I'm calling."

"Oh?" Eve sank into her desk chair once more, the flower order forgotten.

"I'm not working with TDC anymore," Cara said. "With Dane gone, it was pretty clear they wanted me out of the way, too. I have a new job, as coordinator for Wilderness Conservation."

"Congratulations." Eve tried to put some enthusiasm behind the words, but this news pained her. Had Cara left her job because she didn't believe Dane was coming back? "That must be interesting work."

"It is. And one of the first things on my agenda when I took on the position was looking into the Mary Lee Mine site. It was one of the last projects Dane worked on and I think he found something wrong up there. I was able to send in some soil and water samples for testing and they came back way out of whack. My group is trying to pressure TDC to do more testing, and to take responsibility for the test results. We're holding a rally and a press conference at the mine tomorrow and I was hoping you'd agree to be there."

"Me? Cara, that really isn't my thing."

"The more people we have present, the bigger impact we'll make, and the more pressure we'll put on TDC," Cara said. "I really think this is what Dane would want us to do. Please? It won't take much of your time."

Eve wavered. She had plenty of work here at the shop, but it wasn't anything Sarah couldn't handle. "I'll think about it," she hedged.

"We're meeting at the grocery store parking lot at eight to drive up to the mine," Cara said. "I'd really, really appreciate it if you could be there."

Eve ended the call and her chair creaked as she leaned back. With her love of flowers and plants, environmental activism seemed a good fit. But she had never been one to make waves or put herself in the spotlight. She preferred to sit back and enjoy the flowers.

She had to admit that if people didn't speak out to protect the environment, how long would it be before the flowers she loved disappeared altogether? She could almost hear Dane asking the question. He had a way of puncturing her fantasy balloons with practical reality.

Still, they had had a lot of good times together. She recalled an outing where they had visited a lavender farm. A farm worker had taken a photo of her and Dane sitting in a field of lavender, all smiles. It was one of her favorite photos and even after they had broken up, she hadn't been able to bring herself to put it away.

Her gaze roamed over the office. The small space didn't have room for much in the way of personalization or decoration, but she had managed to squeeze in a small bookcase, which she filled with a few figurines and pictures that were meaningful to her, including the lavender fields photograph. She scanned the shelves and realized with a jolt it wasn't there. The space it usually occupied, second shelf down, all the way over to the right, was empty.

Had Sarah moved it for some reason? No, she wouldn't do something like that. Had someone else taken it, then?

But why? Who would want a picture of her and Dane together?

Fear chilled her. Anxious not to be alone one moment longer, she collected her sweater and purse, and left via the rear entrance. She felt better once she was outside. Plenty of people were out and about this early in the evening: shoppers, diners, other people headed home from work. She waved to a couple she knew and forced herself to walk calmly to her car. She thought about calling the commander to tell him about the missing picture, but quickly discarded the idea. He'd think she was a nut. First she couldn't find the safe deposit key. Now she had misplaced a photograph. And who kept a photograph of a man she broke up with six months ago?

There was probably a good explanation for all of this. She should have looked behind the shelf. Maybe the picture had merely fallen down. Or maybe Sarah did have it. She'd find out tomorrow. Meanwhile, she was going to go home and not think about it. Ignoring problems might not make them vanish, but sometimes it was the best coping mechanism. If only everything in life could be dealt with so simply.

# *Chapter Six*

Tuesday morning, Grant dialed his ex-wife's number and waited for the phone to ring. He would have preferred to call his daughters directly, but he had learned the hard way that they both seldom answered. He could have texted, but communicating that way wasn't the same as hearing his girls' voices. Since they were both on spring break, he hoped by calling early he would find them at home.

"Hello." Angela's voice was cool and professional—her telephone voice. Caller ID would have shown her the call was from him, but she always answered as if speaking to a stranger. Perhaps that's what they had become, in the end.

"Hello, Angela," he said. "Are the girls around? I'd like to speak to them." No small talk, asking how she was doing or what was new in her life. She refused to respond, so he'd given up.

"I'll see if they're available." As if they were busy executives, not teenagers.

"Hey, Daddy!" Janie's greeting made his heart lift. He pictured her, smile full of braces, red-gold hair in a wild tangle, hazel eyes sparkling. "When are you coming to visit?" she asked. "I've missed you so much."

"I've missed you, too, Pumpkin," he said. He ignored her question about a visit. Taking any kind of leave from a job he had just started was out of the question, but work had kept him away from them all their lives, and he hated repeating himself. One day, when they were adults with jobs and responsibilities, maybe they'd understand. "What have you been up to?"

"I got an A on my English paper about subversive feminism in *Jane Eyre*," she said.

"That's great." Though what in the world a sophomore was doing writing about something like that he didn't know. Janie was scary smart sometimes. "Did you get the packet of stuff I sent you?"

"I did! The park looks so interesting. Like the real Wild West. I can't wait to see it."

"This summer," he said. As much as he looked forward to the girls spending two months with him, he worried they'd be bored within a week. Montrose, Colorado, didn't offer the social opportunities of Washington, DC. But he'd do his best to make the visit worthwhile.

"I don't want to wait until then," Janie said.

"It's only another couple of months," he said. "In the meantime, look over the stuff I sent you and think about everything you want to do and see while you're here."

"I will."

"Can I talk to your sister now?"

"Beth is being a pain right now. Don't take it personally." Translation: Beth was still refusing to talk to him because, as she had said in their last heated exchange before he left, it was bad enough that he'd been gone all the time while they were growing up. Now he was moving thousands of miles away without even considering them.

The words hurt more than any bullet. All he could do was keep the lines open and hope that one day she would talk to him again. "Tell her I said hello and I love her," he said. "And I love you, too."

"I love you, Daddy," Janie said. "And Mom says I have to get off the phone now because we're going sailing with some friends of Darryl's, which will probably be really boring. Goodbye!"

She ended the call and he laid down the phone. Darryl was Angela's new husband, a lobbyist who had set Grant's teeth on edge every time they met. This was the man he had abandoned his family to.

*Walk it back*, he silently chided himself. No good came of wallowing. He turned his attention to the next item on his lengthy to-do list. The background check he'd ordered on Eve Shea.

No criminal record. Not even a speeding ticket. Her business, Eve's Garden, had a good reputation and appeared to be making a reasonable profit. No marriages. No bankruptcy. In her time as a reporter with the *Montrose Daily Press*, she had won two Press Association awards.

He closed the report and swiveled away from the monitor. He had no reason to believe Eve was faking her lack of knowledge about what had happened to the contents of the safe deposit box, but he had to be sure. For the integrity of the case and for his personal integrity, he needed to know he hadn't let his attraction to her interfere with him carrying out his duties.

His intercom beeped. "Yes?"

Faith Martin's voice answered. "Sir, we've had a request for assistance from the Montrose County Sheriff's Department. They'd like our help with crowd control at the Mary Lee Mine."

"What's going on up there?" he asked. Hazardous waste remediation at the Mary Lee was one of the projects Dane Trask had been working on when he disappeared. More recently, Officer Jason Beck and Trask's administrative assistant, Cara Mead, had been attacked when they tried to investigate the mine site. And of course, the mine had been the focus of the press release someone—presumably Trask—had sent to Eve.

"Some protesters are holding a press conference there this morning, and MCSD is concerned there might be trouble. And since the mine is in the Ranger Brigade's jurisdiction, they thought we could help."

"The mine is private property within the public lands we monitor," Grant clarified. "But yes, we can help. Who's in this morning?"

"Lieutenant Dance is here, and Officer Hudson."

"Thanks."

Grant pulled on a black windbreaker against the late spring chill and went in search of Dance.

Lieutenant Dance looked up from his computer keyboard at the commander's approach. One look at Grant's face and he sat up straighter. "Something's up?" he asked.

"You and I are helping with crowd control for a press conference at the Mary Lee Mine."

Dance unfolded his muscular frame and pulled on his own windbreaker. "You drive," Grant said. Dance knew the location of the mine better than he did.

Whether or not there was trouble at the mine, it was a beautiful day to be driving backroads in the wilderness. Hillsides glowed a soft pink with wild crocus, and aspens unfurled lime green leaves like splashes of Day-Glo paint against the more somber hues of pinion and fir. A hawk traced wide circles across an expanse of turquoise sky unmarred by even a single cloud.

"I saw a poster about this meeting at the coffee shop this morning," Dance said as he turned the cruiser off the highway and up a jagged dirt road. "Something about a press conference to bring to light TDC's failure to address matters of grave environmental concern."

Grant nodded. "Words most likely to get TDC Enterprises and their lawyers riled."

"Riled enough to cause trouble?" Dance asked.

"Not physical trouble," Grant said. "I think they'd be more likely to employ their lawyers to send letters threatening legal action and expensive lawsuits."

Dance nodded. "So maybe we'll have a nice couple hours in the mountains." He gunned the vehicle up a steep washed-out section of road. "Maybe without a lot of company. Not many people will want to risk their cars on this road."

But when they arrived at the mine gates, Grant was surprised to see at least two dozen cars and vans, and he estimated more than fifty people gathered around a wooden platform constructed of pallets. A couple of people held shoulder-mounted television cameras, while others carried microphones and recording equipment.

A quartet of stern-faced men and women in suits stood to one side of the platform, scowling at the growing crowd. Probably the lawyers, Grant thought, as he strode past a cluster of people who carried signs that read TDC Pollutes and Don't Let Corporate Greed Destroy the Future.

He faltered and did a double take as he recognized the woman who held the latter sign. Eve Shea met his gaze and lifted her chin in a defiant gesture.

He veered off course and walked over to her. "Hello, Ms. Shea," he said.

"You might as well call me Eve," she said, lowering the sign.

"Are you a member of Wilderness Conservation?" he asked.

"No. Cara Mead asked me to come. She's the coordinator for Wilderness Conservation now."

And Cara—his officer, Jason Beck's fiancée—had been the one to discover that TDC's supposed efforts to clean up the old mine site had, so far at least, resulted in even more contamination at the site, contrary to what was shown in the reports TDC had filed with the Environmental Protection Agency and others.

So maybe TDC had fudged their data, or even outright lied, but Grant wasn't sure that made them dangerous.

"Why are you here, Commander?" Eve asked.

"We're here in case anything gets out of hand," he said.

She pushed a wayward strand of hair out of her face. "It's a press conference."

"And a protest." He indicated her sign.

She looked down at the sign. "Someone handed me this when we got here. I think it's mainly to give the news cameras an interesting visual."

She made an interesting visual, he thought, the wind lifting strands of her hair to float around her like a veil, her cheeks flushed from either sun or emotion, a soft blue tunic over black leggings and boots clinging to her curves. "I was going to call you today and let you know my investigators didn't find any signs that your locks were forced," he said.

"I didn't think so, but I guess it's good to have it confirmed," she said. "Maybe I really did misplace that deposit box key."

"A good set of lock picks or a key could have opened your door without leaving behind any evidence," Grant said. "Did you find anything else missing?"

"Not from my home, no."

Something in her voice or her facial expression alerted him. "Did you find something missing from somewhere else? Your shop?"

"It's probably nothing," she said.

"What is it?"

"I had a picture of myself and Dane, in a field of lavender. For years it has sat on a shelf in my office. Now it's not there."

"When was the last time you saw it?" he asked.

She shook her head. "I have no idea. It's one of those things that has been there so long I don't really even notice it anymore."

"When did you notice it was missing?"

"Yesterday evening. I was finishing up work for the day and looked over, and realized the spot where it usually sat was empty."

"Could it have fallen behind the shelf, or been moved?"

"I looked this morning, but I couldn't find it." She shrugged. "I'm sure it's somewhere. I mean, who would steal a photograph?"

"Hello, everyone." The voice, overly loud in the speakers that had been erected on either end of the platform, was jarring. Cara Mead, all five-foot-three of her, in black trousers and a purple jacket, leaned back from the mic and tried again. "We're so glad you could join us on this beautiful day in this beautiful place."

Grant wasn't sure he would have termed the piles of gray rock and old building materials that formed the backdrop of this scene as beautiful, but it had a certain untamed appeal. "As you may already be aware, TDC Industries accepted a contract last August to mitigate contaminants at the Mary Lee Mine, removing or quarantining harmful substances like mercury and arsenic, and returning this place to its natural beauty. Instead, recent test results show there are actually more of some contaminants than before."

"Eve Shea, this is a pleasure."

Grant and Eve both turned to look at the man who had spoken. Taller than Grant by at least two inches, he had the sharp features and deep tan of a man who spent a lot of time outdoors.

"Toby Masterson." He offered his hand to Eve, ignoring Grant.

"My assistant said you stopped by my shop while I was out yesterday," Eve said. She shook hands, but immediately afterwards folded her arms tight across her chest.

"I was disappointed not to hear from you," Masterson said.

"I've been busy. And since I don't know you…" She shrugged.

"But you know Dane Trask. And I'm looking for him. I think you could help." He rested his hand on her shoulder and squeezed. Eve grimaced.

"Why are you looking for Dane?" Grant asked. He

wanted to tell the man to take his hands off Eve, but sensed she might resist that approach.

Sure enough, Eve took care of the matter herself, shoving Masterson's hand away. She moved over, putting more distance between them. "If Dane wants to stay away he must have his reasons," she said. "I won't help anyone find him."

She looked at Grant, not Masterson, when she spoke, and he felt again that spark of desire, almost painful in its intensity.

"Still, I'd love to get together and talk," Masterson said.

"I don't have anything to say to you." She started to turn away, but Masterson moved to block her.

"Then listen to me," he said. "I knew Dane Trask from Welcome Home Warriors. He could be a great guy, and he did a lot of good work. But he had a dark side, too. He could be really dangerous. I think he could be dangerous to you."

Eve's face blanched china white, and she put a hand to her throat. "Dane would never hurt me," she said.

"You hurt him," Masterson said. "He was going to ask you to marry him and instead you dumped him."

"He understood. We weren't right for each other."

"He was an expert at hiding his emotions. You know that." He took a step back. "Take my advice and be careful. And don't think you need to protect him from anyone. Worry about protecting yourself."

He turned and left them, shoving through the crowd of reporters and onlookers, until Grant couldn't see him anymore.

Grant moved closer to Eve. "Are you all right?" he asked.

She took a deep breath. "I'm okay." She stared after Masterson. "I didn't like him."

"Neither do I. But maybe you should listen to him."

She glared at him. "What do you mean?"

"We don't know why Dane did what he did—why he left his job and the people who cared about him to hide out in the wilderness. Why he wrecked a really nice truck or sent you that cryptic letter. But one explanation is that those aren't the actions of a mentally stable man. Maybe something happened to change him. To trigger him."

She shook her head, but he slid his hand up to cradle her cheek, stilling her. "Maybe Dane is dangerous," he said. "Maybe you do need to be careful, and stay as far away from him as you can."

"Since he isn't here, that shouldn't be a problem," she said.

"I should have said I think it would be better if you stayed away from anything to do with Trask—like that safety deposit box, or this rally."

She pulled away, color rising in her cheeks. "I don't like people telling me what to do," she said. "And I really don't respond well to scare tactics." She raised the sign again, as if prepared to use it as a weapon, then turned her back on him.

Grant stepped away, stung a little, but continued to watch her.

Toby Masterson had his eyes on Eve, too, and the look on his face had made Grant want to punch the man. Was that his cop sense at work—or plain old-fashioned jealousy?

# Chapter Seven

"I'm sure that picture of you and Dane was in your office on Monday morning," Sarah said when Eve asked her about it Tuesday afternoon. "We had a slow spell and I tidied up a little bit and dusted your bookcase."

"And you're sure the picture was there?" Eve asked.

Sarah nodded. "I'm sure because I wondered why you kept it out, since the two of you weren't a couple anymore."

"I kept it out because I really like the photograph." Eve glared. "Dane and I are still friends, even if we aren't lovers."

Sarah held up both hands in a defensive gesture. "All right, all right. I just worry that if you aren't really over him, you'll never make room in your life for someone else."

"What self-help book did you get that out of?" Eve asked.

Sarah grinned. "I could write the self-help book on that one. I've raised three girls and a boy who are constantly falling in and out love."

"What's the latest with Robby?" Eve asked, glad for a switch in subject.

"Let's look for that photograph and I'll tell you all about it."

While the two women moved furniture and looked everywhere they could think of for the missing photograph, Sarah regaled Eve with a description of the previous day's outing to find the perfect tuxedo for prom. "You know Robby," she said. "He wanted something different, but not too different. He wants to stand out, but not too far out."

"In other words, he's a typical teenager." Eve yanked open a file drawer and stared at the paperwork shoved in so tightly there was no way the picture could be inside. "What did he end up with?"

"He went with a pretty traditional black tux, dressed up with a purple-and-gold paisley vest and a white ascot. Sort of the Regency fop look—though when I said that, he had no idea what I was talking about, which led to a discussion of Jane Austen, Georgette Heyer, and my love of Regency romance novels that had him rolling his eyes. But he seemed satisfied when I told him the girls were bound to find him irresistible."

Eve sank into her desk chair. "Tell him when he's ready for the big day, whatever flowers he wants are on the house. I don't think we're going to find that picture. It's just disappeared."

"I'm sorry," Sarah said. "Are you really upset?"

Was she? "I did like the picture, but I'm more upset by the idea that someone may have come into my office and taken it. Why would anyone even want it?"

"It's a mystery, all right." Sarah leaned back against the door frame. "But maybe you'll meet someone soon whose picture you'll want to put in its place."

At Eve's sour look, she laughed. "I can't help it if I'm a hopeless romantic. I want to see you happy."

Eve sat up straighter. "I don't need a man to be happy."

"No, but you do need a man to make a baby, and I know how much you want to be a mother."

"Maybe I'll find a sperm donor." Even as she said the words, her throat tightened in fear. Sure, women did a wonderful job raising children on their own every day, either out of necessity or by choice, but did she really want to do that? Maybe she was old-fashioned, but she had a hard time letting go of her dreams of a happy family—a child or children and two parents.

"Who are you going out with this weekend?" Sarah asked.

"I'm thinking of taking a break." She focused on her computer screen, hoping Sarah would get the message that she didn't want to talk about it.

But her friend wasn't so easily deterred. "Don't tell me you're giving up so soon."

"Maybe this isn't the way to go about it," Eve said. "I don't seem to be hitting it off with any of the men I've dated, or else they're not interested in me."

"What about that professor from the university?" Sarah asked. "I always thought the two of you had a lot in common."

"He told me—to my face—that he preferred younger women. I took it to mean he usually dated his students."

"Ewww." Sarah wrinkled her nose. "Okay, well, what about the insurance salesman?"

"He tried to sell me a life insurance policy on our first date. I don't know, it just set the wrong tone. Then there was the man who spent most of the date on the phone with his ex-girlfriend. Or the guy who brought his dog along on the date."

"You like dogs."

"I love dogs. But this one sat between us the whole time and growled at me. At the end of the evening the man told me things weren't going to work out between us because his dog obviously didn't like me."

"What is wrong with men?" Sarah asked.

"Maybe I'm being too picky," Eve said.

"No," Sarah said. "You want what you want, and it isn't these guys." She sighed. "You and Dane were good together—until you weren't."

"Dane and I are never getting back together," Eve protested.

"No, hear me out," Sarah said. She straightened. "You don't want or need Dane anymore, I agree, but maybe he's your type, so you need to find someone like him—only better. A good-looking, mature man who wants a family. An athletic, outdoorsy type. Maybe former military."

"I don't know. Does such a guy even exist?"

"Face it, that's what you were attracted to. It's why you're attracted to that police commander with the Ranger Brigade."

"He's FBI," Sarah corrected her. "And I already told you he isn't right for me. He already has two almost grown daughters."

"That doesn't mean he doesn't want more children. Maybe he loves children. Maybe he's secretly longing to find the right woman to raise more children with."

"Maybe he's a great cook and loves to clean house, too," Eve said. "I mean, as long as we're fantasizing about the perfect man, let's go all the way."

"He doesn't have to be perfect," Sarah said. "He just has to be perfect for you. There's someone out there for you, I know there is."

"I wish I had your faith." Eve straightened. "Now come on, we both have work to do. We'd better make sure we have plenty of supplies for corsages, wristlets, hair clips and boutonnieres," she said. "Lots of carnations and baby roses and ribbon."

"I'll get right on it."

After Sarah left, Eve tried to concentrate on proofing the order for the Salazar wedding. But Sarah's words kept echoing in her head. Was it true she had a type of man she was drawn to? But what if her type was all wrong?

She sent in the order form for the wedding, then called the wedding photographer and discussed getting some shots of the bouquets and table arrangements to use in her portfolio and possibly in future advertising. She put together a Get Well Soon arrangement for a woman who broke her arm in a climbing accident, then returned to her computer to get the contact information for the head of a local charity for whom they had supplied flowers for a fundraising banquet, to see if she needed more flowers this year.

She was engrossed in plans for a new summer sales flyer when the front buzzer sounded. "Hello? May I help you?" Sarah asked.

"I'd like to speak to Eve. Ms. Shea."

The voice was unmistakable. Eve rolled her chair back a few inches and looked out at Grant Sanderlin. He wasn't in uniform, or a suit, but dressed casually in dark jeans and a polo shirt.

"Oh, Eve!" Sarah practically sang the words.

Sarah stood, smoothed her slacks and walked out to greet him. "Hello, Commander," she said.

"I'm not in uniform. Why don't you call me Grant?"

Aware of Sarah watching them while pretending to sort greeting cards at the stand in the corner, Eve struggled to keep her expression smooth. "What can I do for you?" she asked.

"I did a little checking into Toby Masterson's background," he said. "I thought you'd be interested in what I learned."

"Why were you looking into his background?" she asked. "Is he a suspect in a crime?"

"I didn't like the way he approached you at the rally this morning. And I could tell he made you uncomfortable. You have good instincts, I think."

Sarah had stopped trying to hide her interest and was watching them openly now. "Maybe we should talk about this outside," Eve said.

"It's almost time for you to close," he said. "Maybe we could discuss this over dinner."

"I don't know…" she began.

"What a great idea." Sarah rushed forward. "I can close up here. You go ahead." She nudged Eve toward her office. "He's your type," she whispered, Eve hoped softly enough that Grant didn't hear.

Eve relented. Having dinner with Commander Sanderlin probably wasn't the worst way to spend an evening, and she was curious to hear what he had learned about Toby Masterson. "I'll just get my jacket and purse," she said, and slipped into her office.

While she was fishing her purse out of the desk drawer, she heard Sarah ask, "Were you ever in the military?"

"I served ten years in the air force," Grant said.

"I knew it. You just have that look about you."

Eve rushed to rejoin them before Sarah could ask any more probing questions. "I'm ready," she said, already moving toward the door.

On the sidewalk, Grant touched her elbow. "Where are you rushing off to?" he asked.

She forced herself to slow. "I was just anxious to get out of there before Sarah started grilling you like an overprotective parent. She's a great friend, but she can't get away from trying to, I don't know, mother me."

He smiled, an expression that transformed his face to such arresting handsomeness she felt warm clear to her toes. She looked away, afraid at any moment her mouth would drop open and she'd assume the vacant, adoring look of a smitten teen. That would be beyond mortifying. "Do you need to get your car?" he asked.

"I left my car at home and walked to work after the rally this morning," she said. "Parking can get very congested downtown and I figure I need the exercise."

"Where would you like to go for dinner?"

"There's a good Himalayan restaurant at the end of the block," she said.

"That sounds good."

The owner's wife greeted them at the door and, instead of seating them at one of the tables in the front room, led them to a secluded booth in the back of the restaurant. Did they really look so much like a couple on a date? Eve wondered.

"This is good," Grant said, sliding into the booth across from her. "It's quiet, so we can talk."

"Tell me about Toby Masterson," Eve said.

"Let's order first."

They decided on an assortment of small plates and

hot tea. Eve leaned back in her seat and cradled a cup of tea. "Well?"

"Toby Masterson really does know Dane Trask from Welcome Home Warriors, the veteran's organization Dane founded."

"Dane was very proud of the work WHW did to help veterans reintegrate into society," Eve said. "He worked very hard at it. But I never saw any sign that he was unbalanced, as Masterson claimed this morning. And he never acted particularly upset over us splitting up. He accepted it was never going to work out between us."

"Why was that?" Grant asked. "Why were you both so certain the relationship wouldn't work? After all, hadn't you been together three years?"

She stared into the teacup. Would it really matter if she told this man the truth? "I very much would like to have children," she said. "Dane wasn't interested. He helped raise his daughter, Audra, and he said he was done. He was very firm about that. If I wanted to stay with him, I'd have to give up my dreams of raising children and I wasn't willing to do that." She met his gaze. "I'm not willing to do that."

He nodded, his expression unreadable. At least he didn't express sympathy with Dane's position. "I never found any evidence of violent or unlawful behavior when I checked into Trask's background," he said. "I can't say the same for Masterson."

"What did you find?"

"Domestic violence charges on two occasions. That was two years ago, when he was first discharged from the army. He's had a clean record since them and took the job with TDC three months ago. Apparently, Trask recommended him for the position."

She sipped her tea. "That sounds like something Dane would do," she said. "He was always trying to find jobs for his guys—that's what he called the men and women who came to WHW for help." She set aside her cup and leaned across the table toward him. "That's another reason I don't think Dane just ran away on a whim. He felt a real sense of responsibility to the people in Welcome Home Warriors. He wouldn't run away and leave them in the lurch. If he left, it must have been because he felt he had no choice."

"Then why doesn't he come forward now and tell us his reasons?" There was no missing the annoyance in Grant's voice. "Why the mysterious messages and inflammatory press releases and other games?"

"I don't know," she said. "I wish I did."

A server delivered their meal, and they passed the next few minutes filling their plates from the various dishes. "This is very good," Grant said after the first few bites. "It's been a long time since I had Himalayan food."

"We have a lot of good restaurants for such a small town," she said. "Though probably not the variety you're used to in DC."

"It's nice to have someone to eat with," he said.

The warmth in his tone touched her. He really was a nice man. It wasn't his fault she was so conflicted over her relationship possibilities. "It is," she agreed.

"Tell me about your flower shop," he said. "How did you get started? I'm not asking as a cop, just because I'm interested."

She told him how she had started working part-time for another flower shop while she was still a reporter. "I was getting burned out on the job at the paper," she said. "The long hours and the horrible pay. The abuse you take from the people you're reporting on and sometimes from the readers, too. I was looking for something new and discovered I had a talent for growing plants and arranging flowers. And a good head for the business side, too. I took a few courses, and when the owner of the shop announced she was retiring, I wrote a business plan, got a small business loan, and turned in my resignation to the paper."

"You took a big risk."

"I've always believed if you weren't happy in your life, then it was up to you to take action to change it." It was why she had broken up with Dane. Why she was considering different ways to have the children she wanted so much. "I figured if things didn't work out, I could always find another job," she said. "Fortunately, things worked out. What about you? How did you end up with the FBI?"

"I worked in military intelligence. When I was discharged, the CIA recruited me, but I wanted to stick with the domestic side of law enforcement, which meant the FBI."

She savored a bite of saag paneer. "Do you like the work?"

"I don't like the politics, but every job has that, to some extent. I like working on cases, and putting some really bad people behind bars. It's important work and I have a talent for it."

He spoke matter-of-factly, not bragging, but not assuming false humility. "And now you're a commander," she said.

"It's different, since my team is made up of men and women from lots of different branches of law enforcement. But we're on our own out here, with a certain degree of independence that allows us to do our job without a lot of bureaucratic interference."

"You get to run the show the way you want." That was one of the things she appreciated about having her own business.

"More or less."

They finished the meal in companionable silence. When she looked up from her plate, she invariably found his eyes on her, but the knowledge didn't make her uncomfortable. When they had eaten their fill and were finishing the last of the tea, she turned her thoughts back to the information he had shared earlier. "If Toby Masterson approaches me again, should I talk to him about Dane?" she asked.

"That's up to you," Grant said. "But I wouldn't recommend engaging with the guy."

"Why did he even seek me out? What does he have to gain from that?"

"A place in the limelight. Or maybe he just wants to get your attention."

She laughed. "Telling me my old boyfriend is dangerous isn't the best pickup line I've ever heard. It could be the worst."

"He's probably harmless," Grant said. "But if he gives you any trouble, let me know."

"And what—you'll threaten to arrest him?"

"Harassing another person is a crime. I can remind him of that."

She could picture that reminder. Grant could look pretty fierce when he wanted to. "I'm sure that won't be necessary," she said.

When the bill came, he insisted on paying it, so she

left the tip. "It's a nice night," he said. "May I walk you home? I'll walk back for my car."

The request was so formal and old-fashioned. Sweet. "I'd like that," she said.

The streets were mostly empty this time of evening, most of the businesses closed for the day, and traffic was light. They left the main business district and strolled past neat bungalows and cottages, many with broad porches and gingerbread trim, painted in soft pastels. Lights glowed in windows and spilled in golden squares on flower beds blooming with daffodils and crocus. The days were starting to lengthen, though the early evening still held an icy chill. Grant shortened his stride to match hers, a companionable presence.

They stopped on a corner to wait for a light. When the signal changed, she started forward, but he pulled her back. "What's wrong?" she asked, startled.

"Across the street. Do you see him? Look out of the corner of your eye. Pretend to be looking at me."

She turned toward him, looking past him to where a man stood on the opposite corner, watching them. "Is that Toby Masterson?" she asked.

"He's been following us for a couple of blocks, staying back and in the shadows. I wasn't sure at first, but now I am."

"He lives in town. Maybe he's just out for a walk or..." Even as she said the words, she knew they weren't true. Something in Masterson's stance made a shiver run down her spine.

"Wait here," Grant said. "I'll be right back."

Before she could protest, he jogged across the street, against the light. Masterson turned away and tried to flee, but Grant caught up to him easily and grabbed his arm. Masterson resisted, but Grant held firm.

Eve waited until the light changed and crossed the street to join the two men. "What is going on?" she shouted over their raised voices.

"I told him to stop following you," Grant said.

"I just wanted a chance to talk to you," Masterson said. "To warn you again about Dane Trask. He's really dangerous."

Grant started to speak, but Eve sent him a quelling look. "Do you know where Dane is?" she asked. "Have you seen him in town? Have you seen him anywhere near me?"

"That's one of the things I want to talk to you about," Masterson said. "I haven't seen him, but I figure you have. He's probably been trying to get in touch with you."

"Why would Dane get in touch with me?"

"Because he hates you."

The words made her shiver again, but she couldn't believe him. "I haven't seen Dane," she said. "And he hasn't been in touch with me." No need to mention the press release and the deposit box key. That had been so cryptic it hadn't even seemed as if he was communicating with her. She was just a conduit for information he wanted to get out there.

"If he gets in touch with you, you need to let me know," Masterson said. "I can protect you."

"The police will protect her," Grant said.

"Right," Masterson sneered. He turned back to Eve. "Call the hotline number." He shoved a business card at her. "I'm in charge of that program and I'll see you get the protection you need."

"You need to leave now or I'll have you charged with harassment," Grant said.

"And I'll charge you with assault." But Masterson took a step back. "Watch your back, Eve," he said. "You think you know Dane, but you really don't."

He turned and jogged down the sidewalk away from them, disappearing into the dusk.

She stared at the card in her hand, numb. Grant put his arm around her. "Are you okay?" he asked.

"I'm fine." She shoved the card into her coat pocket. "That was just so…strange. Why would he be so certain Dane would want to get in touch with me? If he does, he has my personal and work numbers. He knows where I live. But all I've had is that envelope mailed to the flower shop. Dane might not even have sent it."

"His fingerprints were on the envelope and the press release," Grant said. "We checked."

She shivered, and his grip around her tightened. Comforting, not confining. "Let's get you home," he said.

He kept his arm around her all the way to her house. Once there, he waited while she unlocked the door. "I want to go inside and check around," he said. "Just to reassure us both."

"All right." She stepped back and let him precede her into the front room. He moved through the rooms quickly but deliberately, not commenting on anything he saw, though she had the sense he took in everything. "Does everything look all right to you?" he asked.

"Yes. And you're scaring me a little." She hugged her arms across her chest. "Why should there be anything wrong?"

"I'm just being overly cautious." He returned to

where she stood beside the front door and took her by the shoulders. "Being in law enforcement makes you reluctant to trust people's motives," he said. "It's a hazard of the job."

"Are you saying you don't trust me?"

"I don't trust Toby Masterson, and I don't trust Dane Trask. You—I trust you." His gaze searched her face, lingering on her lips.

She leaned into him, drawn by heat and masculinity and her own desire to be closer. To know more. When he dipped his head toward hers she rose up on tiptoe to meet him, her lips pressed to his. He slid his hand from her shoulders around to her back, and pulled her to him. The heat of contact seemed to melt into her, dissolving a stiffness she hadn't even known she'd been holding.

The gentleness of his kiss surprised and touched her, yet when she pressed for more, he responded with a skill and passion that made her sigh. Sensation danced from her lips through the rest of her, until the tips of her fingers tingled and her toes no longer felt the ground. He tasted of wine and spices, and smelled of a subtle aftershave and a fragrance all his own, warm and male and undeniably attractive. She dug her fingers into his shoulders, feeling muscle, and surrendered to the joy of the moment. How long had she been waiting for this and hadn't even realized?

He was the first to pull away, keeping hold of her but putting a little distance between them. "Are you sure you'll be okay alone?" he asked.

Was he hinting that he'd like to stay? As nice as that kiss had been, she wasn't ready for that yet. "I'll be fine," she said. "And thank you for everything."

"Thank you."

He bent his head again, but this time only brushed his lips to her cheek. Then he let himself out. She leaned against the closed door, smiling to herself when she thought she heard him whistle. Grant Sanderlin might be all wrong for her in the long run, but in this moment, he felt very right.

# Chapter Eight

"Something's very wrong with this picture," Grant said. He studied the map of the Ranger Brigade's territory, colored pins tracking locations where Dane Trask had supposedly been sighted. At least a dozen pins studded the map, scattered as much as a hundred miles apart.

"These are just the reports we thought were the most reliable," Officer Hudson said. "We set aside all the obvious outliers, like the woman who said she saw an old man with a dog hitchhiking along the highway just outside the entrance to Curecanti Recreation Area. Or the guy who was sure he saw a man disguised as a woman in a café near the lake."

"It doesn't seem likely that one man, traveling on foot, would have covered so much territory in the month he's been missing," Lieutenant Dance said.

"Lotte and I tried tracking around some of the sightings," Rand Knightbridge said, one hand on the head of his search and rescue dog. Lotte, a Belgian Malinois with black-tipped blond fur and brown eyes that looked as if they had been outlined in kohl, studied the map as intently as any of the human officers. "We didn't find anything. Every trail went cold."

"I put pressure on TDC to share any information

they received from their reward hotline," Officer Beck said. "They promised their full cooperation, but then they only turned over a handful of useless reports."

"Maybe that's all they've gotten," Dance said.

"Or maybe they're hoping to find Trask before we do," Beck said. "They strike me as very anxious to have him contained."

"Do you think he has some dirt on them?" Knightbridge asked.

"Don't you?" Beck asked.

"Unless you believe knowing Trask's motives for leaving will help us find him, let's focus this discussion more productively," Grant said. He picked up a pointer and indicated a spot on the national park's southeastern section. "The largest concentration of sightings is in this area," he said.

"It's one of the accessible areas of the park to the public," Dance said. "More people are going to equal more sightings or supposed sightings."

"Why would Trask stay in such a populated area?" Hud asked. "He's a former army ranger. Why not stay in the back country, and reduce the risk of discovery?"

"For a while someone—we assume Trask—was taking food from campers and leaving behind items as a form of payment," Beck said. "The items left have been identified as belonging to Trask."

"The last of those reports occurred ten days ago," Beck said. "Has Trask moved on?"

"He strikes me as too smart to leave any traces behind unless he wants us to see them," Hud said.

"I agree," Grant said. Previously, Trask had left behind items that seemed to be deliberate messages for law enforcement, though Grant wasn't sure they had interpreted all these communications correctly.

"We'll concentrate today's aerial search here." Grant drew a circle an approximate fifty-mile radius from where Trask's truck had crashed in the bottom of the Black Canyon of the Gunnison. "It's unlikely Trask was in that truck when it was driven or pushed into the canyon, so we'll focus our search above the canyon rim. We'll stay away from the campgrounds for now."

"The campground area has the most pins," Hud said.

"We'll be using FLIR to look for a heat signature of a human being," Dance said. The Forward Looking Infrared goggles could be used day or night, and would allow them to see a man who wasn't visible with the naked eye. "If we try that in the campground area, we'll just spot every camper and their dog."

"Trask might come into the campground for food," Grant said. "But I'm betting he's got a base set up somewhere close by but off the beaten path."

"If he's in a cave, you won't spot him," Knightbridge said.

"We may not spot him anyway," Grant said. "He could be anywhere out here, or he might have left the country. We just don't know. But we have to start somewhere."

He turned away from the map. "Dance is with me. Beck and Knightbridge, I want you to check out the complaint we got from the Forest Service about traffic through the State Wildlife Area. A car theft ring was using that area last year as a place to stash vehicles until they could part them out or ship them to Mexico. I want to make sure they aren't back in business. Hud, I want you to talk to Audra Trask. See if she's heard anything from her dad, or remembered anything that might help us locate him. Reynolds, are you still working on that antiquities act violation?"

"Yes, sir. I've traced the stolen items to a buyer in Dallas. I have a phone conference set up with him and an agent in Texas this morning." Theft of Native American and ancient peoples' artifacts was an ongoing problem in part of their territory, Grant had learned.

"Good." He checked the duty board. "Redhorse is off today and Reynolds is participating in Rigging for Rescue training over in Ouray. Spencer, you'll need to hold down the fort here."

"Yes, sir."

He could have sent Spencer or anyone else on this surveillance mission. A stack of paperwork several inches thick required his attention and there were those who would have said doing the legwork on a case wasn't the best use of his time. But he had taken a personal interest in this case, and he had never been one to spend all his time sitting behind his desk.

Or maybe it was only that he had a personal interest in Eve Shea. Finding Trask would set her mind at ease and maybe give the two of them a chance to move forward. Anything he could do to make that happen was time well spent in his book.

"You do realize that's the third time you've watered that ivy, don't you?"

Eve blinked at the puddle of water collecting at her feet. How long had she been standing here, drowning the poor plant? Embarrassed, she set aside the watering can and looked around for something to wipe up the spill.

"I've got it," Sarah said, and began tearing off paper towels and using them to blot the spill. "Everything okay with you?"

"I'm fine," Eve said, though in truth she was groggy from a lack of sleep. Her evening with Grant—and the kiss that had ended the night—had left her tossing and turning. If only he were younger. If only he wasn't already a father. If only, if only… When she had finally fallen asleep, she had been disturbed by dreams featuring the Ranger Brigade commander and Dane, facing off with swords in an arena full of spectators. By the time her alarm had gone off this morning, she had been anything but refreshed.

Sarah finished mopping up the water and stood. "Okay, I was going to keep quiet and not be my usual nosy self, but now I have to know. What happened on your date last night?"

It was a question she and Sarah had discussed dozens of times in the last six months. Eve had welcomed the chance to rehash and analyze her many dates.

But last night felt different. "It wasn't a date," she said. "He wanted to fill me in on some developments in the case."

"Sure he did." Sarah's smile produced deep dimples at the corners of her mouth. "That's why he showered and shaved and got dressed up to come see you in person instead of making a phone call."

Eve didn't try to argue. "We had a nice dinner at the Sherpa," she said.

Sarah nodded. "Okay. Not fancy, but good. Did you enjoy it?"

"It was all right." She stowed the watering can under the front counter and took out a roll of ribbon and scissors. With prom season just around the corner, it wouldn't hurt to get a head start on making corsage bows.

"Did he kiss you?"

The scissors slipped and she narrowly missed nicking her wrist. She'd sliced the ribbon crookedly, and focused on evening it up. "That's none of your business."

"Which must mean yes." Sarah didn't sound offended. "And since you have never balked at sharing details with me before, I think this man must be someone special."

"I hardly know him," Eve protested.

"The heart knows before the mind does, sometimes."

"Is that supposed to be profound?" Eve asked. "Because it doesn't even make sense."

Sarah smiled and disappeared into the back room. Eve glared after her. As much as she loved her friend, the woman could be insufferable.

The front door chimed and Cara Mead, dressed in a paisley wrap dress and chunky sandals, strolled in. "Cara, it's good to see you," Eve said, grateful as much for a reprieve from Sarah's questions as she was to see her friend. "Did you come to talk about flowers for your wedding?" Yesterday, Cara had asked if Eve could provide the flowers for her wedding to Ranger Brigade officer Jason Beck in the fall.

"I don't really have time today," Cara said. "But we should definitely make time soon. I'm hoping you'll have some ideas, because I'm drawing a blank."

"It helps to consider the season and your budget. And you might try keeping a notebook where you jot down ideas of things you've seen or read about, and you want to copy for your wedding."

Cara nodded. "I'll ask Jason what he thinks, too."

"Good idea." Some grooms wanted to be more involved in weddings these days. "If you didn't come to talk flowers, what else can I do for you?"

"I wanted to thank you for participating in our protest yesterday," Cara said. "It really helped with our numbers. It looked good on TV, and the higher-ups like that."

"I was glad to help," Eve said.

"I'm hoping I can persuade you to do another favor for me," Cara said, coming to stand across the front counter from Eve.

"Do you need a donation for a fundraiser?" Eve asked. "I could do that."

"That's very generous of you, but no," Cara said. "I need a volunteer. Someone to go up to the mine with me to collect soil, water and rock samples for testing."

"Is that legal?" Cara asked. "Isn't that private property?"

"I own stock in TDC," Cara said. "It was part of my compensation package. While the mine is private property, TDC is in charge of it while they're doing mitigation. As a TDC stockholder, I think I have a right to check their work."

"I'm not sure TDC would agree," Eve said.

"Probably not." She shrugged.

"What does Jason say?"

"I haven't told him I plan to collect more samples," she said. "I'm not sure he'd understand."

"I don't know," Eve said.

"Please!" Cara leaned closer, her voice lower. "I can't ask just anyone. It has to be someone I trust. And I really think this is important."

"Of course protecting the environment is important, but—"

"I don't mean for the environment," Cara said. "I mean for Dane. I think he discovered something at the Mary Lee that wasn't right, but when he tried to reveal his findings, his life was threatened and he had to go into hiding. If we can figure out what he found and go public with the information, Dane can come home."

Eve stared at the younger woman. The whole proposal sounded like some wild fantasy. "Dane wasn't the type to run from danger," she said. Then again, he had never struck her as the type to be vague or play silly games. Which made his recent behavior all the more baffling.

"Dane is smart," Cara said. "And resourceful. He's doing what he believes he has to do."

*Then I wish he'd leave me out of it*, Eve thought. But Cara had sparked her curiosity. "If I agree to help you, what do I have to do?" she asked.

"Go on a hike with me. I know a back way into the mine site. We'll slip in, collect the samples and be gone in a matter of minutes."

"Dane should have never involved either of us in this," Eve said. "I wish he hadn't."

"But he did," Cara said. "I think it's because he knew we would help him." She smiled. "Help me out and when he comes back home we'll both chew him out about it."

"Why are you so set on doing this?" Eve asked. "Do you think you'll get your old job back when Dane returns? Do you even want that?"

"I just…" Cara shook her head, then took a deep breath and said, "My brother was murdered in Houston—years ago. His murderer was never found, and as bad as losing him was, knowing I couldn't do anything to help him was worse. Now Dane is accused of all these things I don't believe he did. If there's something I can do to help him, I'm not going to pass up the chance."

"I'm sorry about your brother," Eve said. "But I can't help you." She would have done a lot for her former lover, but this was too much. And when she saw Dane again—and she had to believe she would—she would tell him so. Maybe they'd have a laugh about it.

Or maybe he would tell her she had let him down. It was a risk she was willing to take.

GRANT AND DANCE met the helicopter pilot at a crop-spraying outfit on the edge of town. When he wasn't spraying farmers' fields, the pilot subcontracted for the government for search and rescue, fire-spotting, and searches like this one.

"You've got a good clear day for this," the pilot said as they readied for takeoff.

Grant said nothing, merely kept his focus straight ahead, intent on breathing evenly. He had never enjoyed flying, and the sensation of hovering over the earth in what he couldn't help think of as a giant mechanical mosquito did nothing to ease his discomfort.

They soared out over rock canyons and alkaline washes, crossing into a landscape of pale green prairie dotted with clumps of dark green trees. Then suddenly, a dark gash split the earth below. The helicopter swung wide and they were over the canyon, a dark shape like a salamander winding beneath them, its legs side canyons, the thin sliver of the Gunnison River far below a silver stripe down its back.

"That's a sight I never get tired of," the pilot said in Grant's headset. "We're almost at your coordinates."

"I've got the FLIR ready," Dance said. "Do you want to take a look?"

Grant took the goggles and fit them on, and studied the images below. Swirls of colors swam in his vision, before taking shape like the patterns on a weather map. Dots of red scattered as the helicopter flew over—a herd of deer or antelope. He focused on another red dot, moving much slower along a dull yellow strip.

"Bicyclist, along the park road," Dance said, scanning with a pair of high-powered binoculars.

"Trask won't be along the road," Grant said. "Move out."

The helicopter turned, chased by its own shadow across more barren terrain now. For ten minutes they flew in a broad arc, but the goggles—and Dance's binoculars—registered no sign of life.

"Wait a minute, I've got something," Dance said from his position behind the pilot. "Not a person, but something that shouldn't be there. Can you bring us in a little lower?"

"Will do."

Grant's stomach lurched into his throat as the helicopter dropped. He pulled off the goggles and looked past the pilot as the aircraft tilted, giving him a view of what looked like a garbage dump.

"What is that?" Grant asked.

"Illegal dump site." Dance lowered the binoculars, scowling. "Looks like construction waste. You can see the track the trucks hauling it have cut across the ground." He indicated a route Grant had mistaken for a forest service road.

"Is that in the national park?" the pilot asked.

"It's in the recreation area," Dance said. "It wasn't there the last time I was in this sector."

"When was that?" Grant asked.

"Two and a half, maybe three months ago."

"Want to take another look?" the pilot asked.

"Michael?" Grant asked Dance.

"I've got a good idea of where it's located," Dance said. "We'll get more information on the ground."

"Take us back to base," Grant said. "I don't think the man we're looking for is here." They would need a tremendous amount of luck to find someone who didn't want to be found in this massive territory, but he had felt a flyover was worth a shot. Maybe Trask had seen them and realized they weren't going to give up looking for him.

Back at Ranger Brigade headquarters, Lieutenant Dance began organizing a team to collect evidence from the illegal dump site. "If we're lucky, whoever did this left something behind that will help us identify them. At the very least, we should be able to determine if this is an active site that they're still adding to. If that's the case, we can set up a stakeout to catch them."

Grant returned to his office to tackle some of the paperwork that was the inevitable burden of command. He had just opened a new file on his computer when his phone buzzed. "Commander Sanderlin."

"Pete McCabe, with the National Park," a deep voice said. "We've got a situation over here we need to pull you in on."

Grant sat up straighter. "What's the situation?"

"We've got a DB found on one of the trails. A woman, late twenties. Her throat's been cut."

"I'll send someone right over."

"Just so you know, I think this might relate to something you're already working on."

"How's that?"

"We found a business card clutched in the woman's hand. A card for Dane Trask."

# Chapter Nine

Grant looked down on the body of the young woman at the side of the trail. Arms flung back, lifeless eyes staring vacantly to the sky, it was hard to picture the beautiful, vibrant person she might have been. "The cut was made with a large-bladed knife, like a hunting knife." The medical examiner, a middle-aged woman with short blond hair, spoke matter-of-factly as she stripped off blue nitrile gloves. "No signs of trouble that I can see. Not even any scuff marks in the dirt. I think he surprised her from behind. She was probably dead before she had time to register what was happening."

Grant pictured it: the woman hiking along, admiring the scenery around her, the man seizing her, perhaps lifting her off her feet, slicing open her throat, then laying her out here beside the trail, as if on display. She lay in the shade, on a bed of pinion needles, their forest-fresh smell wafting up to mingle with the stench of death.

He turned to the park ranger beside him. McCabe was in his late fifties, his tanned face creased with fine lines, his hazel eyes almost lost in the many folds. "You said there was a business card?"

"Here." McCabe passed over a clear evidence bag.

The card inside was white, with a red-and-black logo for Welcome Home Warriors and the name Dane Trask, with a phone number, in black lettering underneath.

"Looks like Trask left this deliberately," McCabe said. "I don't know if he's taunting us or what."

Grant slipped the evidence bag with the card into his jacket and looked at the woman again. "Who is she?"

"Marsha Grandberry, aged twenty-two, a student at Western State, according to the ID in the wallet she had with her."

"Did she know Dane Trask?" Grant asked.

McCabe shrugged. "That's for you to find out."

Jason Beck, who had been talking to a small group of civilians gathered behind the barriers the park service had set up at the trailhead two miles back, came loping down the trail. "What have you got?" Grant asked.

"Her boyfriend and her best friend—her roommate, actually—are back there waiting," he said. "They came as soon as they got the word from one of the rangers. They both say Marsha didn't know Trask. She didn't have any connection to Welcome Home Warriors or to TDC Enterprises. She was studying botany and came here today to get some photos she needed for a presentation she was working on for a class." He had been avoiding looking at the body, but glanced that way now as two technicians lifted the shrouded figure onto a gurney. "Why would Trask kill her like that?"

"We don't know that the murderer was Trask," Grant said.

Beck nodded. "He must have handed out a lot of business cards. So you think someone is trying to make him look guilty?"

"This is an area of the park where we've had the

most sightings of Trask," McCabe said. "And the knife sounds like something a former army ranger would have."

"Anyone who's been following this case knows those things," Grant said. "But we also know that Trask is smart. He hasn't done anything I've seen so far without a reason."

"Like I told you, he left the card to taunt us," McCabe said. "He thinks he's smarter than law enforcement."

"He didn't have a reason to kill Marsha Grandberry," Beck said. "No one I've interviewed about him has mentioned anything about violence."

Toby Masterson had warned Eve that Trask was violent, but his accusations hadn't rung true to Grant. Still, he couldn't discard them. "We'll check the card for fingerprints and the body and the surroundings for any DNA or other evidence," he said. "We're not ruling out any suspect at this point."

He left Beck to oversee the forensics team and headed back down the trail to his waiting cruiser. Sun beat down on the back of his neck, and his boots crunched in the red gravel of the trail. If Trask had murdered this woman, a stranger to him, then he was indeed as dangerous as Masterson had warned. Was he a danger to Eve as well?

Grant needed to call and break this news to her before she read about it in the paper, and reiterate his warning for her to be careful.

Head down, preoccupied with these thoughts, he was startled to hear a woman's voice call his name.

"Grant!"

He jerked his head up as Eve jogged toward him. Her face was drawn with worry. "A colleague at the paper called to tell me he'd just heard the rangers found a woman murdered in the park." She gripped his arm, fingers digging into his muscle through the thick fabric of his jacket. "He said they think Dane killed her. That has to be wrong. He wouldn't do something like that."

Aware of people looking in their direction, some of them probably from the media, Grant put one hand at her back and steered her around to the passenger side of his cruiser. "Let's go to headquarters where we can talk privately," he said. "I'll bring you back to your car later." She didn't look in a fit state to drive right now. She slid into the passenger seat and buckled the safety belt, lips pressed tightly together, as if she was struggling to hold back a flood of words. That was one of the things he appreciated about Eve: she knew how to be patient, how to wait for the right time to speak, and she hadn't shown a tendency to jump to conclusions.

Indeed, she waited until they were in his office with the door closed before she spoke. "Dane wouldn't kill someone," she said. "Not unless it was in self-defense. Was this self-defense?"

Grant sat, not in the chair behind his desk, but in a side chair. He motioned for her to take the chair beside him. "This wasn't in self-defense," he said. "And don't ask for more details, because I can't tell you."

She visibly shuddered. "I don't want details. But do you really think Dane killed her? Why?"

He spoke slowly, choosing his words carefully. It was always a balance, giving those close to a case the information they wanted, and protecting evidence in a criminal case. "There was something left at the scene that might have belonged to Dane," he said. "It's one piece of what will eventually be a whole body of evidence. It doesn't mean Dane is guilty."

"But it doesn't mean he's innocent, either," she said. "And you don't have to speak so circumspectly. My reporter friend told me one of Dane's business cards was left on the body."

"How did he know that? Who is this reporter?" Anger tinged Grant's words.

"I'll give you his name, but don't be angry with him. He said an anonymous caller phoned the paper. He called the park and they confirmed they had found a dead woman, but wouldn't say more."

"What's his name?" Grant grabbed a pen and a pad of paper from the corner of his desk.

She gave him the name and phone number of her friend. "Do you think you can trace the call?" she asked.

"Probably not," he admitted. They would try, but a brief call, probably made from a cell phone, was unlikely to yield much information. "But we'll want to know exactly what was said, what the call sounded like, and things like that." So much of investigating a crime was collecting as much information as possible, never knowing which piece might be the one to complete the puzzle.

"Dane wouldn't kill someone," she said again. "And he certainly wouldn't call a reporter and brag about it. I was always after him to do more to promote Welcome Home Warriors in the media. The only time he ever sent out a press release about the group was when I wrote it for him. He really isn't someone who seeks the limelight."

"If I had asked you before all this happened, you would have said he wouldn't purposely wreck his truck, abandon his home and daughter to live in the wilderness, raiding campsites for food and sending cryptic messages about his former employer," Grant said.

"He isn't raiding campsites," she said. "Cara told me he always leaves something of value, which I think shows what an honest and honorable man he is."

Hearing her defend her former lover abraded Grant's nerves like sandpaper. "You didn't answer my question," he said. "You have to admit what Dane Trask has done is not normal behavior."

She bowed her head, hands clasped tightly in her lap. "No," she said softly. "It isn't. But that doesn't make him a murderer."

"We're going to do everything we can to find the person who did this," Grant said. "The right person."

She nodded, and sniffed. His chest tightened. Was she going to cry? Because of something he'd said?

But when she lifted her head, her eyes were dry. "Is there anything I can do to help?" she asked.

He hesitated, then slipped the evidence bag from his pocket and showed it to her. "Do you recognize this?" he asked.

She stared at the card, swallowed hard, then nodded. "Dane carried those with him everywhere." Her eyes met his. "He must have handed out hundreds of them. He gave them to every veteran he met, to families and friends of veterans, to potential employers, to donors. He even pinned them on bulletin boards and left them with tips at restaurants. He tried hard to directly reach people he could help, even though he resisted dealing with the media." She looked at the card again. "Anyone could have put that card there to throw suspicion on

Dane. But if he did kill that woman, he wouldn't leave his card. That's just stupid."

"Maybe he wanted us to know. Maybe he was taunting us, letting us know we'd never catch him."

"He wasn't like that." She sounded exhausted, her shoulders slumped. "I know you haven't seen evidence of that, but Dane was a really good man."

"If he was so good, why did you break up with him?"

He hadn't meant to speak the words out loud. Eve stared at him. "I told you why Dane and I split up. But maybe you don't believe me. Maybe you don't want to believe me." She stood.

He reached out, as if to stop her, but the look in her eyes froze him. "I'm sorry," he said. "I shouldn't have said that."

She turned away. "I'd better go now."

He stood also. "I'll take you back to your car."

"I'll ask one of your officers to do it. I'm sure you have more important work to do."

"I'll call you tonight," he said.

"Don't." She shook her head. "It would really be better if you didn't."

She walked out of the office, shutting the door firmly behind her. He stared after her, fury warring with shame. The one woman he'd met in forever he felt a true connection with, and he'd let stupid jealousy—over a man she was no longer with—ruin things. Was he forty-five or fourteen? He ran his fingers through his hair and dropped into the chair behind his desk. When he found Dane Trask, he was going to punch him. Or maybe Trask should punch him. It was a toss-up which would feel more deserved.

Two DAYS LATER, Eve stared at the headline on the front page of the local newspaper. HUNT FOR TRASK INTENSIFIES AS WOMAN FOUND MURDERED IN NATIONAL PARK. The story below the headline named Dane as the chief suspect in the death of Marsha Grandberry, a local college student. Eve felt sick as she read the details of the crime, and had to sit down.

For once she was alone in the shop, Sarah having taken the morning off for a dentist appointment. Of course her friend would ask questions about this latest development, but at least Eve would have time to absorb this new information and come up with some kind of response. But what could she possibly say? She and Dane were no longer close. She had no idea what was going through his mind these days. Was it possible he had snapped and was indeed responsible for a woman's death?

The bell connected to the front door sounded and she looked up, smile pasted on her face, prepared to greet a customer and pretend nothing out of the ordinary had happened. The smile dropped when she recognized Cara Mead. "You've seen the paper," Cara said, nodding at the sheets open on the counter in front of Eve.

"Yes, and I can't believe it," Eve said.

"You can't believe it because it isn't true," Cara said. "Dane wouldn't kill anyone, much less a woman he didn't know who wasn't hurting anyone." She slid onto the high stool at the front counter and dropped her purse to the floor beside her. "And all that nonsense about one of Dane's business cards being left behind. As if he's a complete idiot, or a homicidal maniac."

"I don't know what to think," Eve said.

"*I* think someone is trying to frame him," Cara said.

"Someone else killed that woman, in an area where Dane had been spotted, and left his business card—which anyone might have because we both know Dane handed out hundreds of the things—so that the police would think Dane was the killer."

"But why do that?" Eve asked.

"So the police would look harder for him? So that if they caught him they would be less likely to listen to anything he had to say." She leaned across the counter and spoke with a new urgency. "That's why we have to go back up to the Mary Lee Mine and get those samples. All the clues Dane has sent us point to something not right—maybe even downright criminal—going on up there. He's counting on us to prove him right."

"So he's letting us do his dirty work?" The bitterness in her voice startled Eve. She had thought she was over being angry or annoyed with Dane and his tendency to be so focused on what he wanted, and what he thought was right, even if others didn't agree. He wanted to go to Mexico on vacation and listed ten reasons why her desire to go to Hawaii instead was a bad idea. He didn't like seafood so they never went to seafood restaurants, even if there were other things on the menu he could have ordered. He had decided he didn't want children and her opinion didn't matter.

"He must have a good reason," Cara said. "Dane was never a coward."

True. Though he had his faults, Dane never backed down from a challenge. If he was wrong, he admitted it and apologized. And he had fought for his country, in some very dangerous places.

But that didn't mean she had to put herself in danger. "I'm sorry, but I don't think more samples are going to prove anything," she said. "We'd better leave this to the Ranger Brigade and local police."

Cara looked disappointed, but not particularly surprised. "Let me know if you change your mind," she said. "I can't just sit around and do nothing. I have to try to help."

"Good luck," Eve said. "But maybe, since Dane got himself into this mess—whatever it is—he's the only one who can get himself out."

## Chapter Ten

Grant surveyed the mounds of rubble scattered over half an acre of what had been, until recently, pristine wilderness. Broken concrete, old timbers, tons of rock ranging from fist-sized chunks to man-sized boulders, were scattered amid the stunted pinions and red rock formations. Deep ruts cut through the sagebrush showed the path of the trucks that had dumped the debris here. The sun beat down on it all, spring fast turning to summer here in the high desert.

"This has all been left here in the last month, I'm sure," Lieutenant Dance said. He nudged an irregular chunk of gray rock with one foot. "I did a patrol down the only road back in here about a month ago and I'm sure I would have noticed those tracks leading from it back here."

Jason Beck picked up a chunk of yellow-gray rock and examined it. "This looks like the same stuff that was at the Mary Lee Mine," he said.

"Wasn't some of that material radioactive?" Dance asked.

Beck tossed the rock aside. "It was. We ought to have this stuff tested."

"I don't know." Dance looked around. "Wasn't the

stuff at the mine just rock? This has wood and metal,
and I think there's even some Sheetrock over there." He
pointed toward the farthest mound. "This looks more
like construction debris than anything from a mine."

"So who would dump construction debris all the way
out here?" Grant asked. "It's a long way from town to
haul all of this."

"Bids for projects usually include the cost of dis-
posal," Dance said. "Landfills charge by the yard and
for a big project that can really add up. Dump the stuff
out here and you pocket the extra." He scowled. "And
the chances of anyone catching you in the act are slim
to none."

"Unfortunately, this kind of thing happens on public land all the time," Beck said. "Mostly it's just a bag
of household trash or a broken appliance. People don't
want to deal with it, so they dump it somewhere out of
the way and make it someone else's problem."

"It doesn't usually happen on this scale," Dance said.
"This goes way beyond a little littering."

"Maybe if we test it, we can determine where it came
from," Beck said.

"We can't test every rock," Dance argued.

"We'll test a few samples," Grant said. "But we don't
have the budget to test everything. I think our best bet
is to get officers to watch the area for a few days and
nights, patrol the area more frequently, maybe see if
we can get a camera or two out here and see if we can
come up with anything."

"They might be done dumping," Dance said.

"They might, but if they've gotten away with this so
far, they might decide to continue," Grant said. "They

might believe they've found a good way to make some extra money without a lot of hassle."

"If I find them, they'll know hassle," Dance said. "It's going to cost the government—in other words, taxpayers—a fortune to clean all this up."

"We'll hold off on cleanup for a bit," Grant said. "Let's see if the people responsible for this show up."

"I'll make a schedule for surveillance and see about setting up a couple of cameras," Dance said.

"I can find out who's got a big construction project going on in the area," Beck said. "This isn't a simple house build, unless it's a monster of a house."

"Good thinking," Grant said. He left Beck and Dance to hash out details while he returned to his cruiser. But he didn't leave right away. He pulled out some paperwork to complete, but sat with it resting beside him, as he stared out at the landscape of turreted stone and sage-covered hills. So different from any view he ever had in DC.

But then, he had wanted a change. A fresh start.

His thoughts turned to Eve. She could have no doubt how he felt about her after the kiss they had shared, but still she held back. He thought he knew why—despite her protests, she was still in love with Dane Trask. Even after his disappearing act, the manipulative SOB had his hold on her, getting her entangled in his troubles.

His radio crackled. "Commander?" Dance's voice emerged from the static.

"I hear you," Grant answered.

"Hang on a minute. I've got something you should see."

Grant looked up and thought he could make out a figure in the distance moving toward him. After a moment, he could recognize Dance, carrying something in one hand.

Grant stepped out of the cruiser to meet his officer. "We just found this up under some of the construction debris," Dance said. He held out a clear evidence pouch. In it was a torn, muddy piece of eight-and-a-half-by-eleven paper with a crude crayon drawing. Grant studied the figure in the drawing, which might have been a man or a monster or even a robot—red crayon tracing a boxy, broad-shouldered figure with an oversize head and a wild tangle of black hair. "It looks like a kid's drawing," he said, returning it to Dance.

"I don't think it came from a mine," Dance said. "There's a name on it." He pointed to a scribble in the corner that Grant hadn't picked up on. "Max" was scrawled in a pale green crayon.

"Log it in," Grant said. "Maybe we can connect it to someone." He opened the cruiser door. "Let me know if you find anything else like this."

"Yes, sir."

Dance went back to the search and Grant started the cruiser's engine. That kid's drawing had made the hairs on the back of his neck stand up. It was so out of place out here. He tried to shake off the feeling. That was the thing about this job. Do it long enough and pretty soon it was easy to see even something innocent as sinister.

Eve LOOKED UP from an anniversary arrangement she was finishing to greet the customer who had just walked in. She was surprised, and pleased, to see Audra Trask. Audra, Dane's twenty-three-year-old daughter, had her father's blue eyes, dark hair and delicate features that must have come from her mother. Audra had always been friendly and welcoming to Eve, never the stereo-type of the jealous only child. "It's so wonderful to see you," Eve said, coming out from behind the counter to embrace the younger woman.

"I've been meaning to stop by and say hello for months now and time keeps getting away from me," Audra said.

"I'm glad you finally made it," Eve said. "What have you been up to?"

"I've been super busy with the preschool." Audra ran a hand through her hair, though this did nothing to tame her thick mane. "That's why I'm here, actually. I need to order some flowers for our parents' luncheon on the twenty-first."

"I'm sure I can help you." Eve moved behind the counter once more and took out an order form. "Do you have something particular in mind?"

"No. I'm hoping you can help me decide."

"Tell me your budget and how many arrangements you're looking for and we'll see what we can come up with."

For the next half hour they looked through pho-tographs of possible arrangements and discussed the merits of carnations versus daisies, possible color com-binations and possible vases. Audra settled on six table arrangements in ceramic containers that resembled stacks of alphabet blocks, with yellow daisies, blue del-phinium and white carnations. "Those are going to be perfect," Audra declared as she signed the order forms. "And at the end of the luncheon, I'll give away the ar-rangements as door prizes. That way I won't have to worry about storing and moving those cute vases."

"You're moving?" Eve asked. She separated the multipart form and slid Audra's copy across to her.

"Only down the street. I'm going to have a brand-new facility, as part of the new elementary school."

"That's wonderful. When will you be moving?"

"We're supposed to be in the new place by the end of August." She folded the papers and slipped them into her purse. "I can't wait. Business has been good, so we could use the extra space. Hey, you should stop by some time and I'll give you a tour of the new place."

"I'd love that."

She expected Audra to say goodbye and leave, but the young woman lingered. "I guess you've heard all this stuff in the news about Dad," she said.

"Yes." Eve kept her expression guarded. "It's been a real shock."

"It's been horrible!" Audra hugged her arms across her middle. "I don't know why Dad disappeared, but whatever is going on, he's not a murderer. You know he isn't."

"I know," Eve agreed. No matter what scenario she put together in her mind, she could never come up with one in which Dane would cut the throat of a woman—especially one she was sure he didn't know.

"And all these stories I keep reading about Dad hiding out in the wilderness, stealing campers' food and stuff." Audra shook her head. "It's ridiculous. If Dad did run away, for whatever reason, why wouldn't he skip to the Caribbean or South America or something? Sure, he always liked hiking and camping, but nobody likes it that much."

Audra's indignation almost made Eve smile. "Have you heard from your father at all?" she asked.

"Not a word. Which kind of ticks me off when I think about it, you know? I mean, he slipped his admin, Cara, a couple of flash drives but he couldn't even drop me—his daughter—a note to let me know he's okay." She studied Eve. "Have you heard from him?"

"It wasn't like a personal note or anything," Eve said. "He sent me a press release accusing TDC of cutting corners with their mine mitigation project. I think he sent it to me because I used to work for the paper."

"Huh." Audra frowned. "This whole thing is just crazy. I'm worried about him and scared for him and I really don't have time for any of it."

"Exactly," Eve said. "I couldn't have said it better."

Audra flashed a brief smile. "Good. When he gets back, we can take turns yelling at him." She hitched her purse up higher on her shoulder. "I'd better get going. It was good to see you again."

"It was good to see you, too."

Audra left and Eve returned to work on the anniversary arrangement. When the doorbell sounded again, she expected it to be her customer, picking up his order, but when she looked up, she was startled to see Toby Masterson, all charismatic smile and rugged good looks.

"Hello, Eve," he said. He crossed to the front counter and rested both palms on the top. Heart pounding, she leaned away from him, determined not the show fear. "I think it's past time you and I had a little talk."

"I have nothing to say to you, Mr. Masterson." Eve said. She focused on the flower arrangement, doing her best to ignore him.

"Actually, I came in to buy some flowers," Masterson said.

Eve wasn't sure she believed him, but she would play along. "What can I get for you?" she asked.

"What do you think is appropriate for an apology?" he asked.

"Roses are a classic," she said. "Though it depends on the recipient and what he or she likes."

"What do you like?" he asked, moving closer, until only the counter separated them.

Eve forced herself to meet Masterson's gaze. "I don't like men who play games," she said. "Or those who lie to me. I especially don't like those who threaten me."

He held up both hands in a gesture of surrender. "Whoa. I never threatened you."

"You said Dane was a threat, which was just as bad."

"I'm sorry if I came on too strong the first couple of times we met." His smile turned ingratiating. "I tend to do that whenever I'm really passionate about a subject."

She didn't return the smile. "Apology accepted. Now I really do have to get back to work." She picked up a spike of lemon grass and pretended to study the arrangement in progress. But she was hyperaware of the man across the counter. She could smell the exotic fragrance of his cologne, mixed with a hint of mint. Chewing gum? A breath mint?

"I'd like to start over with you," he said. "The truth is, beautiful women always make me nervous."

It could have been the worst pickup line ever, but he managed to make it sound sincere. "What do you want, Mr. Masterson?" she asked.

"Toby," he said. "And really, all I want is to go out with you."

She stared at him. "Do you mean a date?"

"Yeah." He tucked both hands in the front pockets of

his jeans and rocked back on his heels. "To tell you the truth, I was always jealous of Dane. I saw him with you a couple of times and stupid as it sounds, I developed this big crush on you." He put a hand over his heart. "I really thought I was too old for that kind of thing, but I guess not." Another smile, endearing this time.

Eve had to admit, he was getting to her. "You saw me with Dane?"

"At Welcome Home Warriors headquarters. You didn't see me. I was just another guy in the background. But you just struck me right away as someone special. And I don't know—I thought he kind of took you for granted." He shrugged. "Maybe that was just wishful thinking on my part."

Dane had taken her for granted. It was one of the things they had argued about, at the end, after he had made it clear no one could change his mind about having more children.

"When I heard the two of you had broken up, I wasted months working up the nerve to ask you out myself," Masterson said. "And then Dane did his disappearing act and I got really worried about you."

"Dane had his faults, but he was never violent," she said. "Certainly not toward me."

"Well, you probably know him better than I did." He took his hands out of his pockets and rested them on the counter once more. "So will you give me another chance? Let me take you to dinner. One date. If it doesn't work out, I promise I'll take it like a man."

For some reason, his choice of words amused her. Still, she was reluctant to say yes.

Masterson's expression sobered. "You're not involved

with anyone, are you?" he asked. "That guy you were with the other night?"

The mention of Grant sent a pain through her. She was so attracted to him—and he was so wrong for her.

She remembered what Sarah had said about Eve having a type. Toby Masterson, with his rugged good looks and military background, was cut from the same cloth as Dane. Maybe she could be attracted to him if she let herself. And she had vowed to date anyone who asked her out until she found the man. "All right," she said. "I'll have dinner with you."

He grinned, and took a step back from the counter. "That's terrific. Is tomorrow night okay? I could pick you up at your place, or here."

"My place would be fine."

She gave him her address and he left the shop and almost swaggered down the sidewalk. Dane had walked like that sometimes, a man in command of his world.

She shouldn't think about Dane now, or whatever had gone wrong with his world. She was making a new life now. Maybe Toby Masterson could be a part of it.

MITCH RUFFINO REMINDED Grant of a scrappy terrier—the kind who growled at anyone who came near, and puffed up its hair to make itself as large as possible. While the vice president of TDC Enterprises didn't exactly growl when Grant entered his office, he did scowl, throw back his shoulders, and make it clear he didn't want this meeting to go on any longer than necessary. "Instead of wasting your time questioning me, you should be out there finding Dane Trask," he said. "The man is a thief and a murderer."

The Montrose County Sheriff's Department was investigating the embezzlement charges against Trask, so Grant was unfamiliar with the evidence in the case. The Ranger Brigade's investigation into the murder of Marsha Grandberry was stalled due to a lack of evidence. Whether or not Trask was the murderer, the Rangers were actively trying to find him because he was someone who had gone missing in their jurisdiction. "We are doing everything we can to locate Trask," he said, no contrition or apology in his tone. He was merely stating fact. And his next words, though some might have read them as conciliatory, held the same note of command. "It would be helpful if you would share whatever tips you've gleaned from your reward hotline."

"I doubt we've received anything that would be of use to you," Ruffino said.

"Nevertheless, I want to see what you have."

Ruffino made a motion as if he was shooing away a fly. "Of course. I'll get back to you on that."

Which wasn't exactly a promise to cooperate, but Grant wouldn't press. "Tell me about Dane Trask's work," he said.

Ruffino's nostrils flared, and Grant was reminded again of a dog. "What do you mean?" he asked.

"What exactly did he do? What was he working on before he disappeared? Who was he close to? How did he have access to the funds you're accusing him of embezzling?"

"I don't see that any of that is relevant." Ruffino tapped his fingertips impatiently on the desktop.

"I'm trying to get an idea of his frame of mind, and what might have triggered him to leave."

"You already know that," Ruffino said. "He left because he realized his theft had been discovered and he would soon be arrested. He ran like the coward he is."

"His military record isn't that of a coward," Grant said. Trask had received several commendations and silver and bronze stars during his military career. None of his actions even now struck Grant as those of a coward.

"Civilian life is very different from the military," Ruffino said, though Grant doubted the man had ever served. "But to answer your question, he was working on several projects for us, none of which could have been related to his disappearance. They were very routine. The kind of thing TDC does every day."

"Which projects, specifically?"

"I don't know offhand. I'll have to get back to you on that."

"Given your interest in Trask, I would have thought you would know exactly what he was working on before he left," Grant said.

Ruffino's gaze hardened. "Then you'd be wrong." He snatched a sheaf of papers from his in-box and tapped them pointedly on the desktop. "I'm a very busy man and I really can't help you. If I knew anything that could aid in finding Trask, he would be found—and in prison, where he belongs."

"Acting uncooperative is a good way to hide what you do know," Grant said. "But it's not a technique that works for very long." He took a step back, toward the door, but keeping his gaze fixed on Ruffino. "Whatever it is you don't want me to know, I'm going to find out. And I'm going to remember that you didn't want to tell me."

The tips of Ruffino's ears flared red, though the rest of his face was bone white. "I don't appreciate law enforcement trying to intimidate me," he said. "I will be filing a complaint with your superiors."

Grant nodded. "You have that right. But it won't stop me from digging."

Ruffino didn't answer, only glared at Grant until the latter turned and left. He had dealt with the vice president's type before—men used to stonewalling and throwing their weight around—until they ran into someone bigger and harder than they were. They would hide behind their power as long as they could, but in the end Grant would dig out their secrets. He couldn't tell yet if what Ruffino hid was criminal or merely venal, but he thought it might connect to Dane Trask, and that made it Grant's business.

He was halfway down the hall when a familiar figure stepped out of a door to his left. Toby Masterson stopped and watched his approach, his handsome face impassive. "What are you doing here, Commander?" he asked when Grant was even with him.

"My job," Grant said.

Masterson looked past Grant, toward the vice president's office, the only office at that end of the hallway. "Then that makes two of us."

Grant started to move on, but Masterson's next words stopped him. "Have you seen Eve lately?" Masterson asked.

"You stay away from Ms. Shea," Grant said.

"Or what? You'll have me arrested?" Masterson laughed.

"If you harass Ms. Shea, I will have you arrested," Grant said.

"Oh, I'm pretty sure she doesn't see my attentions as harassment." Masterson leaned against the doorjamb, arms folded across his chest. "But maybe I'll ask her when I take her to dinner tomorrow night."

Fury choked off Grant's words, at the same time his stomach clenched with nausea. Masterson's expression told him the words were no bluff. Eve, who had rejected Grant, had agreed to go out with Masterson, a man she had previously said she was afraid of. The truth of the situation might have buckled his knees if he hadn't braced himself.

He whirled and staggered away down the hall. It felt like a stagger, at least, though his steps were firm and even. Masterson's laughter trailed him all the way out of the building, long after it would have been possible to hear him.

Once safely in his cruiser, he let out a string of curses, forgetting his Lenten vow, forgetting everything but the pain that knifed at his heart.

# Chapter Eleven

Several times, Eve had almost called Toby to cancel their date. Only Sarah's encouragement had made her keep the obligation. "You're just jittery because he's so much like Dane," her friend had observed. "It's natural, because Dane really hurt you. But I think Toby is exactly your type. In fact, I think these nerves are your subconscience's way of telling you that."

Under other circumstances, Eve might have rolled her eyes at Sarah's logic, but what did she know? In the past six months she'd been on more dates than she could count where she felt exactly nothing for the man. Feeling something—even doubt—might indeed be a good sign.

Her fear eased a little when Masterson arrived, looked handsome and perfectly respectable in dark gray slacks, a dark gray shirt and polished black shoes. Exactly the kind of outfit Dane had favored. He surprised her by handing her a bouquet of dahlias and lilies. "I figure a woman who owns a florist's shop must love flowers," he said.

She buried her nose in the blossoms, touched by his thoughtfulness. "Don't worry," he added. "I didn't patronize one of your competitors. I stopped by after I was sure you had left for lunch and Sarah helped me pick out something. She said these were your favorites."

"Thank you," Eve said. "Let me put these in water and we can go."

When she returned from the kitchen, Toby was standing by the door, studying a small landscape painting that hung there. She glanced at her desk, a few feet to his right. Was it her imagination, or did the papers there look rearranged?

"You look lovely," he said, pulling her mind out of its paranoia. "Thanks for agreeing to go out with me."

"Thank you for asking."

The modest sedan he led her to surprised her—somehow she had pictured him on a motorcycle, or some expensive muscle car, or even a tricked-out pickup truck like Dane. *He's not Dane*, she reminded herself. That was a good thing.

He took her to a Mexican restaurant with candlelit tables around a central fountain. He was smart and funny and so different from her initial impression of him that she wondered how she could have been so wrong. Over margaritas and chiles rellenos with shrimp, they talked about books and travel, his childhood in California and hers in Oklahoma. By the time the server brought two servings of flan, she was warm and slightly buzzed and thoroughly charmed.

"If I do ever see Dane again, I'm going to have to thank him," he said, looking at her over the candles. "If it wasn't for him, I might never have met you."

She sighed. "I hope he comes home soon," she said. "If only to explain himself. Of all the people I might have guessed would do something like this—wrecking his truck, disappearing—I never, ever would have suspected Dane."

"I'd have said the same thing six months ago," Toby said. "But after you and he broke up, he changed. I think you broke his heart."

Some of the happy buzz faded. "No!" she protested. "It wasn't like that at all." If anything, she had been the one most hurt by the break-up, by the knowledge that Dane hadn't—and never could—love her enough to change his mind about having more children. More than once she had berated herself for holding on to such romantic, even fanciful notions, but she couldn't shake the belief that if Dane had truly loved her, he would have wanted to give her the one thing that would most make her happy. Instead, when she had suggested the split, he hadn't protested at all, merely agreed and started packing the things he kept at her house. That in itself was a kind of rejection.

"Maybe it was just coincidence, then." Toby scooped up a spoonful of flan. "But about that time he started behaving, well, erratic. Wild mood swings. Paranoia. I even wondered if he was on drugs."

"I can't believe it," she said.

"So he didn't give you any kind of a hint that something else was upsetting him?" Toby asked. "Something at work, maybe?"

"No. Dane liked his job, but he didn't talk about it much. I wouldn't have known what he was talking about anyway. None of that technical stuff interested me."

"So he never talked about the projects he was involved in? I'm surprised. I would have thought he'd want to share that with you."

She shook her head, and took a bite of flan, hoping that would ward off more questions.

"I don't guess he's been in touch with you since he went on the lam," Toby said.

This struck her as such an odd choice of words. She opened her mouth to change the subject but—maybe under the influence of that margarita—she said, "He sent me a letter about a week ago. Well, not really a letter. It was a press release, accusing TDC of falsifying reports or something. It was a wild accusation, with no proof behind it."

Toby sat up straighter. "What did you do with it?"

"I certainly didn't take it to the newspapers. It would have been completely irresponsible." She pushed away the half-finished dessert. "To tell you the truth, the whole thing ticked me off. As if Dane only wanted me to do his dirty work."

"Like I said, he had changed recently."

"I don't want to talk about Dane," she said. This was beginning to feel less like a romantic date and more like an interrogation.

Toby took her hand. "Of course not," he said. "Let's talk about what you would like to do now. We could go for a drink somewhere."

The last thing she needed was another drink. As the effects of the one—large—margarita began to subside, she could feel a headache coming on. "It's late," she said. "I think I'd better go home."

The warmth in his smile didn't waver. "Of course."

At her house, he got out of the car and escorted her up the walk. In the shadows before her front door, he pulled her close, and she didn't resist. She accepted his kiss, and did her best to respond, but even as his lips touched hers, she had a flash of tilting her head up to Grant, feeling his arms pull her close…

She shoved the memory away, and tried to focus on Toby. But the moment felt flat and mechanical. After a few seconds, she eased out of his grasp and he stepped back. "Thank you for a lovely evening," she said, then hurried into the house, disappointment replacing her earlier happiness. Maybe the problem wasn't with the men she dated; maybe the fault lay with her. She had a knack for falling for the wrong men.

THE DAYS WERE growing longer, the evenings less chill, so after work Saturday, Grant decided to go for a run. He hoped a jog along one of the park trails would clear his head and maybe help him come to some insight about this case. And the physical exercise might work off some of the anger and frustration that filled him every time he thought of Eve with Toby Masterson tonight. Logic told him he had no claim on the woman, but logic rarely triumphed over emotion, in his experience.

He changed into running clothes and shoes and set off down the same trail where Marsha Grandberry had been found, her throat cut, Trask's business card clutched in her hand. The crime scene tape and evidence markers had long since been cleared away, and at this time of day in the off-season, Grant had the trail to himself.

But the murder nagged at him like a rock in his shoe. Everything about the scenario felt wrong. Why would Trask kill a random woman he didn't know? There had been no sign of assault or robbery or any concurrent crime. The evidence pointed to a killer who had stepped out of the underbrush, killed the woman and left her for someone to find, with Dane Trask's business card clutched in her right hand.

It simply didn't fit with the picture Grant had of Dane Trask.

So, if he believed Dane Trask wasn't the murderer, that left the theory that someone else had killed the woman and tried to frame Trask.

But that theory presented plenty of problems, too, not the least of which was, why? The police were already looking for Trask, along with any number of private citizens hoping to cash in on the $25,000 reward offered by TDC. Did the killer think Marsha's death would put even more pressure on Trask? It probably had, but it was a weak motive for murder.

He jogged up the trail, gradually finding a rhythm, feet pounding the soft dirt, breath coming hard but regular and strong, heart pumping. He tried to settle into that zone, mind empty except for his focus on his next breath, his next step.

Something kept distracting him, a feeling that as empty as the landscape appeared, he wasn't alone out here.

He stopped, let his breathing slow, his heart rate return to normal. He took a drink from his water bottle and scanned the scrub oak on either side of the trail. Was that movement in the underbrush in the distance a rabbit or deer, or something more menacing? He knelt and checked the revolver holstered at his ankle, pretending to re-tie his shoe. He liked to think years on the job had given him good instincts, but he felt a little foolish. This place was so empty, but was the killer lurking out there? Was Dane Trask?

And, as impossible as it seemed to him, were Trask and the killer the same person?

He reached the three mile mark on his jog and turned to retrace his steps. Six miles was enough for one afternoon, and he wanted to get home in time to Face-Time with his daughters on the East Coast before too late at night.

By the time he reached the trailhead, orange and pink streaked the sky and the adjacent Black Canyon was already shrouded in darkness. Grant hit the button on his key fob to unlock the cruiser, then slid into the driver's seat. He started the engine and was about to back out when he noticed something stuck under the driver's side windshield wiper. He opened the door and leaned out to snag it, then stared at it, a cold feeling in his gut.

"Welcome Home Warriors," the card proclaimed in red lettering. "Dane Trask" was centered below this, in black letters, along with a phone number.

Grant flipped the card over. In bold black marker on the back of the card was a scrawled message: "I didn't do it."

## *Chapter Twelve*

Grant knew from long experience that cases rarely presented themselves as neatly or smoothly as depicted on television or in the movies. Most solutions came after long, frustrating slogs through piles of data and hundreds of hours of legwork. Many cases were never solved. Accepting this was part of the job, and one he had learned to deal with.

And then a string of seemingly unsolvable cases would come along to strip away all his calm indifference and frustrate him as if he was a rookie fresh from the academy. "We haven't had any luck tracking down the origin of the drawing we found at the dump site," Dance reported at the Wednesday morning meeting to review ongoing work. "We checked the rosters of all the preschools and elementary schools around town, but none of them have a Max registered. We showed the drawing around, but no one recognized it."

"As for the other debris, there's nothing we've found that ties it to any one location." Beck continued the report. "We think it might even be from several locations."

"Surveillance, both live and with cameras, hasn't turned up anything, either," Dance said.

"Unless you count deer, coyotes and one curious bear," Beck said.

"We think maybe whoever was using the site is done or got spooked and abandoned it," Dance concluded. "We'll continue to check regularly, but right now, we can't justify the resources, and the public lands people are agitating to get the place cleaned up."

"All right, but I want us to have someone there when they start hauling away stuff," Grant said. "Just in case anything turns up."

Beck made a face. "Let's hope it's not a body."

"Unless it's Dane Trask's body," Hud said. "That would solve a lot of problems."

"And create more," Officer Redhorse said.

"Speaking of Trask," Grant said, anxious to move things along. "After I spoke with Mitch Ruffino, TDC handed over some transcripts of calls to their reward hotline that were, essentially, useless." He glanced at his notes. "The usual collection of people who thought they might have seen Trask buying gas or in line at the movies, or hitchhiking out by the lake. None of them could give a solid description of the person they saw, and the descriptions they did give didn't really sound like Trask. One woman said she had seen Trask in a dream, at the bottom of the lake, playing poker with a redheaded woman and a man in a black hoodie."

Laughter traveled around the table. Grant waited for it to subside. "I have a feeling if they got anything less off the wall, TDC is keeping it to themselves. The vice president, Mitch Ruffino, made it clear he didn't want us poking into the company's business."

"I've always felt like they wanted to get to Trask before we did," Beck said.

"Because Trask has dirt on them they don't want us to know?" Knightbridge asked.

"That could be why he left in such a hurry to begin with," Beck said.

"But then why stick around?" Grant asked. "And don't say it's to see justice done, because if that was the case, he would have come straight to us and told us whatever he knew and let us take care of it."

"Commander, there's a call for you on line one." Sylvia's voice interrupted the conversation.

"Take a message and tell them I'll call back."

"Sir, she said to tell you it's your ex-wife and this is an emergency."

The bottom dropped out of his stomach at his words, and he snatched up the phone, aware of the others' eyes on him. "Angela? What's going on?"

"It's Janie. She's run away."

His vision blurred for a moment, and he had to remind himself to breathe. "Run away? When?"

"I found the note this morning. Apparently she left some time in the night. She said she's going to see you!"

A little bit of relief edged out the fear. He had imagined his younger daughter wandering the streets alone, or perhaps with the wrong kind of friends. Instead, she was headed to see him. But there were almost 2,000 miles between her mother's home and his, and a young girl on her own was so vulnerable. "How did she plan to get here? Did she fly?"

"I don't know," Angela snapped. "That's why I called you. You've got connections, haven't you? You can have police looking for her."

"Of course. Have you tried calling her phone? Or texting?"

"She doesn't have her phone with her."

"You mean she left it there? Why would she do that?"

"She doesn't have her phone because we took it away from her, as punishment for breaking her curfew last weekend." Angela sounded as if she was having to force out the words. "That was the punishment we all agreed on—break curfew and you lose your phone."

He wasn't going to argue about the punishment, or spend time finding out why Janie had broken curfew. "I'll start a search for her right away," he said. "Do you have any idea what she was wearing? What she took with her?"

He made notes of what she told him and promised to get back to her as soon as he knew anything. "Is everything all right?" Dance asked when Grant hung up the phone.

"My fifteen-year-old daughter decided she wanted to come see me and took off in the middle of the night," he said, somehow managing to keep his voice calm. "We need to find her before she gets into trouble."

"If you'll give me the description and photo, I'll put out a bulletin," Dance said.

Grant started to protest that he would take care of that, then thought better of it. The information would probably be better accepted coming from someone who wasn't so closely connected to the situation. "Thank you, Lieutenant," he said. "I'll text everything to you as soon as we're done here."

"I think we've got enough," Dance said. The others nodded.

They left and Dance stood by, waiting. "We'll find her," he said when Grant had given him all the information. "I know that doesn't really help you much." He offered a crooked smile. "My daughter is only nine months old. I can't imagine how I'd feel if she decided to head cross-country on her own."

Grant picked up the phone to call Angela and tell her he'd started the ball rolling, but instead found himself dialing Eve's number. "Hello?" she answered, sounding wary.

"Hi," he said. "I just…" He cleared his throat. "I just heard from my ex-wife that my younger daughter, Janie, decided to take off cross-country to see me. She left a note for my wife and went out sometime last night."

"Oh, Grant!" The words, so full of sympathy and understanding, made his eyes sting.

He swallowed hard. "We're going to find her," he said. "Law enforcement all along her probable route will be looking for her." He couldn't afford to believe they wouldn't spot her. They'd try the airlines, and the bus stations. Maybe the trains, too? He made a mental note to confer with Dance on that.

"Of course you'll find her," Eve said. "And she's your daughter, so she's smart and probably more aware of possible dangers than your average teenage girl. She'll be careful."

Was Janie more aware? It wasn't as if Grant had talked about his work much with the girls. When he had been with them, he tried to shelter them from the ugly side of what he did for a living. Had he talked to them enough about looking out for themselves and being safe? "We'll find her," he repeated. "And then I'll ground her. Maybe until she's eighteen." He forced a chuckle. "It's a good thing I only have two children. Otherwise, I might have even more gray hair."

"Let me know when she shows up," Eve said.

"I will. I just wanted you to know." He started to say

more, to ask about her date with Masterson, but stopped himself. That wasn't his business, was it, even though he couldn't stop himself from being concerned about her and her safety. "Thank you for that."

There didn't seem to be anything else to say. He ended the call and stared, unseeing, at the stacks of paperwork in his in-box. He wasn't having any luck finding a man who was hiding out practically under his nose in a national park. How was he going to find a girl who could be anywhere across two thousand miles of country?

EVE HUNG UP the phone, her stomach twisted in a knot. The pain in Grant's voice as he talked about his daughter had reverberated through her. But with it had come the pain of his last words. He was thankful he only had two children.

*This isn't about you*, she reminded herself. It was about a hurting father, and a daughter who wanted to be with him so badly she was risking a cross-country trip to see him. She said a prayer that Janie would be found safe, and very soon.

Sarah emerged from the back of the store, carrying an arrangement of daisies, delphinium and carnations in each hand. "These are the last two from the cooler," she said, and nestled each vase into a corrugated box designed to keep them from shifting during travel. "Are you sure you want to handle all of these by yourself?" There were six similar arrangements, requiring a series of large delivery boxes.

"If I need help, I'll recruit someone when I get to the school," Eve said. "It's been a long time since I visited and I want to see the new facility that's being built." She also didn't want to lose touch with Audra. Just because things hadn't worked out for Dane and Eve didn't mean Eve wanted to lose his daughter's friendship.

"Well, have fun," Sarah said. "I'll hold down the fort here and finish that batch of corsages." Orders for proms were coming in daily and, knowing the tendency of people, especially teenagers, to procrastinate, Sarah had suggested making up a quantity of corsages in advance that could be finished quickly with ribbon of the buyer's choice, for those who waited until the last minute to shop. It was yet another idea that made Eve pray Sarah wouldn't decide to one day leave and open her own flower shop.

Canyon Critters Preschool sat next door to a busy construction site five miles from the entrance to Black Canyon of the Gunnison National Park. A large sign proclaimed the site as the future home of Canyon Elementary. The small, squat building that housed the preschool was made of sand-colored stucco, which matched the surrounding rock uplifts, so that at first glance the school seemed carved out of the environment. As Eve parked her van near the back entrance, the sound of singing children reached her ears, high-pitched voices chanting the words of a half-forgotten nursery rhyme set to tinkling piano music.

Smiling to herself, she slid open the van's side door and retrieved a rolling cart, onto which she loaded the boxes of flowers. She maneuvered her awkward burden through the back door and down the hallway to an open room. A woman dressed all in red—red tights, red corduroy jumper and a red sweater—looked up from a copy machine. "Can I help you?" she asked.

"I'm looking for Audra," Eve said, and indicated the flowers. "I've brought the arrangements for the luncheon."

"Oh!" She closed the lid on the copier. "I'll get her." She scooted down the hall, a blur of crimson. Eve looked around the workroom, which was crammed with boxes of copy paper, stacks of picture books, foam mats, poster board, the copier, a worktable with a paper cutter and a stapler, and stacks of boxes with handwritten labels for Christmas, Halloween, the Fourth of July, and every other holiday Eve could think of.

"Please don't look, it's a horrible mess." Audra spoke from behind Eve.

Eve turned, smiling, to greet Audra. The woman in red flashed a smile, then squeezed past them to return to her copier. Audra and Eve embraced. "The flowers are beautiful!" Audra exclaimed. "Let me show you where to put them."

When they were well away from the copy room, Eve leaned over and asked. "Why is that woman dressed all in red?"

Audra laughed. "Her class is studying colors. She has an outfit for every color on their list. The children love it." She led the way down the hall to what was clearly a lunchroom, with labeled cubbies, stainless dispensers for milk and juice, and half a dozen large round tables surrounded by plastic chairs in primary colors. A white paper cloth draped the tables, and paper chains hung from the light fixtures overhead, bright and festive. "We'll just put one of these on each table," Audra said, lifting one of the arrangements from its protective cardboard.

"I can do that," Eve said. "I know you're probably busy."

"I'm always busy," Audra said. "But I could use a break. The parents won't arrive for another hour and these things always get me so keyed up, I need something physical to occupy the time."

"Then do you have time to show me your new building?" Eve asked, as she untangled another arrangement from its box. "I saw all the construction when I pulled in."

Audra made a face. "The construction has been a huge pain, but I keep reminding myself that in the end, it will be worth it."

They finished setting out the flowers and Audra stood back and admired the scene. "Everything looks wonderful," she said. "The parents will approve—or at least, most of them will, and that's really the best I can hope for. Some people simply can't be pleased. And the children will love it."

"Let me return this to the car," Eve said, indicating the cart and empty containers.

"I'll go with you and we can walk across to the construction site," Audra said.

The sun beat down, but with the soft warmth of spring, not the intense heat of summer. A light breeze stirred a field of yellow balsam across the street, and cooled the air further. "The day care and preschool are going to be at this end," Audra said, indicating the section of the building huddled up against a massive mound of red and yellow stone. "The back wall will actually be flush with the rock, so no windows there, but the construction superintendent tells me it's going to make for fantastic insulation. He says the design was a finalist for some kind of industry award, so I guess that's good."

They climbed a small hill and skirted around a section of chain-link fencing. "If anyone sees us, they'll yell about us being in here without hard hats," Audra said. "But I don't think they're working today. Actually, I haven't seen anyone over here all week, so I don't know what's up with that, but they're making great progress."

Metal girders and studs, like pieces of an erector set, rose from concrete piers that lined a deep excavation in the rock. Audra walked right up to the edge. "You should have seen all the rock they took out of here," she said. "It was crazy."

Eve stayed back from the edge, not being fond of heights. "The lunchroom and lockers will mostly be in the basement," Audra said. "With some offices and storage. The classrooms will all be up top, with plenty of light. Those rooms without a lot of windows will have skylights, so that everything is sunny and cheerful."

"It looks much larger than your current facility," Eve said.

"Oh, it will more than double our capacity," Audra said. "But they've apparently done studies and they think we'll need it. Lot of young families are moving into the two new developments going up nearby, hence the need for the new elementary school, and the younger children, including children of the teachers, will be able to enroll here. So it will be convenient for everyone."

"And profitable for you," Eve said.

Audra laughed. "That, too. I even accused my dad of pulling strings so that I got the contract for this space, so he wouldn't have to support me, but he denied everything."

"How could your father have influenced that?" Eve asked.

"Because this is one of TDC's projects. You didn't know?"

Eve shook her head. But then, what difference did it make? "I'm sure the fact that you were already here had something to do with the decision," she said. "That, and your school's wonderful reputation."

Audra beamed. "I am really proud of what we've accomplished here." She glanced around and her smile faded. "We'd better go. Somebody is coming and I don't want to get scolded."

She led the way around the fence, but as they started across the parking lot toward the preschool, Eve recognized a familiar figure emerging from the white car on the other side of the construction site. Toby Masterson looked their way and waved, then continued onto the site.

Audra returned the wave. "Do you know him?" Eve asked.

"He's Toby Masterson," she said. "He works for TDC. I'm not sure what his job title is, but he's been over here a lot lately." She shrugged. "He asked me out a couple of times. He's good-looking, but too old for me."

"When was this?"

"The most recent time was last week." She laughed. "I'll say one thing for him, he's persistent. But I'm really not interested in dating anyone right now, you know? Too much drama. I have enough going on in my life. Why?" She nudged Eve. "He is pretty hot. If you're interested in him, I'll put in a good word for you."

"No, that's okay."

Eve tried to push aside the sick feeling in her stomach as she drove back to town. It wasn't as if she and Toby had any sort of binding relationship. They had been on a single date. He was free to see anyone he wanted. Audra was young and beautiful—any man would be attracted to her. But the idea that he had pursued Audra at the same time he was pursuing Eve felt wrong somehow.

She had never had these kind of doubts about Grant. Was it because he was a law enforcement officer? No, she had never believed cops were less vulnerable to corruption than anyone else. But Grant had a way of making her forget her worries when she was with him. Only when they were apart did the worries creep in.

"Did you get to see the new school?" Sarah asked when Eve returned to the shop.

"Oh, yes. It's going to be beautiful. Lots more room." She collapsed and folded the flower carriers and returned them to the storeroom.

When she emerged again, Sarah was looking at her expectantly. "Anything else?" Sarah asked.

"I saw Toby Masterson while I was there." She hadn't meant to say it, but she couldn't keep the information to herself. Sarah would tell her if she was overreacting.

"At the preschool? Does he have children?"

"No, he was at the construction site. TDC is doing the build and I guess he has some role in that."

Sarah leaned across the counter, elbows propped, settling in for a long conversation. "You never said how your date went with him on Saturday," she said. "I've been trying to not be so nosy, but clearly, I'm a failure at that, so how was it?"

"It was okay," Eve said. She forced herself to supply the details her friend would want. "We went to that Mexican place on Main—Mariposa. It was really good."

"So the food was good—what about the companionship?"

"He was nice. Charming and funny. Considerate."

Sarah frowned. "Why do I sense a 'but' at the end of that sentence?"

Eve shrugged. "The evening was nice. But it wasn't special. Maybe I'm just too picky."

"Aww, honey." Sarah's expression softened. "You deserve special. We all do."

"After we saw Toby at the construction site just now, Audra told me he'd asked her out, too," Eve said. "She said he'd really pursued her."

"The way he pursued you." Sarah straightened, watching Eve carefully.

Eve nodded. "The thing is, as nice as the date was, I couldn't shake the feeling that he was trying to get information from me about Dane. Maybe that's why he wanted to go out with Audra, too." Talking about her feelings had helped clarify them, and she realized that this was what had been bothering her all along.

"I think you should trust your instincts," Sarah said.

They both looked up as the door chime sounded and a customer entered. "I'll take care of her," Sarah said. "You take some time to pull yourself together."

Eve nodded, though already she felt stronger, more certain that she was on to something. She went into her office and closed the door, then sat at the desk and dialed Cara's number.

"Hey, Eve!" Cara answered. "Please tell me you've changed your mind about going up to the Mary Lee Mine with me."

"No, but there's something else I needed to talk to you about," Eve said.

"What is it?"

"Do you know a man named Toby Masterson?"

"Yeah, I know Toby," Cara said. "Why are you asking?"

"Did he ever ask you out? Recently? Since Dane disappeared."

"He did! How did you know?"

"Because he asked me out." She didn't mention she'd actually had dinner with him. "And Audra. I think he's trying to find out information about Dane."

"He didn't get anything from me. And he backed off pretty quick when I pointed out that I'm engaged to an officer with the Ranger Brigade. He probably wants to pick our brains so he can collect that $25,000 reward for finding Dane."

"Did you know Toby at TDC?"

"Only vaguely. I know Dane got him the job there, and that they met through Welcome Home Warriors. But I don't really know anything about him."

Eve sighed. So much for thinking Toby was interested in her for herself.

"You sure I can't persuade you to go with me to the Mary Lee?" Cara asked. "I really don't want to go by myself."

She still didn't want to go, but she believed women ought to stick up for each other. Maybe the three women in Dane's life needed to do that more than most. "All right," she said. "But it's going to be a few days before my schedule is clear. I'll let you know."

"Whenever you're ready. Thanks so much."

Eve waited until the shop closed that evening before

she retreated to her office once more and punched in Grant's number. He answered right away. "Have you heard anything from Janie?" Eve asked.

"Not yet." The strain in his voice was heartbreaking.

"Someone will spot her," she said. "We can't give up hope."

"I appreciate the sentiment," he said. "It was good of you to call."

"I wanted to know about Janie, but there's something else, too. Something I need to talk to you about."

"What is it?"

"I don't really want to say over the phone. Can we meet somewhere?"

"Is this about Dane?" he asked.

"It may be connected."

"I'm pretty lousy company right now," he said. "And I don't feel like going out to a restaurant. Can I stop by your house?"

"That would be perfect." She didn't really feel like talking about this in public, either, in case she broke down and embarrassed them both. She hadn't done anything to be ashamed of, but the knowledge that she had, once again, misjudged a man made her feel vulnerable.

*Chapter Thirteen*

Grant parked in the driveway behind Eve's sedan, again noting the Eve's Garden logo on each side of the car. Red, pink and gold tulips bloomed in the beds in front of the house, lilacs budding behind them. The flowers made the house look like a home, simple and welcoming.

Exhaustion made every step drag, but he forced himself to stand straight and tried to look alert as he rang the doorbell. As much as he wanted to unburden himself to Eve, he was here in a professional capacity. He'd focus on whatever it was she had to tell him that related to his case.

But when the door opened, she took one look at him and held out her arms. He went to her and when her arms tightened around him, the comfort in the gesture left him too moved to speak.

She led him inside, poured a glass of wine and set it and a plate of cheese and crackers in front of him. "I bet you've hardly eaten all day," she said. "And you don't look as if you slept much last night."

"I can't sleep, between worrying about Janie and wondering what got into her head that she decided to do such a foolish thing."

"Fifteen-year-olds behave foolishly," she said. "So do fifty-year-olds, sometimes. So do we all."

He nodded, and sipped the wine, some of the tightness in his stomach easing.

"Tell me what you're doing to find her," she said. "Maybe that will help."

"We've sent Amber alerts, with her picture and description, all over the country, and we've contacted all the airports and bus and train stations, too. We've distributed flyers and I've contacted every law enforcement officer I know personally all over the country and asked for their help."

"Then you have a lot of good people looking for her," she said. "And she didn't just leave to wander the streets. She isn't hiding, not wanting to be found. She's headed here, to see you. So they're going to find her."

He nodded. Everything she said made sense to the part of him that was a law enforcement officer.

The part of him that was father to a headstrong girl wasn't so easily persuaded. "I'm frustrated that I can't do more from this distance. I want to go out and personally look for her."

"You need to be here," she said. "Waiting in case she shows up."

He drank more wine. "Her mother blames me. Her sister does, too. None of them were happy about me coming here to take this job. But they weren't that happy with me when I lived in DC either." Whatever he had done, it had never been enough for them, he realized. "What is it you wanted to talk about?" he asked.

"I don't think you're going to like what I have to say." She sat hunched, hands on her knees.

"I know you went out with Toby Masterson Saturday night," he said.

She straightened. "How did you know that?"

"I ran into Masterson at TDC on Friday and he made a point to tell me." He helped himself to a slice of cheese and some crackers.

She didn't like that, he could tell. He ate and sipped the wine, watching her. "How was the date?" he asked after a while.

She shrugged. "I should have listened to my initial instincts and turned him down again."

He sat forward, temper rising. "Did he do anything—?"

"No, no. He was a gentleman. But I knew from the first he wasn't right for me."

"Then why did you go out with him?"

She looked away, cheeks slightly flushed. "You're going to think it's really silly."

"Try me."

"After I broke up with Dane, I had this sense of time running out. I'm thirty-six years old. I really want to have a family. A husband and children if possible, but if not, I intend to have children on my own." He didn't miss the lift of her chin, and the note of defiance in her voice.

"There's nothing silly about that," he said.

"That's not the silly part. I told myself that I owed it to myself to do everything I could to find the right man. So I vowed to go out with anyone who asked me. Provided they weren't married or had some other big warning flag against them. I registered with a couple of online sites and I've pretty much stuck with that plan. I've dated a lot of men in the last six months."

"But you haven't found the right one."

"No. And sometimes I get discouraged, but since I couldn't put my finger on any one thing that was wrong with Masterson, I told myself he deserved one chance. After all, what was one date?"

"But now you feel differently." He kept his voice even. Dispassionate. "Why is that?"

"The date was fine at first. I was having a good time, even. But then Toby started asking me about Dane. Why did I think he disappeared? What did the two of us talk about? Did he talk about his work? Had he been in touch with me since he disappeared?"

"He was probing you for information."

"Yes. And then, this morning, I delivered some flowers to the preschool run by Audra Trask, Dane's daughter. She took me next door to show me the site where TDC is building a new elementary school, with attached preschool, which Audra will run. While we were there, Toby Masterson drove up. He didn't speak, but he waved. When I asked Audra if she knew him, she said yes, that he had asked her out several times, as recently as last week. She turned him down but, I don't know, it just didn't sit right with me." She shook her head. "So when I got back to the shop, I called Cara Mead."

"Trask's administrative assistant."

"Yes. And she said Trask had asked *her* out, too. Then I was sure his interest wasn't so much in the three of us, but in what we could tell him about Dane."

"Maybe he's after the reward money."

"He probably is. But it feels like there's something more there than that. After all, he had a relationship with Dane through Welcome Home Warriors. When Toby talks about Dane, I get a sense he feels, I don't know, betrayed or something." She shrugged. "I don't know why I'm telling you this, I just felt you ought to know."

"I appreciate it." He set aside his empty wineglass. "It's good to see you again."

She moved in beside him and took his hand, her skin soft and cool against his own, the soft fragrance of her perfume tickling his senses. "It feels good to be with you, too." She leaned in and kissed him.

Her lips were soft and warm, and she tasted of wine and something faintly sweet, though maybe that was merely his imagination translating his emotions to physical sensation. He slid his arms around her and she pressed against him, the tips of her breasts brushing his chest, vanquishing the weariness that had dragged at him like chains.

She opened her mouth against his and clasped him tighter. He responded by deepening the kiss, trailing his hand down her spine, then stroking the sides of her breasts. He wanted her so fiercely he feared losing control, and wondered if it would better for both of them if he left now.

But he remained fixed in place, kissing and touching, united by longing and joy.

"Come to bed with me," she whispered. "Make love to me. Now."

For a moment he wondered if his imagination had conjured the words. He broke the kiss and looked into her eyes, and found desire as strong as his own reflected back to him. "You're sure?" he asked.

She nodded. "Oh yes."

He wasn't a man who had to be asked twice. He stood, still holding her hand, and let her lead him to her room.

EVE MOVED WITH a floating sensation, buoyed by desire—and the heady sensation of taking control. Exactly
what felt right. For the past six months—longer even—
she had made decisions based on what she wanted for
the future.

Tonight, she was doing what she wanted for now. She
wanted to be with Grant. To feel his arms around her,
her body entwined with his. To take and give pleasure
and savor every sensation without analysis or hesitation.

In the bedroom, she switched on several small lamps,
which cast a soft glow in the corners of the room and
beside the bed, a simple queen-size mattress and old-
fashioned iron frame, topped with a white coverlet. She
began to undress slowly. He sat on the edge of the bed
and watched. She ignored him, trying not to feel self-
conscious, aware of his eyes burning into her.

When she was naked, she walked to the bed and
slipped under the covers. Only then did he undress, revealing a body that was every bit as sturdy and muscular as she had anticipated. She felt the power in that
body when he crawled into bed beside her and pulled
her into his arms, and reveled in the feel of his taut,
bare flesh sliding against her own.

Neither spoke, yet she felt an intense communica-
tion between them, as he caught and held her gaze, then
began to trace the contours of her body with one hand,
the other cradling her head. She had the sense that he
was memorizing her, learning her the way a blind man
might learn unfamiliar terrain.

He shaped his hand to her breast, and when she
sucked in her breath as his palm brushed her nipple,
he asked, in a hushed voice, "Do you like that?"

"Yes."

He bent and took her in his mouth, and she let out a groan—not of pain, but of pleasure.

Every movement was like that—exploration, discovery, deeper exploration. She followed his lead and began her own expeditions, learning the taste of his skin and the sensitivity of each inch of flesh. Her body hummed with heat and trembled with wanting, impatient for completion yet wanting this sense of being the center of his focus to never end.

By the time he accepted the condom she handed him and unwrapped it, she thought she could hardly bear more pleasure. And then he filled her and she forgot everything that had come before, as he stroked her with one hand, while steadying himself to thrust and withdraw, exquisite friction stoking the fire within until she exploded in light and heat.

He stilled for a moment, as sensation coursed through her in waves. Only when she was still, panting beneath him, did he begin to move again, stronger and deeper, until a second climax like the aftershock of an earthquake shook her, and he cried out with his own release.

Afterwards they slept in each other's arms, the sleep of two people who had no room left to worry about any heartache the future might bring.

# Chapter Fourteen

Grant woke to a buzzing noise, persistent and out of place. He didn't want to open his eyes and spoil this pleasant, floating feeling of such peace.

"Grant, your phone." Eve's voice, soft in his ear. She was part of his dream. She nudged his side. "Maybe you'd better answer it."

He opened his eyes, and stared into her face, still soft with sleep, her hair mussed, eyes a little puffy. Yet she was the most beautiful sight to wake up to. He smiled, and she smiled, too. "Your phone," she prompted.

He shoved himself up and turned toward the bedside table, where the phone danced in a circle, like a bumblebee stuck in a flower. The bedside clock showed 7:10 a.m. Too early for a routine call. He snatched up the phone. "Hello?"

"Grant Sanderlin?"

"This is he," Grant said.

"Bryce Larkin, Philadelphia PD."

"What can I do for you, Officer Larkin?"

"I think we may have found your daughter. Or at least, we have a good idea of where she is."

All remnants of sleep vanished. Grant sat up on the

side of the bed, heart pounding hard. "Where is she? Is she all right?"

Eve moved in behind him, one hand on his shoulder. The contact made him feel steadier.

"She took the bus from here, headed for Grand Junction, Colorado. Right now she's probably somewhere south of Salina, Kansas."

Relief flooded him, making him weak. He cleared his throat. "Have you spoken to her?"

"No, but we were able to talk to the bus driver and he says she's fine. He's agreed to keep an eye on her until his next stop, which is Denver. I'm calling to see what you want to do then. You could have someone pick her up in Denver, or the bus company people have agreed to keep tabs on her until she reaches Grand Junction. You could pick her up there."

His first impulse was to drive to Denver, to see Janie that much sooner. But his sense of duty told him to stay here, with his active case, and trust others to look after his daughter. "Grand Junction," he said. "If you're sure they'll keep track of her."

"I spoke to one of the head honchos and he promised to put a priority on this. As it was, we were able to track her down because when she bought her ticket, the agent was suspicious and made her fill out her full name and address. She didn't even try to lie."

Grant laughed, as much from relief as anything else. "Thanks for everything."

Larkin gave him the name and number of his contact with the bus company. After Grant talked to the man, he felt much better. He double-checked the arrival time of the bus in Grand Junction and made a note in his phone calendar.

Eve rested her head on his shoulder. "Thank God she's okay," she said.

"How did she get from DC to Philadelphia?" he wondered. "We're going to have a long talk when she gets here."

"When will she be here?" Eve asked.

"I'm going to meet her when the bus gets in a little after five in the morning." He turned and pulled her into his arms. "I want you to meet her while she's here."

Her body tensed. "Do you think that's a good idea? I mean…won't it confuse her, or set up expectations?" She bit her lip, her eyes downcast.

The warmth of the previous night began to seep away. *What about my expectations?* he wanted to say. *Are you telling me I shouldn't have any?* "You're my friend," he said. "That's all she needs to know." He tried for a more cheerful tone. "You can't blame a father for wanting to show off his girl."

She smiled, and if the expression was a little forced, he chose not to see it. "Of course," she said. "I'll look forward to meeting her."

Relationships—and even relationships that didn't happen—were full of complications. Navigating them was one of the givens of adulthood. And as much as he would have liked to stay in bed and make love to her all day, he stood. "I should probably get dressed and head to the office. I have a lot to do. You probably do, too."

She nodded, and pulled the sheets around her, covering her body as if to say it was off-limits to him now. Why? It was only one of many questions he wanted to ask her, but now was not the time or place for such a discussion. People said all the time that the key to a strong relationship was discussion, but they rarely mentioned how hard it was to make the time for complicated conversations, or how impossible it could feel to find the right words—words that healed rather than hurt, that mended rather than made the rifts worse. Most people weren't cowards, but they all had the instincts to protect themselves from hurt.

AFTER GRANT HAD LEFT, Eve telephoned Cara. "If you're still determined to go out to that mine, I can go with you today," she said. Better to do something active than to sit at home fretting about Grant and his daughter and life in general.

"Yes! I'd love that," Cara said. "And thank you. Thank you so much."

They agreed to meet at Cara's office at one. Eve spent the morning in the flower shop. When Sarah came in at noon, she took one look at Eve and said, "What happened to you?"

"What are you talking about?"

"You just look…different. Happier."

Eve laughed. She was not happy. She was miserable. Grant's phone call first thing this morning about his daughter had brought her crashing back to the reality that he was a man with two children who didn't want more. She felt like the butt of a very mean-spirited joke on the part of the universe. "Nothing has happened to me," she said. "Except we've been really busy. Your idea to make prom corsages ahead of time was genius, but I'm afraid we might even run out of them." She went over the tasks that needed doing that afternoon, then excused herself to meet Cara before Sarah probed further.

Cara greeted Eve with her usual enthusiasm and agreed to drive to the mine, in a truck that turned out to belong to her fiancé, Ranger Officer Jason Beck. "Are you planning to tell Jason about this?" Eve asked as they headed out of town.

"I'm going to tell him tonight," Cara said. "He won't like it, but there's not a lot he can say after the fact. I think he's accepted that, even after we're married, I'm going to do what I think is important. He doesn't seem overly bothered by the idea."

"Times have changed," Eve said. "I remember my father objecting to a trip my mother had planned with friends and she ended up canceling. She said that kind of compromise was part of marriage, but I couldn't help thinking she was the one who always compromised. And my grandfather used to tell my grandmother what to cook for dinner and where she had to shop. And she went right along with it."

"Of course compromise is important," Cara said. "But it's better to work out things together than for one person to be expected to give in."

Eve wanted the chance to build that kind of partnership. As much as she wanted children, marriage was so much more than that. And yes, she wanted it all—love and companionship and a family and a partner for life. Anything less felt like settling. She had tried to explain all that to Dane, but she didn't think he had understood.

"Have you set a wedding date?" she asked.

Cara shook her head. "We know we'd like it to be in the fall, but we haven't pinned down an exact date yet. We want to plan a trip to New Hampshire to meet Jason's parents. And we want to wait until after everything with Dane is resolved. The investigation is demanding so much of Jason's time. I understand that isn't going to change—that's his job. But with my connection with Dane—we'd just like to have it behind us."

"I understand," Eve said. In a way, her own life felt on hold until Dane resurfaced, or they at least had some explanation for his behavior.

"Hang on, this part gets a little bumpy," Cara said, turning off onto a steep gravel road. They were in the Curecanti Wilderness now, a landscape of yellow and red rock, stunted pinion trees and silvery sagebrush. It looked so barren, and yet as they trundled over the rough road, Eve could make out wildflowers—yellow daisies, red paintbrushes and pink primroses—amid the weeds. Cattle and deer grazed in the distance and a red-tailed hawk wheeled overhead.

They turned off again, onto a narrower gravel road that Eve remembered from when she had attended the protest rally at the mine. That day she had traveled to the mine with six other people crammed into an SUV, everyone chattering and laughing and discussing the plans for the protest. All conversation had ceased when they turned off onto this road, however, since it was so bone-jarringly rough. It was all they could do to hold on and keep from being tossed out of their seats, despite their safety belts.

"Wow, they've really done a lot of work on this road," Cara said as the truck ground up the steep grade. Gravel ticked against the undercarriage as the tires found purchase, but gone were the deep ruts and head-sized rocks they had been forced to navigate before.

"We'll have to park outside the gate, out of sight of the security cameras, and hike in," Cara said. "But don't worry. I know the back way in. We'll get in, collect the samples, and be out in under half an hour."

The nerves that had been hiding beneath their happy conversation now reared up like a monster that had been lying in wait. "Didn't I hear something about you getting shot at one time when you came up here?"

"That was a long time ago," she said. "When I still worked at TDC. The people who shot at me and Jason are behind bars now. They weren't trying to kill us, anyway. They were only trying to scare us off."

Cara talked as if this had happened years ago, instead of only last month. "I'm just a little worried about trespassing," Eve said. "Especially if there are cameras."

"Don't worry. There aren't any cameras where we're going. I checked when we were here for the protest."

They could see the gate now, a massive structure, with tall iron bars extending ten feet on either side of the road. Cara stopped the truck and shifted into Reverse. "The place where we need to park is just back there," she said.

"Wait a minute." Eve craned her head forward to look. "That gate is open."

Cara looked. "Hmm," she said, but continued to back up, turning sharply to take the truck into a gap in the brush, where it would be almost hidden from anyone who didn't know it was there.

They climbed out of the truck, and Cara put on the backpack that contained the sample containers and some other things they might need. She handed Eve a bottle of water and they started into the woods, keeping well away of the open gate and the camera they could clearly see mounted on a post beside it.

After ten minutes of rough hiking, Cara stopped to get her bearings, then turned uphill. "It's just a little way through here," she said.

The ground, though uneven, wasn't too steep, and there was plenty of room to walk between clumps of sagebrush and scrub oak. The air smelled of sage and warmed earth, and if not for the tension that made her jump at every snapped twig or tumbled rock, Eve might have enjoyed herself.

"It's just up here," Cara said, striking out toward a stretch of barbed wire fencing. She looked all around and, apparently satisfied there was no one to see them, stepped on the lower strand of wire and lifted up the top strand. "Go ahead through."

Eve hesitated. "Go on," Cara urged. "We don't want to stand around here too long."

Eve ducked under, then turned to hold the wire for Cara. Her friend led the way along the fence until they came to a cleared area. Cara stopped. "This can't be right," she said.

"What's wrong?" Eve asked, keeping her voice to just above a whisper.

"This doesn't even look like the same place," Cara said.

Before them lay a neat expanse of green interspersed with newly planted saplings, each tree carefully outlined with a little rock wall. Wood chip paths and two iron-and-wood benches added to the feel of a park. "When I was here before—even as recently as the day of the protest—this was all a jumble of rock and tree trunks and old timbers and mining equipment," Cara said. "Not just a few rocks, but a mountain of them. Truckloads and truckloads full."

"Where did it go?" Cara asked.

"They must have hauled it away." She moved forward, down one of the paths. Far ahead they could make out a little stone building. "I remember that building," Cara said. "But nothing else looks the same."

She shook her head. "This whole place is creeping me out. Let's get our samples and leave."

They managed to scrape up enough dirt and gravel to fill two sample bottles, and added water from the creek to a third. Eve wasn't optimistic they would find anything out of the ordinary, but she didn't mention that to Cara, who seemed so upset. "They were supposed to be cleaning up the mine waste, right?" Eve asked.

"Yes, but how could they have done all of this so quickly?" Cara said.

"I'm not sure I understand why you're so upset," Eve said when they were safely back in the truck.

"Dane sent me here because his findings didn't match up with the results TDC was reporting to the government," Cara said. "At least, I'm pretty sure that's why he gave me those two flash drives with reports I think were from here. And when Jason and I came here—the day someone shot at us—the samples we collected then tested positive for a lot of nasty stuff that wasn't supposed to be here."

"Then the protests and your agitating did what they were supposed to do," Eve said. "They forced TDC to literally clean up their act and do what they were paid to do."

"Yes, but…" She shook her head. "It still doesn't seem right."

"Maybe we'll know more after the results of these tests come back," Eve said.

"If there really isn't anything wrong with that site," Cara asked, "why did Dane feel he had to leave?"

Eve said nothing. Only Dane could answer that question, and for whatever reason, he wasn't talking.

"THE DISTRICT ATTORNEY's office has decided to formally charge Dane Trask with the murder of Marsha Grandberry." Faith Martin reported this news to Grant when he arrived at the Ranger Brigade office Thursday morning after leaving Eve's place.

"On the basis of what evidence?" Grant asked. "We don't have fingerprints or the murder weapon or any evidence tying Trask to Grandberry." They had recovered very little evidence of any kind from the murder scene or the body. No hairs or fibers or DNA, and certainly no witnesses who had seen anyone in the area near the time when Grandberry was killed.

"He was known to be in the vicinity of where her body was found. She was killed with a blade very similar to one he was known to carry. The method of her killing is described in the indictment as one with which he would be familiar." Faith looked miserable as she relayed this news. "I don't think it's a particularly strong case, but public sentiment is very much against Trask, and the DA is under a lot of pressure to indict. Also, I understand TDC Enterprises was one of the chief donors to his campaign, and they've been pressuring for Trask's indictment as well."

Grant had no words to express his disgust over this turn of affairs. "Get me the evidence file for the Grandberry murder," he said.

"Yes, sir." Faith retreated from the office and Grant pulled up the Grandberry file on his computer. There was very little there—an inventory of everything found on the body, including Dane Trask's business card, crime scene photographs, some measurements, the coroner's report.

Faith returned shortly, carrying a cardboard banker's box. "This is everything," she said, sliding the box onto the corner of his desk.

Grant slipped on gloves and began laying out the evidence on the credenza to one side of his desk: Grandberry's clothing, which had shown no sign of sexual assault. Her backpack and its contents: water bottle, map, the wrappings from the sandwich and the core of the apple she had eaten for lunch. The wallet, keys and phone from her pocket. He switched on the phone and keyed in the security code typed on the piece of paper attached to the phone that someone—Hud?—had obtained or figured out.

The home screen showed the usual display of applications and files—messages, emails, photographs, etc. Idly, Grant began scrolling through the photographs. The last pictures she had taken before she died were of scenery—dramatic views into the Black Canyon, vignettes of wildflowers, some artistic shots of the sky.

He stopped at a selfie she had taken in the parking area near the trailhead. A pretty young woman smiled up into the camera, the sign for the trail over her right shoulder. Grant started to move on, then stopped. Over her left shoulder, he could just make out a figure. Was that a person? Another tourist, perhaps? Using his thumb and forefinger, he enlarged the photo as much as possible, but only succeeded in making the background blur. Still, he thought there was something there.

Phone in hand, he went in search of Officer Hudson.

He found Hud at his computer, combing over a printout. He looked up at Grant's approach. "Hello," he said.

"I'm just going over the inventory we made of items from that illegal dumpsite. I'm hoping something unusual pops out at me, but so far I'm not having any luck."

"Put that aside for a bit," Grant said. "I need you to work on something else for me." He handed Hud the cell phone. "Take a look at that photograph, will you?"

Hud took the phone and studied the image. "This is the woman who was murdered on the trail, isn't it?" he asked.

"Yes. According to the time and date stamp on that photograph, she took it before she set out on her hike."

"All right," Hud said. "What am I looking for, exactly?"

"There over her left shoulder. Is that another person?"

Hud squinted, then enlarged the image. "I think so," he said.

"Can you enlarge that image and sharpen it up enough to get a clearer picture of that other person?" Grant asked. "Maybe clear enough to get an ID?"

"Maybe," Hud said. "Do you think this might be a potential witness?"

"It might be," Grant said. "Then again, it might be a photograph of her killer."

## Chapter Fifteen

The early morning cold cut through Grant's leather jacket as if the garment was made of gauze, but he had forsaken the warmth of the inside of the bus station in order to be that much closer to his daughter's arrival. He shared this chilly space with a man and a woman who both stood at the other end of the building, smoking, and a short woman with a large paunch who had introduced herself as a representative of the bus company, apparently there to make sure he was reunited with his daughter and maybe to persuade him not to sue the company.

More people filed onto the platform as the bus's 5:00 a.m. arrival neared. Grant shifted from foot to foot, not so much to warm his numb feet, but to burn off some of the nervous energy that raced through him. He was exhausted from yet another sleepless night, jittery from too much caffeine and sick to his stomach with worry that something would go wrong and Janie wouldn't be on the bus. Angela had called him at midnight, interrupting the little sleep he had managed to snatch, to alternately sob and berate him for the entire situation. "She gets her stubbornness from you," she said. "She never would have done this if you hadn't encouraged her to be so independent."

Grant had resisted the urge to hang up on her, letting her rant and not saying anything in his defense. He had learned the hard way that responding only riled her more. Better to let her cry it all out, and promise to call her as soon as Janie was safely with him.

The squeal of brakes signaled the big motor coach's arrival. People around him began gathering duffels and tote bags and suitcases. Grant started forward but the bus company rep—Alicia or Felicia or something like that—put a hand on his arm. "Your daughter will get off last, with the driver," she said. "It's already been arranged."

A second employee came out to corral the departing passengers behind a length of yellow tape. With a burst of diesel exhaust and the hiss of brakes, the bus lumbered to a halt. After a few seconds' delay, the doors opened.

The passengers who emerged looked tired and pale, shoulders slumped, feet dragging. They climbed down alone or in twos or threes, men and women, a few children. When at last the bus seemed empty, Grant waited, gaze fixed on the open door. "Where is she?" he asked.

"She's coming," Alicia said.

And then she was there, looking very small and young and a little afraid, her strawberry-blond hair streaming down from beneath a bright pink knit cap. An older man in a bus driver's uniform stood on the step behind her. He said something to her and pointed, and she turned her head and met Grant's gaze.

Her face lit up in a smile that made his heart leap in his chest. And then she was in his arms, hitting him with the force of a wrecking ball, his arms squeezing her tight. "I didn't mean to worry you, Daddy," she said. "I just wanted to come see you, and everything was fine, really."

"We'll talk about it later," Grant said. He tilted her head up and looked into her eyes. "Right now I'm just happy to see you."

"I'm happy to see you, too," she said. "The bus driver told me someone was meeting me here and I was hoping it was you and not the cops." She giggled. "Of course, I guess you are the cops. But I really wanted it to be a surprise."

The bus driver joined them and Janie turned to him. "This is Eddie," she said. "He drove all the way from Dallas and looked out for me."

Grant shook the man's hand. "Thank you."

"You've got a good girl, there," Eddie said. "Never gave me a bit of trouble. Not like some, I can tell you."

Grant thanked the bus company rep and collected Janie's bag. Then father and daughter headed for his cruiser. In the vehicle, Grant handed Janie his phone. "You need to call your mother. She's beside herself with worry."

He waited, not moving, while she telephoned her mother, who greeted her with a wail, then shouting, and finally, tears. "I'm sorry, Mom," Janie said, over and over, tears running down her face. Finally, Grant could stand no more. He took the phone from Janie and said, "It's okay, Angela. She's fine. We're all tired. I'm going to take her home now."

"Her home is here," Angela said, but without much venom.

"She'll call you later," Grant said. "After we've all

had some rest." He started the car and headed out, then glanced at his daughter again. "You want to tell me what happened to your phone?"

She squirmed. "I sort of lost it."

"You *lost* it?"

"Mom took it away."

"Because you broke curfew. Why did you do that?"

"It wasn't on purpose!" Her voice rose. "I just sort of, lost track of time. Anyway, it was no big deal."

He struggled to find the right words to say. He hated not being involved in the day-to-day of raising his children—the discipline and tough stuff as well as the good times. But since the girls didn't live with him full time, he had to turn over all of that to Angela. "Your leaving to come here was a big deal," he said.

"I don't know why everyone is so upset," Janie said as they cruised through the dark streets of the still-sleeping town.

"Don't you?" Grant asked. "You aren't smart enough to figure it out?"

He couldn't see her very clearly in the darkness, but he could hear her shifting around. "I wanted to see you, and if I had told you ahead of time, you and Mom wouldn't have let me come," she said. "And it worked out all right. No one gave me any trouble. I always paid attention to where I was, and the people around me, and I always tried to sit right behind the driver, so that if anybody bothered, the driver could intervene. And I left a note, so everyone would know I didn't run away or do anything stupid."

"Setting off by yourself across the country wasn't very smart, sweetheart," Grant said.

She didn't say anything, but turned her head to look out the window.

"How did you get to Philadelphia?" he asked.

"I took the train. I was going to take the bus all the way, but when I put my starting point and my destination in a trip planner online, it suggested the train to Philly, so that's what I did. It was fun. I'd never been on a train before, or a bus either, except a city bus or a school bus. Traveling across the country is really different."

He stopped at a red light, and studied his daughter in the illumination from a nearby streetlamp. She looked older than she had when he had last seen her, less than two months before, and she had navigated a two-thousand-mile journey with the aplomb of a seasoned traveler. She was growing up, yet she was still a child, her fearlessness a testament to how untouched she still was by the ugliness of the world. He longed to protect her from that ugliness for as long as he could.

She turned and met his gaze and smiled, and he had to look away, so she wouldn't see the sudden tears that stung his eyes. "Where did you get the money for the tickets?" he asked after a while, when they were on the highway, away from town.

"I took it out of my savings account. I know that money is supposed to be for college, but there's a lot in there. I missed you and I really wanted to see you."

Any residual anger melted at those words. "I'm glad you're here now," he said.

She shifted to look out at the passing scenery, bathed in the golden glow of sunrise. "It's so different here," she said. "Very barren and kind of stark. But I like it. Do you like it?"

"I do," he said. "Though it took some getting used to."

"Where do you live?" she asked.

"Not far from where I work, in a little cabin." The cedar-sided A-frame was small, with only two bedrooms and a single bath, but large windows afforded good views of the park and surrounding high plains.

"Do you like your job? Is it very different from what you did in DC.?"

"It's different," he said. "But also a lot the same. I'm still commanding a group of men and women who solve crimes, but here we oversee a bunch of territory and cross a lot of jurisdictions." There was more paperwork and more politics, but also more freedom to do things as he saw fit. The mixture appealed to him.

"So, Dad, do you have a girlfriend?"

The question jolted him. He thought of Eve. He felt closer to her than he had any woman in years, but what were they to each other, really? "You and your sister are the only girls in my life," he said.

Janie rolled her eyes. "Do you have a woman friend? Are you dating anyone?"

"Not exactly." He still wasn't sure where he stood with Eve.

She angled toward him. "Well why not?"

"Why are you so interested?"

"I don't think you should be alone. After all, Beth and I are growing up and we're going to go off to college and probably get married ourselves one day. And Mom remarried. Why shouldn't you?"

Her picture of the future, with her and her sister distant and himself alone, pained him. "I'm busy with work," he said.

"You can't let work get in the way of a personal life," she said, sounding about fifty instead of fifteen.

"I think I can take care of my personal life," he said.

"Well, you haven't been, have you, if you're not dating anyone." She sat back in the seat, a sly smile tugging at the corners of her mouth. "Besides, if you got married again, especially to someone a little younger, I could have a little brother or sister. I think that would be really awesome."

The car swerved, and he forced himself to keep his eyes on the road, Janie's giggles filling the car. He cleared his throat. "Don't you think I'm a bit old to start raising another child?"

"Well, you're old, but you're not ancient or anything. Besides, with modern innovations, you could live to be over a hundred. You've got plenty of time to raise another kid. But you've got to get out there and find a woman to have them."

"You sound like you've got all the answers."

"Just some of them. I read a lot." She said this with such a straight face he didn't dare laugh.

"Tell me about this case you're working on," she said. "The one that's taking up all your time."

"You know I can't tell you about an ongoing investigation," he said.

"Dad!" She sat up straight, her right hand in the air, palm up. "I solemnly swear I won't share anything you tell me on social media or with the press or with any of my friends—who aren't here and don't care anyway. Besides, there's bound to be stuff in the papers already. You can tell me that."

She did have all the answers, he thought. "All right," he said, and told her about Dane Trask disappearing, the accusations against him of embezzlement, and now murder, about TDC Enterprises and the protests at the Mary Lee Mine, and about the frustration of not being able to find a man who was so near yet so elusive.

"Wow." Janie shook her head. "I think I'd have to be pretty terrified to crash my truck and live off stolen food from campers in the desert. Do you think this guy has maybe lost his mind or something like that?"

"I've learned not to make too many assumptions," Grant said. "Anything is possible. We won't know for sure until we find him."

"What if you don't find him?" she asked.

That was one possibility he wasn't willing to consider. "We'll find him," he said. "It's what we do."

"TDC IS HOLDING a press conference at the Mary Lee Mine this afternoon." Eve was in the middle of filling their latest round of prom orders Friday morning when Cara's call came in. "I thought maybe you'd want to go."

"I'm too busy with work to go anywhere," Eve said, passing a spool of purple ribbon to Sarah. "You'll have to tell me all about it."

"We got a fancy invitation in the mail this morning," Cara said. "Wilderness Conservation, I mean. It says they're going to unveil the newly mitigated mine property. They're rubbing our faces in it."

"You wanted them to clean up the property, right?" Eve asked.

"Sure. But I still can't shake the idea they are up to something shady."

"Let me know how the press conference goes," she said. "Now I really have to go."

She hung up the phone and grabbed another stack

of clear plastic clamshells to hold the latest batch of corsages and boutonnieres. But she had boxed up only one when her phone rang again. "What is going on?" she complained, prepared to silence the call until she recognized Grant's number.

"Hello," she said.

She hadn't meant to put any significant emotion into her voice, but Sarah looked over, eyebrows raised in question. *Who is that?* her friend mouthed.

Eve shook her head and turned her back to Sarah. "How are you?" she asked. "How is Janie?" Grant had texted her early this morning to let her know that Janie had arrived safely.

"She's still asleep," he said. "The poor girl is exhausted. I don't think she slept all that much on the bus."

"You're probably exhausted, too," Eve said. "You should try to get a nap."

"No chance of that. I just heard TDC is having a press conference up at the Mary Lee Mine this afternoon. I'll need to be at that. That's why I'm calling, actually. I wondered if you intended to be there."

"No. I mean, we're kind of swamped here at the shop."

"I thought maybe since you were at the protest you'd be interested in what they had to say."

"I really only went to the protest as a favor to Cara."

"The thing is, I need to bring Janie with me. I know that at fifteen she thinks she's all grown up, but I'm not really comfortable leaving her here by herself, so far out of town, when my job has such unpredictable hours. And I thought this might be a good, low-key way for the two of you to meet."

Of course it would. And she was touched that he

wanted her to meet his daughter. "I'll see if I can find a way to be there," she said. "I'd love to meet Janie." *And to see you again.* But saying that out loud felt like inviting a jinx. She was enjoying him now. She didn't want to develop anything with him that depended on the future.

She ended the call and turned back to the flowers, trying to ignore Sarah's stare. Finally, her friend started, "Are you going to tell me who that was or are you going to make me beg? And before you answer, I know that it's none of my business and I'm too nosy for my own good, but I'm your friend and I really do care about you. I haven't heard that tone in your voice or that expression on your face in a long time."

"What expression?" she asked, startled out of silence. "What tone?"

Sarah smiled. "You looked all…dreamy. Soft." She wet her lips. "You're going to kill me for saying this, but you looked in love."

"Oh please! There is no such look."

"There is. And I have to say, I've never seen it on your face before. Not even with Dane."

Eve felt a little sick. Coming from any other person, the words might have been an insult, or a criticism. But Sarah didn't insult or criticize. She only told the truth, even when Eve didn't want to hear it. She tried to focus on the bow she was tying on a corsage, but ended up with the ribbon in a tangled mess. She pushed the flower away. "That was Grant Sanderlin."

"The Ranger commander?"

Eve nodded. "He wants me to come to the TDC press conference at the Mary Lee Mine this afternoon so that I can meet his daughter. She's visiting from DC."

"Awww, that's so sweet." Sarah slid the snarled corsage over and began untangling the ribbon. "You should go. I'll handle things here."

"Sarah, it's too much. You know it is. We're swamped."

"Prom isn't until next Friday night. The kids and their moms won't start picking up the corsages and boutonnieres and hair flowers until that morning. We've got a whole week, and if we work late every night, we can get it all done."

The idea made Eve tired, but she knew Sarah was right. "Maybe I can hire some extra help," she said. "Maybe from a temp service."

"That might be good, but when do you have time to interview someone or post ads or anything?" Sarah asked.

"I'll think of something," she said.

"In the meantime, go to the press conference. Meet Grant's daughter." Sarah's smile turned to a smirk. "So I take it you two have been sneaking around behind my back."

The words—and the expression that accompanied them—surprised a laugh from Eve. "Right. Because you're just too nosy."

"Guilty!" Both women laughed, and Sarah leaned over to hug her. "I'm just happy that you're happy. And I think Grant is a really great guy."

"There's nothing serious going on," Eve said. "We've only been out a couple of times." Though one of those times had been spent entirely at her house, and mostly in her bed. So that didn't exactly qualify as a traditional date.

"You've waited a long time for the right man to

come along," Sarah said. "No sense wasting time when he does."

"I don't know about that," Eve said.

"Go to the press conference," Sarah said again. "You might as well meet his daughter and see what happens from there."

## Chapter Sixteen

Eve followed a train of cars up the gravel road to the Mary Lee Mine, where men and women in orange safety vests directed them to a level parking area just inside the gate. As when she had been here for the protest, a platform had been set up near the former mine entrance, but instead of a backdrop of piles of rock and broken timbers, now this temporary stage was backed by a row of new saplings and newly sprouted grass.

Eve searched for Grant in the crowd of people who pressed around the stage, but couldn't spot him. She recognized some of her fellow protesters, as well as some TDC employees and people from town.

"Hello, Eve. It's good to see you."

The hair rose on the back of her neck at the words and she whirled around to see Toby Masterson standing behind her. He moved in, uncomfortably close. "I've been trying to call you since our date."

She had silenced every call. After her night with Grant, she had no wish to see Toby again. Maybe she should have told him that the first time he called, but she'd hoped he would get the message without her having to be so blunt. "I'm not really interested in going out with you again," she said now. "I'm sorry, but it just didn't work out for me."

His expression darkened. "I thought you had a good time."

"I did," she said. "But I'm looking for something… different in a relationship." She cringed at the words. There was really no graceful or truly kind way to do this.

"You're kidding," he said. "I think I deserve at least one more chance."

She shook her head and tried to turn around again, but he took her arm and pulled her to face him once more. "Is there someone else?" he asked. "Someone you prefer instead of me?"

"Let go of me." She tried to tug her arm from his grasp, but he held on tight. "We had one date. I don't owe you anything."

Several people had turned to stare at them now, so he let her go and took a step back. "I'm sorry you feel that way," he said, and left.

She faced forward again, a neutral expression fixed on her face, but her knees shook and she felt out of breath. She had turned down second dates from a lot of men, and been turned down herself. None of those encounters had left her this shaken.

Promptly at one o'clock, TDC vice president Mitch Ruffino mounted the steps and stood behind the podium. "Welcome, everyone," he said. "TDC is pleased to have you witness the unveiling of the results of our hard work at mitigating the Mary Lee Mine. What was once a toxic waste site is now a nature preserve that will be a model for similar projects to come."

He beamed in the roar of applause that followed,

though not everyone around Eve was clapping. She noticed Cara standing with Jason, arms crossed, unsmiling.

Ruffino moved to the mic again. "There are a number of people who were instrumental in making this happen that I need to introduce you to." There followed a roll call of men and women in suits and ties who paraded across the stage and waved. Eve went back to scanning the crowd for familiar faces.

Then she spotted Grant moving toward her, a smiling teenager at his side. "Eve, this is my daughter, Janie," he said, stopping before her. "Janie, this is Eve Shea, a friend of mine."

Janie looked from her father to Eve, and her grin widened. She held out her hand. "Pleased to meet you, Ms. Shea," she said.

"It's a pleasure to meet you," Eve said. "How do you like Colorado so far?"

"Well, I haven't seen very much of it," she said. "But what I've seen, I like." She looked around them. "This looks like something out of a movie. Like a mountain man or a bear could jump out any minute." She slipped her hand into the crook of Grant's arm. "Dad says he's going to take me hiking and stuff when he has some time off."

"Not very exciting for you in the meantime," Eve said.

"No, but it's not like I'd be doing that much back in D.C., either."

"We're trying to decide what she'll do while I'm working," Grant said. "I'm not happy about leaving her by herself while I'm away. But the office really isn't the place for her."

"And I'm way too old for a babysitter." Janie rolled her eyes. "I mean, really!"

"I could use some extra help at the shop," Eve said. "It's prom time and we are seriously slammed." She turned to Grant. "Sarah and I were talking about it just this morning. We need some temporary help, but we're too busy to write out an ad or interview people. Janie would be perfect."

"What kind of shop do you have?" Janie asked before Grant could speak.

"I have a little flower shop in Montrose," Eve said. "The work wouldn't be terribly exciting, but you could help fill orders and answer the phone, and you'd learn a little bit about flower arrangement and plant care. It might be interesting for you. And I'd pay."

Janie's eyes widened. "Dad, that sounds perfect!" she said.

Grant looked skeptical. "Eve, are you sure?"

"I'm absolutely sure," she said, beginning to get excited about the idea herself. "It would solve your problem and mine. I wasn't kidding about needing the help."

"Dad, please!" Janie hung on his arm. "I want to do it."

"All right." He turned back to Eve. "If you're sure."

"I'm sure. You can drop her at the shop at nine, or at my house if you need to get to work earlier. If you need to work after we close, she can come home with me and hang." She turned to Janie. "How does that sound?"

"It sounds awesome." Janie hugged her, a quick, tight embrace that sent a surge of happiness through Eve.

"Thanks," Grant said. "You've taken a real load off my mind."

Cara and Jason joined them and Grant introduced

Janie. Jason nodded toward the podium, where another man in a suit had taken over the microphone and was droning on about TDC's great environmental record. "What do you make of all this?" he asked.

"I think TDC is anxious for good publicity after all the negative news over Dane Trask," Grant said.

"They cleaned up this place amazingly fast," Cara said. "Considering the state it was in only two weeks ago."

Jason moved closer and lowered his voice. "It's possible TDC hauled everything from the Mary Lee to that illegal dump site," he said.

"You should test the stuff at the dump site and compare it to the test results we have from here," Cara said. "If they match, that would be proof, wouldn't it?"

Grant nodded. "Do it," he said. "But we may need more than that to build a case."

"Uh-oh," Janie said, looking past her father.

Grant and Eve both turned to look at her. "What's wrong?" Grant asked.

"There's a guy over there who is really giving us the stink-eye." She jerked her head to indicate behind them.

Eve looked over Grant's shoulder and drew in a breath. Toby Masterson was scowling at them, and if looks could kill, they might all be dead right now.

JANIE WAS WAITING on the sidewalk when Eve arrived at the flower shop Saturday morning. She held out a to-go cup. "I hope you like mocha latte. It's my favorite, even though Dad thinks I'm too young to drink coffee." She rolled her eyes. "Even Mom thinks that's silly."

"Thanks," Eve said. "It's my favorite, too."

"See, I knew I liked you." Janie skipped behind Eve

into the shop. "Oh, wow, this place is so cool." She sucked in a deep breath, eyes closed, chest expanding. "And it smells so good." She opened her eyes. "I really love flowers."

"I hope you still love them after you've worked with them all day." She led the way to the storeroom and showed Janie where to stash her backpack, then gave her a tour of the shop, naming the various plants and flowers they passed.

"Should I be taking notes?" Janie asked. "I'm never going to remember all of this."

"It's all right," Eve said. "There won't be a test." She switched on the lighted Open sign. "But speaking of tests, why aren't you in school?"

"Oh, my school is on this weird quarterly plan— three quarters on, then one off," she said. "But they're staggered so that some kids go to school while others don't. It's supposed to make better use of resources and keep you from forgetting stuff over long breaks. Anyway, it's my quarter off."

Eve nodded. "All right. I'm going to start you off by going through the loose flowers in the cooler. Pull out any wilted or browning blossoms. Then we'll have room for flowers that come in this morning's delivery." She took the girl to the cooler in the back and showed her how to look for browning leaves and drooping flower heads and set these blooms aside.

"So, what do you think of my dad?" Janie asked. She twirled a daisy, not looking at Eve.

"I think he's a great dad," Eve said. "I know he was really worried about you, and so happy you're here now."

Janie made a face. "I mean, what do you think about

him, you know, as a man?" She cast a sideways glance at Eve. "Like, to date."

Eve bit back a smile. Nothing subtle about this kid. "Your dad is a great guy," she said.

"Have the two of you been out? I mean, he introduced you as a friend, but I wasn't sure what he meant by that."

"He meant, I'm a friend."

"He really likes you, I can tell." She dropped the daisy in the bucket they had set aside for flowers to be discarded and faced Eve. "I think you should go out with him," she said. "I know he's older than you, but he's good-looking, don't you think? And I see older guys with younger women all the time. And it's not like you're a teenager or anything. Would it be so weird?"

Eve couldn't help but laugh at this onslaught. "It takes two people to decide to date," she said.

"But I can tell he really likes you. Yesterday afternoon at that press conference thingy, he couldn't keep his eyes off you. But he's probably shy, because of the age difference and you're so beautiful and everything. So I think you should ask him out."

Eve felt her cheeks heat, whether from the information that Grant had been watching her, or Janie's comment that she was beautiful—or the knowledge that she wasn't being entirely truthful with this sweet girl about her and Grant's history. She put a hand on Janie's shoulder. "Let's just see how things develop naturally," she said. "Okay?"

Janie shrugged, and Eve left her to finish the flowers.

At ten, Sarah arrived, bringing the mail. "Lots of junk, as usual," she said, handing the bundle to Eve.

"But there's a letter in there for you." She winked. "It looks personal."

Janie emerged from the back room. "Hello."

"Janie!" Eve motioned the girl forward. "Sarah, this is Janie Sanderlin. She's visiting her dad for a little while and will be helping us out."

"Is your dad the Ranger Brigade commander?" Sarah asked, glancing between the girl and Eve.

"He is," Janie said. "And I'm really excited about working here." She turned to Eve. "Maybe I should have told you before, but the only other job I've ever had is babysitting."

"You'll do fine," Eve said. "Sarah, would you show Janie how to package the prom flowers while I look through this mail?"

"Sure thing," Sarah said. "Come on. We'll get the packaging knocked out pretty quick, and then I'll show you how to make bows."

The pair retreated to the workroom while Eve stood over the trash can in her office, sorting the mail. More than half went straight into the recycling bin, she filed a few bills to pay later and then she finally came to the letter Sarah had mentioned.

The letter was in a thin, prestamped envelope, the kind sold over the counter at the post office. The address was in block printing, but the sight of it sent a shiver up Eve's spine. She picked up a letter opener and slid it under the envelope flap.

Dear Eve,
I haven't seen anything that looked like my press release in the newspapers, so I'm guessing you decided not to pass it on. I was counting on you

to help me out, since I'm not really in a position to do these things myself. That's probably hard for you to understand, but I'll explain more after all this is over.

I know we had our problems there at the end, but we had a lot of really good times together before that. I still love you, even if it wouldn't work for us to be together. For the sake of that love, would you help me out here?

No matter what you hear, I haven't done the things they're accusing me of. I can't tell you more because I don't want to put you in any danger. Please believe that.

If you still have that press release, please send it to someone who will dig more into that story. They'll be surprised by what they find.

Love,
Dane

GRANT MADE IT a point to get to the flower shop shortly before six o'clock Saturday evening. As much as he appreciated Eve's offer to take Janie home with her, he wanted to spend as much time as he could with his daughter. Angela had agreed Janie could stay in Colorado until her new semester started in three weeks. He was even trying to persuade Beth to fly out the last week so they could all be together.

Half a dozen people crowded the shop when Grant arrived, and it was several seconds before he spotted Janie in the crush. She stood next to Sarah at a table next to the flower cooler, chatting with people who waited in line and stapling paperwork.

Eve, who stood at the cash register, ringing up sales,

looked up as he entered and smiled, but didn't stop working. Grant stepped to one side and waited for the rush to ease.

Ten minutes later, the last customer stepped up to the register. "Dad!" Janie raced across the shop and stopped in front of him. "Is it six o'clock already? I've had the most amazing time."

"Hello, Commander," Sarah said, joining them. "This is quite a daughter you have here." She put a hand on Janie's shoulder. "She's been a huge help to us today. I don't know what we did without her."

"It was fun," Janie said. "Sarah's been teaching me how to make corsages. My bows are still a little lopsided, but I know if I keep practicing I'll get really good at it."

The last customer left and Eve followed them and switched the sign to Closed, then locked the door. She leaned against the door for a moment. "What a day," she said.

"You're not usually this busy, are you?" Grant asked, one arm across Janie's shoulders.

"Prom time. We're getting lots and lots of orders." Eve straightened and came to stand with them. "Sarah had the idea to advertise in the school newspapers and it's really paid off."

"I was telling the commander what a big help Janie has been," Sarah said.

"You did a terrific job today," Eve said to the girl. "I hope you'll come back Monday."

"Of course I will." Janie turned to her father. "That's the plan, isn't it? Please say yes."

He nodded, amused by Janie's enthusiasm for this new job. "That's the plan."

Eve patted Janie's shoulder. "Will you help Sarah straighten up the back room while I talk to your dad for a minute?"

"You bet." Janie raced off, Sarah following in her wake.

Grant turned to Eve. Something in her expression had caught his attention. "Is something wrong?" he asked.

"Come into my office."

He squeezed in, then she shut the door behind him, then picked up an envelope from the desk. "I had another letter from Dane today," she said. "I don't know what to make of it."

Careful to handle the letter only by the edges, he unfolded it onto the desk and leaned over to read it. He cringed inwardly at the declaration of love, but pushed on. "That press release accused TDC of falsifying reports, right?" he asked when he had finished.

"Yes," she said. "But the mine site has been cleaned up. At least, it looks clean. Is he trying to say it isn't?"

"That part about not saying more because he doesn't want to put you in danger," Grant said. "That makes me uncomfortable."

She hugged herself. "The whole situation makes me uncomfortable."

He pulled her close and she rested her head on his shoulder. "Thank you again for taking in Janie and giving her something to do," he said.

"Are you kidding?" She smiled up at him. "She really has been a tremendous help." She laughed.

"What's so funny?" he asked.

"We had a very serious conversation this morning, in which she tried to persuade me to ask you out. She pointed out that, despite our age difference, you are actually pretty good-looking, and going out with you wouldn't be so horrible, would it?"

He wasn't sure whether to be appalled or flattered. "What did you tell her?"

"I told her I thought we'd see how things developed naturally."

He pulled her closer, hands on her hips. "And how would you say things are developing?" he asked. "Naturally?"

Hands on his shoulders, she pressed her forehead to his. "I love being with you," she said. "The other night was...special."

"But?"

She stepped back. "But I want children. I'm not willing to compromise on that."

"I know. And I'm not suggesting you compromise." But he was forty-five. He'd be close to retirement age before any child he had now graduated high school. He'd made so many mistakes with the girls, and they had all suffered for it. How could he go through all that again? "I need to focus on Janie while she's here," he said. "We'll talk more later."

She sighed and looked away. He wanted to pull her close and tell her that everything would be all right. But how could he make that kind of promise when he knew not every problem had a solution, and not every ending was a happy one?

He collected Janie and drove home. Once inside, she dropped her backpack and headed for the kitchen. "What's for dinner?" she asked. "I'm starved."

"How about spaghetti?" He moved to the pantry and took out pasta and a jar of sauce. "There's meat thawing in the refrigerator. Get it for me, okay?" He took off his jacket and shoulder holster and draped them over a chair, then unbuttoned his cuffs and began rolling up his sleeves.

Janie opened the refrigerator and took out the package of ground beef. "You can cook?" she asked.

"Don't act so surprised."

"You never cooked when you lived at home."

"I didn't have to. Your mother is a very good cook."

"Well yeah, but everyone likes a night off now and then, right?"

He winced. Would Angela have liked if he had offered to cook every once in a while? He had never even thought about it. Only when he had been out on his own, forced to learn his way around a kitchen or subsist on takeout, had he really discovered a talent for making at least basic meals. "You can set the table," he said.

He unwrapped the meat and dumped it in a skillet, then set water to boil for the pasta. Janie arranged plates and flatware on the little table in the middle of the kitchen. "I like it here, Dad," she said. "Maybe I should stay."

He could only imagine what Angela would say to that idea. And he was pretty sure the novelty of a new place would give way to the reality of living in a remote area with most of her friends and her mother and sister two thousand miles away. "It's great having you here, Pumpkin, but you need to go home to your mom and sister," he said. "I'm going to miss you, though."

"I can come back after school is out, right?"

"You can come back as often as you like. But no more surprise visits, okay? When you want to come see me, you let me know and I'll buy you a plane ticket."

"It probably would be nicer to fly than all that time on a bus. But it was an adventure, you know? It's good to have adventures."

"You and your sister have certainly been my adventure."

"Ha! That's something, coming from a cop." She looked around. "What do you want me to do now?"

"I forgot to collect the mail on the way in. Check the box, will you?"

She left to check the mailbox, bouncing as she moved, full of energy even after a long day. He watched her go, the familiar tightness of loss in his chest. He was going to miss her when she went back to her mother. The house would be emptier, and so would his life. Raising children was so hard—but he couldn't think of anything more rewarding.

Could he do this again?

He pushed the idea away. Maybe he'd learned some things, but he was still the same person. He had the same job and the same habits, none of which seemed compatible with the demands of raising a family. How often had Angela reminded him of that? He might have fallen out of love with her, but he couldn't deny she was usually right.

# *Chapter Seventeen*

"We got the test results from the dump site." Tuesday morning, Jason Beck dropped a stack of papers onto Grant's desk. "And some new results from the Mary Lee Mine."

"When did you test the Mary Lee Mine?" Grant asked.

Beck flushed. "Someone from Wilderness Conservation took the tests the day before the press conference and forwarded the results to us."

If Grant had to guess, he would pick Beck's fiancée, Cara Mead, as the anonymous tester, but since these results were unlikely to ever end up in court, given their uncertain provenance, he let it pass. "Summarize the findings for me," he said.

"The results from the dump site show some of the same findings as the first tests from the Mary Lee Mine," Beck said. "Traces of uranium and thorium."

"Some," Grant said. "But not all?"

"No, sir. There are a couple of other things—asbestos, for one—that never showed up at the Mary Lee."

"So we can't be sure the debris actually came from the Mary Lee?"

"No, sir. I believe it did, but we can't be one hundred percent sure."

Grant glanced at the reports. "With these findings, we can't even be fifty percent sure. An expert witness would tear this apart in court."

"Yes, sir."

"What about the latest tests from the Mary Lee?" Grant asked.

"They come back clean. Whatever TDC did up there, they got rid of the bad stuff, in a hurry."

"So they did what they were paid to do. Dane Trask doesn't know what he's talking about."

Beck frowned. "Dane Trask?"

Grant shook his head. "Never mind. Ask Hudson to come see me when he gets a chance."

"Yes, sir."

When Beck was gone, Grant pulled up the copy of Dane's letter that he had scanned in. He had logged the letter into evidence, but he hadn't mentioned it to anyone else yet. He wanted time to try to figure out the significance of the correspondence, if any. Was Trask a nutcase who was fixated on getting his former employer in trouble? Was he paranoid, imagining danger where there was none?

Then again, it appeared the man might have been framed for murder. That might make anyone wary. As for the embezzlement charges, Grant didn't have enough knowledge of that case to pass judgment, though Dane didn't act like a man who had stolen a bunch of his employer's money. In those cases, the guilty party at least attempted to skip town. Dane kept hanging around, even with a price on his head that had would-be bounty hunters coming out of the woodwork. Apparently, a park ranger had arrested a man just two days ago who was stringing trip-wires across trails in the area of the park where Dane had been most frequently spotted.

Worse than Trask's vague accusations against TDC was his declaration that he still loved Eve. She hadn't commented on that part of the letter. Was that because she didn't care—or because she cared too much?

Two minutes later, Officer Hudson sauntered in. The man walked with a kind of swagger, as if all his joints were a little loose. "Beck said you wanted to see me?" Hud said.

"Any results from that photo from Marsha Grandberry's phone?" he asked.

"Not yet," Hud said. "But I'm working on it. I've got a computer program that sharpens photos pixel by pixel. It can do some amazing things, but it takes time."

"Let me know as soon as you have something." Ever since he had found that photograph, he couldn't shake the idea that the picture showed something significant. He might be all wrong. What looked like a person might turn out to be a tree, or if it was a person, it might be a tourist from Akron who hadn't seen a thing.

But sometimes in an investigation, you did get lucky. They could use a little luck with this one.

"THANK GOD THAT'S over with for another year." Sarah shut the door to the shop Friday at six and flipped the sign to Closed.

"I can't believe that cooler was full this morning and now it's empty," Janie said, eyeing the cooler that was empty of everything but a few rosebud arrangements and loose flower petals.

"Ladies, we sold one hundred and twenty-five corsages, fifty-seven boutonnieres and two dozen hair arrangements," Eve said. "Definitely a new record."

Janie whooped and Sarah joined in. "Go home, Sarah," Eve said. "Take lots of pictures of Robby and his date."

"I'm on my way." Sarah already had her purse in hand. "I told him he wasn't to leave the house before I got there. And he can't anyway, because I have his keys."

"I can't believe she took his keys," Janie said, as Sarah hurried down the sidewalk away from them.

"I guess parents have to learn how to outsmart their children." Eve sagged back against the counter. "How do you feel about ordering in pizza for dinner? Your dad texted me that he has to work a little late."

"He texted me, too, and pizza sounds good."

"You don't mind coming to my house with me, do you?" Eve asked. Part of her was looking forward to having the girl over. Over the past week of working together, the two of them had become good friends. Janie was funny and optimistic, and a hard worker, too. Grant deserved part of the credit for that, surely.

"No. I want to see your house," Janie said.

"All right. Do me a favor and stash these roses in the back cooler. I want to shut this one down and first thing Monday we'll give it a good clean-out."

"Sure thing." Janie hugged the four bud vases to her chest and headed for the back room, while Eve leaned into the cooler to flip the switch at the back.

When the door buzzer sounded, she didn't recognize the chime at first, since they were closed and she'd seen Sarah lock the door. Then a hand clamped over her mouth and strong arms yanked her backwards out of the cooler.

"Don't struggle, or you'll just get hurt," Toby Masterson said. The blade of his knife flashed in the overhead lights, then she felt the sting of it against her throat. "You come with me now, and everything is going to be all right."

JANIE EASED OPEN the door of the big walk-in cooler and stood for a moment, searching for a place to put the bud vases. Sarah had explained this morning that flowers like these, that didn't sell by Saturday night, could sometimes be used in other arrangements Monday morning. Rosebuds would be blooming roses in mixed arrangements or for corsages. Longer-lasting flowers like mums and alstroemeria could last a week or more if cared for properly. Running a flower shop was a balance between always offering fresh, beautiful flowers and wasting as little as possible.

She spotted space on a shelf in the back and hurried to put the roses there, then paused to admire the bucket of pink carnations that was all that was left of the stock they had used for prom. Eve had mentioned that next Wednesday she had a huge order of flowers coming in for a big wedding. Janie really hoped she would get to help with those arrangements, and maybe even get to go with Eve when she delivered the flowers to the church and the reception hall. Spending her break here was turning out to be so much more interesting than hanging out at home with Mom and Beth and her friends.

She left the freezer and started back toward the front of the shop when the sound of a man's voice made her freeze. The voice was low—too low to be her dad's. They were closed, so it wouldn't be a customer, would it?

On tiptoe, and holding her breath, she crept to the curtain that separated the workroom from the rest of the shop. She stood right behind the curtain, straining to hear.

She didn't know exactly what she was hearing, but she knew it made her afraid. Scuffling sounds, like a struggle. Then something heavy being dragged over the floor. The man's voice again, the words indistinct, but like he was giving orders. Then the sound of the door opening, the door chime sounding, and then…nothing. So silent she could hear her own breath heaving in and out, and her heart pounding.

After what seemed like forever, but was probably only a few minutes, she eased back the curtain and peered into the front of the shop. The first thing she noticed was the sliding door of the display cooler open. Flower petals littered the floor around it. Had they been there before? Maybe. They had all been pulling things in and out of that cooler all day.

She took two more steps forward, until she could see the whole shop. Empty. "Eve?" she called, almost a whisper. Then, a little louder. "Eve?"

No answer. She wanted to cry, but she forced back the tears. She had to think. What to do? What would her dad do?

Hands trembling, she picked up the phone receiver and dialed. Then she sank to the floor behind the counter, where anyone watching wouldn't see her. "Dad?" she asked when he answered. "Can you come to the flower shop right away? I think something really bad has happened."

THE FURY IN Toby's eyes startled Eve, and the knife in his hands frightened her, but the thought of what he might do if Janie suddenly walked in on him terrified her. So she made no protest when he tied her hands roughly behind her back. He held the knife to her throat again. "You make a sound and I'll cut you," he said. "Do you understand?"

She nodded, and he dragged her toward the door. He gave no indication that he had any idea Janie was in the store, and this knowledge sent a flood of relief through Eve. Janie would probably be confused and frightened when she came back to the front room and Eve was gone, but she had a good head on her shoulders and would probably call her father.

Grant would think of something, she told herself, comforted by the thought. Grant would take care of Janie, and help Eve.

Out on the sidewalk, she stumbled alongside Toby to the white sedan she remembered from their date. Toby opened the passenger door and shoved her inside. "Don't try anything stupid," he said. "I can still hurt you bad."

"I won't," she promised. All she wanted was to get him away from the flower shop before Janie ran out or he spotted her through the front window.

She remained silent as they drove through town and headed toward the national park and the wilderness land that was part of the Ranger Brigade's jurisdiction. "Where are we going?" she asked.

"We're going to find Dane Trask," he said.

"Do you know where he is?" she asked, surprised.

"No. But when he finds out I have you, he'll come running, and then I'll have him."

"I don't think I understand," she said. Why would Dane come running?

Toby grinned. "You don't? Let me put it another way. I'm setting a trap to catch Trask. And you're the bait."

JANIE'S WORDS WERE like an icicle to Grant's heart. "Take a deep breath," he said, as much to his daughter as to himself. "And tell me what's going on."

"I think someone broke into the shop, right after we closed. I was in the back cooler and heard a man's voice, then some thumping sounds and…" She made a sound like a sob. "When I came out, Eve was gone."

"Where are you now?" Grant asked. "Are you somewhere safe?"

"I'm on the floor behind the front counter."

"Do me a favor. Go into the back room. Wait there. I'll be right there."

"I love you, Daddy."

"I love you, too, Pumpkin."

He ended the call, moved into the main room of headquarters, and scanned the men and women working there. "Beck! Dance! With me," he ordered and headed for the armory at the rear of the building.

By the time Dance and Beck reached him, Grant had opened the locker containing SWAT gear and began passing out body armor, helmets and weapons. "What have we got?" Dance asked, accepting a sniper rifle.

"A possible kidnapping," Grant said. "The flower shop where my daughter is working. She just called to say someone—she thinks a man, but she only heard his voice, she didn't see him—came in after closing. She heard a struggle and when she came out of the back room, the shop's owner, Eve Shea, was gone."

"Eve Shea is Dane Trask's girlfriend," Beck said.

"Was," Grant said. "They split up six months ago."

"Do you think Trask has her?" Dance asked.

"I don't know who has her, but we're going in prepared for anything. After we assess the situation, we may call in reinforcements. Right now, I need to go make sure my daughter is all right."

On the way into town he called the Montrose Police, then dialed the number for the shop. It rang and rang, but finally Janie answered. "Eve's Garden, how can I help you?" She sounded so adult it hurt to hear.

"Janie, it's Dad. How are you doing?"

"I'm okay," she said. "I'm sitting here by the back door with the phone. Nobody else is here."

"We're on our way. The Montrose police are coming, too."

When the two Ranger cruisers pulled onto Main, two Montrose squad cars were already parked in front of the flower shop. A sergeant met them on the sidewalk. "No sign of activity inside," he said.

"My daughter is in there, in the back," Grant said. "She says no one else is in there. Let me go in first and get her."

"The door's unlocked," a second Montrose officer said. "We tried it, but didn't go in."

Grant pulled on gloves, then went in. Everything looked pretty orderly. The door to the display cooler stood open, and there were a few flower petals on the floor, but otherwise, nothing looked out of place. "Janie!" he called. "You can come out now."

Seconds later, Janie pushed back the curtain that separated the front of the shop from the workroom. She was very pale, and stared at the group of armed men, wide-eyed. "Come here, honey," Grant said, and she ran to him and buried her face in his side.

He hugged her close and patted her back while she cried a little. Dance and Beck and two Montrose officers searched the shop from front to back. "It's clear," Dance said, emerging from the back a few moments later.

Grant gently pushed Janie away and handed her a handkerchief. "Take a minute to calm down, then tell us what happened," he said.

She sniffed and scrubbed at her eyes with the handkerchief, suddenly looking very young. He wanted to pull her close again, to shield her from all the danger and ugliness in life. Instead, he took out a recorder. "I'm going to record this, so we have a record," he said. "You tell me everything you remember."

She started from when she took some vases of rosebuds to the back walk-in cooler, through hearing the man's voice and the sounds of struggle, up to when she called him. Her voice shook a little as she relived it all, but she remained tough. "I couldn't hear what the man was saying, and I didn't recognize the voice, but it was deep—deeper than yours."

He switched off the recorder. "You did a good job," he said. He turned to the others. "Talk to people in the shops on either side and across the street and see if they saw anything."

"We'll start processing the scene for evidence," the Montrose sergeant said.

Janie turned toward the display cooler. "I don't know if those flower petals were on the floor before or not," she said. "But I think Eve was in there when the guy came in and grabbed her."

Grant patted her shoulder. "Try not to worry about it,

Pumpkin," he said. "You did what you could—now it's our job to find her." Every second counted. Grant had no idea what Eve's kidnapper intended, but his job was to get to them before the man could act on his intentions.

# Chapter Eighteen

"What is going on here? Has there been an accident or something?" A woman's voice rose out on the sidewalk.

"Sarah!" Janie called, and Eve's assistant pushed past one of the Montrose officers and rushed up to them.

"Janie, what is going on?" she asked.

"Eve's been kidnapped," Janie said, and started crying again.

The color left Sarah's face and she turned to Grant. "Eve's gone?"

He took her elbow and walked with her a little way from Janie, who continued to sniffle and mop at her face with the handkerchief. "Janie was in the back room and heard a man's voice and sounds of a struggle. When she came out, Eve was gone and the shop was empty. She said this happened not too long after you left. Did you see anyone near the shop when you left—in a car parked nearby, or on the sidewalk?"

Sarah shook her head. "I didn't notice anyone. But then, I was in a rush to get home and see my son and his date before they left for prom."

"Was there anyone in the shop earlier in the day who acted suspicious? Anyone angry about anything?"

"No. Nothing like that." She glanced at the cops

swarming the shop, taking photographs and measurements, dusting for fingerprints. "After my son and his date left, my husband and I decided to go out to eat. We were driving past and I saw all the cop cars and I had to see what was happening."

She turned as a bulky man with a broad face and thinning blond hair came into the shop. "I'm Dale McLean," he said, putting an arm around Sarah. "What's going on?"

"Someone's kidnapped Eve," Sarah said.

Janie joined them and Sarah put her arm around the girl. "You were so smart to call your dad right away," she said.

"I'm worried about Eve," she said.

"I'm sure your father and his men will find her." Sarah looked at Grant. "You're going to be busy a while, aren't you? Working? I can take Janie if you like."

He hadn't even thought about what he would do with Janie while he searched for Eve. He looked at his daughter. "Would you mind going home with Sarah?" he asked.

"I guess not," she said.

"I'm sure you'd rather be at your own place, but I'd appreciate the company," Sarah said.

"All right," Janie said.

She went to the back room to retrieve her backpack. "Thank you," Grant said. "I wouldn't want her to have to stay at my place by herself."

"Of course not. She's a great kid, Commander. You should be proud."

"I am."

After Janie and the McLeans left, Beck and Dance returned, bringing with them a young black woman with close cropped hair and large, wide-set eyes. "This is Isabel Hart," Dance said. "She works at the sandwich shop across the street and may have seen our guy."

Grant fished out his recorder again. "I'm Commander Sanderlin," he said. "Tell me what you saw."

The woman looked around nervously, then said, "I went out to water the flowers in the planters by our door a little after six and I saw a man come in here," she said. "I remember because he shoved the door really hard and made a grunting noise. That's what made me look up. I thought the door must have stuck." She shrugged. "I didn't think a lot about it after that. I went inside."

"Was the sign on the door turned to Open or Closed?" Grant asked.

"I don't know. I think he was blocking the sign so I couldn't see it."

"But you're sure about the time?" Grant asked. "Just after six."

"Yes. Because we have a special that runs from six to eight and I had just rung up my first one of the evening."

"What did the man look like?" Grant asked.

"Tall. Dark hair. Not fat or thin." She shrugged. "His back was to me, so I didn't see his face."

"Thank you, Ms. Hart." Grant switched off the recorder. "We may have more questions for you later. We appreciate your help."

She left and Dance said, "He might have forced the door, or picked the lock. It's a pretty basic lock. There's an alarm, but it wasn't set yet."

"He could have had a key, too," Beck said. "If he'd been in the shop before or knew Ms. Shea, he could have swiped the key or borrowed it and had a duplicate made."

The Montrose sergeant returned. "We've put out an APB with Ms. Shea's description," he said. "We haven't found anyone who remembers any kind of trouble with her and a man, or even a disgruntled customer. No ex-husband in the picture."

"She dated Dane Trask for a couple of years," Dance said.

The sergeant's eyebrows rose. "Maybe he came back for her?"

"The man the woman across the street described fits Trask's description," Dance said.

"We're not ruling out anything at this point," Grant said. He gave the Montrose officer the description Ms. Hart had shared. "Are there any security cameras that might show the area around the shop?"

The sergeant shook his head. "A couple of places have cameras inside, but none of them are focused on the street. We'll keep talking to people, and we'll put out this description, in case anyone recognizes someone."

He left and Grant turned to Dance. "I'm going back to the office. Keep me posted."

On the drive back to the office, he scanned every car he passed, hoping to see Eve, or a man who fit the description Ms. Hart had given. He refused to think what might be happening to her and focused instead on why someone might have taken her. Had Dance returned out of some misdirected version of love, determined to take Eve into exile with him? Maybe the man really had lost his grip on reality.

Eve had no fortune, or wealthy family, so ransom seemed out of the question. Had someone been stalking her, one of her former dates who believed she was in love with him, or even a stranger who had decided he wanted her?

Back at the office, Hud met him just inside the door. "I've got that image you were waiting for," he said. "The one from Marsha Grandberry's camera."

Dully, he followed Hud to his computer and studied the enlarged and enhanced image of a dark-haired man, squinting into the sun. "It looks to me like he's definitely watching Grandberry," Hud said. "Judging by the trees around him, I'd put him at about six-two, approximately 180 pounds." He paused. "He fits the description for Dane Trask."

Some of the fog cleared from Grant's mind as he studied the picture. Though still slightly blurred, the image was recognizable. "It's not Dane Trask," he said. "That's Toby Masterson." The two men did resemble each other, superficially. Looking at this image, it struck Grant that Masterson could have been the man who opened Trask's safety deposit box. He could have used a fake ID, or stolen one from Trask, either at work or at Welcome Home Warriors.

"Who is Toby Masterson?" Hud asked.

"He works for TDC. He knows Dane Trask from Welcome Home Warriors." And he had dated Eve. "It's very possible he killed Marsha Grandberry," he said. "And I think he kidnapped Eve Shea. He fits the description we got from a witness and Eve went out with him at least once, and he's tried to date the other women in Dane Trask's life—Cara Mead and Trask's daughter, Audra. I think he's obsessed with Trask." He clapped Hud on the back. "Get me everything you can on Masterson. I especially want to know the make, model and plate number of the vehicle he's driving."

They were going to get this guy, but how long did they have before it was too late?

MASTERSON SWITCHED OFF his headlights and they barreled down the highway in the darkness. "What are you doing?" Eve cried. Was he trying to kill them both by speeding blindly along these twisted mountain roads?

He didn't answer, but suddenly swerved left, bumping onto a rough gravel road. She tried to make out some landmark in the darkness, but that was impossible. She didn't know how Masterson could even see to drive, it was so dark out, with no moon and few stars and no other light for probably miles. The car rocked wildly from side to side and she tried to brace herself with her feet, but banged her head hard against the side window. "Are you trying to kill us?" she shouted.

He slammed on the brakes, throwing her forward, though the seat belt he had fastened around her kept her from catapulting through the windshield. She strained her eyes to see him in the dark, but could only make out shadows. She thought she heard him breathing hard over the rumble of the car's engine.

He grabbed her, and she cried out, startled, and then in pain, he was squeezing her so hard. "Where is Dane hiding?" he asked. "You must know. You two were lovers. You said he'd been in contact with you since he left. Why? Did he want you to meet him and run away?"

"I don't know where he is," she protested. "He never told me anything. And we're not lovers. Not for a long time."

He shoved her away. "No, you're not Dane's lover. You're sleeping with that cop, that Ranger Brigade commander. You'd do that old man but you could hardly stand to kiss me." He swore at her, then put the car in gear and they rocketed forward once more, but not as fast as before, and after a few seconds, he switched on the headlights.

The high beams illuminated a landscape of rock and sagebrush, the road two faintly discernable ruts climbing steeply. Not the road to the Mary Lee Mine, she thought. "Where are we going?" she asked.

"I know a back way into the park," he said. "We're going to look for Dane." He sounded calmer now. More sane.

She assumed he meant the National Park. "It's a big park," she said. "How will you find him?"

"Because I've got you. He'll want to save you. He's got a hero complex, did you know that? It's why he started Welcome Home Warriors. He wanted everyone—all the townspeople, and all of us veterans—to look up to him. That Dane Trask, what a great guy." He laughed. "People aren't saying he's so great now."

"But Dane did help a lot of people," she said. "He helped you get a job with TDC."

"I got that job on my own," he said. "Dane just took credit for it."

Was that true? She tried to remember, but she hadn't paid that much attention.

"And then he stole all that money from TDC," Toby continued. "Everybody thought he was such a hard worker, winning all those awards, and putting in all those long hours, when in fact, he was siphoning off money from the jobs he worked."

She started to protest that that didn't sound like Dane, but could TDC really make those accusations without proof? Toby continued talking. "When he found out everyone was on to him and he was going to be arrested, he tried to fake his own death, pushing that truck into the canyon. But then he was stupid enough to keep showing up. He couldn't lay low and keep quiet. People like him, always wanting to be in the spotlight, can't ever do that."

The Dane she had known and loved hadn't been one to seek the spotlight. He had never been shy or timid, but he never went out of the way to tout his own achievements. Had love blinded her to his faults?

"The people at TDC were on to him for a long time," Toby said. "But they had to be careful. They had to collect a lot of proof. I talked to one of the people who was investigating Dane and he told me all kinds of things they found out about him. They said he was selling drugs to some of the guys at Welcome Home Warriors. Some of those men and women were fighting addiction and instead of helping them, Dane was making money off their weakness. Disgusting."

Eve listened, dazed, trying to take it in.

"The guy at TDC told me they thought Dane had a secret safety deposit box where he kept records of all this stuff. I did some snooping and figured out where it was, but when I looked inside, it was just a bunch of pictures and stuff. He was too cagey to keep anything incriminating, I guess."

"You broke into Dane's safety deposit box?" She shifted to face him, even though she could see him only dimly in the light from the instrument panel. "How did you get the key?"

His teeth flashed white as he grinned. "Dane mentioned once that he had given you a key. I don't remember how it came up, but I went to your house while you were at work one day to look around. You really should have better security. A woman living by herself can't be too careful."

She felt sick, knowing he had been in her house, had pawed through her things. And to think she had kissed this man!

"And then he murdered that woman. Everybody said they didn't see it coming, but I did. I knew he had that kind of violence in him. You didn't believe me when I tried to warn you, but now you see it's true, don't you?"

She didn't answer. She couldn't.

"Don't you see?" Toby's shout reverberated through the darkness. "He has to be stopped. The police won't do it. Your precious Ranger commander won't do it. So I have to do it." He wrenched the car off the road, careening wildly.

"Stop!" Eve screamed. "You'll kill us both!"

He braked hard, skidding and slamming into a rock outcropping. The airbags exploded, filling the air with choking white dust. Eve felt the impact against her chest, and bowed her head, eyes watering, disoriented in the darkness. In the sudden silence her own ragged breathing filled her ears. The driver's door opened with a metallic protest, and a cold breeze raised goose bumps on her arm. Then her own door opened and Toby pressed his knife to her chest.

She went rigid, steeling herself for the first cut. But instead of stabbing her, he sawed at her seat belt, then dragged her from the car. "Come on," he said. "We walk from here."

## Chapter Nineteen

"Masterson's car isn't at the airport or the bus station or the train station." Lieutenant Dance stood at the front of the room, briefing the members of the Ranger Brigade, as well as Montrose County Sheriff's deputies, Colorado Department of Public Safety officers and Montrose Police Department officers who had mobilized to search for Toby and Eve. Men and women filled every seat in the Sheriff's Department classroom, and stood shoulder to shoulder along the walls, many clutching cardboard cups of coffee. Grant had positioned himself in a back corner, arms crossed over his chest, jaw clenched. "We checked hotels in Montrose, Delta, Grand Junction and all the surrounding communities and the car isn't there," Dance continued. "We've alerted gas stations, campgrounds and any other place they might have gone. We're drawing a blank."

"He could have taken her to a private residence," a woman in the crowd said. "If the car is in a garage somewhere, we'll never see it."

"Masterson rents an apartment midtown," Dance said. "We've had the place staked out since shortly after he took Ms. Shea. He hasn't been there. He hasn't been in contact with friends, family, or people he knows from work. We put a trace on his cell phone, but the battery is either dead or he's removed it. In any case, he hasn't used it to make any calls, and he hasn't purchased anything with his credit cards."

"What's his history?" a man asked. "Has he done anything like this before?"

"He's got a couple of domestic violence charges dating back three years," Dance said. "Both involving physical altercations with a woman he was dating at the time. They were both charged. But nothing since then."

"Somebody said he dated Ms. Shea?" someone else asked.

"He went out with her one time that we're aware of." Dance looked to Grant for confirmation. Grant gave a curt nod. "Her coworker at the flower shop said she recently turned him down for a second date," Dance continued.

"Maybe he didn't like that," a woman said.

"Maybe not," Dance said. "Right now, we don't care about his motivation so much unless it gives us a clue as to where he is now."

"We need to focus on the National Park," Grant said.

The rustle and creak of uniforms and weaponry filled the room as everyone shifted to look at him. Grant pushed his way toward the podium. "Grant Sanderlin, Ranger Brigade Commander," he introduced himself. "Masterson was obsessed with Dane Trask. He tried to date Trask's administrative assistant and his daughter, and only succeeded with Ms. Shea, who had a long-term relationship with Trask that ended six months ago. New evidence has come to light this evening that leads us to believe it was actually Masterson who murdered Marsha Grandberry in the park, and left one of Trask's

Welcome Home Warriors business cards on the body in an attempt to frame Trask. Masterson and Trask worked together at Welcome Home Warriors, so Masterson had easy access to those cards."

"What evidence?" a man asked.

"Ms. Grandberry took a selfie with her phone at the trailhead, just before she set out on her hike. An enlargement of the photograph shows Masterson standing nearby, watching her."

A murmur spread around the room. "It's a big park," someone in the back said. "Where do we start?"

Grant pulled a map of the park from his jacket and pinned it to the wall behind him. He used a pointer to indicate a section ringed in yellow highlighter. "We've had several confirmed sightings of Trask in this general area. We think Masterson may take Ms. Shea here, in an effort to lure Trask out of hiding." It was, at best, an educated guess, but for now it was all they had.

He stepped back from the podium, and Dance took over to assign areas for the various groups to patrol. Grant left the room, signaling to Carmen Redhorse to accompany him. "I'm headed to the Dead Horse Trail," he said. "Masterson killed Ms. Grandberry there, so he may return with Eve. I want you and Knightbridge as backup."

"Yes, sir," Redhorse said. "Are we going in on foot?"

"Yes." It was a risky move, carrying with it the danger of being ambushed, but in that rough country, he didn't see any other approach to take.

"If I may, sir, I think we should send officers in from both sides in a flanking maneuver," she said. "It's rough country there, but it is possible to approach from the south and east."

"Good idea. No more than a couple in each group," he said. "We don't want to sound like a herd of buffalo closing in on him."

"No, sir."

He left her to the details and returned to his cruiser. He sat, the engine and lights off, the radio turned down so that the chatter was a low murmur. He had called Janie and talked to her before going into the sheriff's department, and she had sounded tired, but calm, and had seemed okay with spending the night with Sarah and her husband, but had made him promise to call her as soon as he found Eve. Her faith that he would find Eve, and that she would be all right, buoyed him.

He closed his eyes and tried to put himself in Masterson's shoes. He couldn't think what the man was thinking, only try to predict based on past behavior. Masterson projected an air of swagger and confidence, which sometimes was a blind for deep insecurities. He and Trask had worked together, had maybe even been friends. Trask had helped Masterson find his job at TDC. Unlike others of Trask's friends, who had defended him when he was accused of theft and murder, Masterson had on more than one occasion tried to persuade people—particularly Eve—that Trask was dangerous.

Possibly, Masterson was jealous of Trask, of the respect and admiration Trask had received. He wanted that respect and admiration for himself. He wanted the life Trask had led.

He wanted the woman Trask had loved.

Grant wondered what an FBI profiler would think of his theories. He didn't have time to wait for a profiler's opinion. He could only act on his own instincts, and his instincts told him Masterson would bring Eve to the national park—to taunt Trask or maybe to trap him. But Grant intended to get to him before he had a chance to do either.

EVE DIDN'T KNOW how long they had been stumbling along in the dark, over boulders and through brambles, falling and getting up and falling again. After her fifth fall she had persuaded Toby to untie her hands. "There's nowhere I can run to out here," she said. "And I can balance myself a lot better if I can use my hands. I'll be able to move faster."

"All right, but if you try to run away, I'll kill you," he said, with all the emotion of someone explaining to a five-year-old that failing to clean his room would result in a lost allowance. He flashed his knife again to cut her free, and she winced as she brought her arms forward and rubbed feeling into them.

"Come on," he said, and grabbed her arm and dragged her after him again.

After what seemed like an hour of walking, the ground became less rocky, and stunted junipers and oaks replaced the sagebrush and weeds. Eve wondered if they were near the rim of the Black Canyon, then wished she hadn't thought of that. In the darkness it would be so easy to stumble into that black void, and fall for many minutes before hitting bottom.

At that moment, Toby shoved her to the ground, then crouched beside her. "What is it?" she asked. But then she heard it—the steady throb of a helicopter, flying low.

"Keep your head down," he said. "Don't look up. We don't want them to see us."

She pressed her forehead to the ground and closed her eyes. Was the helicopter looking for them? How would it ever find them down here in the darkness?

The throb of the chopper grew louder and louder, then receded, never passing directly over them. When they could no longer hear it, Toby stood and pulled her to her feet. "Come on," he said. "Let's go."

A short while later she sensed another change in the terrain. Though it was darker than ever, the little moonlight that was available blocked by trees crowding in around them, the ground was smoother underneath. "Are we on a trail?" she asked Masterson, who hadn't spoken in perhaps an hour.

"You get an A," he said. "Clever girl."

A trail meant they were in the developed area of the park. Development meant people. Hikers wouldn't be out this time of night, but would park rangers?

Janie would have alerted Grant to her disappearance by now. Eve couldn't know how much the girl would have heard or seen from the back room, but Grant would be looking for her. How would he ever find her here in the park, miles from the flower shop and even miles, by now, from Toby's car?

She looked up, trying to gauge from the sky how many hours they were from dawn. More people would come to the park with light—climbers and hikers, campers and anglers. With them would come a better chance of being spotted. She just had to hang on until light.

Toby stopped so suddenly she plowed into his back. He grabbed hold and held her against him, an embrace she didn't welcome but could do nothing to fend off. Not without risking the knife he still carried in one hand. She could feel it now, resting against her left shoulder. "What was that?" he whispered, his breath hot in her left ear.

"What?" she asked.

"Listen!"

She listened, holding her breath, and heard…nothing. "I don't hear anything," she said after a long moment.

"I heard something," he said. "Over to our left." He gestured to the side of the trail.

Was it Grant? she wondered. Had he somehow guessed where she was?

"Maybe it's Dane," Toby said.

"That's what you wanted, isn't it?" she whispered.

"Not yet," he said. "This isn't the right place for it." He released his hold on her and shoved her forward once more. "Come on. We have to keep going."

"WE'VE GOT SOMETHING from the aerial mapping the Forest Service chopper crew did." Hud approached Grant at the Dead Horse trailhead, where he and his team were assembling.

"What is it?" Grant grabbed the report and pulled his reading glasses from his shirt pocket.

Hud leaned over his shoulder. "That little red blob there—that's a heat source. It could be a couple of deer or an elk bedded down, but where it's located, the chopper crew thinks it was people—possibly one big one, but maybe two. They weren't moving."

"They probably heard the helicopter and froze," Grant said. He tried to hide his disappointment. It might be Eve and Toby, but the information was too vague to tell.

"There's more." Hud flipped to a second page in the

report. This was a fuzzy black-and-white photograph of what looked like a wrecked car. "They got this, about a mile and a half from the heat source," Hud said.

Grant squinted at the photo. "It's hard to tell much about it. Maybe it's been there a long time."

"Uh-uh," Hud said. "They spotted it because they were getting a heat reading from the engine. It was still warm. And it gets better." He turned to a third page. This was a close up, blurry but legible, of a license tag. "That's the tag number for Masterson's car. For whatever reason he abandoned it and started walking. They're headed this way."

Grant let out a breath, feeling twenty pounds lighter. "All right, everyone," he said in a normal tone of voice. "Let's get in place. We've got confirmation that our targets are headed this way."

"What's the plan?" Dance asked.

"I want you positioned across the trail, about 100 yards out, hidden in the brush. I need two officers on this side of the trail."

"Spencer and Reynolds are on their way," Dance said. "They should be here soon."

"Radio them to position themselves near the trail, about fifty yards apart. I'm going to be on the trail. If I can intercept Masterson, you three can close in from both sides. Redhorse will be behind me, about fifty yards farther south on the trail. Hud will be fifty yards north. Remember, he's got a hostage, so do everything you can to avoid endangering her. I'm gambling we can catch him off guard."

Plans made, they moved toward their positions to wait and pray they could stop Masterson, before he killed again.

*Hold on, Eve,* Grant sent a silent message. *I promised Janie I'd bring you home safe.* He had never made a promise he wanted to keep more.

EVE WAS TIRED, her body heavy, every step an effort. They must have walked miles over rough country, and that after working on her feet all day, then being terrified for most of the night. "I have to stop and rest," she told Toby. "I can't keep going."

"You can sleep when you're dead," he said, with no hint that he was making a bad joke. "Keep going."

"But where are we going?" She didn't move. She didn't think she could. She sank to the ground. "I need water, and food," she said. "I haven't eaten since breakfast." The shop had been too busy to stop for lunch, though she had insisted Janie eat the sandwich Grant had sent with her.

Masterson knelt beside her and pulled a water bottle from his pack. She unscrewed the lid and drank, the water so good and cool going down. He took a long drink, too, then dug a protein bar from his pack and passed it to her. He took one for himself as well and for several minutes they ate in silence.

"Do you think that helicopter earlier was searching for us?" he asked.

"Probably." She saw no sense in lying. Masterson wasn't stupid. "But they couldn't have seen us. It was too dark."

"They use infrared," he said. "We did some of that in the army, looking for insurgents. They use it to map forest fires and stuff, too. It operates on heat signals. You can spot a person in pitch black from 800 feet in the air with those things."

The last bite of the protein bar stuck in her throat. Did that mean the helicopter had seen them? That it knew where they were? She tried to hold onto the hope that bloomed within her, but it died too quickly. Rescuers might know where she was, but Toby still had that knife, and he was close enough to kill her with one thrust.

"Did you take the picture I had in my office of me and Dane?" she asked. "The one of the two of us in a field of lavender?"

He didn't speak for so long she started to repeat the question. "You looked so beautiful in that photograph," he said. "So happy. When I saw it, I realized how completely Dane had fooled you. I took it so you wouldn't be reminded of him."

As if she could forget a man she had been with for three years simply because his picture was gone. But Toby's sudden honesty made her bold. "Did you kill Marsha Grandberry?" she asked.

"What?"

She forced the words out. "Did you kill Marsha Grandberry? That college girl whose throat was cut on the trail?"

"No! Dane killed her. He left his business card so everyone would know he did it. That's how messed up he is."

Masterson worked with Dane at Welcome Home Warriors. He would have had access to Dane's business cards. And he wanted everyone to know how terrible Dane was. "I just wondered," she said. She forced herself to stand despite her wobbly legs, suddenly anxious to move. If they kept going on this trail, they would eventually reach a trailhead, and a road. And someone who could help her.

Toby rose beside her. "You believe me, don't you?" he asked. "Dane killed that girl, not me."

"Of course," she said. But he was the one with the knife. He had held it to her throat and she had believed he had been ready to kill her.

They moved again, Masterson just behind her, almost stepping on her heels with each stride. She walked with her head down, trying to see where she was going, an impossible task in the darkness, though overhead, above the trees, the sky had lightened from charcoal to ash.

She sensed more than felt movement somewhere to her left, and lifted her head to listen. Had it been a deer, or a large bird—or a person? She glanced back at Toby, but he gave no indication he had heard. So she kept walking, ears straining for any hint of sound. Twice more she thought she might have heard something, but when no one appeared and Toby didn't react, she told herself she was imagining things.

Then a dark shape loomed, ten yards in front of them. "Police! Freeze, with your hands up!"

She tried to comply, lifting her hands in the air, but Masterson tackled her from behind and dragged her back against him. She felt the sting of the knife at her throat. "Don't move or she's dead," he shouted.

"You're surrounded, Masterson." She recognized Grant's voice now. "You'll never get away alive. Don't make things worse on yourself."

"If Eve dies, her blood is on your hands, Commander!" he shouted. The knife pricked, and a hot dampness bloomed. She closed her eyes, willing herself to stay strong, to push back the panic.

"We know you killed Marsha Grandberry," Grant said. "We have a picture of you with her at the trail-head."

"No one would believe how dangerous Dane Trask is," he said. "I had to show you how dangerous he is." His hand shifted, and she gasped as the knife nicked her again.

"Eve, are you okay?" Grant asked.

"She won't be okay much longer if you don't let us through." Toby's voice sounded ragged, higher-pitched. "Get back."

The shadow receded a little. "I'm moving back," Grant said. "Don't do anything rash. We can talk."

"I want you all to back off," he said. "I want you to let me go."

"You have to let Eve go first," Grant said.

Toby laughed, a wild, choking sound that sent a chill through Eve. "That's not going to happen," he said. "Do you think I'm stupid?"

The explosion deafened her, and the back of her head was wet. She fell forward, Toby collapsing with her. She struggled away, to her knees. Then Grant was lifting her, cradling her. "Eve, are you all right?" he asked.

Was she all right? She put a hand to the back of her head and felt something sticky, but there was no pain. "I don't know," she said.

"I need a medic here!" Grant shouted, and two men rushed forward, pulling her from his arms and shining lights on her. Others rushed past her to Toby, who lay crumpled on the ground behind her.

One of the medics shone a light in her eyes, while the other probed at the back of her head. "Hang on a minute," the second man said. "This is gonna be wet, and probably cold." He dumped what must have been a half gallon of water over her, drenching her hair and the back of her shirt, then handed her a dry T-shirt. "You're gonna want to take a shower when you get home," he said. "But none of that blood and other stuff was yours. You're gonna be just fine."

Grant moved forward to hold her close once more. "You're sure she's not hurt?" he asked the medics.

"She's okay. Just blowback from the other guy."

She tried to turn to look at Toby, but Grant held her head. "You don't want to see," he said.

"What happened?" she asked.

"He was shot in the head," he said. She could feel him shaking. "It wasn't a shot I'd have risked in a million years. It was way too close to you. But the shooter knew what he was doing, I'll give him that."

"He must have had a hell of an infrared sight." A man in a visored helmet and body armor joined them. He raised the visor and she recognized Lieutenant Dance. "It wasn't one of our guys, Commander."

Grant shifted her in his arms and faced Dance. "Are you sure about that?"

"I'm positive. Reynolds and Spencer were covering that side of the trail and they got held up by a deep gully they had to navigate in the dark. They didn't show up until after Masterson was shot."

"Someone was trailing us, to my left, for a long way down the trail," Eve said. She cleared her throat.

"It wasn't one of us," Dance said.

Both men looked at her. She closed her eyes and opened them again. "Dane had a sharpshooter's medal from the army. And he had a bunch of guns. He took me with him to the shooting range a couple of times, but I didn't really like it."

"You think Trask shot Masterson?" Grant asked.

"I don't know," she said. "But I think he would have risked a shot like that. To save someone he cared about."

"I'm going to see what I can find out," Dance said, moving past them.

Grant kept his arm around her, and together they walked back down the trail. Eve leaned on him heavily, exhausted, wet and cold, trying not to think about what might be clinging to the back of her.

Grant took her, not to her house, but to his. He showed her his shower and she stood under the hot water until it ran cold, the spray forceful and stinging, washing away some of the horror of the evening, and a lot of her tears. When she finished, she found he had laid out a stack of thick towels, and a T-shirt and sweatpants that were several sizes too big for her, but soft and warm and smelling of fabric softener, and of him. She held the shirt to her nose and inhaled deeply, wanting to stay in this warm, humid sanctuary forever.

But a growing chill and her growling stomach forced her to open the door and step into the hall. She found her way to the kitchen, where Grant stood over the stove, scrambling eggs. "You can make the toast if you want," he said, nodding toward the loaf of bread laid out beside the toaster. "I called Janie and let her know you're okay. She was really worried."

"Poor kid." She fed two slices of bread into the toaster. "How is she doing? I was terrified she was going to come out of the back room while McMasters was there."

"She's a little shaken up, but she's a real trouper. She

called for help right away and gave us the information we needed to find you."

"She probably saved my life, and I'll be sure she knows it."

"Sit down and we'll eat." He had made tea, too, and she drank a large mug of it, sweetened with honey, and ate scrambled eggs and toast with strawberry jam and neither of them said anything until their plates were clean. Grant carried the dishes to the sink, then sat across from her. "Do you want to talk about it?" he asked. "You'll need to make a statement at some point, but that can wait if you're not ready."

"It's all right. I can talk about it." Talking was better than silently reliving the events of the night in her mind, though she imagined she would do her share of that, too. She told him everything from the moment Toby had grabbed her in the flower shop.

"He actually told you he wanted to use you as bait to get to Trask?" Grant interrupted when she got to that point in her story.

She nodded. "Yes. I don't know if he envied Dane or resented him. He had read or been told all this terrible stuff Dane had supposedly done, and I think he really believed it. Maybe he felt betrayed by that. He thought Dane needed to be stopped and he was the person to do it."

"I guess it worked, to a point," Grant said. "He managed to lure Dane out of hiding."

"We don't know that," she said.

"No, but we know someone killed Toby Masterson. Someone who was expert enough to risk that kind of shot. You don't take that kind of risk for just anyone."

She bowed her head. If what he said was true, Dane

had saved her life. She didn't know how that idea sat with her. Not that she wasn't grateful to be alive, but it was a heavy debt.

Grant slid his hand over hers. She turned her palm up to twine her fingers with him. "I know you still love Dane," he said.

She jerked her head up, startled by the words. "No! What makes you think that?"

"The two of you were together so long. After you broke up, you admitted you couldn't find anyone else, even though you dated a lot of men. I read that last letter he wrote you, where he said he loved you…"

"Maybe he loves me, but I don't love him. Not in that way." She leaned toward him, compelling him to look into his eyes. "I love you," she said. "Not Dane."

He squeezed her hand tighter. "I love you, too," he said.

Her smile felt as wobbly as her voice sounded. "Then I guess we're both really screwed," she said.

"What do you mean?"

She let go of his hand and leaned back. "I only seem to fall in love with men who don't want children."

He cleared his throat. "About that—I'm man enough to admit I was wrong."

She couldn't speak, only stared at him, waiting. He took her hand again. "I love you," he said again. "And I want to have children with you—if that's what you want."

"You said you had raised two children and couldn't handle any more."

"I lied. Having Janie here with me proved that. I thought I wasn't cut out to be a father, because I'd done such a poor job with Janie and her sister. But she's a great kid, and she loves me in spite of everything, so I must have done something right. I'd like to have a chance to do even better this time around."

"You're not just saying that to get me back in your bed?" she asked.

He laughed, and she laughed, too, breaking the tension. "I love you," he said a third time, and kissed her. "And I think you'll make a wonderful mother."

She buried her face in his shoulder and they held each other for a long time. "It's a little scary," she said after a while. "Marriage and children and the whole nine yards."

"Yeah," he said. "It's a gamble, but I'm feeling lucky. Aren't you?"

She looked into his eyes, shining with love, and couldn't stop smiling. Right now she felt like the luckiest woman in the world, not only because she had survived, but because she had found what she had been looking for, for too long. She thought—she hoped—that it had all been worth the wait.

\* \* \* \* \*

# LET'S TALK
## *Romance*

For exclusive extracts, competitions
and special offers, find us online:

 facebook.com/millsandboon

@MillsandBoon

@MillsandBoonUK

**Get in touch on 01413 063232**

For all the latest titles coming soon, visit
**millsandboon.co.uk/nextmonth**

# MILLS & BOON

## THE HEART OF ROMANCE

---

## A ROMANCE FOR EVERY KIND OF READER

**MODERN**

Prepare to be swept off your feet by sophisticated, sexy and seductive heroes, in some of the world's most glamourous and romantic locations, where power and passion collide.
**8 stories per month.**

**HISTORICAL**

Escape with historical heroes from time gone by. Whether your passion is for wicked Regency Rakes, muscled Vikings or rugged Highlanders, awaken the romance of the past.
**6 stories per month.**

**MEDICAL**

Set your pulse racing with dedicated, delectable doctors in the high-pressure world of medicine, where emotions run high and passion, comfort and love are the best medicine.
**6 stories per month.**

*True Love*

Celebrate true love with tender stories of heartfelt romance, from the rush of falling in love to the joy a new baby can bring, and a focus on the emotional heart of a relationship.
**8 stories per month.**

*Desire*

Indulge in secrets and scandal, intense drama and plenty of sizzling hot action with powerful and passionate heroes who have it all: wealth, status, good looks…everything but the right woman.
**6 stories per month.**

**HEROES**

Experience all the excitement of a gripping thriller, with an intense romance at its heart. Resourceful, true-to-life women and strong, fearless men face danger and desire - a killer combination!
**8 stories per month.**

**DARE**

Sensual love stories featuring smart, sassy heroines you'd want as a best friend, and compelling intense heroes who are worthy of them.
**4 stories per month.**

---

To see which titles are coming soon, please visit

## millsandboon.co.uk/nextmonth

# MILLS & BOON

## HISTORICAL

### Awaken the romance of the past

Escape with historical heroes from time gone by. Whether your passion is for wicked Regency Rakes, muscled Viking warriors or rugged Highlanders, indulge your fantasies and awaken the romance of the past.

# MILLS & BOON
## *True Love*
### Romance from the Heart

Celebrate true love with tender stories of
heartfelt romance, from the rush of falling
in love to the joy a new baby can bring,
and a focus on the emotional
heart of a relationship.

# MILLS & BOON

## MEDICAL
### *Pulse-Racing Passion*

Set your pulse racing with dedicated, delectable doctors in the high-pressure world of medicine, where emotions run high and passion, comfort and love are the best medicine.